Ballard's War

Ballard's War

Tom Holzel

iUniverse, Inc.
Bloomington

Ballard's War

iUniverse books may be ordered through booksellers or by contacting:

iUniverse
1663 Liberty Drive
Bloomington, IN 47403
www.iuniverse.com
1-800-Authors (1-800-288-4677)

ISBN: 978-1-4620-1723-2 (pbk)
ISBN: 978-1-4620-1724-9 (ebk)

Printed in the United States of America

niverse rev. date: 05/26/2011

Chapter One
Berlin, April 8, 1941

The lieutenant's secretary recognized the approaching tattoo of his high boots on the cold marble floor of Berlin Abwehr Headquarters. Inge Schmidt stood ready as he burst through the office door. Falling in step behind him she took the leather greatcoat from his narrow shoulders in a single practiced motion with one hand, while handing him the packet of the morning's mail with the other. Dutifully she followed him as he marched through her antechamber and into his own office. By the slightest trace of a smile she knew he had spotted that the wood parquet floor had been freshly polished. Inge was bribing the cleaning lady with American cigarettes to clean their floors weekly instead of the usual monthly polishing. She got the cigarettes from Mueller, the supply sergeant, whose uniform she washed and ironed at home.

Inge stood by as her boss swiveled into the green leather chair behind his carved mahogany desk as graceful as a ferret she thought and reflexively checked that his inkwell was full. Satisfied, and snapping its brass cover shut, he finally glanced up at her.

"Did anything interesting come in overnight, Frau Schmidt?" he asked, dropping his hooded eyes quickly at her attentive returning gaze. He shuffled hurriedly through the envelopes. She was an attractive young woman, he realized. Today she wore a taupe dress with gold buttons down the side modest, yet classy. Her bright yellow hair was pulled back into a tight bun. Her high cheekbones and alert expression made it difficult to tell her age which was twenty one. He had hired her only six months ago to replace his previous secretary whose husband had been transferred to Hamburg. She had been an inspired choice.

1

She shook her head. "Nein, Herr Leutnant Only routine matters. Oh, except this urgent message." She handed him a formally hand addressed envelope.

His dark eyebrows furrowed briefly, detecting an irregularity. The letter had a Berlin postmark dated yesterday, April 7, 1941. Familiar handwriting. He opened the letter it was a birthday greeting from her to him! He looked up, shocked. Trying to smile pleasantly, he fumbled for words. Finally he uttered an awkward "Very nice, very thoughtful, Frau Schmidt. I didn't think anyone knew. Thank you." Quickly he averted his eyes to check the other letters.

Inge looked at her boss with admiration, No, she realized, it was more than that. He was slender and only of medium height her height actually with black hair plastered back on his head and the high officers' "white walls" of nearly bare skin around his head to above his long ears. His dark, moody eyes seemed too large for his narrow, saturnine face but they shone luminously with the fires of unquenchable intelligence and, she believed, deep passion.

Returning through the tall doorway to her own office, Inge sat down at the graceful, inlaid table she was using as a desk. This two office arrangement was rather fancy for a mere lieutenant. But he was clearly one of the admiral's favorites. Perhaps it was a reward for his brilliant work on analyzing the workings of the Norden bombsight. She didn't quite understand it all, but somehow he had been able to create a working model of the top secret Allied bomb aiming device by merely watching how the British bombers flew off their targets. Combining their offset with known wind speed, he had calculated the type of gear train such an instrument would need. His analysis had created a mild sensation at the Luftwaffe, and a rush to duplicate the device for German bombers.

She opened the folder of letters to type but she couldn't keep her thoughts from dwelling on the lieutenant. She realized it had been more than a bit forward sending him a birthday greeting. He was about six or seven years older than her, she estimated—a perfect catch. He had become remote and somber since his wife had died several months ago. Inge recalled how helplessly he had asked her if she would sew the obligatory black armband onto the sleeve of his

2

uniform. Fighting to hold back the tears, his hands were trembling as he held the uniform out for her. She knew he would wear this sign of mourning for at least six months. Some men wore them for an entire year! She felt the cloth ring had drawn a black curtain between them, distancing him from her even more than when his wife was alive.

Was he aware of her growing affection for him? He coolly rebuffed all her advances, no matter how subtle. She sometimes wished he would not be so correct about it! She heard the squeak of his chair tipping back, and the rustling sound of him methodically flipping through his letters and dispatches.

Lieutenant Werner Stumpfnagel had recovered from the embarrassing moment with his secretary in his characteristic fashion by throwing himself into his work. He spotted another hand addressed letter in his mail and set it aside. This one was written in a horrible script, probably that of a mental case. Or a foreigner. Also a Berlin postmark, he noticed. He quickly scanned the remaining envelopes for signs of importance. All appeared routine and uninteresting. He returned to the awful handwriting. What a scrawl. And the writer was using one of those new Rotring fountain pens that used a tube to apply the liquid ink instead of a metal nib; there was no shading to the script. Another nut case? The handwriting was obviously that of a foreigner, probably an American. Penmanship was losing out fast in the modern world, ever since the invention of the typewriter, Stumpfnagel mused. And the American barbarians were losing it the fastest. Still, this writing was particularly atrocious. He slit the letter open. It was written on women's pink stationary and egad it was ten pages long.

> April 7, 1941
> Sehr geehrter Herr Leutnant Stumpfnagel;
> I possess intelligence that will give Germany a chance to win the war, and I want to give it to you. But there are some problems. First I must convince you that, as things stand and in spite of what the public believes, unless some radical measures are undertaken now, Germany will lose the war in the next few years in utter destruction.

Ach, im Gotteswillen, yes, Stumpfnagel realized. He tilted back in his hair, his hand going up to shade his eyes from the light streaming through the window. Another rip snorting crank. Their warnings came every month or so, as regularly as the full moon. Flying saucers from the North Pole, enemy death rays, a poisoned water supply that sapped one's manhood, and so on and so on. What was on this one's mind, he wondered.

> Second, you are naturally going to think that I am a madman. But read this letter through. Then you will realize that, mad or not, the information I possess is of such inestimable value, that I will immediately fall under another suspicion, that of being a double agent an American "plant" hoping to offer you true information of minor value in order to mislead you in some major direction. Except there is nothing minor, about what I am offering you.

Hmmm. He's clever to bring up the lunatic angle himself, Stumpfnagel thought. So he's a clever, nutty foreigner. They'll probably only deport him. However, the word "double agent" used in time of war is nevertheless reckless . . . how much money does he want?

However, unless you are thoroughly convinced of my authenticity, we cannot meet. Otherwise you will only try to do your duty and arrest me. So I am outlining here a small part of my intimate knowledge of the German and Allied war apparatus.

> You will need a lot of intellectual daring even more than when you correctly divined the operation of the Norden bomb sight, of which the allies are still so proud, simply by recording our flying patterns and their off sets to the target.

"How the blazes . . . !" Stumpfnagel blurted out. It is impossible for an outsider to know about his Norden bombsight analysis. And this

4

American fruitcake makes it sound as if my suppositions are correct. This fellow can't be an American, Stumpfnagel snorted. He's an insider. This is a stupid joke being played on me by one of my agents. Or Supply Sergeant Mueller down the hall, who never has enough to keep him busy. He read on.

> How do I know that? Because my sources are at the absolute highest, most reliable levels within the Allied and German governments. For example:
>
> 1. In two days, on the evening of April 9, the British plan to carry out a major air raid on Berlin. This is in retaliation for "Operation Castigo," the German bombing raid on Belgrade last week.
> 2. On the same day, General Bakopoulos, the Greek Commander of Salonica, has been ordered by the Greek Supreme Command to surrender his 70,000 men to German forces. This move opposed by the British will nevertheless cause them to withdraw their Expeditionary Forces from the region.
> 3. Tomorrow, the 8th, Luftwaffe bombers plan to strike the British aircraft factories in Coventry.

As interesting as these items may seem, they are minor intelligence matters, but they, will quickly prove my bona fides. However, Germany is not going to reverse the coming Allied onslaught no matter how much such advance notice I give of Allied tactics. Instead, Germany must actively change its strategy. Here are some changes upon which you must embark at once.

> 4. Cryptography. The Polish underground supplied a model of the Enigma machine to the British two years ago. Three Enigma rotors found in U-33 (sunk on 12 Feb. by H.M.S. Gleaner) have compromised the Naval code. Your own Abwehr code was broken on 12

January. Soon all Enigma transmission will be read routinely by the Allies.

Wilhelm Fenner of the Cipher Center is the key obstacle here. As clever an administer as he is, he nevertheless imperiously describes the "impossibility" of breaking the billions of code keys and will fight everything I have to tell you. So, here fresh from the Bletchley Park decoding factory north of London, are your next month's codes:

IYWER DWKLS YDOPW GCXZS
WKLPO HGATR TVCWL FLOPN
UYBNA WPMNH YCWER KIDXB
HWGPO YBXSE MZSRE IUBFL
UAWER PNFUT VFIRE LUFDS
QXZRE SLUIP JYOGT NBGEA
XCZVF UBWER DAHIO PPUTV etc.

Stumpfnagel called to his secretary. "Frau Schmidt, take this up to Knoblau in the code room immediately. Have him call me when he's checked it for authenticity." He continued to read.

5. The V-1 pilotless flying bomb will be hopelessly inaccurate to be of military value, as will the very expensive V-2 ballistic rocket. Dr. Robert Luster is working on the former, and Werner von Braun the latter, both under the direction of Colonel Dornberger. It is essential to give the former of these low priority projects the fullest support to improve its military value; the latter project must be canceled. Of equal importance is the Me-262 twin jet fighter being proposed by Willi Messerschmidt. Coupled with the He 296 air to air kinescope guided rockets, it will be your only hope to keep British and American bombers from reducing Germany to ashes. (Yes, American bombers. Nothing will stop President Roosevelt from joining the war at the first opportunity.)

6. Chief of the General Staff Heinz Guderian must be given advice on implementing "Barbarossa," the invasion of the Soviet Union, adopted by the Führer himself on February 3rd for a spring offensive. Yes, Russia must be conquered to provide Germany with food and oil, but American and British, intelligence are certain that Germany's entry into Yugoslavia two days ago (with Greece to follow) will result in a serious delay in commencing Operation Barbarossa. This means fighting the Russian campaign through the mud and mire of fall and the bitter cold of winter. The German Army of 190 Divisions, expecting a ten to twenty week Blitzkrieg against two hundred Soviet Divisions, is prepared for neither. When it is discovered that the Soviets have the manpower to form over three hundred new Divisions within six months, the German drive is sure to falter.

7. Worse yet, the Eastern Armies' "Vulture" code is almost completely broken. By the time the invasion takes place in late June, Stalin will learn everything transmitted about all German East Front movements. At first the Russians won't be able to do anything about it. But as the attack drags into winter, it will help the Soviets finally wear out whole German armies. Yes, you will kill many more Russians than you lose Germans but they have men and machines to burn. Germany does not.
    There are many other areas that we will discuss. But this sample will suffice for now.

Stumpfnagel felt the hair crawling at the back of his neck. He swiveled in his seat to cast more light on the pink stationary. His stomach began to churn as it did in the presence of extreme danger. He didn't know what this guy was talking about, but he had few of the earmarks of a crank. There was none of the characteristic struggle of all lunatics—never quite pulled off to insist they are rational. Even the cleverest of them generally assemble a few interesting but insignificant facts and blow them all out of proportion. This guy was talking about the most secret of grand strategies. And of both sides! Stumpfnagel pulled his uniform jacket closer to him to banish a chill. What kind of prank was this?

> All right, you are asking yourself What next? The first thing is to establish whether the information I have is valuable or not. But it is essential you do so without sounding a general alarm. The easiest way is to wait to see whether my claims prove true. The bombing plans should serve nicely: Then talk to Major Dornberger about his secret weapons.
>
> Second, I have written especially to you because, if properly handled, this opportunity will let the German nation seize victory from the jaws of defeat. But Germany can not win the war only by reacting to the many warnings I can give about Allied operations. To win she must change her strategy significantly. Unfortunately this will present enormous difficulties for the German leadership.
>
> Not the least of which is how to get Herr Hitler to change his mind on some of his many pet projects—many of them seriously misbegotten.

Stumpfnagel scowled. He was aware of Hitler's constant meddling in the smallest military matters. Top ranking officers had complained about it to their mistresses, many of whom were on the Abwehr payroll. But it rankled to hear it coming from a foreign spy.

> One other point: knowing the Gestapo's reputation for blind and ferocious defense of the Fatherland, if they find out about me, Heinrich Mueller's reflexive reaction will be—regardless of the inestimable value of my information—to turn all of Germany

upside-down to root out what to him will appear as
an incredible security breach. If that happens, I will
vanish and you will get nothing.

Stumpfnagel smiled weakly. The American was right about the
Gestapo, but he had little to worry about. If any of his predictions were
correct, the Abwehr would guard him like the family jewels.

As I said, I have chosen you because you have
a good mind an excellent mind able to deduce
conclusions from facts, no matter how outrageous
they may seem or where they may lead.

The lieutenant grimaced. This American spy was laying it on a bit thick.
He realized no American spy could possibly know half of what this
person claimed. And, he thought, what he knows about me and the
Norden bomb sight, why only a dozen or so of the Abwehr staff were
in on it. That and a few Luftwaffen generals. It's the fatal flaw of this
prank, Stumpfnagel recognized. Soon he's going to be asking for a
small "investment" of money in his next great "can't lose" scheme.

I will reveal myself to you after you have satisfied
yourself of the great value I can be to the Fatherland
and when I am given convincing assurances for my
personal safety. That's the one area I don't have
any suggestions. But if I even smell a trap I'll
disappear.

Mad or not, the man is no fool, Stumpfnagel mused, and a great
prankster to boot. What's next?

If you decide we should meet, publish your answer
in the personal column of the Berliner Zeitung. I
expect it will take about a week. After that, we
can plan how to help Germany win the war. I know

things look good right now. But in a year, they won't.
Hochachtungsvoll,
RTB, a friend of Germany.

"Herr Leutnant," a voice called to him from afar. He looked up. It was his secretary peering around his open doorway. She had a concerned expression on her face, her very pretty face, he realized once again. She was a charming young girl who had married a pilot in the Luftwaffe. Her husband had died in a training accident in less than a year, making her once more available. He realized she had eyed him speculatively more than once. But he believed his correct behavior toward her made it clear that he could not possibly get involved. At least not yet. "I've been ringing your telephone. I thought you had fallen asleep."

"No, not asleep, Frau Schmidt," he answered. "Just concentrating. Who is it? I can't take any calls right now."

"It's the Foreign Office," she replied with a worried look on her face. She could not understand how a person could shut himself off from the world so completely. It was eerie.

"They're looking for 'an intelligent male escort.' Someone who plays chess."

"Oh, for God's sake. For tonight? With whom?" He was sick and tired of performing for the idiots at the Reich Chancellery. But they controlled the purse strings.

"A chess playing female," he said disgustedly. "That means she'll be as ugly as boar. What about Mueller down the hall?"

"No they specifically asked for you. It's for next Saturday night. A Donizetti opera with a reception and dinner. Smoking jackets for civilians. The Italians are putting it on. It sounds like fun." She laughed at him gaily.

"All right Frau Schmidt," he replied wearily. "But I can't believe how they push us around. See if you can find out who she is—and if they expect me to sleep over, too."

Not realizing his weak attempt at, humor, Inge gave him a shocked look and closed the door behind her.

"No calls," he shouted after her: He returned to the letter and reread it completely, slowly this time, trying out alternate possibilities. The German grammar was imperfect, as would be expected from a foreigner. But a prankster could purposely use imperfect German as well. Well, what difference did it make? He would just wait to see if the British did attempt to bomb Berlin tomorrow. Fat chance of that. Göring had promised if a single bomb fell on Berlin, the people could call him "Miller." German anti-aircraft would have a field day: like shooting ducks at a gallery.

He looked at his watch and was astounded to discover it was nearly lunch time. He stood up and thought about eating at the canteen. Or should he bring back some food and join his secretary who economically brought her own lunch to work? It was a pleasant interlude to eat quietly with her, neither saying much. He tried to put the bogus letter out of his mind. What did the trickster expect him to do make a fool of himself by rushing off to Canaris with this ridiculous red herring? Yes, that was it exactly. But who was after him?

He shook his head to empty it of the irritation this idiotic prank was causing him. Still, if half the items mentioned in the letter were true, the answer the American was hinting at was too incredible to contemplate. Jesus Maria, it was clearly impossible. He stopped and cleared his mind. Impossible never stopped Sherlock Holmes. It means this American—if that's what he really is has access to, or has penetrated, the highest levels of the Allied and German military intelligence circles. One could count on the fingers of one hand the people with this type of access. The American flyer, Colonel Charles Lindberg, came immediately to mind: a darling of the air forces on both sides of the Atlantic. But Lindberg a traitor? That was clearly impossible.

So it was a trick. He sat back in his chair, ready to move on to the next task: Yet the implications of what the American was hinting at would not leave him; they rolled around in his mind, ricocheting off as different possibilities. What if it were not impossible?

Germany was on top of the world. Hitler had just rolled over Yugoslavia and Bulgaria. Rommel was about to retake Cyrenaica. The British were cowering across the channel, losing aircraft to the Luftwaffe faster than they could produce them. The Greek Army was being rolled back. And in spite of their sideline glowering, the Americans were completely unprepared for war. No one in his right mind would state with the certainty of this "Friend of Germany" that things would not only get quickly much worse, but that she would lose the war. Stumpfnagel snorted. It was utter rubbish. The American was right about one thing. If anyone else had received this letter, the dogs would have been let loose in full cry. At least he would give the crazy American a quick hearing before throwing him out.

Chapter Two
APRIL 9, 1941

The next morning Lieutenant Stumpfnagel received his packet of mail and dispatches from Inge Schmidt in their usual well worn ritual. But this time he stopped short before he got to his own office. Inge, following behind, almost bumped into him. "Anything on the English air raids last night?" he asked, turning to look at her.

Caught off guard by this departure from their routine, she flustered for an answer, then quickly pulled herself together. He realized once again how attractive she was.

"Why yes, Herr Leutnant," Inge answered. "A large force of British bombers dropped incendiary on Stadtmitte in Berlin. They caused a lot of fire damage. It lit up the sky. Didn't you see it? Goebbles is downplaying it on the radio this morning, saying it was a suicide mission of bombers which had got turned around and lost their way."

"Any news from Greece?" He could smell the fresh scent of her, standing so close to him, still expecting to follow him into his office. She was still trying to puzzle out this breach of their morning routine. He had instructed her to read all his mail in order to put the most important items on top of the pile.

"Oh, yes, there was one item," she said after a moment's thought. "General Bakopolous, or Bakoupulos—I can never get the Greek names right . . ."

"Surrendered his garrison of 70,000 men," Stumpfnagel finished for her.

"Why yes. Fifty-thousand they said. How did, you . . . ?"

She saw a rising light of excitement flare up in his eyes. Was he going to kiss her on the spot? Her cheeks flushed at the thought.

"The code report from Herr Leutnant Knoblau?" he asked. He was not going to kiss her. Something else had got him incredibly excited. They were speaking to each other in sentence fragments. Just as when he was working on the Norden bomb sight.

"The yellow flimsy," she said, running her finger down the pile and pulling out the report from the sheath of papers in his hand. Stumpfnagel scanned it rapidly. He found he was holding his breath.

"Come into my office, Frau Schmidt, and sit down," he ordered her. "I need your help. We have got some very unusual business to attend to."

Stumpfnagel swiveled behind his desk and immediately began to reread the code report.

> Security Rating: TOP SECRET
> Memo to: Lieut. W. Stumpfnagel
> From: Lieut. R. Knoblau, Chief, Code Department.
> Abwehr IV/3
> Date: 8.4.41
> Ref: Handwritten code sample in letter dated 7.4.41
> A group of twenty-seven (27) Enigma code blocks of the subject letter, with the writer's representation that these groups purport to be next month's correct code grouping, was examined.
> The code group was that of "Vulture," the code variation to be used by General Paulus for the Eastern Army Groups preparation of the defensive reinforcement of the Eastern Front.
> Incredibly, the code is correct, even though this grouping has not yet left Abwehr headquarters. Thus, the information can only have come from someone within this headquarters. Six (6) people have normal access to these codes, and a possible twenty-two (22) might have conceivable access. Their names are listed below.

> Security interviews were begun on 8.4.41 at 1545
> hours.

Stumpfnagel looked up abruptly. "For God's sake, Frau Schmidt," he shouted. "Where's the decrypt?"

"The what?" she asked, a look of concern dancing on her face. Had she done something wrong?

"The decrypted message," Stumpfnagel answered. "What did it say?"

There was a sharp rap on the office door. Without waiting for an answer, the door pushed open. In marched Lieutenant Knoblau followed by the Security Officer, Helmholz, and then—the Admiral himself.

"I'm sorry, Herr Leutnant," Knoblau started to say. "The codes were real and so duty required I . . ."

Admiral Canaris sat down in the chair Inge had just vacated and began genially:

"Good morning, Herr Leutnant. It seems you have uncovered another great mystery." He beamed at the lieutenant, but the gruff joviality did not cover the piercing stare that would soon demand convincing answers.

"Jawohl, Herr Admiral," Stumpfnagel answered. "But the correct code is just one subject. In a letter dated 7th April, this . . . this benefactor predicted this morning's bombing of Berlin and the surrender of General Bokapoulos in Salonica."

"What?" Canaris blurted out. "Show me." He slipped on his reading glasses and reached his hand toward Stumpfnagel. The lieutenant pulled the letter out of the file and handed it over.

The group of men stood around uncertainly, shifting their weight from one leg to another, while the admiral read the ten-page pink letter. "Hmmm," and other grunts escaped from him as he carefully read—and then reread the entire ten pages. He looked up abruptly.

"Himmel Herr Gott noch mal," he muttered. "This is not just a local security issue."

I don't think so, sir," Stumpfnagel replied.

And the reason you didn't bring this to my attention when it first came in?"

15

"Herr Admiral, the likelihood of this coming from anyone but a lunatic . . ."

"Ach, ja, natürlich. "Canaris' face screwed up tightly in intense thought. "Jesus Maria, I don't know what to make of it either." He stood up. "But the Ami is right about one thing."

"Herr Admiral?"

He picked the right man to send it to." Canaris turned and pushed the others out through the door in front of him. "Keep working on this, Herr Leutnant. Make it your first priority. Keep me closely informed. At least daily until we have something solid on this . . . this "Friend of Germany."

"As you order, Herr Admiral."

After lunch, Stumpfnagel found the other two reports he had asked for: a chemical analysis of the paper and ink used on the letter, and a handwriting analysis of the penmanship. The chemical analysis was brief and to the point.

> ABWEHR RESEARCH LABORATORIES, Berlin the 8.4.41.
> Case Nr. 140141-34.
> Paper: Conventional wet-laid paper, 98% rag content, 2% hard wood pulp. Sulfite-based slurry. Laid surface, tinted pink. Watermarked BVS. Source: a standard, better-class, German-made ladies' stationary.
> Ink: Unknown composition of dyes containing quick—drying carriers never before seen. The application of the ink (i.e., the writing) was not, as first appearances suggest, by means of the new tube-fed fountain pens from Hamburg currently making their appearances (the so called "Rotring" pens). Rather, the ink of this sample was apparently pressed in place in the form of a viscous paste by means of a captured ball bearing, leaving a circular groove in the paper. It would seem the ball bearing must have a microscopically roughened surface in

order to apply the ink without skipping. The ink paste might be administered under pressure.

Conclusion: Writing instrument not know to us or any of our world-class expert consultants and literary historians. Please supply any additional particulars and samples to the above office at the earliest possible opportunity if available.

In rising excitement he turned to the handwriting analysis.

Sample Nr. 1A-4567.

Analyzed by Senior Staff Graphologist Frau Dr. Hedwig Stutz. Berlin, the 8.4.41.

The writer is described as an adult male, probably an American, handedness unknown. A full analysis is not possible because of the Rotring-type pen used, now popular in many schools, which eliminates all stroke shading. Nevertheless:

The first impression is one of a person nearly totally untutored in simple penmanship. This is beginning to become typical of the Americans, but this sample is an extreme example. It is as if the writer had learned penmanship by reading a book without being required to perform the most basic drills.

Yet this primitive script, though sloppy in the extreme, is nevertheless completely legible and in fact easy to read, a sign of someone who demands to make himself understood. In fact the spare precision of the writing suggests an extremely logical mind, which accretes no excess intellectual baggage. There is no sign of deceptiveness or duplicity, except one—to hide a deep sense of resentment.

17

Stumpfnagel reflected on that assessment. No duplicity? Well, fanatics don't need to lie, so convinced are they of the truth of their cause.

> Mathematical brilliance of the highest order is indicated by very high extensions into the upper zones along with many quasi-numerical formations. Were these extensions not grounded in reality, as this script most certainly is, the writing would be that of a mad scientist—someone who dreams of achieving great things, but does not possess the capacity to carry them out.

> However, the strength of the down strokes, the fact that all upper zone strokes are finely connected to the middle zone rather than left floating, and that the embellishments in the upper zone are clever and well integrated, aiding legibility rather than hindering it, indicate without question a world-class mathematician, physicist, chess player, or other highly original and intellectually superior person.

The middle-zone letters are well formed, and widely spaced, indicating a person whose daily life is well organized. The lower zone loops are full, gracefully round and, most tellingly, strongly formed, indicating strong sexual proclivities, as well as the athleticism and the executive decisiveness of a man of action.

> Underlying the powerful and realistic intellect is an unresolved emotional bitterness that casts a shadow over everything this person does. Unrelievedly straight-line strokes beginning in the lower zone and traveling to the middle zone, totally lacking in curvaceous softening, indicate a deep, pervasive resentment. Pleasant, spacious curvatures in the middle zone indicates this resentment is

18

well-hidden in everyday life. Indeed, the writer seems to have a delightful sense of humor and a sensuous flair for living. He is usually genteel and cultured: But behind this pleasant facade lies a road map with every purposeful step taken to avenge a burning sense of some great perceived wrong. This neurosis will color or motivate everything the writer undertakes, including his most brilliant intellectual achievements.

Summary: In my thirty-two years of analyzing hand writing, I have come across few examples of intellectual virtuosity of this caliber. And none in people still living.

The writer has an ability to analyze any quantifiable situation to a depth and complexity that the average genius could barely follow. He could then manipulate the results into a brilliant synthesis. He may have no living peer in this talent.

However, this is not the same as analyzing unquantiflable situations, such as politics, or the assessment of character, in which he has no special skill.

With drive supplied by the tension of his inner conflict, and a direction guided by his extraordinary intellect, to paraphrase Aristotle: 'give this man a lever and a place to stand and he will move the world.'

The report slipped from Stumpfnagel's hand. God in heaven, the unflappable "Aunt Hedwig" had fallen hard for the American. So this "genius" had come to Germany offering his services for the good of the Fatherland. But he must want something in return. Maybe something

19

he'll tell us about later, when we'll either be so grateful we can't say no, or—more likely—we won't even know we're giving him what he wants. But who could he possibly be? What could his motive be? Powerful strangers never offer their services for nothing. Stumpfnagel stopped trying to force an answer. With this genius' level of brains and passion it means it won't be money he's after. The lieutenant felt like an athlete getting an unexpected second wind. He picked up his telephone and had Inge put a call through to Colonel Dorenberger.

Chapter Three
APRIL 18, 1941

Stumpfnagel came away from his meeting with Oberst Dornberger shaken. He had described his reason for visiting the Colonel at the Stettin military compound north of Berlin in the most roundabout terms. He was startled by the Colonel's utter frankness. Stumpfnagel had met Colonel Dornberger a year ago. The two had played a spirited game of chess which the Colonel lost gracefully, but not without a fierce battle. Dornberger had remembered their chess game instantly, and had opened up completely, telling him everything about the Planned V-1 jet missile and the first plans of the unbelievable A-4 rocket. Yes they were well along on the design of this liquid-fuel rocket of astounding capability, the Colonel had admitted. Rocket engine tests were proceeding nicely. When finished, the A-4 would be able to drop a ton of explosives four hundred kilometers away! And fly there many times faster than the speed of sound!

It would strike its target, and only after the explosion died down, would survivors then hear the roar of the rocket's approach! But it would not be cheap. It all seemed like a futuristic dream.

Traveling back to Berlin by train, Stumpfnagel felt a growing sense of exultation swell in his breast. This "Friend of Germany" had him as excited as he had been over any intelligence matter in years. Passing quickly through the Stettiner Bahnhof in Berlin, he was lucky enough to spot a taxi for the short ride to his office. He declined Inge's proffered packet of mail and asked her to bring in her dictation pad.

"Take out a personal ad in the Berliner Zeitung," he said to her. "Let's see, today is Friday, too late for tomorrow. But Sunday should go." It was his neutral tone of command, a tone of voice that said "this

21

order is simply my job and has nothing to do with our relationship.' It was a little thing, done unconsciously Inge was certain, but she noticed how most natural leaders all seemed to make their orders more palatable by separating their official demands from their personal behavior.

> Dearest Suitor:
> We have yet to meet, but your thrilling promises make my heart leap. I see many problems ahead, particularly with the elders, for we cannot gain their ears, so important to our future plans, without much preparation. Please write how we can meet. I long for more of your kind words which promise so much. And I will remain faithfully yours.
> W.S.

Stumpfnagel did not have to wait long. Monday morning's post brought a scribbled pink reply:

> Berlin, April 20, 1941
> Dear Herr Lieut. Stumpfnagel:
>
> I see my trust in your intellectual capacity was not misplaced. Yet I still feel a bit queasy in offering myself up into the hands of one of the most—how shall I put this inoffensively—one of the most effective intelligence agencies in the world.
>
> Think also on another point: I will be giving you top intelligence information, but you will never be permitted to learn how I obtain it. At least not at first. I know this essential aspect of any arrangement we come to will cause the Abwehr some serious heartburn, but it's either that or no deal. This means you will have to judge my value

based on the quality of the information I give you, not its provenance.

That is always difficult for the convoluted mind of most intelligence officers, another reason I chose you. Remember too, that I do not want to be in the position of merely reciting new intelligence data month after month. For Germany not to lose the war, we must become much more aggressive than that. I will telephone you soon. Think of a safe place for us to meet. Safe for me, that is.

Vty,

Robert T. Ballard

P.S. I need current identification papers. I assume you can supply them?

"Gott im Himmel!" Stumpfnagel muttered. "Here goes my career, one way or the other."

Chapter Four

Inge Schmidt put her hand over the telephone and pressed the buzzer under her desk. She had never used it before. It meant come quickly. Stumpfnagel bolted through the door.

"I've got your American on the line," she hissed, her hand covering the telephone mouthpiece. "Shall I start to trace it?"

Stumpfnagel thought for an instant. "No need," he said. "Put him through—but record it."

He returned to his office and picked up the telephone, remaining standing. "This is Stumpfnagel."

"Herr Leutnant Stumpfnagel," a cheerful voice replied. "This is Robert Ballard speaking. I wonder if you've given any thought to how we could meet safely?" It was a strong tenor voice. The German accent was good, but not perfect, just like his grammar.

"Herr Ballard," Stumpfnagel replied in his most professionally genial manner. "How nice of you to call. Yes, I do have a suggestion. There is a large diplomatic function being held at the Staatsoper this Saturday—a reception and the performance of Lucia di Lammermoor by the La Scala company. The cream of Berliner society will be there—civilian, diplomatic and military. It's not an absolute guarantee of safety, of course, but it's as close as I can reasonably come. Besides, it'll be fun." He paused. His suggestion elicited no response.

"Oh, say, I've just got a brain storm. I myself am required to escort an official guest, but my secretary, Frau Inge Schmidt, is dying to go. She's an attractive young women, a widow. You could take her."

24

Inge's face burned with pleasure at hearing Stumpfnagel's words. He saw her smile and turned away. The ominous pause on the line continued.

Stumpfnagel felt a little panicky at the American's lack of response. He didn't know how his light banter was being taken.

"Listen to me, Herr Ballard, I know what you're thinking. There's no need to worry about your immediate security. I've had three men check out your—your credentials, shall we call them over the telephone. And I met with Colonel Dornberger myself. Most astounding what you've come up with. I can't imagine how a foreigner can have the access you claim to, but whatever the means you're using, they certainly deserve the Abwehr's fullest attention.

"If I don't have this access, where do you think I'm getting my information from?" Ballard asked. There was suspicion and exasperation in his voice.

Stumpfnagel was immediately on guard "It's a little bit like a good magic trick, Herr Ballard. Alternate explanations are so well disguised, they don't come readily to mind. How would you react if you were me?"

"With the proof I have given you, it would take me a day or two to bring my prejudices in line with the facts."

"Well, you are quicker thinking than me, Herr Ballard. But in any case, the things you have mentioned are useful to the Reich no matter how you obtain them."

Stumpfnagel shifted the telephone to his other ear. "Listen Herr Ballard, we can fence all day. You need me as much as we want the information you seem able to get. No other German intelligence agency will give you this opportunity—you said so yourself, and you're right about that. I give you my word as an officer that nothing will happen to you at the opera. You might even have a good time."

A pause.

"When was the last time you enjoyed the undivided attention of a pretty girl?"

Another pause. They were getting longer.

"OK," Ballard sighed. "I also need papers and an invitation to the party. How do you want to handle the transfer?"

25

"Well one way is to stop all the spy-chasing business and just come up to headquarters and have your picture taken." There was another ominous silence on the line. "You could meet your date."

Another pause. Then a chuckle. "Shit, Stumpfnagel," Ballard snorted, half in disgust. "Are you sure you're not an American yourself?"

Stumpfnagel's heart soared. He was taking the bait.

"Tell you what," Ballard said. "Does your photographer have a Leica camera?"

"That little Swiss camera that shoots still pictures on movie film? He better have one," Stumpfnagel replied. "With his budget he's got just about every piece of photographic equipment ever made."

"Why not give your secretary the camera. I can meet her for lunch right now and she can take my picture for the ID."

Stumpfnagel agreed instantly.

"There's a cafe down the street from you on the Bendler Strasse across from the U.S. Embassy. The 'Pirandelle.' Have her meet me there. But Lieutenant Stumpfnagel," Ballard said in a threatening growl. "She is to be alone. And don't take all day." He hung up.

Stumpfnagel was flushed with excitement. "Frau Schmidt, get your coat. You're going to meet the American."

"Me? I am?" she exclaimed. The excitement put an instant bloom in her cheeks as well. They strode down the hallway, the lieutenant leading her by her arm, their heels clopping in step loudly on the polished marble floor.

"Now Frau Schmidt," Stumpfnagel said at the Abwehr building entrance. "Calm yourself." She was flitting about like a drunken butterfly. "This is a business lunch. You are to be attentive, feminine, and as pleasant as possible to the American. Even flirt with him, discreetly of course. Answer all his questions truthfully. If he likes you, it might see you to the opera."

"Oh, Werner," She cupped her hand over her mouth. "Excuse me, Herr Leutnant. I didn't mean . . ."

"It's quite all right. I know exactly what you mean, Frau Schmidt. Now get going. Drink in everything you can about him. Here is Hahn's camera. He took her scarf from around her neck, leaning up to her to

26

remove it. She felt slightly faint at their sudden closeness. "And give him this." In her handbag he placed a heavy object wrapped in her scarf.

Inge Schmidt peered through the windows of the cafe searching the tables. It was 11:40. None of the few early diners seemed to be there alone. A car pulled up behind her and the door was pushed open.

"Frau Schmidt?" a voice said coldly. "Get in."

"Herr Ballard?" she asked tremulously.

"That's right. Now move it, Liebchen."

She slid into the front seat and fell back into it as the car roared away. Ballard turned left at the first street corner and made an abrupt U-turn. He pulled back up to the Tirpitz Ufer intersection and pulled over, scanning it up and down for any cars that might be following him. No one seemed in unusual hurry. He drove around for a few minutes, always with his eye on the rearview mirror.

"No one will follow you, Herr Ballard," Inge said nervously.

"How would you know?"

"Because he trusts you. And he sent me right out to meet you without calling anyone."

"But he could have had me followed after you left, nicht Wahr?"

"I suppose so. But getting a car is not that easy. There are forms to fill out . . ."

Ballard burst out laughing. "Of course, I forgot. I'm in Germany," he said, looking at her fully for the first time. She was very pretty, like a grown-up Heidi. A widow, the lieutenant had said. And a potential date. Hmmm.

"Well, in that case, where would you like to eat?"

"Eat?" she asked blankly.

Yeah, you know, lunch—Mittagessen." He looked at her incredulously. "You really are his secretary, aren't you?"

"Of course," she muttered. She was crestfallen. He could tell she was not a trained agent.

He parked the car across the street from where he had stolen it. How easy that had been. They walked to a nearby indoor cafe.

Ballard kept looking back over his shoulder, and scanning the street in front of them. His anxiety was making Inge nervous. She reached into her coat pocket.

"He told me to give you this." She handed him the object in the scarf. He unwrapped it to find a Walther PPK .32-caliber pistol. "It's his own," she said.

Ballard's jaw dropped. "Do you know why?" he asked. The girl shook her head. "It's to shoot you with, in case they come after me." Her face turned white. "Well, I guess he really does trust me. Come on," he said, slipping the gun into his trench coat pocket. "This looks like a good spot."

Chapter Five

"Now, Frau Schmidt," Stumpfnagel said excitedly. "Tell me everything."

"Well first off, he's quite nice," she said with some reticence. "Quite a bit taller than you Herr Leutnant, maybe by fifteen centimeters. He's slender at about seventy-five kilos and good-looking, a gentleman with good breeding—no question about that. And so easygoing once he relaxed. He has dark blonde hair and gray eyes. A cute little dimple in his chin. I have his pictures here."

She pulled out the Leica. "He showed me how to use it."

"He did, did he?" Stumpfnagel asked sourly. "Is there anything this guy doesn't know?"

"He knows about the opera," she answered. "He even asked me to it." She gave Stumpfnagel an enormous, evil smile.

Stumpfnagel barked out a forced laughed. "This Ami sure moves in fast, doesn't he?" Stumpfnagel said. "Did you accept?"

"But of course, Herr Leutnant. "You yourself told me to flirt with him. What better way than to sit with him and agree to his every suggestion?"

"Agree to his every . . . ? Frau Schmidt, you ought to be ashamed of yourself, throwing yourself at a perfect stranger like that—and a foreigner," Stumpfnagel snorted. He could see that she was enjoying herself enormously at his expense. Why was he so upset?

"Why Herr Leutnant. I was only following your orders," she replied with mock hurt pride. "To the letter." She thrilled at rubbing his nose in the American's implied attraction to her. In fact he had been merely curtly professional. Yet how delightful it was to have the shoe be on the

29

other foot with "her" lieutenant. And it seemed to be working. Instead of her pinning for him and receiving no encouragement whatever, he was positively jealous of the American's attention. She couldn't wait for the opera.

*　　*　　*

"Aha, Herr Leutnant Stumpfnagel, there you are," a voice behind him called. Stumpfnagel turned to look up at the tanned superior smirk of Oberlieutenant Wolfgang Treuherz from the Diplomatic Office. At his side stood a black-haired pixyish women with a perfectly styled pageboy haircut. She was dressed in a simple but elegant black dress. She wore only a stunning pearl necklace and, of course, no makeup. Nor did she need any. Although diminutive, she nevertheless possessed a startlingly curvaceous body which seemed to tremble ever so slightly as she moved. My god, Stumpfnagel thought, trying not to stare; is it possible with her figure she is not wearing a brassiere?

"Permit me to introduce to you Frau Sabina Pergolesi, wife of the late Segniore Rodolfo Pergolesi of the Italian Embassy," Trueherz purred, bowing to her slightly. "This is Herr Leutnant Werner Stumpfnagel of the Abwehr. He is reputed to be an excellent chess player," Treuherz said, drawing himself up to full height. "Although I myself have never played him."

"And a good thing, too, Herr OberLieutenant," Stumpfnagel shot back. "One wouldn't want to mar an otherwise perfect reputation."

Treuherz bolted his head backwards as if he had been slapped. Sabina tried to suppress a snort—a little cat-laugh—and her face, previously sad and unfocused, illuminated Stumpfnagel with a warm smile. The lieutenant felt scorched by the heat of her gaze. What powerful sex appeal this little kitten exudes, he thought, and then blanched. Wait `till Frau Schmidt sees her: If I so much as smile at this one I'll never hear the end of it.

"So pleased to meet you, Herr Leutnant," Sabina replied, taking the lieutenant's hand and shaking it firmly. Did she trail off with just the slightest caress? It all happened too quickly for Stumpfnagel to notice for certain . . .

30

"Yes, well, I think I can leave you two together for a moment," Treuherz said blandly. The duty of introduction completed, his eyes began to flit about the crowd, hoping to alight on someone more congenial to butter up or insult, depending on relative rank.

"Frau Pergolesi," Stumpfnagel said a bit defensively. "I'm very pleased to meet you." Embarrassed at her frank gaze, Stumpfnagel found himself unable to look her fully in the eye. "But let me warn you that I must first actually conduct a small bit of business. I am to meet someone who is being escorted here by my secretary. So I must keep a lookout for them: After that, I will be able to pay you my complete attention."

"Oh, I don't require you to pay me any attention at all, Herr Leutnant," the little women said archly, casting her eyes aside. "There's already far too much attention being paid here for my liking."

As they circulated in the opera house entrance foyer, with its splendid baroque decorations encrusted in cream and gold, all accented by a ceiling of sky blue, Stumpfnagel both saw and felt the eyes of dozens of men latch onto the shapely Sabina as they passed by. It was stupid, he knew, but he couldn't help feeling proud of himself, more masculine somehow, being seen escorting such a sultry beauty.

But where were Frau Schmidt and the American agent? Stumpfnagel cruised slowly through the crowd, Sabina formally holding on to his arm. More then once he felt the liquid pressure of her full breast pressing momentarily against his biceps. She smelled like a young baby. The combination of her body prodding his, and her delicious odor made him notice the first stage of arousal, something that had not happened to him in months, since his wife had died.

He knew most of the people in the room. That was part of his job. As usual, there were a few strangers wandering about. A group of heavily medallioned senior Italian officers he had never seen before—all looked senile, as if they had been pulled off the battlefields of the First War and exiled to maneuver only at diplomatic functions. A trim, mustachioed man with a dark haired young woman he would want to check them out later, but they were undoubtedly foreign embassy personnel—code clerks, or something else low-level. And two swarthy

31

foreigners—Argentinean businessmen by the looks of the gold they sported on their hands and in their mouths.

"You do play chess, is that not so?" Frau Pergolesi asked demurely. He could see that she was used to being stared at, and carried it off with great aplomb. He was certain she enjoyed it, but would die rather than admit it. Her German, like her figure, was exquisite.

"Yes, I enjoy playing very much," Stumpfnagel answered. His eyes swept the room for the hundredth time, seeking out the golden-haired Inge Schmidt and the American whose face he knew only from photographs, and not finding either. "In fact I am a local champion at the Charlottenburger Chess Club."

"Oh, what fun. Perhaps we could play with each other some afternoon." She looked up at him. Her face was as perfect as a Botticelli Madonna. As with many beautifully-formed small people, her age was impossible to estimate. But for an instant her self-assured face flashed a deep glimpse of pain and desperation.

"When did your husband die?" he asked, stopping to face her directly.

"Oh, nearly five months ago," she answered lightly. "I'm living with my mother now in the Tiergarten section of Berlin. Although they all consider me Italian here, my family and I are really all German. I just spent my university years in Florence, where I met my future husband at an embassy function." She looked up at Stumpfnagel with an odd smile. "Just like this one."

They were standing in an alcove just outside the bustle of the crowd. Stumpfnagel was still scanning the crowd nervously. He had heard that Americans are always late. He felt a tug at his arm. It was the mustachioed man and his young companion. They had approached unnoticed. The man peeled off his mustache. The women slipped off a silly brown costume wig. It was Inge Schmidt and the American!

Stumpfnagel almost muttered a curse. The two of them had been here all the time, watching to make sure no one was watching them. Instantly, Stumpfnagel's intelligence training returned.

"Herr Ballard—I congratulate you. You had me completely fooled. I, ah, guess that means you win the bet and I pay for dinner tonight," Stumpfnagel extemporized for the small woman's benefit.

Ballard looked quickly at her and then at the lieutenant with a questioning stare.

"And Frau Pergolesi," Stumpfnagel continued seamlessly, "Let me introduce to you Frau Inge Schmidt, my secretary, and Herr Robert Ballard, an American diplomat."

The group shook hands all around. Stumpfnagel noticed his secretary's intense examination of Sabina. She stared at the little woman with animal fascination.

Sabina ignored Inge completely, and looked up briefly at Ballard. "Another foreigner," she said impassively. "I suppose they treat you well?" She turned away, not expecting an answer, and finally managed to look over Inge Schmidt, examining her with air of a fashion model generously stopping to smile briefly at a pretty milkmaid. Stumpfnagel saw a hostile glare developing on his secretary's face.

"Frau Schmidt," Stumpfnagel said, interrupting the intense gazes between the women—good god, they were staring at each other like snake and mongoose angling for the kill. Inge tore her eyes away from the small woman and looked up at her boss, feigning a bland expression, but a hurt look of jealousy hovered across her face. If you're going to 'sleep over' with that, her expression said, I'll never speak to you again.

Stumpfnagel was caught momentarily speechless at the effort of breaking off the animal intensity that had sprung up between the two. "F-Frau Schmidt," he muttered, and then cleared his throat. "Could you be so kind as to take Frau Pergolesi over to the bar. We will join you there in a just a few minutes. Herr Ballard and I have some very boring business to discuss, but it won't take long, I assure you."

The two women linked arms like the dearest of friends, all broad, cheerless smiles, each plotting how to find out as much as possible about the other as polite conversation would permit.

The two men watched them walk out of earshot. "Good God, Herr Ballard," Stumpfnagel said. "What the hell was going on between those two?"

"Beats the hell out of me, Herr Leutnant. But if that little vixen doesn't have some general in her bed by midnight—hmmm, now there's an idea—you can call _me_ Miller."

Stumpfnagel turned to study the American. He was prepared for anything, but perhaps not for what he saw. As Inge reported, the man was in his mid-forties with dirty blond hair, and cool, gray eyes. But the easygoing manner she described was barely evident. This evening Stumpfnagel saw only the hard glare of a man of action.

His eyes flitting nervously about, scanning the room continuously, and only looking up at Stumpfnagel for the briefest moments. He was keeping a watch out for any sudden movement toward them. The lieutenant recognized the type—the natural leader who always knew exactly what to do, and while charming when necessary, able to spring into the crudest action when the situation called for it. Yet there was an American variation—the absence of the rigid fanaticism that usually accompanies such men.

Within seconds of studying him, Stumpfnagel realized that Ballard was not a lunatic, and not a put-up by one of his men. He was surely an American—no German could fake that. Yet there was also an indefinable aura about him that made him seem almost larger than life.

"Well and good, Herr Ballard," Stumpfnagel said, exhaling his held-in breath in a long sigh. "I believe you. You've got a direct line to Roosevelt' and Hitler. Where does that leave us?"

Ballard let out a deep sigh as well. "Finally," he muttered. "I never realized how hard it would be to try and give away the goose that lays the golden egg."

"Maybe it would have gone faster if you had tried to sell it to us," Stumpfnagel suggested.

"Well actually I will be selling you something further down the road. But before we discuss my price, I think we ought to get to know each other better." Ballard gave Stumpfnagel a mock leer, testing the German for a sense of humor. Instead a look of dismay crossed Stumpfnagel's face. "What's wrong?" Ballard asked, moving his back against the wall. His hand dove into his pocket.

"It's the women," Stumpfnagel answered wearily. "They're being interviewed by the Gestapo." He gestured across the hall. A tall, almost foppishly-dressed man, complete with monocle, was regaling the ladies with witty repartee. He had snagged two glasses of Sekt—German champagne—off the tray of a passing waiter and was handing one to each of them. They were both holding their hands to their mouths, laughing.

"Why don't you go and break it up?" Ballard asked.

"No, that's Oskar Faulheim. He's an expert. If I do that he'll get suspicious. And besides, I don't want to leave you alone. Otherwise he or one of his stinkards will try to interview you. The less they know about you the better. Let's, just hope the girls haven't spilled the beans."

"And if they do?"

"It means he'll pry into your existence until he finds out who you are and whether you pose a threat. That would not be easy to deflect—even for us. Technically, our jurisdiction is outside the Reich, theirs is inside. But we'll take care of you. Yet if they push it, they could hold you for questioning."

"Then let's go and introduce me," Ballard, suggested.

Stumpfnagel looked startled.

"Act like we've got nothing to hide. Hell, it might keep him off my trail for a while longer than having me scurrying about."

"Ballard, you are a genius." Stumpfnagel eyed him appraisingly. "Do you play chess, by any chance?"

"Never lost a game yet," Ballard answered lightly. Yet he looked serious.

Chapter Six

Ballard was delighted with the first act of the opera which he had seen several times, but never performed with such verve. Somehow the version that had crossed to the United States had lost much of its Latin energy. Inge Schmidt was a delight as well. She was an adorable creature, almost too wholesome to think of. Idly he wondered if she would be available. During the intermissions, they chatted amicably in their orchestra seats. Ballard noticed flashes of acute intelligence in the young woman's quick wit—a wit she tried to disguise under the reins of strictly proper, self-deprecating behavior.

As they talked, Inge could not help herself from repeatedly glancing up at the box where Lieutenant Stumpfnagel anal the Italian woman were seated. They seemed to be thoroughly enjoying themselves. Inge could not fail to notice with what rapt attention the small, dark-haired woman hung on to every word of the equally dark lieutenant.

"They look like they were cut from the same cloth, don't they," Ballard remarked casually.

"Hardly," she snapped. "The lieutenant is a gentleman."

"Why Frau Schmidt," Ballard countered "What sharp teeth you have." He laughed at her distraught stare. Inge dropped her gaze at the box and joined weakly in the laughter.

"You care for him greatly," Ballard said. It was not a question.

"Really, Herr Ballard, you Americans are all alike—frank well beyond the point of intrusiveness. You really should learn to mind your manners." The smile left her face. He saw a look of anxiety that made her blink her eyes.

36

"Don't worry Liebchen," Ballard said outrageously. 'That Pergolesi women won't be the least bit interested in your lieutenant."

"Oh, no?" Inge pouted, fully expecting to be soft-soaped. "And why not?"

"Because I fancy her myself," Ballard said smoothly. "Stumpfnagel doesn't stand a chance."

Inge burst out laughing, yet behind her laughter he saw the tears.

"Mr. Ballard, you are . . ." she was momentarily lost for words. " . . . something else."

After the opera the two couples met in the grand foyer. Stumpfnagel was anxious to reassert his authority over the situation, an authority undermined by the demur Italian women hanging so cozily on his arm, and by the stream of daggers emanating from his young secretary's eyes while she ostentatiously clutched at Ballard's arm as if she needed help walking.

"I suggest we escort the ladies home, Herr Ballard," Stumpfnagel said as they waited in line to retrieve their overcoats. "And then attend to the state-important business we have to transact."

Ballard noticed a moue of disappointment forming on the dark women's face. He seized the moment.

"An excellent idea, Herr Leutnant. And since I am living near where Frau Pergolesi lives, and you and Frau Schmidt both live in Wilmersdorf—do you not? Perhaps I should escort Frau Pergolesi home, and you Frau Inge Schmidt."

"Why that's an absolutely perfect idea," Inge burst out. She disengaged the other women's grasp of the lieutenant's arm and clutched on to it herself like a lifesaver thrown to a drowning man. Sabina Pergolesi, caught off guard by Inge's sudden rush forward found herself standing in the crowd, momentarily manless. Ballard reacted quickly.

"Frau Pergolesi," he purred, taking her reluctant arm into his with courtly grace. "I would be honored if I might escort you home. That is, if this gentlewoman could be persuaded to first spend a brief moment at a local watering hole on the way."

"Watering hole?" Frau Pergolesi said, blanching at the prospect of spending even a moment in some dank dive with this pushy American.

"Kempinski's is the place I had in mind, the Wild West Bar," Ballard continued smoothly, naming the most glamorous restaurant and nightclub in the city of Berlin. He had totally ignored her look of distaste, but was pleased to see it transform into one of spiteful pleasure.

"Kempinski's?" Sabina Pergolesi repeated, drawling out the magical syllables, her eyes growing wide at the luxe of the fabled place. "If you mean the Kempinski's on the Leipzigerstrasse, Mr. Ballard," she continued, switching to flawless English, and drawing her arm more intimately into his, "then this gentlewoman would be delighted to accompany you. Of course you mean just the two of us, don't you?" Only then did she condescend to nod briefly in the general direction of Inge and the lieutenant who were standing by flatfooted, watching with astonishment Ballard's seduction of the Italian woman.

"The lady's pleasure is my pleasure," Ballard said, continuing his courtly dance. How pleasant to speak English again. "Shall we go?" She followed wordlessly, clutching his arm and beaming up at him adoringly.

Ballard turned to the lieutenant. "Thanks for the invitation, Herr Leutnant. I'll call you first thing in the morning to set up our meeting. And Frau Schmidt, it was delightful meeting you."

Stumpfnagel and Inge saw the American's stride falter as the dark women jerked his arm for that last remark.

"But Herr Ballard . . ." Stumpfnagel protested. He did not want to let him go. And then muttered, half in awe, "Thunder and lightning; I hope he can handle that hellion . . ."

"I'm certain he's just the man to do it," Inge agreed.

"What did you say, Frau Schmidt?" He asked, the American's aura fading with his retreating footsteps. He bent toward her to hear better. She smelled his eau-de-cologne, the sweet-sour odor of '4711.' It suited him perfectly. For an instant she had the urge to kiss him, just as a lark. Surely he would understand. But the moment passed too quickly.

"Perhaps we could stop for a nightcap, too," she said eagerly. I know a nice little restaurant near the . . ."

"Frau Schmidt! We are on duty, and I am still in official mourning." Stumpfnagel acted shocked.

"For just a beer, Herr Leutnant," she continued in a downcast voice. "It's a family restaurant. To celebrate our acquisition of the American spy." She looked up at him hopefully, clutching his arm even tighter.

She saw the thought captivate him briefly. But then his face turned official. "If we have acquired what we think we have, it will require more than a toast with beer," he replied, his face brightening as if he had just successfully threaded his way out of a dangerous mine field. He unclasped her grip on him and restored it to proper pressure by laying her hand lightly on his forearm. "And then it will be done correctly, and with the proper list of guests."

Patting her hand on his arm in a fatherly manner, he straightened his, posture and escorted the glum-faced Inge Schmidt out the entrance portals and into the cold night air.

Chapter Seven
APRIL 28, 1941

It was already 11:15 a.m. Monday morning and Stumpfnagel was pacing around Inge's office like a caged animal.

"Did we scare him away Frau Schmidt?" the lieutenant asked. "I thought we had him, for sure."

"I'm certain he'll call, Herr Leutnant," Inge said soothingly. "You know how those Italian women like to stay up until all hours. They may not have woken up yet." She gazed at him with serene satisfaction. There, but for the grace of God, go, you, her smile said.

"Is that so, Frau Schmidt," Stumpfnagel snapped. "And how, may one ask, would a properly-reared German lady know how late Italian women stay up?"

"Oh, it's common knowledge, Herr Leutnant," Inge replied, refusing to be drawn into an argument over such fundamental realities. What do men know anyway, she thought smugly. If I hadn't been there to rescue you . . .

The thought was interrupted by the telephone. At the same instant, Admiral Canaris burst through the door, his gaze speared Stumpfnagel like a lance, his eyebrows raised in a questioning stare.

"Herr Leutnant," Inge said, covering the mouth piece with her hand and resuming instantly her, professional manner. "It's the American."

The lieutenant threw up his arms to signal his despair at the gross irregularities of this crazy project. He picked up the telephone while motioning to Canaris to listen-in on an earphone attached to Inge's extension.

"Herr Ballard," Stumpfnagel said in his most genial manner. "I'm so relieved you finally called. I was beginning to think Kempinski's didn't agree with you."

"Oh, God in heaven, don't even mention Kempinski's," Ballard groaned. His voice was hoarse and low. "I'm telling you, Herr Leutnant, if they didn't serve the finest champagne in all of Germany, Frau Pergolesi and I would be dead now. I don't even remember how I got home."

"And Frau Pergolesi?" Stumpfnagel asked. Out of the corner of his eye he saw Inge smirk.

"Well she's not here, if that's what you mean," Ballard answered. "Listen, about our meeting . . ."

"Now, now, Herr Ballard," Stumpfnagel said, his tone switching to that of a stern schoolmaster. "We're not going to let you wriggle out of that just because you have forgot how to hold your liquor. Tell me, do you have the Kempinski bill?"

"Of course. How can you leave a place like that without the bill to show-off to your friends and mortify your enemies?"

"Well, I'll bet it came to a small fortune. Listen to me: let the Abwehr reimburse you for it. Why don't we meet for a little dog hair—is that not the American expression? And maybe a late lunch. You name the place, and Frau Schmidt and I will come alone. I'll pay your Kempinski bill and give you your Foreign Resident Permit."

All Stumpfnagel heard was a groan. "And besides, I think after the haste with which you deserted Frau Schmidt last night, she at least deserves to witness how your cavalier behavior is rightfully punished."

Canaris' eyes popped in dismay. He shook his head violently. This American-style familiarity was going too far.

"Son, of a bitch, Stumpfnagel," Ballard laughed weakly. "You've got some set of balls, treating your master spy like an errant lackey. And blatant bribery, too.

Well, OK, I accept. Bring 655 Reichsmarks and the fair Inge. If you promise we won't be tailed, we can meet at the same restaurant I took her to the first time. Say two o'clock. I should be conscious by then."

"You have my word, Herr Ballard," Stumpfnagel answered. "And be sure to . . ." He startled and looked up at Canaris. "He hung up."

"Well, no matter," Canaris said jovially. "You seem to know how to handle him better than I would. Good work, Herr Leutnant. The bribe was the perfect touch. Suck the bugger in. Money and women always work wonders. But RM 655, Gott im Himmel no wonder the poor bastard is hung-over. Say, wherever did you get that Italian tart from? Frau Schmidt says . . ."

Canaris caught the look of shock shooting from the lieutenant to his secretary. Her head dropped abruptly, her cheeks burning with shame.

"I . . ." Stumpfnagel stuttered.

"Yes, well, ah," Canaris harrumphed with the faintest glimmer of an embarrassed smile. "It seemed to have worked in any case. Keep up the good work.' And remember, daily reports to me, no matter how insignificant." Amidst the silent glower of anger by the lieutenant at Inge Schmidt, Admiral Canaris beat a hasty retreat.

Chapter Eight

APRIL 28, 1941; 3:20 P.M.

Admiral Canaris paced around in his office at a furious clip. In his hand was the "Basic Allied War Plan" which Ballard had given Stumpfnagel at their late lunch. It mentioned the Allied certainty that Japan would soon enter the war.

"Why don't we just haul him in and make him tell us where he's getting this information?"

"And how would we do that, Herr Admiral—torture?" Stumpfnagel asked, shocked at his own temerity.

"Torture?" Canaris spat out disgustedly. "No, of course not. That's for those animals at the Gestapo. You're a clever administrator, I just don't see why you can't reel him in like all the others. He's setting us up for some clever scheme."

"He is certainly not like all the others," Stumpfnagel replied quietly. "And he is certainly more clever than anyone I've ever met. He doesn't want to be brought in. He doesn't want to get rich quickly. He doesn't even want to meet you. I had to promise that if his intelligence was as good as he claimed, he'd have his freedom. Otherwise he said he'd disappear. That's the arrangement."

"Well, arrangements can be changed," Canaris bellowed.

"Of course, Herr Admiral. But are we willing to risk losing him just to satisfy some bureaucratic niceties?"

"Bureaucratic niceties? Just whose side are you on, Herr Leutnant? Those regulations are there for a reason: to prevent us from making costly mistakes. They are tried and true, the distillations of years of military experience . . ."

43

"None of which have anything to do with a master spy of this caliber, Herr Admiral," Stumpfnagel broke in. "And I believe he will disappear if we put him under surveillance. He's extremely clever in those matters. But, if that's what you want me to do, I'll . . ."

"No, no, for God's sake, don't scare him off. You're right, of course. It's just so damned frustrating to think someone is operating a huge spy network right under our very noses, and we can't even find a trace of it."

"You've tried to trace it?" Stumpfnagel asked, alarmed. "So those were your men outside the restaurant. They made me look very bad. I had to apologize to Herr Ballard about a "mix-up." I thought we had agreed . . ."

"I know, I know, that's why I'm so upset," Canaris said, raising his arms up in a gesture of helplessness. "I thought it could be discretely done. It wasn't. I promise I won't interfere again. And if you're satisfied with him, I don't need to meet him, yet. What was it he said about a major defection?"

"He said that a top Nazi—someone extremely close to the Führer—was planning to steal a plane and fly to England." As soon as the words came out of his mouth, Stumpfnagel realized how ridiculous the story sounded. It made Ballard look like he was trying too hard to impress them.

"Someone extremely close to the Führer?" Canaris repeated coldly, his bushy eyebrows fluttering with incredulity. "Did he say when?"

"May 10th," Stumpfnagel answered. "He said he'll let us watch the escapade if we, ah, agree to his terms in spying for us."

"Gott verdammt, now this really is too much," Canaris blurted out, all the exasperation returning to his voice. "An American spy is telling us about a top Nazi defector? How the hell does he get that kind of information? We are supposed to be sucking him in to do what we want, and instead, he's doing it to us! A top Nazi defector—this has got to be just so much bunk. He is trying to hoodwink us, and it will be during this "top Nazi" defection caper where he takes us to the cleaners." He swung his troubled gaze around to his lieutenant. "What do you think?"

Stumpfnagel bowed his head and scratched his neck in a gesture of uncertainty. He closed his eyes tightly and rubbed them. Then he looked back at his boss. "I know it all seems impossible, but the American has given us unbelievable intelligence items so far, Herr Admiral. I've had most of them checked out. This so-called top party official defection is only two weeks away. If he really lets us in on it, surely that'll be all the proof we need." Stumpfnagel blinked his eyes. He looked directly at the admiral. "He's not asking us to put up any money, so what difference does it make what we think is impossible or not."

"Ah, Herr Leutnant," Canaris replied with a slight smile softening the hard expression on his face. "Always the chess player. But what if our top Nazi is some boarder guard, or a customs official—"high-ranking," mind you—who slips across into Switzerland to live off the graft he's swindled from smugglers. Your master spy's report will be true—sort of—but inconsequentially so. I still thinks it's some kind of double-cross. And the blow will come just before the so-called defection—which he'll expect us to stop."

"If that's the case, we'll know it's a setup," Stumpfnagel replied coldly. "And the Abwehr will be glad to pay his room and board. Permanently which won't be for too long."

"Won't be for too long, ha-ha-ha, you're absolutely right," Canaris chuckled, nodding his head. He sat down. His two dachshunds raced away from Stumpfnagel to their master. They rolled over each other, demanding to be chucked under their ears. Canaris stopped talking and sat staring absentmindedly out the window, stroking the dogs. "Well, all right. As far as I'm concerned, he's all yours. I won't interfere." Canaris turned to gaze at the lieutenant. "But whoever the so-called defector is, let the caper run through to the end."

"Run through?" Stumpfnagel asked.

"Otherwise we won't know whether or not it's just bait for us to swallow. If we cut it off, we'll never know if the American is counting on us to break it up. Then we won't find out about the real value of your Mr. Ballard's sources."

Canaris wrapped his overcoat around himself more closely and shivered even though his office was pleasantly warm. "Has he named his price yet?"

"His price? We promised to give him RM1000 a month and pay his rent, and supply him with an automobile and ration cards for gasoline, food and clothing."

"No, no. You know what I mean. Didn't he say at one time he'd eventually ask us to buy into some scheme of his? After we earned his trust?"

"Oh, yes, of course. He hasn't brought that up again. It isn't going to be money he's after." Stumpfnagel looked away. Suddenly he jerked up.

"What is it?" the admiral asked. He knew the sign of his young aide's brain attacks.

"Why don't we offer Ballard desk space here—an office, even—here in Abwehr headquarters?"

"He's practically hiding out from us and you think by offering him a desk he'll jump into the net all by himself?"

"We can put a desk in that large walk-in closet off Frau Schmidt's office. It's monstrous for a closet. We'll put an armoire in her office to hang the coats."

Admiral Canaris eyed the lieutenant shrewdly. "Go ahead, try it. I'll bet you a bottle of Scotch whisky he doesn't accept."

Chapter Nine
MAY 10, 1941

Ballard and Stumpfnagel flew to Munich on one of the few remaining civilian flights and borrowed a car from the local Abwehr office. They headed northwest to Augsberg. Lieutenant Stumpfnagel drove carefully and kept the Ford on the road by a series of little jerky tugs on the wheel.

"Herr Leutnant," the American said wanly, "Have you been driving for long?"

"Oh, yes, for years," the lieutenant answered blandly. "But actually, I never got a chance to practice much. And now that gasoline is in such short supply . . ."

"I'm getting a bit carsick, Herr Leutnant," Ballard said, not the least interested in Germany's deteriorating fuel situation. "Do you mind if I drive for a while?"

"You know how to drive, too?" the lieutenant replied inanely. His mind was racing furiously. Was this it, a roadside set-up?

"I normally drive ten to fifteen thousand miles a year, my good friend," Ballard answered tersely. "Now pull over here before I embarrass both of us.'

Stumpfnagel looked at the American's face. He did look a little green around the edges. It couldn't be a trick. "It's no difference to me," the German officer answered. "Let's wait until we get to a more convenient stopping point."

"No, goddamn it," Ballard said, seizing the wheel and jerking it to the right. "Let's stop right here!"

The car swerved over to the side of the road, the tires sending up a storm of dust as they slid to a stop. Ballard popped out of the passenger side and stood in front of the car, propping his gangling

47

frame on the front hood with his arm, breathing heavily. After a minute, he walked around to the driver's side. Stumpfnagel slid over. Ballard noticed him holster his sidearm, but said nothing. He pushed the seat back as far as it would go, put the car in gear and, looking briefly in the rear-view mirror, accelerated the car back onto the road. Soon they settled down to a steady eighty km/hr.

"You drive fast," Stumpfnagel said reluctantly.

"And smoothly," Ballard muttered. Some color was returning to his face.

"I thought for a moment . . ."

"I know what you thought, Herr Leutnant," Ballard said angrily. "You thought I was going to pull some two-bit Hollywood stunt—cops and robbers—like you see in the cinema. If that's all you think I'm good for, it's going to take forever to help you save Germany."

Stumpfnagel blushed furiously. The American was completely right; he had made a fool of himself by thinking of Ballard as he would any ordinary defector—like an adolescent thrill-seeker, as so many of them were.

The countryside passed by in a ribbon of serenity. Every small farm plot was intensively cultivated. Cows grazed in the fields with an occasionally herdsman waving to the automobile. Dogs barked at their passage.

"I . . . I apologize, Herr Ballard, Stumpfnagel finally muttered. "It won't happen again, such a lapse of . . . of intelligence."

"You're forgiven, Stumpfy," Ballard said with a smile. "Look, there it is—Haunstetten Airfield."

They drove past the main building, a large Messerschmidt design center and aircraft factory and drove to the Air Field Operations Center. A few gliders were parked near the end of the field. Stumpfnagel showed their Abwehr passes to the guards who scanned them perfunctorily and returned to their game of Skat.

Ballard gazed at the airfield landing strip. He tapped the lieutenant on the shoulder. He pointed to an airplane being gassed up from a fuel truck by a hand pumper.

"It's the new ME-110," Stumpfnagel said proudly, recognizing the twin-engine aircraft as Germany's fastest heavy fighter. "It's a two-seater with the aft-seat facing backwards for a rear gunner. Oh,

48

look, it has the extended-range fuel tanks, too." The lieutenant turned to Ballard. "Seven hundred additional liters. Those are the tanks the pilots can drop after they're used up. Something we learned from you Americans."

Ballard said nothing, a smug look of satisfaction on his face. "Do you mean this is the plane . . ." Stumpfnagel immediately dropped his voice to a whisper. "that our so-called `important party member' is going to use?"

What did you expect him to use, Herr Leutnant—a Fiesler Storch?"

"We . . . I'm not sure we expected anything at all to tell you the truth, Herr Ballard," the lieutenant replied. "Or perhaps if your tip is real, an important local figure, the Gauleiter of Hannover, or something."

"Who is going to fly to England in a spotter plane?" Ballard asked, affecting the smirk he was using on the German officer to express extreme doubt. "It would take him most of the night just to get to Hamburg."

"I could ask the duty officer who the plane is being gassed up for," Stumpfnagel said.' He began to turn toward the desk. Ballard grabbed his arm.

"So that after everyone realizes what happened, she'll remember that a young lieutenant from the Abwehr was asking questions about the plane before it took off," Ballard whispered.

Stumpfnagel's head fell. The American was running circles around him. But he was not putting on superior airs as any normal German would. But then, Ballard wasn't a German; he was an American. What a difference.

The two men walked a few steps out to the front of the building. It was a clear early evening and the sun was more than halfway to the horizon. A Mercedes saloon roared up to the gate. A tall man stepped out of the rear of the roadster, resplendent in the blue-gray flight uniform of an Air Force Captain. He wore high pilot's boots, a pale blue shirt and a dark blue necktie. Stumpfnagel could just see the edge of a flat gold watch encircling his left wrist, and a gold identity chain the right. As soon as he stepped out and swung the door shut, the Mercedes quickly pulled away, its supercharger singing.

Ballard tapped his friend on the shoulder and pointed.

"Ja, I see. A Luftwaffe captain," Stumpfnagel replied. "Kind of dumpy for a pilot." He froze in shock. There were the bushy eyebrows referred to by Allied propagandists as a "beetle brow," the familiar lantern jaw, complete with five o'clock shadow. Together they painted an all too familiar picture.

"Oh in God's Will, Ballard. Now just look at that. There's a real big shot for you. That's . . ." Stumpfnagel froze in mid-sentence. He spun on his heel and grabbed the American by his lapels. "Herr Ballard," he hissed. "You don't mean to say it is the Deputy Führer himself who is defecting?"

"Calm yourself, Herr Leutnant," Ballard said breezily. "And watch the show."

Stumpfnagel could not remain still. He tore open a pack of Egyptian "Muratti" cigarettes and began to puff on one furiously. "I must call the Admiral immediately," he snorted, but stopped abruptly. The call would certainly be recorded by the Gestapo.

"We've got to stop him Herr Ballard. This defection is far too serious . . ." Stumpfnagel, turned to intercept the tall officer striding towards them. Ballard grabbed his friend's arm and spun him around in a complete circle. "Herr Ballard?" the young lieutenant said confused. Ballard clenched his fist and gave the reeling officer a quick, sharp jab on the jaw, jolting him and sending his cigarette flying in a smoking arc. The lieutenant's knees buckled and Ballard caught him and let him slither to the ground.

"Herr Leutnant," Ballard called out in a loud voice. "Are you ill?"

The tall Luftwaffe officer stopped at the door just as Stumpfnagel collapsed to the ground. He looked over at them with tense concern written on his face, torn between getting on with his mission, and helping a fallen officer.

"It's nothing to worry about, Herr Deputy Führer," Ballard said. "He's been feeling a bit faint from his wounds. I told him to sit down while waiting for his wife to arrive. But he kept pacing back and forth. Now maybe he'll listen to me."

The captain bent down to examine the lieutenant. "He has a bruise on his chin."

50

"Obtained when he fainted this morning," Ballard said facilely. "From getting out of his hospital bed too quickly."

Stumpfnagel groaned and opened his eyes. He stared directly into the face of Rudolf Hess.

"Well, he seems to be in good hands, Herr Doktor," Hess said standing up. "Now I must be off on my training mission."

"Yes, please go on," Ballard said: "You won't want to be landing after dark."

"No, I certainly don't want to do that," the tall pilot said. He stood up and eyed Ballard appraisingly.

"I know how awkward landing on these small country air fields can be after dark," Ballard continued. "But at least you have your parachute."

"Bailing-out is hardly an acceptable way of landing an aircraft," Hess tittered nervously.

"Well good luck however you, land," Ballard said, and turned to his recumbent friend, patting him on the cheek. Stumpfnagel began moaning quietly. "It looks like my patient is coming around. I only hope he's learned his lesson this time."

"His lesson?" Hess said, stopping again and turning to face Ballard suspiciously.

"To listen to the doctor," Ballard said. He smiled broadly at the Deputy Führer and then returned his attention to the muttering lieutenant, who was unsuccessfully struggling to sit up. Hess could not see Ballard's hand holding his friend down by the collar.

Rudolf Hess' face froze. "The doctor" was the code name of Joseph Kennedy, the American ambassador to Great Britain, and an ardent supporter of Germany. Kennedy was his backup in case the Duke of Hamilton failed to gain Churchill's ear with Hess' message. Was this strange "doctor" trying to tell him something? He looked at the dazed officer. No, the poor fellow could not be acting this convincingly. Hess stood up and strode quickly through the operations waiting room to his parked aircraft. He climbed onto the wing and hoisted himself into the cockpit. An airman helped strap him in, then hopped off the wing. No sooner was he clear than the left engine belched smoke, caught, then roared to life. The plane began to turn in the direction of the runway when the other engine burst into smoky life. Within a few seconds both engines ran cleanly and the menacing fighter accelerated toward the takeoff position.

Ballard looked at his watch. It was ten minutes past six.

"Herr Leutnant, look at this," he said, helping the young officer to his feet. He supported his friend at the shoulder and faced him toward the poised Messerchmidt.

"What happened?" Stumpfnagel asked.

"In your haste to interfere with this operation, your face contacted my fist. Look, there's your swallow leaving for Capistrano," Ballard said, pointing to the fighter roaring down the runway. It lifted off and immediately made a wide, shallow turn to circle the airfield, far too low according to safe flying regulations. A small knot of people watched the departure. Two bright points of light marked the exhaust flares of the powerful craft as it turned north.

"Wait. Is that . . . ?" Stumpfnagel said.

"Hush, my friend," Ballard said, covering the lieutenant's mouth with his hand. "The enemy hears too."

"You . . . struck me?" the lieutenant asked.

"And thereby probably saved your career. You can thank me later. Let's see if we can find something to eat." Ballard escorted the shaky lieutenant out the door and into the passenger side of the Ford. Ballard could just hear the faint drone of the Messerchmidt fighter disappearing in the distance. He noticed larks resuming their singing in the still evening air.

"Listen to that, Herr Leutnant," Ballard said. "What music do those singing birds remind you of?"

"Music? What music?" the officer babbled. He was still not himself.

"The larks. Richard Strauss' `Four Last Songs,' Dummkopf," Ballard said disgustedly. "Christ, Stumpfy, the way you behave in public, It's getting so I'm embarrassed to take you anywhere."

Chapter Ten

MAY 12, 1941

Admiral Canaris' eyes glowed with an enthusiasm the lieutenant had not seen for the past year.

"Gott im Himmel," Herr Leutnant," he said, "that must have been a sight. To see that lunatic Hess just walk out to his aircraft, and you standing there knowing—knowing—he was fleeing to England. What a thrilling sight that must have been. How did you ever keep yourself under control?"

"Ah, well, it's a good thing Herr Ballard was there . . ."

"To have given you fair warning, that's what did it. Still, I couldn't have resisted the urge to accost him," Canaris said with a big smile. "Goebbels has just issued a statement on the radio saying that Hess has been suffering from acute mental problems for quite some time now. Hah, Goebbels has no love lost for Hess, that's for sure. He's going to enjoy playing that tune."

"But if that's true, why was he still second in line to succeed the Führer after Göring," Stumpfnagel asked.

"Hah! An obvious question, that. And one pointedly not raised in the newspapers either. So you know it's a painful issue." Canaris crossed over to reread his report by the light of the window. "Herr Hess left in the evening of the tenth, Hitler got his letter hand delivered at noon yesterday. They arrested his poor adjutant Pintsch, you know. That's their "kill the messenger" mentality. Yet the Führer didn't let Goebbels issue his broadcast on Deputy Hess' condition until 10 a.m. today, the 12th—twenty-two hours after he learned of the event. Here's a transcript of the key part of the speech, by the way.

> The National Socialist German Work—ers Party hereby announces that Party Comrade Hess, who has not been allowed to fly due to an illness he suffered years ago, has somehow succeeded in obtaining an airplane against strictest orders of the Führer, and on Saturday evening, May 10th, he took off from Augsburg. He has not yet returned. We regretfully re port that a letter he left behind seems to leave no doubt that he suffered from mental derangement, and it must be feared that he has fallen victim to hallucinations. Under these circumstances, it is possible that Party Comrade Hess has either jumped out of his airplane or he has died in an accident.

"Ah-ha," Stumpfnagel muttered. "Does this mean what it sounds like?"

"Of course," Canaris answered briskly. "The Führer was waiting to see how the adventure would turn out."

"He really thinks he can still call off his war with England at this stage?" Stumpfnagel asked, his mind taking on its working demeanor of analyzing the situation like an unusual chess move.

"Precisely, my boy. Hope springs eternal. And by God, that finally explains Dunkirk. We have never been able to figure out why that Austrian corporal prevented us from finishing off the British Army when we had the chance. This explains it."

Stumpfnagel winced at the use of a nickname for Adolf Hitler that could land a less well-connected person in jail.

"He still thinks he can make a deal with the Brits, even now?" Stumpfnagel shook his head in wonder. Hitler the great strategist . . ."

"Of course. Especially now. You know, he likes the British. They're Anglo-Saxons, just like us. God in Heaven, the Duke of Edinburgh-Mountbatten—is a German. Born as "Battenberg." Anglicized his name."

"And, just on the side, the Führer wouldn't mind at all if he could keep the limeys out of our hair during our upcoming domestic dispute with Mother Russia," Stumpfnagel added, joining in the seldom seen levity of Admiral Canaris. "Let us alone to make the world safe against Bolshevism."

"Precisely. You've got it," Canaris joshed. Then his face became serious. "Absolutely astounding how this Ballard fellow found out about it. I can't imagine how he gets his information." A pained look came over the admiral's face. "Can't we find out? I feel so . . . so foolish handing the High Command this priceless top level stuff, and pretending I'm not telling them how I get it only because I want to "protect my sources." If they knew it was coming from a single American spy, and that I have no idea where he gets it from—and that he's got free run of the Reich—Jesus Maria, they'd slice him up to find out how he gets his information—right after they dissected me."

"And kill the golden goose in the process," Stumpfnagel added.

"Oh, of course," Canaris answered. "And curse him for dying while they were cutting him up. Can't we check him out with our consulate in Boston?" He paused. "All right, let's recap the situation: One, we've got a spy who has information the likes of which we've never seen before."

"Two, he's delighted to give it to us as long as we leave him alone," Stumpfnagel added.

"Right," Canaris agreed reluctantly. "And we'll take what he gives us. Three, he's leading up to something, some deal he wants to make with us later on."

"But he's not asking us to promise anything now," Stumpfnagel said. "Because he feels—probably rightly so—that by giving us this fantastic information, we'll be delighted to help him out when the time comes. Hell, he's counting on it."

"And maybe we will be delighted to help him," Stumpfnagel replied. "Even so, he's not telling us what his price is now."

The admiral had a perplexed look on his face. "Why not, Herr Leutnant?"

Both men were standing. Stumpfnagel sat down to think about it. Instantly the dogs ran up to him, demanding to be scratched behind their ears. It was this complete acceptance of him by the admiral's dachshunds that completed the admiral's trust in his young lieutenant.

Stumpfnagel furrowed his brow in concentration while he chucked the dogs behind their floppy ears.

"He must feel he has to bring us over to his point of view, somehow," Stumpfnagel answered. "To some point of view that we wouldn't believe or accept at this time."

Canaris stared at his lieutenant. "Wouldn't believe at this time? Like his claim that Germany will lose the war? Well, I certainly don't understand it. But, ah, you seem to have his trust. I'll leave him in your hands. Drop everything else. Ballard was your priority assignment, now he's your only assignment. Milk him for everything he's got. What does he want to do next?"

"He wants to meet with Professor Doktor Robert Lusser, the head of the pilotless bomb experiments," Stumpfnagel answered, his lips pursed in thought. "I plan to take the train with him up to the Peenemunde test grounds."

"Well go to it my boy," Canaris beamed. "Good Lord, if we get any more tips like this Hess thing, we can shut down all the other agents and just rely on your Mr. Ballard. We'd be far ahead from an intelligence point of View, and think of the money we'd save."

Chapter Eleven
MAY 23, 1941

Ballard pointed to Frau Schmidt's telephone—his way of asking if he might use it. His own telephone had not been installed yet, but a bottle of Dewar's scotch had mysteriously appeared on Stumpfnagel's desk the day after the installation order had been placed.

How strangely lacking in manners he is, Inge thought. But actually, never offensively so. She nodded in acquiescence.

"It's to Frau Pergolesi," he said for no reason. He misdialed halfway through the number and had to begin again.

Inge smiled to herself. He had moved into an office in the room across from hers that was a converted walk-in closet. He and the lieutenant had been working closely on some operation that even she knew nothing about. One thing she did know, if her lieutenant was brilliant, the American was a genius. And usually so unflappable. Watching him misdial made her laugh inwardly. Except for their first meeting, it was the first time she had seen the imperious American uneasy. In one minute he is directing generals how they should run their war, in the next he behaves like an adolescent screwing up courage to ask a girl for a date. For the first time she saw him at something where he seemed to be afraid of failure.

"Hello, Frau Pergolesi," Ballard said. Inge could hear how he vas trying to calm a trembling voice. She had to laugh. Men: how powerful and yet how weak.

"No, Madam, I wish to speak with Frau Sabina Pergolesi." Ballard wiped his brow. With all their technical miracles, why hadn't the Germans put in air conditioning yet, he wondered. Or was making

57

people comfortable against the Prussian moral code—like joyous sex in America?

"Ah, yes, Frau Pergolesi. So nice of your mother to get you to the telephone. This is Robert Ballard." He spun around, his back to Inge, and propped himself on her desk. Her mirthful gaze was adding to his discomfort.

"Ballard, Ballard," he repeated anxiously. "The American. We were introduced at the Staatsoper by Herr Leutnant Stumpfnagel." He pointedly omitted mentioning Kempinski's. Ballard slipped off Inge's desk and looked at her in despair, making wild eyes which asked why women were so impossible to converse with in a normal manner.

"I was wondering if I might take you out to dinner tomorrow night, Friday." Another long pause. Inge could just make out the reluctant tone of the speaker at the other end of the line.

"Well, any day is fine with me, Frau Pergolesi. My dance card is rather empty." Ballard gave a weak laugh, and gave Inge another shrug.

"We could do that, of course, yes." Inge saw Ballard grimace. "I'll ask the lieutenant and he . . . I'm sure he'll be able to find someone to bring along."

Inge's eyes shot up. Ballard was making a date for Stumpfnagel—and a woman! She pretended to become engrossed in reading a file, her face burning at the intensity of her interest in this conversation.

"Hold on, maybe I can ask him now. He's in the other room." Ballard handed the telephone to Inge and walked into Stumpfnagel's office. "Say Werner, would you and a date like to have lunch with me and Sabina Pergolesi this Saturday afternoon? She won't go out with me alone."

Stumpfnagel laughed and nodded agreement. He raised his forefinger in the air to indicate an idea. "She's a chess player! We could play chess at the club, he said. But tell her they only serve beer!"

Ballard took the telephone from Inge. "Yes, he can make it. The lieutenant wants to know if you'd like to go to a chess match next Saturday." Pause. "You would?"

Ballard's face fell. "Well, great, it's all set then. First we'll have lunch. Shall I pick you up at noon? Now remember, just you—don't bring your mother." It was a last attempt to save his reputation with Inge and the lieutenant, who were pretending not to notice the unaccustomed difficulty the suave American was having maneuvering this women to his will.

A heavy silence descended on the two offices, broken only by the rustling of pages being turned, as each person returned to reading the battle dispatches and other official correspondence. The question of who Stumpfnagel was going to bring to the chess club hung in the air like a black sulfurous cloud emanating from the desk of Frau Inge Schmidt, and completely filling the room. Ballard could feel the tension rise like the slow accretion of electricity in the air before a mountain storm. Everyone was waiting for the discharge to clear the air.

Frau Schmidt sat at her desk with burning cheeks, turning the same sheet of paper over and over again, pretending to be gainfully occupied. The minutes dragged on, while Stumpfnagel, also rustling pages in his office, said nothing. Tears slowly filled Inge Schmidt's eyes and she fumbled for a handkerchief to blow her nose. She was about to leave for the ladies room and have a good cry when her intercom buzzed. She took a deep breath before answering it.

"Jawohl, Herr Leutnant." She could not keep a choking sound out of her voice.

"Frau Schmidt, I wonder if I might ask you to work next Saturday," Stumpfnagel said. There was tension in his voice, too.

Inge sucked in her breath. "Yes, of course, Herr Leutnant." Her shoulders slumped. Tears streamed silently down her cheeks. Ballard looked away.

"It's to accompany Herr Ballard and his lady friend with me to the chess club," Stumpfnagel continued. "You know, lunch, the chess club. Have I ever shown you my chess club?"

Inge Schmidt jolted up as if struck by lightning. "No you never have, Herr Leutnant," she said: "And, yes, I would very much like to have lunch with you."

She fell back in her seat. She rose to go to the wash room, crying freely now, but with such a radiant smile on her face, she didn't care who saw her.

59

Chapter Twelve
JUNE 15, 1941

General Heinz Guderian shook his head at Stumpfnagel decisively. "I appreciate your warning about our Enigma code. If true. We will check out the current code groups by setting up a false alarm and watching if the Soviets pay any attention. But no, under no circumstances are we going to supply the eastern armies with winter uniforms. Hitler would see that as treasonous caution. If we do not conquer Russia within three months . . ."

"Yes?" Lieutenant Stumpfnagel replied. Ballard sat by morosely, his eyes shifting nervously. He saw Stumpfnagel was getting nowhere.

"The Fuhrer's Directive Number 32 of June 11 specifies quite clearly that Russia must be conquered quickly in order to move the German Expeditionary Force from the Transcaucasus into Iraq. This would bring the Arab world against the British and tie up a major portion of the British manpower defending the Middle Eastern oil fields. That, and the entire 'Siege of Britain'" depends on our rapid success. The Führer would never permit any indication that his schedule might not be met."

Stumpfnagel looked questioningly at Ballard and took a deep breath. "But think how much greater the Führer's displeasure will be when your armies are immobilized by mud, frozen by cold and exhausted of ammunition," Stumpfnagel said.

The general's aides had risen, anxious to escort him and his strange American guest out.

"Easy for you to say, young man," the general replied. "But we are nearly two hundred full-strength, crack divisions against a few more Russian divisions, which are who knows how well armed. Their numerical tank advantage is nullified by armor that is too thin, their two million infantry are poorly trained and commanded. The Führer has declared that many Russians will desert, so hated is the, Soviet command."

"Well, your intelligence is quite wrong about that," Ballard said, speaking up for the first time. "If you count the troops the Soviets have on the Finnish boarder, and those in the Caucuses, they have 360 divisions, not 211. They have nearly five million men under arms—or will have by June 22nd."

Guderian swung his shocked gaze toward the lanky American. "What do you know about our intelligence, Herr Ballard," Guderian asked sharply. His expression—was pained at the need to rebuke this odd, civilian visitor, but having no authority to do so.

"Just that once Hitler informed the general staff they were going to invade Russia, the Abwehr's foreign intelligence activity was deliberately restricted to determining only changes of conditions on the eastern front. No one at the general staff was ever asked for an overall assessment of Soviet war making capability, nor was Admiral Canaris permitted to offer one. Once Hitler's decision had been made, any news that did not reinforce intelligence chief of Foreign Armies East Colonel Kinzel's estimates was not welcomed. As you well know."

"And I suppose you, from America, know more about the Soviet preparedness than General Koestring, who is on the spot in Moscow," an aide blurted out, deliberately failing to control the sarcasm of his voice.

"As Military Attaché, Ernst Koestring travels around in that huge car of his with two Soviet Secret Service agents at his side at all times," Ballard answered. "He is allowed to see nothing they don't want him to see. Lieut. Col. Kreb's assurances of 22 April that the Soviet army has not yet reached two hundred divisions is also wrong. As for Blumentritt's estimate of a two week war—well, that's a sick joke. Tell me, Herr Major von Moeltke, since you believe yourself to be so well informed, how many Soviet tanks do you expect to come up against?"

"It's none of your business, but since you ask, perhaps as many as ten thousand T-60s and 70s and some BT7s," the aide snapped back, "against our far superior Panther, Tiger and King Tiger Panzers."

"You mean against your far superior 3500 tanks," Ballard said casually, glancing at his fingernails. "At a three-to-one numerical disadvantage. But you forget two salient points." He looked up at the aide with an expression of bored condescension. The aide refused to be drawn in.

"What then," the aide bristled finally.

"The Soviets actually have 24,000 tanks," Ballard said steadily, "so you'll actually be outnumbered seven to one. And while most of them are inferior, they are not seven times worse. Part of this numerical superiority consists of their thousand or so new T-34 tanks which have enough frontal armor to stop any anti-tank munition in the German arsenal."

"T-34 . . . ?" the aide stuttered.

"A BT-7 variation with a 76.2mm gun. Built at the Komintern factory in the East with great secrecy," Ballard smiled harshly. "And your intelligence is so certain, yet you haven't even heard about it. Interesting."

He turned in his seat to face the aide directly. "Of course the one thing that is certain today is that you're going to accept this information with the same grace as all bad news from your intelligence agencies is accepted—as near treasonous defeatism."

Von Moltke stepped from Guderian's side toward Ballard, teeth clenched, his face reddening with rage. Ballard stood up, wondering whether he was going to be physically attacked. The aide began to circle him like a dog sniffing for advantage before leaping at his throat.

Ballard turned as if to take his leave. "Herr General, most of what you've said is true. It's what you're not taking into account that will do you in."

The general looked directly at Ballard. His expression was one of wary interest coupled with extreme distaste at being lectured by a civilian.

"Many Russians will revolt—especially the Ukranians—except Herr Hitler's assault on the partisans, the Jews, and his fanatic desire to extinguish Bolshevism and everyone connected with it, will quickly turn against us a perfect fifth column the German Armies would otherwise employ against Stalin's' forces."

Ballard spoke offhandedly, in an insultingly confident manner, as if lecturing at an officer candidate school. What made it all the more infuriating, was that as soon as the words were spoken, the group recognized them immediately as their worst fears unveiled. Von Moltke was frozen in position, inches from Ballard's side, glaring up at him with burning hatred, just daring Ballard to make a move toward him, just to touch him. Ballard again turned away.

"Some other unacknowledged factors are the Russian ammunition supply and your codes. The British, and especially the Americans, will provide the Soviets with an endless supply of munitions and, as we warned you, they will read every radio transmission you make. At first the Russians won't be able to do anything about it. By the fall, your tanks will be bogged down in the mud, ammunition will be short in supply because your automatic weapons—which you pride yourself on having so many of—will have chewed up ammo at a rate never before experienced. By then your offensive actions will be anticipated. You'll go broke and then you'll start to freeze."

"Herr Ballard," von Moelke, snapped. "This little speech is quite outrageous. We don't know how you managed to bamboozle the Abwehr into setting up this meeting, but I can assure you the Herr General is completely aware of the strategic importance of supplying his troops with sufficient ammunition and materiel."

Ballard had ambled over to Guderian's side. Almost casually, as if leaning over to whisper a confidence, he reached down and lifted the general's sidearm and held it to the old man's head.

"Gentlemen—everyone except the general please leave the room."

Von Moelke slapped at his own sidearm. Ballard fired a shot just over his head. The aid fell over backwards in surprise, wrenching his ankle.

"Please, gentlemen," Ballard said pleasantly. "Leave all the foolishness to me. Now all of you, get out. The general and I want to have a little conversation under four eyes."

The aides were standing around with their hands in the air, awaiting instructions from Guderian, who sat with a shocked expression on his stony, aristocratic face.

"Leave us," the general said sharply, angry at his aides not for what had happened—one man shot at, his own life threatened—but for having got him into a situation where such an outrage could happen. Canaris himself would have to make the apologies.

"We will deal with Herr Ballard after he ventilates himself."

The aides withdrew reluctantly, von Moelke limping pitifully, and swung shut the massive door to the general's study. Ballard immediately uncocked the pistol and laid it on a side table. He pulled out a sheath of documents.

"You are not here to kill me," the general said disapprovingly.

"Of course not," Ballard replied, arranging his papers. "You would be dead already. I've come to show you what will happen to your men if you don't take my advice."

A grimace passed over the general's face. For a moment he thought perhaps he had not fallen into the hands of a lunatic. Well, he would play along to see what this crazy foreigner wanted. Guderian stood up, the better to look at the documents laid out on his desk. They were photographs of men at war, he saw, German soldiers, haggard beyond belief.

"You know so much about our intelligence. Do you know the penalty for shooting at a German officer?" the general continued, picking up another photocopy. He studied the scene of a winter road lined with the bodies of German soldiers, abandoned in place as they had died of their wounds on the way to the airstrip, or were plowed aside to keep the road clear. Arms and legs stuck out of the snow at odd angles as far as the eye could see. The men assumed the position in which they had died—on stretchers, on the backs of their comrades, or hobbling in alone. After freezing solid, they were swept aside by periodic snowplows, their carcasses assuming tortured new positions, their frozen bodies forming a grotesques forest of limbs, rock hard arms and legs reaching out for help that would never come. The sound of an alarm bell could be heard ringing faintly through the study doors.

"Death by firing squad, I imagine," Ballard replied. "Unless there are extenuating circumstances."

The general studied each photocopy wordlessly. Scenes of men lashing at exhausted horses in desperate attempts to pull artillery out of frozen ruts, dead teams of horses lying in the road side gutter, their legs pointing upward in stricken gestures of hopelessness, men dragging their wounded comrades to a drafty first aide tent while snow swirled around them like a shroud.

"These . . . where did these come from?" The general whispered. He looked up at Ballard with a haggard expression.

"I cannot tell you that, Herr General. Even if I did, you would not believe me."

"This whole Russian invasion business is unbelievable," Guderian said somberly, putting the pictures down. "Did you know that the Führer has canceled my plan to use my tanks as a spearhead to penetrate to the Dneiper? Our only solid hope of a decisive victory?"

"Yes Herr General, I do. "Ballard replied. "You are to hold the Panzers back to support classic infantry encirclement. A great waste of opportunity. Perhaps in this, his finest hour, Herr Hitler, the great risk-taker, has lost his nerve."

The general looked sharply at Ballard, then continued to study the photographs. "You know too much, especially for an American. More even than my own people . . ." He stared at Ballard keenly, studying his face. Ballard returned the look evenly. He saw the general's stern gaze become watery and unfocused. It was impossible to tell what he was thinking. This was always the hard part. The questions about where the information had come from, followed by outraged incredulity, and then rantings of "impossible," "lunacy" and so on.

The general picked up his telephone.

"Here is Guderian. Call off the alarm. Return to my office without sidearms. Have my staff car ready to drive Mr. Ballard and Lieutenant Stumpfnagel back to the air port."

Ballard raised his eyebrows slightly, either in mild surprise, or as if signaling something. The general gave a curt acknowledgment.

"And nothing sneaky, either," he said into the telephone, the German phrase being "Keine jüdische Sachen"—No Jewish business.

He returned his attention to Ballard for one moment more. "I will rethink the Russian front supply situation." Then he turned to his own stack of papers. There were no thanks, no accusations, no demands for explanations. And no agreement to change anything.

Ballard collected his photocopies and began carefully to incinerate them in the fireplace, one by one. The general walked around and retrieved his sidearm lying on the side table. He held it in his hand for long seconds before holstering it and closing the leather flap. At that moment, aides burst through the door, their faces distraught with tension, ready to throw themselves at Ballard's throat to rescue their general. They stumbled to a halt at the scene before them: the general was sitting absent-mindedly at his desk. Ballard was kneeling by the fireplace. Neither man spoke. Both wore solemn faces, but Ballard's was placid, the general's troubled.

Stumpfnagel entered, his face white with anxiety. Once again the crazy American had thrown his own career into the most serious jeopardy. Kidnapping a general, shooting at an officer, it would be a court martial followed by execution or at least exile into a prison battalion.

Ballard stood up and faced the general. He brought self to attention, clicked his heels and bobbed his head, a necessary military social grace taught to him by Stumpfnagel. The general did not look up, but nodded briefly as if responding. The meeting was over. Ballard grabbed Stumpfnagel's arm and pulled him out the door. They retrieved their coats from cold-faced attendants and jumped into the waiting staff car. An MP major slipped into the front seat and ordered the driver to proceed. Stumpfnagel could not contain himself.

"What in God's name prompted you to take the General hostage? Have you completely lost your mind?"

Ballard shook his head, and pointed to the MP. The ride continued in silence. At the airport, the MP opened the door for them. "It is only my General's strictest order that prevents me from beating you two into bloody pulps," he said icily. "The next time you feel like visiting the general, Herr Leutnant, especially in the company of this American Schweinehund, I would bring along a company of SS guards, or you won't be leaving so easily." He saluted involuntarily, and jumped back into the car.

Stumpfnagel burst out in hysterical laughter that was almost a crying fit.

"Jesus Maria, Ballard, now I've seen everything. How in God's name did you get us out of this one alive? What did you tell the General? What did the General say? Is he going to winterize the Sixth Army? Do you know it's a mandatory capital offense to shoot at a German officer?"

Ballard turned his eyes toward Stumpfnagel as if seeing him for the first time. It was a look of pity.

"Stumpfy," he said tersely. "Control your emotions. Do you think this war is a goddamned game that you play by rules of social etiquette? Think of the Führer. Does he play by the rules? This is real life, Lieutenant. Nothing is more serious, not your officer's code of conduct, not your capital offenses, not your blind respect for rank. If we do not save the Sixth Army at Stalingrad, Germany will lose the war. It's that simple. Now stop your damned Katzenjammer and see about getting us back to Berlin."

"But what could you possibly have told the General that would convince him to listen to you?" Stumpfnagel cried.

"I showed him pictures of what would happen to his troops in the grip of a ferocious winter. Without proper equipment they would fall everywhere, dead and dying. I don't know if he even thought about where they came from. Maybe he didn't need to know or didn't care. Logic didn't enter into it. All he saw was German boys and men, maimed, mangled, frozen. That was enough to make him realize the tremendous consequences of not taking the simple precautions we recommend."

"But where did you get such pictures? Last winter we hardly lost any men at all. And besides, the general has seen enough of death on the battlefield not to be swayed by photographs. Herr Ballard, are you not telling me something? Is the General going to do anything?"

"He didn't say he'd do anything. But why would he tell me? I'm just an ill-mannered messenger boy." Ballard hesitated. "Guderian is the . . . the deepest German general I've met. He said he'd 'rethink' the situation. I think he'll do what he can, probably behind Hitler's back. We took our best shot. The rest is up to him—and the German soldier."

Stumpfnagel leaned up against the airport counter to light a cigarette, his hands still shaking with excitement. He took a deep drag and exhaled. "God, I don't know what I'm doing schlepping a nutty Amerikaner around. I can just see it. The others you want to visit are going to ask Guderian's staff what you wanted from them. Once they talk to each other, no one's going to have a thing to do with us."

"On the contrary, my friend of little faith," Ballard shot back. "Guderian's staff won't utter a word about what happened. They'll put up a stone wall to any requests for information," Ballard leered at Stumpfnagel with a maniacal grin. "That alone will make everyone extremely interested to see us. And if Guderian goes ahead and re-equips his armies we will have accomplished what we set out to. Up `till now." Ballard spotted a newspaper on a seat across the waiting room and walked over to it. He picked up a day-old Voelkische Beobachter. He fanned through the pages, an annoyed grimace on his face. "Say haven't your Nazi editors ever heard about crossword puzzles?"

Chapter Thirteen
JUNE 19, 1941

As the audience drifted out of the meeting room, Admiral Canaris turned from the group of officers he was conversing with and motioned to Lieutenant Stumpfnagel to join him.

"Herr Leutnant, I think you know these gentlemen."

He motioned quickly to the assembly. "Oberst Schenkel from the Wehrmacht signals department, Generalmajor von Piekt from the Oberkomando der Wehrmacht, and Kommandant Kurzecke as well. And, on loan from the Luftwaffe, General von Hoescht. Gentlemen, this is Leutnant Stumpfnagel, who has been running our new espionage ring, 'Operation Boston.'"

"Herr Leutnant, we have discussed briefly the valuable, ah, well, the extremely valuable information your American spy ring is producing," von Piekt said in a high-pitched voice. He was a Junker through-and-through, and often found it difficult to speak to officers as low-ranking as a captain, to say nothing about a lieutenant. His open admission of Ballard's worth was high praise indeed.

"Yes, almost too good to be true," the Luftwaffe general broke in, a brilliant, taut, condescending smile on his face. Short and almost white-blonde, von Hoescht was, as usual, preened like a movie star. The leather of his high boots was polished to a sheen that made them look wet with fresh paint. "What is the ringleader's name—Herr Ballard?"

"Herr Admiral," Stumpfnagel said, his face stricken. "I thought we agreed to keep the details of the operation secret."

"We are, we are, Herr Leutnant," the admiral replied hastily . . . All of these men are sworn to absolute secrecy. But too many of the tips we got from your friend affected their commands."

"Such as your remarkable knowledge about our strictly secret jet fighter," the Luftwaffe general broke in again. "It's one of our most highly guarded projects. Only a handful of people know about it at all."

"And the general wishes to know how 'Boston' found out?" Stumpfnagel asked worriedly.

"I insist on knowing," von Hoescht answered. "The Luftwaffe can't afford to have traitors in such important places."

Stumpfnagel looked at Canaris deeply crestfallen but said nothing. Canaris watched his lieutenant and then turned to von Hoescht. "The arrangement you have agreed to is to shield 'Boston' from the demands of other agencies. If we gave you such special access, everyone else would demand it, too. And in the fight for the provenance of every detail, the details themselves would get lost."

"And so?" the general asked. "Is he working for us or are we working for him?"

"We made a bargain . . ." Stumpfnagel said sheepishly.

"A bargain?" von Hoescht shrieked, turning to confront the lieutenant. "If we make a bargain with some traitor, we can break the bargain. Who the hell is calling shots in this little melodrama—him or us?"

"Now, now Herr General," Admiral Canaris tut-tutted. "Just tell me the information we have been supplying the Luftwaffe has not been of the highest quality . . ."

"Ja, it's been good. Too damned good," von Hoescht answered sullenly. "Well, thank you Herr Leutnant. I can see I have to work on your chief a little longer." He turned to Canaris and looked at him bitterly. As far as the general was concerned, Stumpfnagel no longer existed.

"And we have our bargain, too, Herr General," Admiral Canaris said briskly. "The Luftwaffe is to keep its hands off in exchange for the information we have been supplying. I expect you to keep up your part of it."

"Yes, yes, of course," von Hoescht replied, disgustedly. "But one can't help wondering what the Abwehr is coming to when it is run by its spies instead of the other way around."

"Now in the Luftwaffe, we do it different," Generalmajor von Piekt interjected in a self-deprecating mock Prussian accent. Except for von Hoescht, the assembly broke out in chuckles.

"At least in the Luftwaffe we know who the boss is, for God's sake," von Hoescht said, attempting to join in the laughter. But his smile lacked conviction.

Chapter Fourteen
JUNE 22, 1941.

On the morning of June 22, the entire country paused to listen to the newscasts describing a huge Blitzkrieg of German troops rushing into the Soviet Union. Operation Barbarossa was underway. All traffic stopped as people pulled over to hear the news. Pedestrians gathered to listen somberly in front of stores which had placed radios on chairs outside their premises. Announcements heralding an important address to the German people caused many to remain at home. After a short Wagnerian prelude, the news came quickly: in the early hours of this morning, June 22, the Luftwaffe had attacked, bombing sixty Russian airfields, and destroying nearly one thousand military aircraft, most of them sitting on the ground. At the same time the mighty Wehrmacht—the German Army—advanced into Russia on a nine hundred mile-long front. It was the largest land invasion in history. The invasion of Poland and Czechoslovakia had been mere training grounds compared to the scope of this enormous offensive.

With all the military traffic heading east, everyone had known that an invasion of Russia was coming. But when it actually happened most were stunned nevertheless.

Hitler had written what he hoped would be a stirring speech:

"German people, at this moment a march is taking place that compares with the greatest the world has ever seen. I have again decided today to place the fate and future of the Reich and our people in the hands of our soldiers. May God aid us especially in this fight."

But he did not himself give it, nor were most as thrilled as he hoped. Propaganda Minister Goebbels was the one who read Hitler's announcement over the airwaves. He realized that the public was wary of expanding the war. "The nation wants peace, and every new theater brings worry and concern," he wrote in his diary. He refrained from publishing maps showing the rapid German advance for fear that the large amount of territory gained would frighten, rather than elate the public.

On the next day Italy and Romania declared war on Russia. A few days later, Finland joined the Germans and invaded Russia from the north. Hungary and Albania soon followed. The "phony war" was over. World War Two was in full swing.

Chapter Fifteen
JUNE 25, 1941

General von Hoescht sat behind his desk erect as a ramrod. On each side, standing nearly at attention, was an aide. Across the desk sat Oscar Faulheim, a pleasant smile of puzzled expectation on his face.

"It's not every day that the Gestapo gets a request to meet with the Luftwaffe," Faulheim said in a puzzled voice. "But I'm always ready to be of service, Herr General von Hoescht. How exactly can I help you."

"Have you met the American, Robert Ballard?" von Hoescht asked tersely.

"Ballard," the Gestapo agent repeated, throwing his head back in thought. "Ja, briefly. Lieutenant Stumpfnagel introduced him to me a few months ago."

"Have you checked him out?"

"I understand he's a code clerk or something at the American Embassy," Faulheim replied breezily. "And that he's quite a good chess player."

"Really?" von Hoescht said, as if genuinely surprised. "And when was the last time he set foot inside the American Embassy?"

Faulheim bent forward, an intent expression replacing the genial smile. "You are saying . . . ?"

"I am saying nothing, Herr Faulheim. I was merely asking a question. In any case, I'm so glad you could stop by to visit." The general stood up. An aide jumped to, unexpectedly bringing the Gestapo agent his coat.

Faulheim stood up slowly, trying to fathom the meaning of this curious conversation. Is this all the general had asked him to make an

74

hour's drive for? Was it a deliberate insult? He scowled inwardly. No. Von Hoescht is a patriot of the highest order. Something is going on with this American, but the general isn't saying what. Can't say. Because it might compromise his own position. And for some reason he can't bring his own security people in on it, either, Faulheim calculated. Perhaps a leak in the Abwehr at the highest level. Hmmm. Most unusual, unprecedented even, for a military man to bring the Gestapo in on a case.

"I will look into the matter discreetly, Herr General," Faulheim said, clicking his heels together and giving the Heil Hitler salute. "And you can personally depend on my complete discretion as well, and the appreciation of the Gestapo."

Ballard spotted Inge sitting at the Abwehr canteen and changed direction to sit with her. He bumped into someone also making a sharp turn.

"Excuse me," Ballard said. "I wasn't looking where I was going."

"For God's sake," the tall man said testily. He had spilled some pudding on his jacket. "Say," the stranger said, eyeing Ballard deliberately. "Aren't you the American I met recently? Where was it . . . ?"

Shit, Ballard thought. It was Oskar Faulheim, the Gestapo agent Stumpfnagel had warned him about. "At the opera," Ballard said resignedly. "My name is Robert Ballard, Herr Faulheim. What brings you to the Abwehr?"

"Why you, of course, Herr Robert Ballard. The American embassy worker who never sets foot in the embassy." Faulheim set his tray down on an empty table. "We should talk. Do you have a minute?"

"I don't know," Ballard said. "Not if you continue to answer my questions with your own questions."

"Donnerwetter, I can't seem to use that trick on anyone anymore," Faulheim said, crestfallen. "To tell the truth, I came here on official business—to find out more about you. Unfortunately, Admiral Canaris was not very forthcoming."

Ballard looked into Faulheim's eager face. The man's eyes sparkled with intelligence and self-deprecating charm. "So the accidental bumping into me was deliberate?"

75

"You noticed that, too? Good God, I really am getting too old for this sort of work."

Faulheim's eyes fell in mock despair.

"There's no need to keep my work a secret to the Gestapo," Ballard said, the hint of a smile forming on his face. This Faulheim guy was not at all what he expected, no surly German machismo, no arrogance. He could as well be a sassy American detective. "I'm an American turncoat doing intelligence analysis for the Abwehr."

"Ha! Now that's what I find so refreshing about you Americans. Utter frankness." Faulheim eyed Ballard appraisingly. "'Turncoat' is not a pretty word. Do you ever plan to return to the States, Herr Ballard?"

"Not if I want to keep my head attached to my body," Ballard said sourly. "But the way the Amis' treated my mother and father, it'd have to be a snowy day in hell before I'd want to go back."

"Snowy day in hell, ha-ha, what an expression," Faulheim retorted, chuckling. "So your American citizenship won't do you much good now?"

"How perceptive of you to notice, Herr Faulheim. But it will work to German benefit just fine, as long as no one informs the Americans what I'm doing. Meeting and drinking and . . . with other Americans is one of my best intelligence tools."

"And 'fucking' you were about to say, Herr Ballard?" Faulheim said giving Ballard a man-to-man leer.

"You really should stop these mind-reading tricks, Herr Faulheim," Ballard answered. "Most unnerving to those of us who don't have the knack."

"But it is rumored that you certainly have quite a knack for getting intelligence. Tell me, do you trade German information to get it?"

"Of course, Herr Faulheim," Ballard replied testily. "As any professional spy would know. This is not amateur night. Tossing out a few intelligence tidbits is the surest way to get important information in return. Surely you're aware of that?"

"Quite aware, Herr Ballard. And aware of the dangers of giving out too much information, while not getting enough in return."

"Really?" Ballard asked, suppressing a yawn. He was becoming irked at this sly needling. "When was the last time you traded information with anyone of consequence? I thought the Gestapo just took what it wanted."

Faulheim faced flushed momentarily. He took a deep breath. "Well, you've got me there, Herr Ballard. I don't have much experience in the spying game, it's true. Just enough to know it is a dangerous business and can backfire at any moment." Faulheim stood up. "I apologize for the cheap trick of bumping into you. I should have known that the best way to meet an American is to just walk right up to him and introduce yourself. But you've answered my questions. The admiral says that you are operating under Abwehr protection. That's good enough for me. So, until we meet again, Herr Ballard, auf Wiedersehen."

Faulheim shuffled off uncertainly, looking for the correct way out. He turned to look at Ballard with a shrug of indecision. Ballard nodded his head to the left. Faulheim smiled gratefully, sauntered out to the hall and turned left.

"Until we meet again?" Ballard asked, trying to mimic the Gestapo agent's Saxon accent.

Chapter Sixteen
AUGUST 2, 1941 .

Sabina Pergolesi sat in the police station staring across at the tall "gentleman" who had been so charming at the opera reception. He was wasting little charm now. She had been asked to report in to the local police station by a routine notice requiring her to renew her Foreign Diplomatic Resident Permit. When she handed it to the clerk, it was whisked away, and she was told to follow. Now she sat here facing Oskar Faulheim of the Gestapo.

"Frau Pergolesi, let me make the situation quite clear," he said, waving her Alien Residence Permit in the air. "Your dear departed husband of Italian citizenship is dead. The Italian government is no longer interested in extending to you, and your mother—both natural born German citizen—the honorary Italian citizenship you have been living under. Thus, at our request, your Italian diplomatic Passport has been canceled. And as a German citizen, you'll no longer be needing this."

Color drained from her face as she watched Faulheim rip the residence permit into small pieces.

"There," he said, as if an unpleasant duty had gone unexpectedly well. "Welcome back to the Fatherland. Now you are just like any other German citizen."

Faulheim lit up a cigarette, and offered her one. She declined. "And fall under the complete jurisdiction of the Gestapo. There is just one matter we are interested in before we let you go." He looked up at her expectantly. "We would like to have everything you know about your Mr. Robert Ballard."

"I'm sorry, Herr Faulheim, I never discuss my personal business with strangers."

She stood up to leave. He sprang to his feet behind the desk and leaning over, clutched the front of her blouse. He forced her back down in her seat. Releasing his grip, his fingers lingered, foundling her breasts. She recoiled in terror.

"I don't want to argue with you gnädige Frau," he said pleasantly. "But unless you answer all my questions now, and to my entire satisfaction, you will be spending the next few weeks in a cell with one of our criminally berserk inmates. He is a brutal man who doesn't know when to stop beating or raping a prisoner cellmate of either sex. But he does have a warm spot in his heart for small, voluptuous women . . ."

She cried out: "Help, help, Herr Policist."

A police captain came warily to the door. "Herr Policist," she said with great relief. "This man is threatening me. Please arrest him. I wish to press charges against him for unlawful destruction of my personal documents, threats against my person, and physically molesting me."

The captain smiled weakly. "I'm sorry Madam, but the Gestapo has the entire jurisdiction in this matter. We cannot get involved in their business. Please do not call out again," he added. "It disturbs the office workers. Auf Widersehen." He closed the door.

Sabina sat back in her chair. So it had come to this. They were closing the noose. Just when she had thought there was a way out. She looked back at Faulheim, hate raging through the tears in her eyes-and hopelessness.

Her gaze dropped. "What do you want to know?"

Chapter Seventeen
AUGUST 5, 1941

It was a beautiful Sunday morning. Ballard lay in bed staring idly out his apartment window. For the first time in years he had nothing that absolutely had to be done right now. It was an odd feeling, and he enjoyed it.

The telephone rang and he hesitated to answer. Who would call on a Sunday morning? Only Stumpfnagel would have the nerve. No, it wasn't even a case of nerve, it was just his incessant attention to detail. Ballard laughed. Just like himself, he realized. Never able to stop plotting for one second. He lifted the handset.

"Ballard here."

"Oh, good morning Herr Ballard," a familiar female voice said. He could not place who it was.

"This is Sabina Pergolesi calling. I hope I didn't wake you."

"No, not at all," Ballard answered, his eyes brightening at once. What luck. A call from the belle of the ball.

"It's such a beautiful day—have you looked outside yet? I thought perhaps you might like to go for a walk in the country. It's warm enough to go swimming. We could take a picnic. I know just the place to go—a lovely beach on the Tegel lake alongside the island of Scharfenberg."

"Why Frau Pergolesi, how nice of you to think of me," Ballard answered. All he could remember was her small pert body, and her subtle but intoxicating aroma. He felt himself becoming aroused. "I'd like nothing better. I've got a car. When shall I pick you up?"

"We could take the car," she answered. But I'm in Tegel right now, visiting an old family friend. "Why don't we meet at the trolley barn and take the old trolley? The Number 28. It starts in Tegel Center and rattles right up to the lake. It would be such fun."

Ha, Ballard thought. She wants to keep our meeting public. No passionate back-seat love-making on a lonely country lane.

"Fine," Ballard replied. "I can meet you in Tegel Center, say at eleven o'clock?"

Ballard returned the telephone receiver to its cradle. He thought for a moment and then called the apartment concierge. "Herr Apfel," he asked. Does your son have a driver's license? He does. Oh fine. I wonder if he'd like to earn a little money today . . ."

Ballard came early and walked a complete circuit around the trolley barn in Tegel Center. After his inauspicious meeting with Faulheim, he had become a bit worried about being followed. No one suspicious seemed about, although with all the coming and going of short-pants wearing Germans of every description, he could have been observed by a dozen Abwehr or Gestapo agents and not noticed any of them.

He had no evidence that he was being followed, but he just found it hard to believe that German efficiency would permit someone as valuable as himself not to be kept under surveillance, even if just to keep him out of trouble. But maybe the Abwehr was indeed keeping to its promise. He had grown to like and trust Lieutenant Stumpfnagel, and his adorable secretary was also nice to be near. But it was clear who she had eyes for.

He spotted the A-15 bus pulling up to its stop. Out stepped Sabina. She too was wearing short pants. Tight little Lederhosen—Tyrolean leather pants that were often handed down from father to son, but worn loosely by men. Hers came from no father. They were made to measure. A set of suspenders with scenes of stags braying were connected to the pants, but so tightly fitted were the pants to her waist, the ornate suspenders served no purpose but to complete the outfit. She wore a white cotton peasant blouse, frilly and loose, buttoned up to her chin. A little colorful scarf touched off her adorable face. At this distance, she could be fifteen years old.

"Frau Pergolesi," Ballard called out, waving his hand. She spotted him, a demure smile forming on her mouth. They shook hands formally.

"So Herr Ballard, we meet again," she said archly. "Perhaps this time we will get home at a reasonable hour?"

"Oh, Frau Pergolesi, honestly, a thousand apologies for that evening," Ballard stammered. God, he could not get over her intoxicating beauty. He felt himself becoming aroused just by the touch of her hand.

"It was all so exciting, just being here in Germany, the lovely opera, meeting you—the most exciting part. And then drinking champagne at Kempinski's with such a beautiful woman—I just got completely carried away."

"Yes, you certainly did. But it was fun, wasn't it? You are forgiven this time Herr Ballard," she said primly. "You know it promises to get quite warm. Have you brought your bathing suit?"

"Bathing suit? I..I hadn't even thought of it. I don't own a bathing suit," Ballard replied.

"Well then let's get you one," she smiled cheerily. "Over there, at that department store."

Inside the store the sales clerk asked Ballard what his waist size was.

"Thirty two inches," He replied automatically. The sales clerk looked at him uncomprehendingly.

"He means thirty-two Zoll," Sabina said, using the term for inches when that English measure was still used in Germany. "But let's measure him to see what that is in the modern world. Here," Sabina said briskly, taking the measuring tape from the sales clerk. "Let me do it." She reached around Ballard's waist, briefly pressing her taut bosom into his stomach. That glorious sensation coupled with the smell of her hair made Ballard feel mildly faint with pleasure. He felt embarrassed at his automatic response, hoping she would not look any lower than the tape-measure.

"Eighty-one centimeters," she said. "Let's say eighty with no clothes on. Come over here Herr Ballard. This color will suit you nicely, and look, only 12 clothing coupon points." She had instinctively picked out the perfect color for him, a sky-blue bathing suit with white trim along the waist and leg holes. A man's bikini. "Put it on under your pants in the dressing room, Herr Ballard. There aren't any changing rooms at the beach."

As they waited for the trolley, Ballard brought up the subject of the bathing suit. "Frau Pergolesi, I don't know if you noticed the size of this bathing suit. I have handkerchiefs that are bigger."

"Oh, yes, the Americans practically wear long pants into the water, don't they," she smiled. "All a part of your Puritan heritage, isn't it?" The trolley trundled up to the stop and they hopped on. "Well don't worry, Herr Ballard. In Germany, everyone wears them small."

The trolley ride took a half-hour clattering through a dense pine forest, ending at a circular ring of tracks around a small square in the sleepy village of Tegelort. They got off along with a dozen other adults out for a day at the beach, and several school students.

"We walk through the woods along the Schwarzer Way to Tegel Lake about a half kilometer," she said. Already Ballard could smell the country air. The scent of pines was strong. It was turning out to be a wonderful day. And he with this gorgeous woman! His mind was rolling over schemes to turn this innocent picnic into dinner and a not so innocent evening out.

They came to the water's edge near the ferry to the island boarding school of Scharfenberg. The ferry consisted of a large metal rowboat, with a tiny dingy attached, propelled by the students themselves as they came and went off the island. Most lived in Berlin and would travel home for the weekends.

The beach dropped down from the pine forest and was comprised of the same yellow sand on which most of Berlin was built. It was an interesting combination, an ocean-like sand beach on a freshwater lake surrounded by pine trees. He didn't know if he had ever been to such a place. The walk had made them both hot.

They spread out their picnic blanket and Sabina began removing her clothes. As Ballard dropped his trousers, he was once again acutely embarrassed by the skimpiness of his new bathing suit. It was absolutely the minimum size a man could wear without something falling out. If anything untoward happened, something would definitely stick out. He looked around. A few other German men were running around, most in equally tiny bathing suits. But Sabina was wrong. Some men had on normal bathing suits. What was she up to?

Two women had taken the tops off their bathing suits and were sunning their naked breasts. My God, he thought, in a country where a man could get arrested for embracing a woman in public, it's perfectly all right for them to appear topless at the local beach.

She took his hand and led him to the water's edge. Only one other couple was swimming.

"Let's swim out to the float," she said. Her bathing suit was smaller than his-and there were two pieces to it. Her breasts stuck straight out, even their undersides were free to the air and his gaze. The Germans may take that kind of exposure with aplomb, Ballard thought, but he couldn't. He felt an urgent tug in his suit. He had better get into the water quickly. "I'll race you," he said.

She took up the challenge and trotted in up to her knees and then dove primly into the water. He followed with a sprint and a flat racing dive. Six strong free-style strokes brought him to the float. In a single motion he vaulted himself up onto it. He turned to look back. She had just surfaced from her dive:

"My goodness, Herr Ballard," she called out. "Where did you learn to swim like that?"

He watched her swim toward him in little ineffective breast strokes. It took her a minute to reach the float.

"How did you get up?" she asked. "I just pulled myself out of the water," he said, realizing that the Australian crawl had not traveled to Europe yet. He jumped back into the water next to her and grabbed her waist. With a powerful scissors kick He pushed her partially up out of the water, but she did not attempt to pull herself on to the float and fell back into the water with him. If she didn't want to get up on the float, what did she want?

"You're so strong . . ." she muttered, holding on to his shoulder as they both treaded water. She floated in closer to him, brushing up against him. She dropped her hand and put it on his waist. She dropped her eyes and pulled herself into him, her legs straddling his under water. He bent his knee slightly so she could sit on it and stop treading water. He felt the warmth of her crotch as she settled down on the top of his thigh, the conforming shape of her inner hip and pubis bones so tantalizingly different from that of a man's.

"It's cold, the water," she muttered, pressing her breast against him. He could see her nipples pressing tautly through the slick wet cloth of her top. It was as if she was wearing nothing. "Maybe we should head back."

"I can't leave the water, just now, Frau Pergolesi. It . . . it would be too embarrassing," he answered, his face flushed in spite of the cold.

"Oh," she said, her eyes still cast down. She reached back and untied her top. It fell into the water, floating aimlessly. She turned to him and softly pressed her naked breasts into his stomach, rubbing them against him slowly from side to side. She reached behind him and grabbed his rump, sliding her hands inside his tiny bathing suit and pulling herself tightly into. his thigh. "To get warm," she muttered.

Ballard seized her tiny waist and enveloped her. With one hand he turned her face upward and began kissing her passionately. The motion untangled their legs. She took the half of his manhood that protruded out the top of his bathing suit into her hand. She squeezed the knob tightly as their tongues slithered in and out of their mouths.

Ballard went underwater and pulled off the bottom of her suit, and then his own. Holding the float with one hand, he lifted her up. He heard her gasp with pleasure as she settled down on him. She was so small, he didn't fit in all the way. They started to rock against each other, sloshing waves against the float, the water gushing in strong swells between their legs.

"Hallo, what's going on here?" said a voice from the side of the float.

They quickly uncoupled and separated. An old man swam around, searching for the ladder.

"We were just wrestling," Ballard answered weakly. Sabina had swum behind him and was trying to put her bathing suit bottom on without putting her face under water.

"Ja, Ja, I know that kind of wrestling," the old man answered peevishly. "Why not swim over to the island and wrestle in private."

They looked at each other and blushed. The island was about one hundred yards away. It would be a long cold swim, and then another on the return. Sabina's lips were turning blue. She was shaking with cold.

"Thanks, old-timer. Maybe some other time."

Ballard jackknifed under the water and took Sabina's bathing suit bottom, straightened it out and slipped it back over her legs. Underwater he stared at the neatly shaven black bush between her legs. He gently slithered his fingers between her legs. They spread involuntarily in spite of the cold. He surfaced and kissed her. She adjusted the suit around her waist and accepted her top from him.

"Swim in," he said. "I'll be with you in a minute."

He followed her halfway in, until he could stand. Then, pretending to be enjoying the view, he desperately engaged in solving a mathematical equation. Anything to get his mind off the lovely Sabina. In a minute he was able to tuck himself in, although the bulge would fool no one. He raced up to their beach towel and wrapped it around himself.

"I'm so cold, I'll never warm up," Sabina said forlornly. The goose bumps rippled up and down her legs as she stood there in her skimpy Lederhosen. "If only there were still taxis to be had . . ."

"What a great idea," Ballard said cheerily. He had put on his long pants and felt less conspicuous. He waved his hand over his head in a circle. A black Opel Rekord pulled up to the edge of the beach and a boy got out, holding the door. Ballard led the astonished Sabina to the car and into the front passenger seat. He turned the heater to high and a blast of hot air engulfed the shivering woman. Ballard jumped in the driver's seat and they drove off.

"Was ist los?" Sabina gasped. "What's going on?" She looked up at Ballard completely perplexed. "This is not a taxi."

"On the contrary, my dear lady. This is the Ballard Taxi Service, courtesy of the Abwehr. Where to now? Your place or mine?"

"What about the driver?"

"He has enough money to get himself home by trolley," Ballard said. "More than enough." He grinned at the petite women crouched like a cat in the front seat of his car.

"Oh Herr Ballard," she exclaimed, her eyes sparkling. "You're so clever." She reached over to give him a hug. Ballard stepped smoothly on the brakes, stopping the car at the side of the country lane. The hug turned into a long passionate kiss. Their hands began to rove over each other's bodies, foundling and pressing, then slipping in under clothing, unbuttoning, tugging, lifting themselves urgently to allow clothing to be shifted, unbuttoned, removed. The windows misted over with the heat of their exertions. For long minutes the car rocked gently on its suspension.

Chapter Eighteen

SEPTEMBER 8, 1941

Captain Otto Skorzeny shook Ballard's hand perfunctorily and turned quickly to that of Inge Schmidt. Clasping her arm in a great sweeping motion he then gallantly kissed her hand—rather too gallantly, Stumpfnagel thought. Skorzeny's eyes sparkled with a charm calculated to leave no doubt that he would be available after hours if the "blond goddess," as he referred to her, were interested to hear a detailed description of the harrowing derring-do of him and his band of paratroopers. Stumpfnagel saw Skorzeny whisper something into Inge's ear. She blushed.

"Now, now, Herr Hauptman," Stumpfnagel was moved to utter from across the room. "Frau Schmidt is still a widow in mourning. You must save your charm for those German women who can appreciated it."

Inge's eyes smirked at the lieutenant's remark.

"Ah, Herr Leutenant," the irrepressible Skorzeny sighed, reluctantly releasing Inge's hand. "The Abwehr always has maintained such high moral standards. Not at all like us crude Army types."

At a beefy six feet, four-inches, Skorzeny loomed over the lanky American by a full two inches, and outweighed him by fifty pounds. Unwilling to pay for custom-made uniforms, Skorzeny had obtained the largest available Wehrmacht-issue uniforms and had them altered to the limit of their available cloth. It was never enough. His large ham-like hands hung out of the sleeve with an extra inch of bare wrist showing. A large, puckered dueling scar ran from his left ear to the corner of his mouth. His dark hair was cut in a brash-cut that added another inch to his dominating height.

Skorzeny reluctantly turned from Inge to Stumpfnagel and Ballard. He eyed the American deliberately.

"It's not every day we get the services of an American spy," Skorzeny said with a questioning grin.

"And not every day that such a spy can give a task to a well-known paratrooper that will let him strike a great blow to the deskbound British who are causing the deaths of countless German soldiers," Ballard replied grandiloquently.

Chapter Nineteen
SEPTEMBER 11, 1941

As usual, Ballard awoke at first light. He tried to resist it, and envied those who could sleep in broad daylight. No matter how tired he might be, he could not. As the first shaft of daylight impinged on his closed eyelid, he would wake up. Next to him lay the beautiful Sabina. She delighted him by insisting they wear nothing to bed each night, "The better to get close to each other at any time," she had said.

Lying in bed with her snoring lightly like a purring kitten, he mused at his good fortune in turning a reluctant date into a sensationally arousing sex partner. As a professor of advanced mathematics, the single-minded concentration of his work had caused him to give his social life short shrift. Unmarried, he usually settled for women who, because they were only moderately attractive, were generally readily available and did not hold out for any unrealistic long-term commitment. None had compared to Sabina's feline sex appeal. Occasionally he wondered what a sensationally attractive woman like her saw in him. He hated to admit it, but from the deep looks of admiration she attracted from high-ranking and well-connected officers, he was certain that she could do much better than him. That she chose him made him feel incredibly virile—and permitted him to slough-off the concern he might ordinarily feel of what she would do once they inevitably tired of each other. She would have little problem finding other attentive males.

Of the few affairs Ballard had engaged in, all had been torrid and brief. He was usually quite reticent, but once his passion was aroused his ardent nature overcame its natural shyness, and he would become romantically bold. Many women found this transformation and his attention flattering, and generally relented. But after three to six months all their little charming characteristics that had aroused him in the first place began to appear more like tricks of the trade. True, none of his flings compared to the intensity of this one, a good part of that could be attributed to the setting. Being a spy in Berlin at the country's golden moment of military glory brought with it an excitement close to the sex act itself. At least this affair would be one he'd remember for a lifetime, even if it didn't last that long.

In a stroke of good luck, Sabina had found a splendid old apartment in the center of town, just a block off the Leipzigerstrasse—the "Broadway" of the city. An old university friend had been transferred to Cologne she said, and was desperate to have someone live in the apartment, lest if found vacant in the current housing shortage and be expropriated by the city government. Sabina quickly moved out of the small apartment she shared with her mother. She had not invited him to move in yet, but they spent most weekend nights there. And Ballard no longer had to speak on the telephone with Sabina's sullen mother.

The other tenants of the apartment block were an odd bag. A number of attractive working girls—some of them obviously well-connected judging by their very stylish dress, a group of diplomats, a few other foreigners, mostly men who kept furtively to themselves-acting out adult fantasies as spies Ballard imagined. Sometimes the two of them would wake up early in the morning to the tumult of music and the shrieking laughter of wild parties echoing through the center courtyard.

Ballard lay back in his bed. For the first time in years, he was able to take his mind off his singular quest to make something practical and long-lasting of his genius—and relax to enjoy the company of others. Perhaps the reason his few female entanglements had been so few and far between—if none the less passionate—was because he had always got himself so wrapped up in his work. He hated half-measures.

He had found that applying his genius in mathematical reasoning to the workings of "history in the making" gave him an extraordinary sense of power, to the exclusion of nearly everything else. And for each blow he helped Germany strike against the Allies, he came one stroke closer to success. The more successful he was, the more urgent his sexual longings became no matter how much he tried to ignore them. Sabina had unexpectedly tapped into his unrealized yearning like a roughneck drilling into a new oil field. He gushed out his pent-up energies so vigorously, he found himself requiring an extra hour of sleep each day. That, and the time they spent with each other meant he was in bed for half the day. For the first time ever, his sex life was beginning to interfere with his work, and not the other way around! Yet so physically infatuated were they that, in bed or out, whenever they were together, they could hardly stop from touching each other.

He reached over to her. Like a cat, she loved to have her back scratched between her shoulder blades. He gently scraped her backbone with his fingernails. She moaned and turned over onto her back, her full breasts lolling on her chest like independent creatures. She opened her eyes and looked at him, a smile of satisfaction building on her face.

"Good morning my darling," she said, shyly pulling the sheet forward to cover herself. "You were very naughty last night."

He looked at her askance.

"Three times, you were naughty, you old goat." She rolled over him and dangled her breast over his penis, using her nipple to push his flaccid member back and forth.

"Oh, dear. Are we too tired this morning?" she pouted. Ballard felt a twinge of desire stiffen his resolve. "Oh, no, I see we're still capable," she said. "Or trying to be. Maybe it needs a little help." With that she took him in her mouth and swiveled her hips around on the bed to offer her sex to his lips. Ballard needed no more encouragement.

They lay rocking in a French embrace for nearly half an hour, gently licking and sucking each other, with no pressure of time. Finally, Ballard discovered pressure of different sort, a welcome pressure that heralded a swelling tide of joyous release. He felt her thighs trembling on his cheeks in mutual expectation, too. Wordlessly glued to each other, they spent themselves serenely in rolling waves of pleasure.

Sabina returned from the bathroom wearing a filmy nightie, "Just to keep off the drafts," she had assured him. She put the coffee on and returned to bed. Ballard was reading yesterday's newspaper.

"Darling," she said. "What does the 'T' of your middle name stand for?"

"It stands for 'Tanaka,' my mother's family name, he said noncommittally.

"Tanaka?" she repeated in English. "That doesn't sound American."

"It's Japanese."

"Japanese? How unusual. You don't look the slightest bit Japanese. Your father must have been an American. Are they still alive, your parents?"

Sabina had snuggled up to him. She lay between his legs and began to fondle his thighs with feline strokes. He smiled. God, she was insatiable.

"No, my father died when I was eight, and my mother died when I was twelve." He turned a newspaper page, pretending not to notice her cuddling. "A long bout of leukemia. I was treated for it, too."

"I don't know leukemia," Sabina said. She was cupping his testicles in her hand as if weighing them, but Ballard realized it would be a while before he could get back into action.

"It's a form of white blood cell cancer," he said. "Radiation sickness." He tossed the newspaper down and spun around to face her. "You sly vixen, you. Let me do that to you to see how you like it." He pressed his hands between her legs.

"Oh well, if you insist," she said mockingly. She lay back on the bed and spread her legs wide. "But don't you dare take longer than an hour."

93

Chapter Twenty
SEPTEMBER 13, 1941

Oscar Faulheim reread the transcripts carefully. Something important was going on right under his nose—he could smell it—yet he could not for the life of him figure out what it was. He didn't like it one bit. He picked up his telephone: "Get me Professor Pfalzer on the telephone. He's at the Technische Hochschule."

He continued to study the file, the photographs in particular. God this woman was absolutely insatiable, he realized. Either she's a great actress, he thought, or she's really in love. Or both. My, my, what a body. So tiny yet so well filled out. I wonder what she's like to have? He shuffled through a dozen grainy photographs showing her and her mysterious American in every conceivable position of sexual congress. Lord help him if he has a wife, Faulheim thought. It would be the easiest blackmail job ever undertaken.

His telephone rang. "Herr Professor Pfelzer? How nice to speak with you again. I have a question: radiation sickness and leukemia—What can you tell me about them?"

Faulheim's face darkened monetarily. "Not over the telephone? Well, if you say so, of course. Why, yes the . . . look why don't we meet over lunch? I'll send a car. Good. Auf Wiedersehen."

He hung the telephone up slowly. "So. 'Not over the telephone.' How very interesting."

After the lunch, Faulheim was more confused than ever. From what the professor had said with much whispering and nervous glances, leukemia and radiation had one thing in common: enriched uranium—the same material it was rumored was needed to construct a uranium-burning bomb of unheard of power. At least the theoretical

94

possibility of such a bomb. No one knew if it could be made to work, but the British and the Americans were also known to be hard at work on such a project.

The Soviets were suspected of having a program. Germany was spending millions of Reichsmarks on producing the one key ingredient necessary to determining the answer—something called 'heavy water.' What Faulheim could not understand is how all of this scientific mumbo—jumbo had any connection to the American, Robert Ballard.

Chapter Twenty-One
SEPTEMBER 14, 1941

"Frau Pergolesi," Oskar Faulheim said with all the charm she had seen him apply so facilely at the Staatsoper. "The Gestapo has gone to considerable expense getting you a lovely apartment. And I think the clear understanding about this little favor was one of quid pro quo. We give you an apartment, you give us information. Unfortunately, while we have kept up our side of the bargain, you are not keeping up your side. Quite frankly, we don't feel we are getting our money's worth."

"Herr Faulheim, I don't know what you mean about my side of the bargain," Sabina said. She felt herself trembling in the presence of this man who could smile so charmingly and yet be so brutal. "I agreed to take the apartment and have Mr. Ballard over. That has happened several times . . ."

"Yes but we are not interested in your unending love life, for God's sake, woman. We want you to find out more about him. Who his contacts are. Who he meets and where. We want to know about his meetings before they happen."

"He doesn't seem to meet anyone. He goes to and from work at the Abwehr, and then goes home to his own apartment or comes to mine. I've never seen him meet anyone."

"That is not a satisfactory. answer, Gnädige Frau," Faulheim sneered. "Not satisfactory at all. To make the situation perfectly clear, let me show you something we wouldn't want to fall into anyone else's hands.

Faulheim opened a large brown envelope and pulled out a sheath of photographs. He turned them over and slid them in front of Sabina.

"Oh my God . . ." Sabina murmured, her face turning white.

"Yes, quite arousing, wouldn't you say?" Faulheim moved around from his desk to view the photos over her shoulder while standing behind her. He clapped his hand on her shoulder, forcing her to remain seated. His other hand slipped inside her blouse, and began foundling her breast. She tried to rear up, but was held firmly in place. She tried to rip his large hand away, but he was hopelessly strong.

Sabina felt herself get dizzy. She wanted to shriek out, but she knew that would be useless. She let her body go slack and closed her eyes. Faulheim pushed her off the chair and onto the carpet. All the while holding her firmly by the neck with one hand, he pulled her skirt up around her waist and stripped off her plain cotton panties with the other. He unbuckled his belt and dropped his own trouser, then rolled on top of her.

She tried to close her mind to what was happening, but the sharp searing pain of Faulheim's insertion forced her to open her eyes. She was not ready for him, she would never be ready for this monster, yet he struggled to push himself in deeper. She spread her legs to make his entry less painful.

"Ah, now, that's a nice girl," Faulheim purred. "You all really do like it like this, don't you? To have a real man shove you around and give you a nice hard fucking."

Sabina began to blubber uncontrollably. "No, Herr Faulheim, please stop it . . ."

"You needn't cry, my dear. This shouldn't hurt much at all," Faulheim said, thrusting himself at Sabina with increasing vigor. "After all, I'm not that much bigger than your Mr. Ballard. And you don't seem to mind him going at you like this one bit."

As Faulheim entered his terminal tempo, Sabina felt herself go completely cold. Nothing was happening to her. She was somewhere else—on the beach, skiing in the mountains, anywhere but being violated on the floor of the Gestapo office by Station Chief Oskar Faulheim. Vaguely she heard him grunting and wheezing at the chore he was performing. So excited he was, Sabina could not image what about . . .

"Arrrgh," Faulheim cried, pushing and shoving at her near lifeless body. Suddenly he pulled back from her and stood up, dripping.

97

"You bloody slut, get out of here at once." he roared. She rolled over on her hands and knees and crawled over to retrieve her underpants. Putting them in her pocket, she stood up and hobbled toward the office door.

"And make sure you start getting some useful information about our Mr. Ballard," Faulheim shouted after her. "It would be just awful if these disgusting photographs should fall into the hands of your mother."

Chapter Twenty-Two

It was an Indian Summer afternoon, with the yellow evening light streaming into Canaris' office like shafts of gold. Skorzeny directed them to their places around the admiral's conference table like a headwaiter seating especially honored guests. He had been dropped off in Hamburg at 9. a.m. this morning after a submarine pickup off the coast of England. He had hitched a ride to Berlin in a bomber returning to the Eastern Front.

"Arabel was running around at the drop like a chicken with its head cut off," Skorzeny began, excitedly. "He had a group of 15 SAS and RAF Bomb Disposal Squad members to do the job of four. They collected the cargo, loaded it onto a lorry and drove off. I've got photos." Skorzeny held up the small Leica. "Nice little camera, this."

"And what about the Lucas repair factory?" Stumpfnagel asked.

"Peter and I alternated watching it from a wooded bog about a kilometer away," Skorzeny said. "On the third day—that was last Saturday—we noticed that no one was returning from lunch. Then the fire department came up and parked their trucks about two hundred meters away. A couple of uniformed types went into the building carrying cases, but not many. Two minutes after they came out, the place started to go up in smoke. They took pictures and we got pictures of them taking pictures, but again, from a long distance."

"Did you check it out closer up?" Ballard asked.

"Did we ever," Skorzeny answered, the gleam returning to his eye. "We bicycled by the next morning and stopped and talked to the locals hanging about. They had cleaning ladies in there by 8 a.m. to wipe the walls down. All they did was complain about having to work on a Sunday. The only structural damage was one outside. corner of the building. It had been knocked down by a crew with sledge hammers."

"To make it look good," Ballard volunteered.

"Exactly," Skorzeny agreed. He and Ballard had become like a single mind.

Admiral Canaris gave a long sigh of weariness. "Well, I guess that means we've got something else concrete out of our famous Mr. Ballard." He pulled out a folder containing radio dispatches. "Here is Arabel's report, just in six hours ago. Herr Leutnant, you read it to us."

Stumpfnagel picked up the report:

Arabel to Stork:

Perfect drop. Explosives recovered and transported to safe house. Charges placed at 3 a.m. on 12 July for detonation at mid-afternoon.

Entire building gutted by flames. Major interior structural damage. Thirty workers killed outright, sixty eight injured. Photos, news clippings follow by courier. A great day for Germany.

"Der Schweinehund," Skorzeny muttered. I'd like to get my hands on him."

"You might just get that chance, old sot," Ballard said. His eyes locked onto Skorzeny's, illuminated by the same daredevil gleam. The two stared at each other like lovers across a crowded room. Stumpfnagel shot a look at Inge Schmidt. She averted her eyes, her cheeks reddening.

Admiral Canaris saw the bond that had developed between the two men. He saw a mutual regard for brains, naked ambition and the unconcealed lust for action—the hallmark of the warrior. He cleared his throat.

"Yes. Well, let's get down to the logistics of our next move," he said warily.

Chapter Twenty-Three

Major Oster found Ballard up in his private war room, filling in the Russian map. Ballard had insisted they keep an accurate track of the Russian campaign. He was obsessed about following the results with detail bordering on fanaticism. Stumpfnagel could not figure out why such accuracy was necessary. "What are you going to do with the information?" he had asked Ballard repeatedly. Ballard only muttered that it was an important part of his intelligence gathering method, but he refused to explain further.

Oster noticed that Ballard and Stumpfnagel now spoke to each other using the familiar "Du" form, instead of the formal "Sie" that their professional relationship would call for. But that was true of a number of the relationships in Canaris' organization. Sometimes the group seemed like one extended family. Von Hoescht had commented on this unprofessional familiarity more than once: "The pernicious influence of excessive contact with soft foreign cultures."

"Herr Ballard," Oster interrupted. "The admiral would like to speak with you." Stumpfnagel looked up, acutely aware that he was not being invited.

Seated in his elegant office, Canaris took orders for drinks. It was late afternoon, and the admiral had found that Ballard waxed eloquent with one or two snorts under his belt.

"Herr Ballard, You have been absolutely correct about the perfidious behavior of our agent Arabel. And about the Engima machine having fallen into British hands. I thank you on behalf of the Abwehr and all of Germany. Clearly the Allies know many of our codes, and once you break one, the others each become easier."

Canaris took a sip of Cognac himself and a deep breath. "Do you have any suggestions on how we might gain maximum advantage from knowing our code is broken, before we replace it? We thought maybe we might draw Stalin out in a grand maneuver that would allow us to capture a few of his Armies."

Ballard sat down with as serious a mien as Canaris had ever seen. The Cognac was doing nothing to break his intense demeanor. "I have thought about it extensively."

"Oh good. I knew you would have," Canaris sighed with relief. "What do you suggest we do?"

Ballard shifted his weight in the leather upholstered club chair that Canaris and Oster now mutually recognized as 'Ballard's Chair' whenever they met. It was oversized and permitted him to flop down and squirm his lanky frame around into the most comfortable position, which changed from minute to minute.

"The Russian feint is good idea. But there is one step that is much more important. You should send a message from Tokyo to Lieutnant-General Oshima Hiroshi at the Japanese Embassy in Berlin describing Japan's decision to enter the War against the Americans."

Canaris and Oster jumped upright in their seats.

"Japan attacking the US," Canaris blurted out. "We saw that in your report on the Allied Joint Basic War Plan. But how does that help Germany?"

"The British will intercept the message. Coming from Japan, they'll give it to the Americans where it'll get the highest priority. They can decode some of the Japanese messages already. If the Americans fall for it, they will immediately reinforce their Pacific Fleet. They can only do that by pulling boats out of the Atlantic. This will result in a rapid reduction of destroyers and sub-hunting aircraft in the Atlantic which will take a great deal of pressure off your U-boats. In addition, the US Navy is woefully under equipped with fuel, ammunition, and fighter aircraft. Everything is currently going to the Brits and the Soviets. If the Americans really believe they're going to get attacked by Japan, the Navy will demand that much of the materiel currently going to the Russians be switched to the defense of the US mainland. This will cause Stalin to run out of ammunition before the Germans do."

"Jesus Maria," Oster muttered. "Talk about grand strategy. Where exactly will the Japanese strike?"

"Who knows," Ballard said averting his eyes. Talk is of a major landing in Alaska to get a secure base on the North American mainland. But I wouldn't put that in the transmission, Herr Major. In fact, I would like any hint of location to remain a secret for now, only because if you mention it at all, you are likely to be required to grill me on it. Higher Authority might think they know the mind of the Americans better than I do, and include the location in the Trojan Horse message. This might result in them overplaying their hand, and the Americans will suspect a trick. If they do think it's a trick, they'll do little until after any attack.

"If the message is vague about location, the US Navy will spend most of its time trying to figure out where the strike will come—and not so much in figuring out how real it is: And they'll feel the need to build up the stocks at all the possible sites."

Canaris was rocking his torso back and forth in his chair. "Goddamit Ballard, that's the most trenchant analysis of global strategy I've ever heard."

"Herr Ballard," Major Oster interjected. He had just lit up his pipe, the only person permitted to do so in Canaris' office. "If the Japanese are thwarted in their attack on the US because we help build up American naval preparedness, won't that mean they might sue for peace earlier, and thus leave the Americans able to throw their entire military might into the European theater?"

"What happens is anyone's guess. But the Allies think what will happen is the following: Japan will attack regardless. They want more Lebensraum, too. And instead of overwhelming a weak US Pacific Fleet, as they would if we don't intervene, they'll take some damage. But once they attack, it will be, too late for them to pull out of the war. As with Hitler and the British, once war starts, the Americans are not going to let the Japanese—or the Germans—say 'Oh excuse me. I didn't really mean to declare war.' In addition, the Japanese High Command would see suing for peace as the vilest form of cowardice. No Japanese commander could ever suggest to the Emperor that having got a little bloodied in the early stages of an invasion that they should simply throw down their sword.

"No. I believe what will happen is after an attack the Japanese will pull back and enter the same period of 'phony war' that Germany enjoyed against the British and French after the invasion of Poland. Licking their own wounds, and building up even faster. But we have one ace up our sleeve that will keep them in the battle much longer."

"What's that?" Canaris asked. Again he found himself utterly entranced by the American.

"The Japanese codes—Purple, Red, Magenta—all of them are Enigma based. Before the war the Germans gave the Japanese their code machines! And these 'secret' Enigmas are simply variations of standard commercial code machines that have been available over the counter throughout Europe for the past decades. The Americans are struggling mightily to crack the Japanese codes the same way the British cracked the German codes. Hell, your own military attaché in Washington, Huns Thomsen, cabled you that one Jap code was broken back in April! It will take a little longer, but they'll eventually break all the Japanese codes just as they are breaking all yours right now.

"If, after the Japanese attack message is intercepted the Japanese switch to a more secure cryptology, well, you'll see a much more tentative war in the Atlantic. The Americans will have much less of an advantage. I am a mathematician by profession, and I have developed a much more secure code for Germany—and Japan."

With his lecture complete, Ballard gulped down his remaining two ounces of Cognac. Canaris was silent for several minutes, running through the possibilities—the dangers, the difficulties of Ballard's bold call to action—and weighing them against the likely outcome. He looked over at Oster. Oster simply smiled in admiration.

"OK, as you Americans say," Canaris intoned, trying to strike a friendly note of thanks. "We'll send a message to Berlin that will appear to come from Tokyo. Why don't you write it? And the new code system you talked about, how are we to implement that?"

"Just say the word. I've given all the details to Hauptmann Hartkopf already. He's raring to go. It will take a year or so to replace all the code machines, and it won't be cheap. But then cheap compared to what? Guderian already knows. He's still using the Enigma machine, but he changes his code every day."

"Yes. Stumpfnagel described your meeting. How did you manage . . . ?"

"Beat's the hell out of me, Herr Admiral," Ballard retorted. "He just heard me out and that was that. He didn't let himself get bogged down with all the petty details."

"Like where that information could possibly come from."

Ballard looked up weakly. "Believing without knowing why—it's the highest form of intelligence—or of faith."

"Or maybe they're both the same thing," Canaris said.

PART TWO

Chapter Twenty-Four

Juan Pujol Garcia-code name "Arabel" to his German taskmasters—paced back and forth nervously in the high, damp grass of the English meadow. His pants were wet from the knee down. His men, nearly invisible in the gloom of the early morning were listening for the arrival of the German Ju-53 transport plane carrying especially disguised packages of 200 kg of high explosives and incendiary.

He did not like this sudden passion the Abwehr had developed for getting him personally involved in operations. His job was to collect and supply information—or "misinformation" as his new chief, Lord Winterbotham at MI-6 called it—to his duped pay masters at the Abwehr—not to blow up buildings. Garcia felt there was something fishy about this new turn of events, either Canaris was getting more desperate than the situation called for, or . . .

"Mr. Garcia," a voice hissed at him. "I think I hear our plane coming."

"What are you whispering for?" Garcia yelled back angrily. There was no question about it this operations stuff was getting on his nerves. Particularly as the two Germans being dropped would have to be killed. Can't have word of this ongoing double-cross reaching back to the Fatherland.

"Turn the lanterns on," Garcia shouted.

His supposed turncoat helpers loped into position, pulling the shielding away from the kerosene lanterns, muttering amongst themselves at the poor showing of their improbable 'leader,' a genuine turncoat German spy. They were SAS men, disguised to look like farmers that Garcia had supposedly recruited. In daylight there faces would never pass the test, no matter how wide-eyed and idealistic they tried to appear. The hard glint of the trained killer always sprang to the foreground.

He was using only six this time. The fifteen of the last operation had been unwieldy and excessive. How many men does it tale to load 450 pounds of explosives into a lorry and execute two unsuspecting technicians? The sound of the plane became a sudden roar. He could just see its faint shape in the black night sky. An object separated from the craft, then two more. Parachutes: the explosives load and two demolition experts. Amazingly, they were right on target. On the last drop they had to hike a half mile through a swamp to find the goods:

"Stacheldraht," Garcia shouted out.

"Erdbeeren," came the correct reply. The SAS men trotted up to the visitors.

"Here let me help you, son," one of Garcia's men said to the German struggling with his chute. Odd looking thing, the SAS trooper noticed. He clipped handcuffs around the wrists of the young man and stripped his weapon from him.

"Verdammt noch mal, was machen Sie?" the young man shouted, and then recognizing the trap, bellowed out: "Herman—it's a trap. Run for your life."

Two short coughs sounded ominously, followed by a groan.

"Sorry mate," an English voice said cheerily. "Mr. Garcia, 'e's not dead. What should I do with 'im?".

"Do your job," Garcia answered bitterly. They would take the second one prisoner and see what they could get out of him. Then he would have a regrettable accident. A single cough broke the air.

"Well, 'e's not going to have to endure the public health services now," the British soldier said, and began dragging the body toward their lorry.

Garcia watched as the SAS men retrieved the parachute with its explosive cargo. Four men staggered out of the darkness, carrying the bulky case in his direction. As they hoisted the wooden crate into the back of the lorry, a sputtering sound erupted from the darkness, not twenty feet away. A curious zipping sound filled the air, like giant mosquitoes on a rampage. He heard heavy thuds, like a carpet being

107

beaten. His men cried out, gurgled, and dropped to the ground. Garcia felt an unbelievably sharp pain in his leg, and then another in his hip as if he had been pierced by a steel spit.

"Cease fire," a voice called out in German. The sputtering stopped. Men rushed up to him and grabbed his arms, pinning him to the truck. Another burst of noise right next to him caused a man on his knees to flip over.

"How many?" a voice asked tensely.

"Two, four, five, plus Garcia. One of them is missing.

"Look under the lorry."

A revolver shot rang out, deafening in its crack, then two more shots. One of the intruders stumbled backwards. A whirring sound combined with the pocka-pocka of bullets striking meat and bone. The air stank with the smell of cordite, hot oil and the salty smell of fresh blood.

"That's six. George is wounded in the arm, but the bastards shot Wolfgang on the drop."

"Goddamned cowards," Skorzeny said. "Shooting a man hooked-up in his parachute." He paused. "Load up the bodies and let's get out of here. That'll buy us a little time if they come looking for them. Stumpfnagel, come out." The lieutenant stepped out from the trees where he had been ordered to remain. No sense in getting Canaris pissed off by having one of his favorite junior officers killed.

"What about Garcia? He's bleeding and he can't walk."

"Here," Skorzeny said, tossing his Sergeant a rope. "Search him, then show the traitor how the Führer ties a knot. Do it where he won't be quickly found."

As Skorzeny loaded his men into the SAS lorry, he pulled Lieutenant Stumpfnagel aside.

"You sit in front with me," he said brusquely. He was still upset by the killing of his man. "I hope nothing else unexpected comes up," he muttered.

"Herr Hauptman," Stumpfnagel said. "There is one other thing. I've got to mail a letter. It's part of the deal we made with Ballard. At your convenience, of course".

Skorzeny looked at Stumpfnagel. "Mail a letter? At my convenience? For Christ's sake, Herr Leutnant, are there any other last minute little surprises you want to tell us about now, or are you going to continue to spring them on us as we go along?"

Chapter Twenty-Five

Bletchley Park, a sooty brick suburb of no city in particular, lies in the county of Buckinghamshire fifty miles northwest of London where the main rail line crosses a branch rail between Oxford and Cambridge. A haughty church spire, perched on a knoll overlooking the clay pits of the valley, marks the town's location. Coming from the eastern coast where they had been dropped off by submarine, Skorzeny's plan was to drive north around the town disguised as American soldiers, then turn south to enter the town from the north, and drive to the Victorian code-breaking castle. They waited until 9 a.m. and drove into town.

Skorzeny pulled up to the Bletchley Park guard house and held out his pass and a requisition form.

"I've got the electrical transformers your professors have been bleeding for. My boys'll install them today and wire them up tomorrow."

"A Yank, are you?" the guard asked noncommittally, taking the forged installation and access permit.

"Electrician's Mate First Class, US Corp. of Engineers," Skorzeny said with a broad smile. "A helping hand from across the sea." He didn't say which sea.

"Let's have a look."

Skorzeny dumped out and pulled back the canvas cover. Inside sat two of his men dressed as American soldiers. They leaned against four large transformer covers and smiled.

"I didn't get any notice of this work," the guard said.

"That's because the guy who did get it would've retired by now, governor. Look at the date of the order. This requisition was approved four months ago. Only we just couldn't rustle up the right transformers.

Oil-cooled these are. I don't know what kind of equipment your boys are running in there . . ."

"And you won't find out from me. All right. Let me have the paperwork. I'll have it straightened out while you and your boys are working." He raised the gate to let the lorry through. After restoring the gate, he entered the guard shack and picked up the telephone.

"Hello, Milli? Edward here at the front gate. Do you know anything about some electrical transformers being installed in the main building today? No? Well they're on their way. Yes, some Yank electricians. You get new electricals all the time? But they're supposed to have the actual signed entry orders attached to the requisitions, not just the transport papers. I am not picking nits. Listen Milli, put me through to the Sergeant of the Guard. He'll know what's going on. Say what? Well then please ask him to call me after he gets back from tea."

The guard hung up the telephone and made an entry in his gate pass diary. "Stubborn women . . ." he muttered angrily. He did not notice a shadow pulling back from his rear window.

Milliescent Ardsley pulled out the RCA jack connecting her headset to the guard shack. That senile old guard, she thought. Here they were, suffering one electrical disruption after another because of that monster code machine the professors had built—'Colossus' they called it—and as soon as the Americans come along to finally remedy the situation, the old fool is worried about German spies. She quickly reconnected herself to Betty Deamon's line. Betty had been telling her about the wife of the new Cambridge Don who had just joined Bletchley last month. My word, if even half of what Betty said was true—and that was the most one could expect from the old biddy—the way they lived in Cambridge, the rampant wife trading, she couldn't wait to ring her Mum and relate all the fascinating gossip.

Skorzeny pulled up to the back of the main building. He had to laugh, only the British would put one of their most modern war activities in a Tudor-Gothic red brick building that almost looked like a poor man's version of mad King Ludwig's castle at Neuschwanstein. Ducks waddled self-importantly in and out of the small pond in front of the building. At the side, uniformed recruits were peeling potatoes on the porch.

111

"Where's the freight entrance?" Skorzeny shouted.

"For the basement?" one of the young men asked.

"Yeah."

"The next turn-in. There's a lift that comes up out of the ground—don't park on it. It's a hand crank job. Hope you have strong arms."

"Thanks, amigo," Skorzeny replied, theatrically bending his forearm to flex his biceps. He drove on. They stopped the lorry and walked up to the rear door and rang the bell. A sergeant opened the door with a surprised look on his face.

"What do you want?" he asked crossly.

"We've got a delivery for you. Some electrical transformers," Skorzeny said, clipboard in hand. He didn't like the looks of this one—a professional soldier.

"Well you can't just storm in here like this. I don't know anything about it. Stay where you are. I'll call the . . ."

Skorzeny raised his clipboard and pointed it at the sergeant. A popping sound filled the air and he pitched over backwards and fell into the hallway. Skorzeny quickly scanned outside to see if anyone had noticed, then returned his machine pistol inside his shirt and quickly ran down the hall. Had anyone heard? He came to a solid oak door. Opening it cautiously, he peered into a large pantry. Aha. This was the cold room for foodstuffs. He returned to the sergeant's desk and retrieved his chair. Tilting it back so the top of the chair back fit under the door handle, he jammed a pillow in between the door handle and the chair back to prevent anyone from jiggling the chair out of the way from the other side.

He ran back to the outside door and signaled to his men by holding up a single finger. Jürgen, dressed as an American corporal, sauntered over to him trying to look bored, and then burst through the doorway, weapon at the ready.

"Stay here. If anyone comes, act drunk and give them a hard time. Don't let anyone downstairs. Kill them if you have to. Say, where's Helmuth?"

"He's hiding at the guard shack to keep the door open in case we have to make a rush for it out of here," answered.

Skorzeny dragged the dead sergeant down the basement stairs. At the bottom of the stairs he looked around. The basement was a rat's warren of cubicles, passage ways, uneven, dirt floors, and bent ceiling beams. He found two large coal heating furnaces the size of ships boilers and dragged the dead sergeant behind them. From there he found his way to the outer foundation, barely lit by tiny, dirty slit windows.

An ancient elevator sat at the ready. A hundred years ago it had undoubtedly been installed as an example of the miracle of the age of reason. Now it looked like a museum piece from the Iron Age. He stepped onto it and began to crank the handle. It grunted, gears spun reluctantly and the wrought iron contraption began an uncertain upward trundle. Skorzeny was whirling the handle around at a furious pace. The elevator cranked and groaned, lurching sedately upward. Soon the super structure clanged into the overhead doors to the outside and the elevator stalled. Skorzeny climbed up to the top of the open framework and pushed the outside doors open. He dropped down and continued cranking madly. The elevator seemed to respond even more slowly. He was about to burst out with his favorite string of German curses when a shadow fell over him.

"Is the pumpin' gettin' yee down, laddie?"

He looked up into the bright daylight. A soldier wearing a frock was bent over, peering down the open shaft. It was a Scotsman.

"It's about to make me split a gut," Skorzeny answered back.

"Why don't you shift the gears?" the Scotsman asked.

"Gears?" Skorzeny asked. He stopped cranking. There, on the cast iron control lever next to the raised markings "Up" and "Down" was a second lever that read "Slow" and "Fast." He pulled the indicator lever to "Fast" and began to crank. The elevator rose smoothly and rapidly upwards.

"By gorrah," The Scotsman said. "And I always t'ought the Yanks werrre so cleverr." He walked away, chuckling to himself.

"Let me thank you at the pub tonight, my friend," Skorzeny shouted. The Scotsman waved his hand without looking up. He was on his way there already.

The elevator pulled up to ground level and Skorzeny waved the truck to back up closer. Three men jumped out, ready to heft their 'transformers' out of the truck. Skorzeny stepped off the platform and tottered backwards, momentarily exhausted by the effort of raising it.

He walked to the cab of the lorry. "I'll take over the lookout job, Herr Leutnant. You help the men."

Skorzeny looked out of the cab. Bletchley Park consisted of the main building—a large, ungainly brick mansion built in the 1850's, surrounded by a gaggle of recently installed Quonset buts in which support staff toiled. Each theater of war had its own Quonset hut as its code-breaking operations headquarters. The grounds were lovely, actually, with just that slightly decrepit air of insufficient pruning that evoked the romantic image of decaying "British Country Life" in which untended plants overflowed their bounds. Army guards congregated in groups and seemed to loiter around the entrance gate and a second delivery gate in the rear but he could see no real organized patrol. Is it possible the British are so lackadaisical about one of their most important secret weapons, Skorzeny wondered. He knew that in Germany, this site would be rigorously patrolled twenty-four hours a day by an SS Company, including a K-9 contingent. Ah, British insouciance . . .

Two raps on the lorry door indicated the freight had been transported to the basement. He got out and motioned Stumpfnagel into the driver's seat.

"Park the lorry at least one hundred meters from here, so if anyone gets suspicious, this won't be the first place they look. Then come down and join us."

Skorzeny joined his men in the gloomy basement. They had distributed the four 'transformers' to each of the four corners of the building, setting them to rest at the base of the four main masonry support columns. Jürgen reached in behind the transformer and pulled out a thick bundle of heavy power wires.

"Heinrich, Ullie, Stefan, go to the other transformers and begin to string up these fake wire bundles as if we had already begun to connect them up," Jürgen ordered. The men fell to. Skorzeny climbed the narrow stairs to reconnoiter outside. So far, everything was going smoothly.

He emerged in the ground-floor hallway to spot his guard frozen at the side of the door, peering out, grasping his automatic pistol. "Jürgen, was ist Los?" Skorzeny whispered.

"It's the lieutenant," Jürgen hissed. "He's in trouble.

Skorzeny rushed to the door. Stumpfnagel was standing in the middle of the back yard, his hands in the air facing the rifle barrel of a British MP. Skorzeny burst through the door. He trotted over to the MP.

"Hey, Sergeant, what's the problem?" he asked with an embarrassed half smile on his face.

"Who the hell are you?" the MP said, half-turning his rifle toward Skorzeny.

"A Yank engineer. My men are Installing the new electrical transformers," Skorzeny replied cheerily.

"What's Harry done this time?"

"He won't speak to me. I think he's a Jerry spy. Look at his face. You can't tell me he's an American."

"Of course he's not American, Sergeant, he's a Pollack. And my best electrician, even though he can't speak five words of English. Come on over to the desk. I'll show you the roster." Skorzeny yelled "Ya ni gavoru po-Angliski," at Stumpfnagel. It meant 'I don't speak English' in Russian. Skorzeny hoped it would satisfy the MP.

Stumpfnagel lowered his hands and smiled stupidly at the MP, then began to follow Skorzeny.

"Eh there. Where do you think you're taking my prisoner?" the MP shouted peevishly.

"Come on Sergeant. Let's walk over to the desk and we'll straighten this out. Your sergeant has got the list."

"You mean 'arold's back?" he asked. "'E missed 'is tea."

The MP lowered his rifle, but did not shoulder it, and followed along glumly.

"We've got a pot going," Skorzeny remarked over his shoulder. "You sound like you could use a cuppa. And maybe a bit of the other."

"You're bloody well right I could," he replied. "And more than just a bit."

"Well, step right in, Sergeant. And your troubles will be over." As the MP stepped through the door, Skorzeny turned to face him. Two loud pops placed bullets in his forehead and through his left eye. He dropped like a stone. Gerhard quickly pulled him inside.

"Shit, did you hear that?" Skorzeny asked.

"No, what?" Stumpfnagel exclaimed, a look of fear returning instantly to his harried face.

"How loud this pistol was," Skorzeny said with an annoyed look on his face. He blew smoke out of the barrel. "I think I've shot out the baffles of the silencer."

Two of his men laughed at Stumpfnagel's bewilderment.

"All right," Skorzeny said. "The main charges for this building are in place. But we're going to need help to find Nissan Huts numbers 3,6 and 8. Place the smaller incendiary charges on each one. All their code breaking records are on paper."

Jürgen disappeared up the basement steps to check the remaining explosives in the lorry. A small ruckus was heard and then a body tumbled down the stairs.

Jürgen followed. "I had to shoot him. He was looking for the sergeant. Got suspicious."

"Fine, good work," Skorzeny answered. "But let's get a move on. No sense in stretching our luck too far." He turned to his men.

"The charges in this basement are in place, ready to go off. None of the dead Brit's have been discovered yet—the two sergeants—nor any of us. We could set the timer for five minutes and get the hell out of here. That would be the smart thing to do. We'd get the building and a lot of them. But we'd leave the Quonset huts untouched."

"You have something else in mind?" Stumpfnagel asked anxiously. This sounded like a change in plans. Stumpfnagel didn't liked changes of plan.

"I do," Skorzeny said. A mischievous smile formed on his face. Stumpfnagel recognized it instantly. A "dare" was coming up.

"The problem is this: from the sign-in sheet at the guard shack I noticed that these propeller-heads work strange hours, mostly from about five in the evening to three or four in the morning. We've got a lot of worker bees in the building, but not many of the queen bees. If we can wait a few more hours, I think we'll have more of the big shots back into the hive." He stopped and raised a finger in the air signaling a brainstorm. Skorzeny walked over to the crate and pulled out a repairman's telephone. "Where do the telephone lines come in?"

Jurgan pointed to the far wall. Skorzeny clipped into a trunk line and listened. It was not being used. He twirled the hand ringer and waited for the operator to come on.

"Hallo, this is Peetah Benchly from the home office calling," Skorzeny said in a wonderful caricature of English 'received speech.' It was so overdone, no Britain could possibly not believe it. "I'm cahling to inform you that Sir Bertrand Russell will be visiting Bletchley Park to give a smahl tahk at 8 p.m. Surprise visit, don't you know. In appreciation for all the excellent work the boys have been up to." Skorzeny loudly sucked up a mouthful of spittle. "Would you be so kind as to inform the guahdd to let Lord Russell and his pahty through at the appropriate time?"

He heard the operator sputter in surprise at the mention of the Great Man. Yes, yes she replied. Leave everything to her. She would take care of it. My word, Lord Russell himself, you don't say.

Skorzeny unclipped from the line. "That woman will spread the word better than the BBC World Service," he laughed. "Now we can install the incendiaries, relax and wait."

Skorzeny and Jürgend ambled across the back lot. One of the gate sentries beckoned to him. Skorzeny broke off and walked in his direction.

"What are you two doing?" the sentry asked casually. His rifle was still slung on his shoulder. He looked sixteen years old.

"Putting in the electrical transformers. We're almost done for the day. We have three little ones to hang up. Then we'll be back tomorrow morning to string the wires and hook them up."

The young man turned away. Skorzeny thought of Ballard.

"I say, young Corporal, none of these huts are numbered. Can you show us where . . . ?" Skorzeny took out a sheath of papers and checked it carefully. " . . . where huts number 3 and 8 are?"

"Oh, quite. Three is over there . . . Really, I might as well take you to them," the young guard replied. "It's not like there's a lot else to do. Say, you haven't seen Sergeant Burns, 'ave you. Old 'arold Burns?"

"The big old guy who smokes those terrible cigars?"

"That's 'im."

"To tell you the truth, he's been a bit under foot. Spent the whole day telling us how to do our jobs. Is there anyway we can keep him out of our hair tomorrow?"

The sentry laughed. "That's old 'arold. 'E's in trouble with the Old Man for not reporting in. Tell 'im to report on the double, could you?"

"I'll do that, mate," Skorzeny said. "Say what's with the rush of people coming in? It's past quitting time and this place is getting busier than Victoria Station."

"Oh, one of the university geniuses is giving a little chat to our resident geniuses. Some egghead bloke by the name of Lord Russell. 'E'll be 'ere any minute."

"I hope we get out in time to beat the rush," Skorzeny said.

"Number 8 is right over here next the entrance," the young sentry said, switching his rifle from one shoulder to the other.

Skorzeny let the sentry lead them to the number 8 hut while Jürgen followed in the lorry. Quickly, he and Jürgen drilled holes and screwed in the lag bolts at the building corners furthest from the doors where they would be the least noticed. They asked the young guard to give them a hand in hanging the 35-kilo 'transformer' in place. The job took less than fifteen minutes. As Skorzeny engaged the boy in idle chatter, Jürgen, pretending to be sorting the wire bundles, deftly set the timer to 8 p.m., and armed the charge.

They moved on to hut number 6 and completed that installation. Building number 3 was at the opposite side of the compound. As they hung the last transformer, Skorzeny pressed a pound note into the boy's hand.

"Here, have yourself a beer or three courtesy of Uncle Sam," he smiled. The youth was shocked at the size of the reward. He looked around furtively and, seeing no one, pocketed the note and ambled off, thanking the "Americans" profusely. A whole pound! He and Jenny would be able to live it up with a real night out on the town.

Skorzeny and Jürgen quick-marched back to the main building. Their arms ached from lifting the heavy loads and holding them in place so long. Skorzeny checked his wrist chronometer. It was 7:08. Fifty-two minutes to go before the charges detonated.

"All right, good, we're in fine shape so far. Here's what we have," Skorzeny said in a relaxed manner, leaning against a wooden column, his men gathered around him and watching their leader intently. He could have been describing an afternoon tea to Inge Schmidt, Stumpfnagel thought. And what a powerfully soothing effect his relaxed behavior had on his men. He realized that his fears were effecting the men and he redoubled his determination not to appear so excited.

Chapter Twenty-Six

Stumpfnagel had worn a groove nervously pacing the dirt floor of the Bletchley Park basement.

"How much longer, Herr Hauptman?" he asked for the third time. It was no use—he could not keep his apprehension from showing through.

"It looks like they've about got most of them in by now, Herr Leutnant," Skorzeny replied in a bored tone, peering out a slit window. He did not like the effect the nervous little lieutenant had on his men. Just as he calmed them down, the little twerp would raise the specter of another danger.

"Jürgen. Can we wire the charges so that they can detonate by wire and if that fails, the timer will set the charges off?"

"Of course, Herr Hauptman. That is how they are set up now."

"Good. I don't like leaving explosives on a timer. You never know who might find them. Maybe with the last minute rush of people coming into the building, we could string the wire behind us out the lorry without being noticed." He motioned for the men to start stringing the wires out in the direction of the elevator.

"Everyone in the lorry," Skorzeny ordered, checking his wrist watch again. The charm had gone out of his voice. Now was the time for fighting. The men bolted out of the cellar and into the back of the truck. "Safeties off. Ready for action," he ordered. He looked at his Rolex chronometer: seven minutes to go. He cranked the elevator down halfway, then jumped down on to the basement floor. Three transformers contained 40 kg of "createring" explosives—relatively slow burning explosives that are best at moving heavy loads like buildings.

They would set off at the same time as the Nissan huts. The fourth 'transformer' in the main building was filled with incendiary explosive, designed to set fire to the wreckage. It was set to go off one minute later. After checking once again that all charges were armed, he ran back and hopped up onto the half-raised elevator, pulled himself up onto ground level, and peered into the back of the truck.

"Guns at the ready, men. String out the wire. After we pull away from the guardhouse and if they haven't gone up already, Jürgen, you blow the charges. As we pass it, Stefan, you kill the guards."

"Don't forget Helmuth, Herr Hauptman," Jurgen said. "He's been hiding behind the guardhouse."

"Donnerwetter, That's right. The whole time," Skorzeny said, stunned to realize he had not spoken to his man for several hours. "Make sure of your shots. Don't worry, we'll pick Helmuth up. We'll head north. You all know the escape route."

Skorzeny shoved Stumpfnagel out of the driver's seat. "Here, use this," he said, handing him his machine pistol. "But only if necessary. I don't want anyone of us to get hurt."

The truck pulled slowly up to the gate. Cars were lined up outside the gate, and only one vehicle could pass through at a time. Skorzeny jumped out and walked up to the guard. He glanced at his watch. Two minutes to go.

"Are we going to have to wait for that entire line to pull in before we can get out?" he asked.

"Let's see your papers, first Capt'n," the guard said amicably. He was a new one.

"I left them with the other guard on the way in," Skorzeny said, putting one hand behind his back to give the hand-signal 'trouble' to his men.

"Oh, so you're the blokes with the electricals no one's heard of. We've been looking for you. Let me call the major, He'll be by in a moment."

Skorzeny returned to the truck and ripped his gun out of Stumpfnagel's hands. He turned and saw the guard lifting the telephone receiver. In plain view of the cars lining up at the gate, Skorzeny aimed through the window. A three shot burst shattered the glass. "Blow it,"

121

he yelled, and ran into the shack. The guard had been knocked to the floor, blood streaming down his face. But he was still alive.

"You bastard," the guard muttered. In his hand was a Webley revolver. "Don't, old man," Skorzeny said, but the revolver continued to swing in his direction. A second burst knocked the guard flat. Skorzeny saw people leaping out of their cars and running for cover. Those in front were ducking and fleeing. The ones further back were pressing forward to find out what was going on.

"Helmuth!" Skorzeny shouted. Some of the sentries had rallied at the sound of braking glass and were dog-trotting apprehensively towards the shack, unsure of what to do. Suddenly an enormous roar filled the air.

The sentries were thrown off their feet. The rest of the windows of the shack blew out—Skorzeny felt shards of glass slash at his back. Two of Skorzeny's men, halfway to the shack with their guns drawn, were knocked over by the concussion. They turned their falls into rolls and expertly dove through the door.

A second roar, and then a third filled the air. Skorzeny could see people jumping out of windows in the Bletchley building, but only a half dozen or so. In side were hundreds.

A brilliant eruption lit the evening sky, making a strange hissing blast: the incendiary. Screams of agony came from the building as flames raced to consume the ancient timber reinforced construction.

Skorzeny crawled outside the shack. Three sentries were lopping indecisively his way. "Help the people in the building, help them!" Skorzeny yelled at the guards.

"We'll hold the gate." The guards turned and ran toward the building, grateful to be told what to do. Where was their officer, Skorzeny wondered.

"Hey you, Yank," a sharp voice yelled at him. A British lieutenant approached, his tethered revolver pointed at Skorzeny. "What are you doing? Don't move."

"For God's sake, man," Skorzeny cried. "I've got one of your men wounded in the shack, there's two dead Jerries in the lorry, the buildings are blowing up and you're asking me what I'm doing?"

"Jerries in the lorry?" the Lieutenant asked, the suspicion on his face turned to fear. He turned toward the truck. "Where . . . ?"

A short sputter from Skorzeny's machine pistol shoved him forward, just as an answering burst from the lorry pushed him back. He crumpled in a zigzag heap to the ground. Two more distant blasts sounded, and then a third—the huts.

"Jurgen, stand guard, but keep down. Where's Helmuth?" Skorzeny ran back into the shack and scrabbled around on the floor. He ripped open the door of a small water closet. Empty. "Stefan, run around the building. See if he's hiding underneath."

People from the cars lined-up to visit Bletchley had overcome their initial fear and were streaming through the, gates around the abandoned cars. The screaming from the building, one hundred meters away, was faint but ghastly when it could be heard in the occasional moments when the roar of the blaze slackened momentarily as the evening breeze changed direction. Where is Helmuth?

Skorzeny spotted a coat closet near the door. It was almost invisible. It had no door handle, just a latch. He popped it open. Helmuth fell to the ground.

"I've got him," he shouted. "Let's get out of here."

He slung the limp body over his shoulder and staggered toward the lorry.

"Jürgen, you and Stefan seize that Rolls Royce and follow us."

"I can't drive, Herr Hauptman," Jürgen protested, running toward the car.

"Then let Stefan drive, for God's sake," Skorzeny roared.

He flung Helmuth into the rear of the truck and hopped into the cab pushing Stumpfnagel out of the driver's seat. With a growl of the engine, he burst through the gate, bashing aside the abandoned Morris blocking the entrance, smashing each other's headlights in the process. Steam spouted into the air from the small car's radiator. He surged ahead and then slammed on the brakes. The Rolls was not moving. Stefan couldn't drive either.

"Stumpfnagel, get out and follow us in the Rolls." Skorzeny pointed to the line of cars behind him. "Here take this. About ten shots left." He handed the lieutenant his Schmeisser machine pistol.

Skorzeny watched in the rearview mirror. As Stumpfnagel trotted toward the car, a British officer approached him, pistol drawn. He fired! "Gottverdammt," Skorzeny cursed. He saw Stumpfnagel fall backwards, his gun sparking as he tumbled and rolled over. Then he stood up! The British officer was lying on the ground, writhing. "Son of a bitch, you bloody little bookworm!" Skorzeny muttered in surprise. "That's going to make that little lady of yours proud." He saw Stumpfnagel, his left arm hanging slackly, jump into the Rolls. Skorzeny floored the gas pedal and accelerated away. He looked in the rear view mirror. The Rolls was pulling out of line and roaring down the road towards them, swerving violently as Stumpfnagel fought to bring the car under control.

They sped out of town without being followed, and soon settled down to a merely fast pace. The light faded to deep twilight. Skorzeny looked at his watch: 10:05. They had been on the road for two hours. In the dusk, Skorzeny had trouble seeing the road. Neither of his headlights worked. He pulled over, the Rolls pulled alongside.

Skorzeny stuck his head out the window and shouted at Stefan.

"I can't see the road without head lights. You lead the way to the town of Halstead. Then its only thirty minutes to the coast at Harwich. You know the rendezvous point near the shore. Pull over out of sight and we'll wait together. Our U-boat pickup is scheduled for between midnight and three."

"The lieutenant is hit in the arm and bleeding," Stefan exclaimed.

"Make a tight bandage. Keep pressure on it. With your hand if necessary. We can't stop now. Los." The Rolls leaped forward. Skorzeny put the lorry in gear and lurched after it. The Rolls was fast and he had trouble keeping up with it.

There was a knocking at his rear window. He turned briefly. Helmuth's face smiled through the glass weakly, alive if not yet fully recovered. Skorzeny knew what must have happened: Helmuth had tried to hide in a tiny closet and got himself locked in. Unable to move, and unwilling to give himself away he remained still. In a hour his circulation slowed down and he had quietly fainted.

Skorzeny felt light-headed himself, but with a sense of elation coursing through his brain. They had accomplished their mission with change left over in a brilliant action that would finally keep British noses out of Germany's business. Now all he and his men needed to do was make their submarine pickup. Once again, Skorzeny felt a deep sense of satisfaction arising within his loins, the feeling he always got after a risky mission that went well. He knew it was partly a reaction from the adrenaline that was pumping through his body, and partly the satisfaction of pulling off a difficult mission. How many men could lead a small band of fighters into an unknown situation deep behind the lines where a single slip-up meant death, and, improvising brilliantly, successfully strike a mortal blow against the enemy? A battalion of infantry couldn't have accomplished as much.

Who would he call for a date when he got home? Now that he was one of them, Stumpfnagel's adorable secretary would be off limits. It was clear who she had eyes for anyway. There were plenty of others, but he had a very special one in mind. Racing down the English country lane, the two red dots of light swinging in front of him like a beacon toward home, his mind delighted in mulling over the possibilities.

Chapter Twenty-Seven

It was another lovely summer day and Sabina and "Robert" as she called him (she would not use the name "Bob" it was far too common, she insisted), decided to return to the Teglersee, the large lake in the Tegel town ship of northern Berlin. This time they decided to take Ballard's car both ways. Ballard had surprised both of them by suggested Sabina invite her mother along, but Sabina became unexpectedly upset at the suggestion. And what the hell am I doing inviting her, he thought to himself. Deliberately building entangling alliances?

"No that would be impossible," Sabina declared sharply. "You know my mother hates the sun." And then looking at the sullen reaction her attack had caused, modulated her reason. "Mother is very old-fashioned, Robert. She is still very angry that I started seeing another man only a few months after my husband died."

"But it's been well over a year now," Ballard exclaimed.

"And it can be ten years from now, Robert," Sabina said curtly. "After crawling home from our first date dead drunk, Mama is never going to change her mind about you. I'm sorry."

Still Ballard was disappointed in her response, and a mild tension built up between the two of them that no amount of snuggling in the car seemed to dissolve.

They parked the car and walked to the beach near the Scharfenberg ferry. Sabina billowed out a blanket on the grassy border of the beach while Ballard began to unpack their picnic. The popping sound of the champagne cork attracted a remark from a passing couple.

"It's a fine thing to be enjoying Sekt when there are men fighting and dying on the front," a young man said sourly. Ballard saw it was only envy. The young woman blanched at her boyfriend's remark.

"Come and join us for a sip," Ballard said pleasantly, waving them over by holding up the bottle and two glasses in his hand.

"You mean join the plutocrats?" the young man said. But he stopped to think over the offer.

"Come on Uwe," his girl friend said, pulling on his arm. "When was the last time we've drunk champagne?"

"When was the first time?" the youth snapped, and pulled up a part of the blanket. The young girl sat next to Sabina.

Ballard poured each glass half full and handed them to the young couple. The girl was a beauty and sharp witted, so typical of working–class Berliners. The young man looked like an auto mechanic. Stolid, self confident of his station in life—which was not high, and self-satisfied.

"Hee-hee," the girl laughed. "It tickles the snout."

"Not bad at all," the young man replied, holding the glass as he might imagine a movie start would to discourse on the caliber of the vintage. "Is it German?"

"It's French," Sabina answered.

"Ah, no wonder it tastes so strange," the youth said. He swigged the remainder of his glass and stood up.

"Many thanks for the unusual experience," he said. "Come on, Hannelore. We should leave these two alone."

"And go back to drinking beer, you mean," she said, making a moue. "It was very pleasant of you to invite us, thank you very much," the girl said, with the exaggerated courtesy the uncultured feel is expected of them in the presence of their betters. The two left, skipping in the sand. The young boy grabbed the girl and kissed her deliberately in sight of Ballard and Sabina.

Ballard laughed. "He's showing us that we may be drinking champagne, but he's still got his girl."

"Robert, that was very nice of you," Sabina said, staring at him wide-eyed. "No German would ever have turned the other cheek like that. They just couldn't do it."

"Different cultures, different mores," Ballard said noncommittally. "Let's see what we've got to eat."

127

Sabina began unwrapping the food she had packed. She set out several jars containing pickled fish: eel, herring, each in a different vinegar liquor, and a smoked whitefish.

She set out two types of fresh bread: a pumpernickel which she enjoyed, and the white Knüppel milk rolls that Ballard preferred and that his ration coupons allowed her to buy. Ballard found himself staring uncontrollably at the young woman opposite him. For the first time he noticed his attraction to her at this moment had nothing to do with sex. Lately she had become gentle and reticent with him, so completely different from the officious sophistication that she usually exhibited. He found that he could spend an hour driving with her in the country and not feel the need to say anything. She had remarked upon it more than once.

"Robert, you haven't said anything since we started. Am I boring you so much?" It was not boredom, he insisted. It was . . . complete comfort to be with her and not have another thought in the world. The thought of their quiet intimacy momentarily frightened him.

"We better drink all the champagne first," Ballard said. "Otherwise the vinegar will ruin, our taste for it."

"That will make us drunk and then you'll try to take advantage of me," Sabina said with a repressed smile.

"Why do you even bring champagne, Robert?" she asked. "You know it doesn't go well with German food."

"But it goes well with Italian food," he replied. "You're Italian. Why don't you make Italian food? But all right. Next time I'll bring beer."

They ate silently, Ballard tasting each type of fish gingerly. He was not used to the North German predilection for sour, cold fish and although he thought he enjoyed nibbling it, he could not eat much of it at a time.

"Sabina, darling," Ballard spoke in-between bites. "I never could figure out why you pretended to be a chess player. You are a clever but very inexperienced player. Maybe someday you'll be good—with much practice. But you haven't asked to play once since the time with Stumpfnagel and Frau Schmidt."

"Oh, Robert, I was so hoping you wouldn't bring that up." Sabina began busying herself with cleanup so she wouldn't have to look at

Ballard. He expected to hear a quick equivocation that Sabina was so expert at.

"I had heard of an attractive officer who is a chess champion. He is single, you know, and has a secure position . . ."

"Ah-ha! So you finagled the Italian Embassy to set you up with Stumpfnagel." Ballard took her chin in his hand and turned her head to face him. "But you two seemed to make the perfect couple. When Frau Schmidt and I were watching you from across the room. Stumpfnagel could hardly keep his eyes off you."

"And neither could Frau Schmidt," Sabina replied. "No, I didn't think I'd stand a chance with her being in his office day-in and day-out. And besides . . ."

"Yes," Ballard prompted, a look of lustful glee on his face.

"Well there was another, more attractive man," Sabina answered slowly. "Also a bachelor." She continued to fuss with the silverware, pretending not to notice his expression. He reached for her hand and tugged it.

"Does Madam care for a little swim?"

"Why, yes, that would be nice," she purred. "But really Robert. You can't stand up like that. You're sticking out again."

"I'll run into the water. No one will notice. Maybe we could swim across to the inland."

"Oh, I shouldn't think so. There are currents. We can just play around at the float." She looked up at him with adoring eyes. None of the guile that usually shaded her expression was present. Ballard got harder than ever.

It had been several days since they had seen each other. He had noticed that he would think of her at the most unlikely moments—moments of repose rather than randiness. It was . . . odd. He sprang to his feet and raced into the lake, hitting the water in a shallow racing dive. In a few strong strokes he pulled his way through the water to the float. There he waited, remaining in the water, anticipating the soft press of Sabina against his body. The water was mild this time. They could stay in for an hour or more. Ballard was glad the beach was not crowded. In his condition in the clear water, wearing the tiny

129

German bathing suit as small as a G-string, he could not let anyone swim too near him.

Sabina swam out slowly in a breast stroke—the only swimming stroke most Europeans know. She paddled delicately up to him and they swam together around to the back of the float. There they practically bumped into the young couple they had given champagne. The two were locked in a conjugal embrace. They looked up, startled, but they remained locked together.

"Great minds think alike," Ballard quipped, and turned away.

"It must be the champagne," the young girl replied, and wriggled shamelessly against her partner, kissing him strongly on the mouth.

Sabina swam out a little further and floated on her back. "Oh, it's heavenly," she said. Ballard supported her rump with his palm, so she no longer needed to kick her feet to keep them from sinking. He slid his hand inside her tiny bathing suit bottom. Her legs opened slightly and his fingers found the lodging they so anxiously sought.

Gently, he twisted and turned his fingers, in slow rhythmic pressure, all the while he scissor-kicked ahead, pulling the two of them forward. Sabina lay on her back in the water, her eyes closed, her lips parted, her legs spread slackly. Soon Ballard's fingers felt little involuntary twitching of Sabina's loins. His foot hit bottom. He could just stand in the water. Sabina spun around, her face flushed with desire.

"Please put it in, darling," she whispered. He stripped off her bathing suit bottom and placed her hips against his. In a single liquid motion, he penetrated her and held her in place. Just in time. Without another movement he felt her loins rippling with jerking thrusts. He felt himself trigger in reflexive response to her. His pulsating emission causing Sabina to arch her back in languorous ecstasy.

She let out her breath in a long sigh. "Oh, God, my darling. It just gets better all the time." Still holding him inside her, she lay her head on his shoulder and held him lightly with her arms. He continued to walk toward shore. She felt him stumble.

"Oh! Where are we?" She looked up. He lifted her up, uncoupled from her, and set her on the ground. They were standing on the shore of the island school. He picked her up and carried her inland. He sat her down on the grass, hidden from the lake shore by a copse of beech trees, her wet pubic bush glistening in the hot sun, its sleek blackness contrasting sharply with the tiny patch of white skin her bathing suit bottom usually covered. The rest of her was a dark copper Mediterranean tan.

The school was on summer vacation and the kilometer-long island was nearly deserted. He lay down beside her and pulled her on top of him, untying her swimsuit top and stripping it off. Her pointed breasts dug into his belly, their nipples taut with desire.

He was half hard again, just rigid enough to replace himself in his favorite parking place. They would rest like this, coupled together but remaining motionless, until his full powers returned, Sabina moving her hips around from time to time to test and stimulate his state of readiness.

"Robert, you mentioned that your mother died over a period of years, and how much that disturbed you as a child. But what disease did she get? And why were you treated for it, too?"

Ballard looked up at the woman lying on his chest. They both felt his member slip lifelessly out of its warm grotto.

"I hinted at it before, Sabina darling. But I have a very strange background. Fantastic beyond belief, actually. I have always thought it would be better for both of us if I kept my background secret. The Gestapo would love to know about it. In fact, I'm surprised they're not snooping around already."

"The Gestapo? Oh, Robert, are you in some kind of trouble?" Sabina asked. She could not look him in the eye.

"No. Not yet, anyway. The Abwehr is protecting me. And will protect me. But I think you should know what you're getting into with me. That is, if you want to get into anything with me, my darling." Ballard sought Sabina's eyes. She turned her head and pressed her breasts into him.

"The reason I've come to Germany is going to sound rather odd," Sabina. "Odd, but very simple. It has to do with how my mother died. I've wanted to tell you about it, but you must keep it a secret."

"Of course Robert. You know I love you."

131

"My father was an American soldier. He and his men entered the city they had just bombed. Many of the civilians had been killed or horribly maimed by a terrible new weapon . . ."

"You mean our use of gas like at Ypres in the last war?" Sabina asked, her eyes falling at the recognition that it was Germany which had first broken the rules of war. "I know that was awful."

Ballard continued as if he had not heard her. "Civilians were strewn all over the place. Those that were not dead were retching their guts out. Although the survivors begged him for help, he and his men could do nothing for them. Except for their own first aid packs they had no medical equipment, and nothing they had would have helped the people in the condition they, were in anyway.

"Soon, even my father, a battle-hardened veteran, could not stand the sight of all the suffering. He turned his men around to make for their staging area outside the city.

As they marched out, he heard a squealing sound. Unable to understand what it could be, he peered into the basement of a collapsed building. It was the basement of a nursery school. In the collapsed ruins he saw a half-naked woman trying to tend to a dozen injured, crying toddlers."

Sabina's face screwed up. It sounded so horrible. She remembered hearing about the seared eyes and lungs of soldiers and civilians alike who were caught in the acrid yellow clouds of mustard gas. After the battle, those who could still see, led the blind out in long strings, each man holding onto the hand of the person behind him.

"She, herself was badly injured, as well, but she had stripped her dress to shreds making bandages to cover the burns of the children. When my father saw the woman, she was half crazy and half dead. She could speak some English and she begged him for water. He commandeered an ambulance at gun point and forced the driver to evacuate the children and the woman to an American field hospital. There they bandaged the kids, but the Americans wouldn't treat the woman because she was an enemy alien.

"All of a sudden my father went crazy. He spent the next few hours looking for a minister and demanded he marry them. He took his new wife back to the field hospital and showed them the marriage certificate: At first they threw him out, but he insisted. Her whole body was pink and she was feverish. The medics didn't know what to do.

As she lay close to dying, in a desperation move a doctor suggested they try a complete blood transfusion. Within hours it made a miraculous difference. When the Allied Command got a report about what my future father had done, they sent an MP to arrest him, but when they learned how his new wife had been so quickly pulled out of danger, they also sent some medical specialists over to observe and then take over the treatment. They had no real experience with this type of casualty, and she became their guinea pig.

"My father was arrested to face a court martial for disobeying orders against fraternization. Marriage was the ultimate fraternization. But because of it, my mother got excellent medical treatment because the Chief Medical Officer of the expeditionary force became personally involved in her case. She was his experiment, and he saved her life.

The two of them were shipped back to America in disgrace; he because of his pending courts martial; my mom, because marrying a complete stranger—and a foreigner at that—made her akin to a prostitute in the eyes of her parents. Although I don't think her parents ever found out. They were never seen again. Nor did my father and mother ever learn what became of the rescued children.

"My mother never recovered her health completely, but she bore me. I too suffered from the same illness that afflicted my mother, but a complete blood transfusion at birth saved my life, too, along with a lot of treatment. It was all very experimental and very frightening. I realized much later that to my mother I was not just her son but all the nursery school children she could not save. I remember once waking up with a fever and crying out and seeing my mother ripping cloth from her nightgown to mop my brow before my father calmed her down. I was like a recurring punishment to her, as if she was being made to atone for the sin of not saving the children by reliving her most horrible nightmares all over again.

"My father died unexpectedly of stomach cancer when I was eight. My mother spoke of him as if he was a god. How he came down out of heaven to find her and her charges. How, among all the sick and dying, he had rescued her and her children. How, when all hope was lost, he made the heaven-inspired decision to marry her. And the wonderful way he took care of her back home, until he himself died as a result.

"She revered him until her last day. She repeated each of the stories of his kindness a hundred times, until I memorized them. Once she learned English well enough, she worked ten hours a day in the US consulate as a translator. It tore her apart to learn of the cruelty of her own people, and once she did learn, she was so ashamed of them, she refused to teach me to speak the language.

"It was my mother who bought me up. It was her utter selflessness that probably saved the lives of the dozen infants in her care. She earned little, money, but everything went to make sure I got through school comfortably and without shame. Avoiding shame was the biggest thing in her life. Avoiding shame for me, that is. She would gladly suffer the most humiliating event if it furthered my life.

"I revere my mother's memory, Sabina," Ballard said, coming out of near trance-like recitation. His eyes were filled with tears. "I've never told anyone before about my background. And this is just the easy part to understand. There's much more that will be totally incomprehensible to you."

"Oh darling, I'm so glad you were able to unburden yourself. I don't understand the half of what you're telling, or why. I don't really need to know . . ."

"My darling, Sabina," Ballard replied. "I don't quite know why I'm telling you all this either." Ballard stopped speaking for a moment. His conscious mind flashed a warning: "Caution! What are you doing?" it asked.

Ballard felt like a man watching a movie of himself. The real him was watching this actor impersonating him to an attractive woman. But the actor was not following the script. "I love you, and I don't want to go on without you," the actor was saying. What's going on with me, Ballard's mind screamed out to the actor. Do you realize what you're saying? Shut up now! As in a nightmare, the actor continued without hearing the commands.

"I want you to know who I am and that I have a very strange background-far stranger than anything you could imagine."

Sabina's eyes filled with tears.

"I love you, too, Robert," she said quietly. "But I love you for who you are right now, and what you have been to me. I don't need to know anything about who you used to be." Sabina rolled off his body. "I don't even want to know." She took her, bathing suit bottom wrapped around his neck and put it back on. She lay down leaning against his side, holding herself up with one elbow.

"I understand that, Sabina," Ballard said. "But there are complications you must know about. If we should . . . marry, we cannot go back to America. We'll have to stay here in Germany."

Sabina sat up, fully alert. "But you would retain your American citizenship, wouldn't you?" she asked apprehensively.

"No. I will undoubtedly be stripped of it as soon as the Americans find out what I have done. I've worked too hard for the German cause. I'll be considered a traitor, and they'll never let me back in. I will have to become a naturalized German."

Sabina turned her face. Her body stiffened as if struck. "Oh Robert," she said, unable to face him. She began to cry, gently at first, then in great heaving sobs.

"Sabina, darling. There's no need to cry. We'll do fine. Germany will win the war—or at least obtain a stalemate. We won't want to live anywhere else. I'll be considered a hero of the Reich. We'll have a great house by the Wansee, lots of kids. It'll be wonderful for us."

Unheeding, she got up and, still crying, walked to ward the water. She slipped in and began to swim across the channel toward the mainland. Ballard was flummoxed. What was wrong now? Why was his citizenship so damned important? He got up and ran after her. What in God's name ever compelled him to even consider marriage?

Diving in, he scraped his head on a submerged root and came up with a bloody forehead. He tried to support her so they could swim at his speed, but she pushed him off, still bawling uncontrollably. "You're all bloody," was all she could blurt out. He swam alongside her mimicking her breaststroke. His shock at her behavior turned to anger. Women! When you ignore them, they throw themselves at you. When you open up, they burst out crying and leave you in the lurch. She was a great lay and a screwed-up broad, just like all the rest of them—and nothing more. When did they ever make any sense?

135

Chapter Twenty-Eight

Oskar Faulheim's assistant poked his head through the door.

"Herr Faulheim," he called obediently. "The letter you asked the bomb disposal group to open, it was from the Pergolesi woman."

"So?" Faulheim shot back. "What was in it?"

"Just an apartment key, Herr Faulheim."

It was a rainy Sunday morning. Robert was reading the Deutsche Allgemeine newspaper. It was slow going: He still had difficulty with the significant difference between the convoluted complexity of formal, written German, compared to the easier spoken version. He and Sabina had not seen each other for the three weeks it had been since the puzzling incident on the island of Scharfenberg. Ballard was certain she would call to explain—maybe even apologize. When he could stand waiting no longer, he called to apologize but for what exactly he hadn't the least idea. No matter at what time he called, her apartment phone never answered.

He waited for her outside the school where she taught. They went to his apartment without saying much. After supper they went to bed and made love quickly and with little passion. Sabina told him that her friend posted to Cologne had returned unexpectedly, and Sabina had moved back into her mother's apartment. Her mother in turn had gone for an extended visit with old friends north of Berlin.

The next morning Sabina was pouring them tea, coffee being almost impossible to get. Since the war started, Germany had clamped a firm lid on any purchases that required hard currency leaving the country. Of these, halting the importation of coffee was the hardship most ubiquitously grumbled about. Tea was rationed but since it could keep in warehouses for years, it was still available.

Their lovemaking seemed rationed, too. Affection had not cleared the air which was still thick between them, and the long moments of silence were awkward rather than relaxing.

"Sabina, may I speak frankly to you about a subject that puzzles me?" Ballard asked her one evening as they prepared for breakfast.

"Of course, Robert," she said, turning to face him, her silk nightgown flaring open and revealing, for an instant the full length of her naked body. His gaze zeroed in on the black patch below her stomach. She set the pot down and retied her robe.

Ballard gulped at the momentary vision. "I often feel that whenever the subject of your mother comes up, you get very defensive."

"I don't know what you mean Robert. I'm very close to my mother. Just like you, we've been through a lot together, especially in the last few years."

"I can understand that, Sabina. And you've told me how she feels about you and me being together. But don't you think you should introduce me to her? Like it or not, we are practically living together and . . ."

"I have told her about you. She does not want to meet you. It's all I can do to keep a civil relationship with her. She is very hurt by what I am doing, and she forbids me to mention you in her presence."

Ballard scratched his head. They were getting nowhere again. "I just don't understand . . ."

"That's right, Robert," Sabina cut in sharply. "You don't understand. Not everyone has the same casual outlook on life and superficial relationships that Americans do. In fact I don't know anyone else who does. Didn't your parents teach you any respect for the opinions of your elders?"

"Sabina, please. It's not my manners we're discussing. I'm just trying to understand why your mama is so dead-set against someone she's never even met."

"And has no intention of meeting. Oh damn it." It was the first time he had heard her swear. "You've made me spill the hot water."

137

Ballard arose to help her mop up the spilled water. As they knelt down, the top of her robe fell open, revealing her thrilling cleavage. Again, Ballard had trouble focusing his thoughts.

"She's not in any trouble, is she?" he asked sheepishly.

"Trouble?" Sabina said. Her voice took on an accusatory tone. "What kind of trouble?"

"That's what I'm asking, Sabina." Ballard stood up. "Trouble with the Gestapo, with the police. How should I know? Any kind of trouble."

Sabina wiped up the water with a rag. She scrubbed furiously, as if trying to clean a deeply embedded stain off the floor. "I don't know what you're talking about Robert. You're just not making any sense. My mama is a wonderful person. Like your mother, and I love her just as much. She saved . . . she has sacrificed a lot for me, too."

Sabina stopped her furious cleaning. Ballard saw by the shaking of her body, bent over her task like a scrubwoman, that she was crying again. For a moment it made him angry.

"Darling, I . . ." he muttered, pulling her up to her feet.

"Oh, Robert," she sobbed. "It makes me so unhappy to have us arguing like this."

He held her in his arms, wanting to help. Her robe had come untied and hung open, exposing the full length of her nakedness. This time she did nothing to cover, herself. Ballard took her into his arms.

"I'm sorry my darling." But he felt thwarted once again. He kissed her tears pensively, and then her lips. She slide her hands up his back, pulling herself into him, electrifying him with her touch. Without interrupting their passionate kiss, he lifted her petite body into his arms and carried her into the bedroom. By the time he laid her down gently on the bed, she was already moaning for him to enter her.

Chapter Twenty-Nine
NOVEMBER 25, 1942

Ballard walked up the wide entrance staircase of the Reich Chancellery building, pulling his coat around him tightly. The frigid December wind whistled around the Roman columns, sucking every bit of warmth out of his tightly wrapped leather overcoat. He could not imagine how the German troops battling furiously at Stalingrad at this moment could live every day in weather far worse than this. Inside, Ballard followed the slow-moving line of officers up red-carpeted stairs. At the top of the wide marble staircase was the entrance to the main hall of the Reich's Chancellery, the center of government of the Third Reich. A dozen men ahead of him was Admiral Canaris, being perfunctorily frisked by SS Guards and then let through the entranceway.

When Ballard got to the inside entrance way, he held up his invitation and Abwehr Pass, which was scrutinized thoroughly and then was meticulously checked off a neat list. He was frisked efficiently but thoroughly. Wordlessly his Swiss Army knife was removed from his jacket pocket, placed in an envelope and a claim tag pressed into his hand.

"Next please," the slender blonde SS captain said with a tone of cold politeness one millimeter short of affront. Ballard stepped through the massive carved wooden doors—Good lord, they must be fifteen feet high he thought—-and into the large reception hall. Most of the guests were already inside. As a person with no rank or real status, Bormann had placed him near the end of the line, in spite of the fact the Führer would be decorating him for his role in crushing the British "Ultra" operation at Bletchley Park.

"The Reich Chancellery is quite capable of making up its own list of invited guests without pernicious foreign influences of that sort," Bormann had snorted derisively when Ballard timidly broached the question of whether he might invite Sabina to the ceremony. Even so the request had been pro forma on Ballard's part. Lately Sabina had become distant, with much of the spontaneity of their earlier relation greatly diminished. Is this it, he thought, the beginning of the end?

Canaris had decided it would be safer to stop hiding Ballard's work under a bushel. As the reputation of Ballard's "Operation Boston" intelligence feats spread, Canaris felt it would be all too easy for the Gestapo to spirit him away at any time for their own interrogation. As someone personally decorated by the Führer, Gestapo Chief Heinrich Muller and his henchman Oscar Faulheim would have to think twice about authorizing any outrageous abductions.

Hitler had been given a heavily doctored "complete report" about Ballard's discovery of the code breaking activity at Bletchley Park, and how he had planned the Skorzeny caper. For his part, Skorzeny was to receive the Oak Leaves to his Knight's Cross. Ballard was to receive the highest civilian award available to non-Germans, die deutsche Ordnung the German Order.

Passing through the great entrance doors, Ballard descended a short set of stairs that encircled the great hall like an amphitheater. A waiter approached offering a tray of Sekt glasses. Ballard snagged two which relieved him of the problem of getting a second drink too slowly. As he hoisted one glass to his lips his gaze fell upon Oskar Faulheim staring at him across the room. Their eyes locked for an instant, capturing each other in mutual fascination, a thin smile forming on the foppish man's face—or was it a sneer. The Gestapo agent tore his glance away and, ignoring Ballard completely, rejoined his small clot of fawning colleagues. Where is his charm, Ballard wondered. Or had that been an act, too? Like the spilled pudding?

Faulheim, Ballard reflected. Odd that he should be here. This was a military occasion. Was he here professionally, or socially? A chill settled over Ballard's shoulders. Or is he still interested in me?

As he stood taking in the view of the large hall and its three hundred guests milling about in so many small circles, Ballard felt his arm being touched. He turned to face Treuherz, the same Oberleutenant who had introduced Stumpfnagel to Sabina. This time his face carried none of the deliberate superiority that characterized its normal repose. He eyed Ballard with the frank envy of one who would also like to get an exalted award for doing nothing but thinking about things.

"Herr Ballard," Treuherz purred, "I'd like to introduce you to Heinrich Hofmann, Hitler's personal photographer." Treuherz moved his hands slightly to the left, indicating the direction he wished Ballard to go.

The two men moved through the crowd. Although both over six feet tall, Ballard noticed that for the first time he appeared to be only of average height. Did Hitler deliberately surround himself with tall men, or are tall men drawn to the centers of power? Or was this audience selected in order to exemplify Aryan racial superiority? It made him laugh to realize that the most powerful man on earth needed such transparent window dressing to bolster his ego.

Treuherz stopped near a tall, curtain-draped column at the edge of the hall. "Wait here a moment, please," Treuherz said in English. Treuherz stepped through the curtain and came out a few seconds later "Mr. Ballard," he continued in English, "permit me to introduce to you Herr Henrich Hofmann, the official photographer to the Führer. Herr Hofmann, Mr. Ballard." Ballard turned to shake hands with the photographer, a dapper gentleman, about age fifty-five he would guess, slickly dressed as if an ex-actor. Mildly salacious looking, too, as if cheesecake might be his favorite photographic subject matter, but wearing a congenial smile. Treuherz was already off, scanning the crowd for someone to bore or insult.

"A pleasure to meet you, Herr Hofmann," Ballard said in German. "Why do you think the Oberleutnant, spoke to us in English?"

"Oh, just to show off, as usual," Hofmann replied laconically. "He doesn't really speak English, you know. He's just memorized about a hundred handy phrases."

"Like the doorman at Kempinski's," Ballard laughed, "who can say `May I get you a taxi' in 20 languages." He eyed the older gentleman speculatively. "To what do I owe the pleasure of this meeting?"

"After the presentation of your medal, for which permit me to congratulate you ahead of time," Hofmann said, "the Führer will be leaving immediately for an inspection trip to Rastenburg." A couple drifted by and Hofmann ceased speaking until they had passed.

"The Führer often holds a little private meeting with his honored guests in one of the more intimate rooms, after the awards ceremony." Hofmann scratched his head as if he had momentarily forgot what he was talking about. He raised his forefinger as the recollection of the subject matter at hand returned.

"However, he cannot stay today. But, because of the illustrious caliber of the gathering for this Führer decoration, some members of Hitler's personal staff are going to hold this gathering in spite of the Führer's absence. This is not unusual. They have asked that you be invited to it."

"Why thank you very much," Ballard answered. "I didn't realize my feats were that well-known." He quickly wondered why they were known at all.

"Fräulein Eva Braun will be at this little gathering," Hofmann continued. "And she has asked that you please join and not feel left out."

Ballard was shocked and flattered at the same time. His situational awareness antenna was instantly raised. If even Eva Braun knows about me, who else does, he wondered. And how much do they know?

Hofmann looked Ballard over like an undertaker meeting a potential client. Was he measuring him for height? "When you leave this hall out the doors you came in, just continue down the main interior stairs, turn right and under the staircase you'll see a little service door. Enter there." The older man nodded wryly, turned and left.

Ballard was puzzled, and felt a pang of fear mixed with an inexplicable excitement. He had made a point of avoiding any contact with the maelstrom of power that Hitler and his closest associates represented, a vortex of savage disregard for even the most primitive norms of human behavior. Yet now that Canaris had felt it better to give him a little "protective exposure," he felt a flare-up of the thrill of action, a sensation he knew had developed into a narcotic habit with him. It made sex seem second rate. He spotted the admiral across the room within a small knot of naval officers and worked his way toward him. Yet the admiral was too engaged to be bothered. Stumpfnagel had not been invited, although he had been decorated with a Close Combat medal for his brave role in the Bletchley Park operation.

Ballard turned and nearly upset the drink of an older officer attempting roughly to scurry past him. It was General Guderian! The two locked eyes.

"Der Amerikaner," Guderian spat out warily.

"Always glad to be at your service Herr General," Ballard said, retreating a step and nodding subserviently.

"I don't want to be seen in the same building as you . . . you foreign gypsy," Guderian sputtered, searching for a word to describe Ballard's unorthodox magic. Strangely, there was no venom in his voice. "But frankly, your information about code, 'Vulture' was completely correct. With Abwehr help—your help, again, I take it—we have been changing all our machines. Your new design, I think." Guderian took a rapid sip from his glass. Almost as a deliberate affront, he was not looking at Ballard as he spoke. "I did have the winter material beefed up. Right now we're in a stalemate at Stalingrad, but we expect to launch operation "Winter Storm" as a major attack next week. We'll learn in the next few weeks if it was worth the trouble. The Führer knows of my unauthorized equipment supplements, but so far he hasn't said anything."

"He's waiting to see how it turns out, Herr General. You've done absolutely the right thing, I can assure you," Ballard purred, delighted to learn his tumultuous meeting had not been for naught.

"Is there anything else you have on your mind?" Guderian asked pugnaciously. He darted a glance at Ballard, then looked up, startled. Ballard caught his glance. The general had spotted his adjutant, von Moelke, across the room, who saw them together. A look of fear sprang across his face at the sight of Ballard so dangerously close to his general. Von Moelke pushed his way through the crowd, limping.

Ballard spoke rapidly: "Please, Herr General, now that you are at the gates of Stalingrad, under no circumstances let the Soviets—or the Führer himself—lure you into taking the city itself. Shell it, sap it, burn it. Encircle it and cut off all traffic to it, especially if you can seize the

143

far side of the Volga River. But do not try to occupy it. Because of its namesake, the Russians cannot permit it to fall, whatever the cost. Stay at the fringes of the city and guard your flanks. But if you attempt to take it—and I know the Führer will demand just that—the Soviets will spend every last man they have to stop you. They've got men without end, you don't.

"While Hitler will demand that von Paulus use up his best battle-hardened veterans fighting for a few square meters of the city proper, the Bolsheviks are right now assembling a major offensive west of the city.

"Look at the map. The Soviet 2nd Guards Army and the 7th Tank Corp. are poised but not engaging. These are extremely powerful units, yet they're not relieving the attack of Stalingrad. Why not? They're waiting for von Paulus to move into the city and get pinned-down in house-to-house combat. Then they'll respond with `Operation Uranus.' A large Soviet combat force backed by 1500 tanks will begin to pinch off the 500,000 men of the Sixth Army. Brave as these soldiers are, they will be no match for the numerically superior Soviet forces.

"Von Paulus has no new forces to replace his losses, which will be high. Generals Zukov and Vasievsky have an unending supply—they have the resources to bring a million combat troops to bear—and they mean to chew you up no matter what the cost. Stalin is just as crazy about defending his namesake city as Hitler is to seize it."

Guderian looked at Ballard as if examining an alien from another planet—cautious but curious about its strange talents. Von Moelke burst onto the two men.

"Herr Ballard, are you imposing yourself on the General again?" he snarled. He could not keep his lips from quivering with anger. His teeth were bared.

Guderian put his hand gently on his aide's shoulder, wordlessly calming him down. "'Operation Uranus,'" Guderian whispered, still studying Ballard's face. Then he turned and pushed his trembling aid in front of him. He did not shake hands or look back.

Ballard felt his heart racing. He looked around for someone to talk to, to calm himself down. The orchestra played a brief fanfare and the guests pulled back from the center of the large hall and began looking expectantly toward the inside entrance portals through which Hitler and his entourage were to appear. Ballard saw Treuherz waving anxiously at him, pointing with sharp twitches of his head in the direction of the room center. Ballard moved forward, trying to brush past the crowd that had formed in front of him.

"And just where do you think you're trying to shove your way to," a loud voice asked brusquely. A Wehrmacht full colonel was deliberately blocking his way through the crowd.

"I'm to get a medal from Herr Hitler," Ballard muttered. The officer fell back in astonished fear.

"I beg your pardon," the Colonel gasped. "I didn't realize any civilians were being presented. Please forgive me. Here, let me at least help you through. Make way," he shouted. "Make way for the 'becoming-Fuhrer-decoration-recipient.'"

Ballard trailed in the wake of the colonel plowing his way through the throng of guests to the inner edge of the circle. In German, 'becoming-Fuhrer-decoration recipient' was a perfectly correct, single word, such is the constructive power of the German language and the bureaucratic talent of the Colonel who undoubtedly made it up on the spot. It was probably his greatest talent.

Ballard saw Skorzeny and several other officers easing their way through the crowd as well. A flushed young SS lieutenant was acting as a protocol menial, lining them up to be presented. He looked aghast at Ballard. A civilian: where to put him? He could not stand anywhere in the front row. To do so would have him superseding military personnel and yet to begin a separate row would also accord him excessive distinction.

Skorzeny looked up and saw the lieutenant's agony of indecision. "Lieutenant, listen up. I'll stand back here with Herr Ballard. You'll be one short up front." He stepped back out of the front row and in conversational tones commanded: "Soldiers, attention. Fill in, left!"

The row of men lifted their hands to their waists, poking their elbows out the requisite stand-off distance and moved left to fill in his spot. The SS lieutenant's eyes bugged: This was not perfectly correct either . . .

"Buzz off, sonny," Skorzeny hissed at the young man dithering in indecision. Just then two guards, all well over, six feet tall, in full SS regalia including gleaming silver helmets, pulled open the grand interior entrance portals. The protocol lieutenant evaporated.

Several aids stepped through the door, followed by Reichsmarshall Herman Göring, supreme commander of the Luftwaffe and a half dozen other organizations, including the SS. Corpulent, yet with slender legs, he nevertheless strode in as light on his feet as a dancer, resplendent in a blazing white uniform of his own exotic design which was filigreed with gold embroidery. "Golden pheasants" Ballard had heard his type called, and Göring himself "the Fat One." A ceremonial golden dagger swung freely from his side, designating no known honor. Yet the Knight's Cross First Class around his thick neck was legitimately won as a daring photographer/pilot in the First War. Hanging upside down in an open biplane, Göring had photographed enemy installations while under heavy fire and earned himself the name the "Flying Trapezist." When he ran out, of film, he turned to his machine guns, strafing the enemy installations he had just photographed.

The Fat One twirled his golden baton in his hand, his alert eyes glancing at the reception line, and noticing instantly the discrepancy of Skorzeny in the rear. His eyes lingered on Ballard, trying to size him up without appearing interested. Ballard saw the flash of cunning in the glance. What he did not realize is with that single view of him, Göring, with his photographic memory would never forget Ballard.

The Reichsminister of Propaganda, Josef Goebbels followed the Reichsmarshall. Although his uniform was much subdued, he was another expensive dresser, Ballard noticed. The tailoring of his uniform was exquisite. He was rumored to have a huge wardrobe. Short and with a right clubfoot, the Reichsminister of Propaganda limped in regally, head held erect, his dark baleful eyes sweeping over the crowd, reflexively sizing them up in order to control them—should the need arise—with raw, rhetorical pyrotechnics that occasionally surpassed Hitler's. At least he had a sense of humor.

Heinrich Hiimmler, chief of the SS was next. His black uniform stood in somber contrast to that of his jovial appearing boss. Himmler's opaque, bored expression concealed the mind of a fiend, Ballard realized—a man able to keep up the appearances of civility as long as he could then get back to work. Ballard shuddered at what that "work" was.

Hitler wore a simple but also well-tailored uniform with only two decorations—his own Knight's Cross won for bravery as a corporal messenger in the trenches of the First World War, and the Nazi party insignia, the stylized spread-winged eagle holding the swastika globe. His expression was one of preoccupation, an executive suffering from overwork, but happy, on occasion, to be able to show the flag. Scurrying behind Hitler was the beefy Reichs Secretary Martin Bormann. Inseparable from the Führer and, now that Hess was gone, with control of his appointments, he was fast gaining a reputation as the second most powerful man in Germany.

Göring gave a brief introduction to the Führer, the proud task he so was happy to perform. A polite round of applause fluttered through the audience. The were saving their enthusiasm for the star of the show. As Hitler approached the two rows of men, a stern voice from behind commanded: "Special Decoration Detachment, Achtung . . ."

As one, the soldiers straightened up, the left leg of each man spreading twenty centimeters to the left, toe still touching the floor, poised.

"Statt!" Six legs slammed back to the vertical, the heels striking the standing heel with a sharp "clack."

At the command Ballard tried to stand up a little straighter and appear a little less relaxed, intimidated by the martial precision that seemed so natural to the rest of the assemblage.

The front row was decorated with dispatch. The Führer was a busy man. Ballard looked straight ahead, frightened even to turn his eyes in the direction of the leader of the German Reich as he pinned the Oak Leaves on Skorzeny's Knight's Cross.

"What kind of adventures do you have in store for us next, Herr Hauptman," the Führer asked.

"Whatever is asked of me, mein Führer," Skorzeny shot back, a grin on his face. A fellow Austrian, he was one of Hitler's favorites.

The Führer chuckled. "When we invade America, I shall send you to capture Texas. Then you can be with your real friends, the other cowboys."

"Jawohl, mein Führer. I should like that."

Hitler moved in front of Ballard, stepping back a bit, the better to gaze at him. Hitler had become far-sighted and he had developed a habit of moving back from an object he wished to see better. As leader of the Aryan race, wearing glasses in public, was out of the question.

"So you're the strange Mr. Ballard," Hitler murmured, tipping his head back to stare up into Ballard's eyes. Ballard, returned the gaze, unwaveringly. He saw the pale, impenetrable blue eyes of a man who had witnessed everything, yet the radiation of genius Ballard expected from this great leader was missing. In its place was a terrifying sense of raw power, genteelly but imperfectly masked. He saw a vast breadth of mercurial cunning, but no depth. Hair-trigger anger momentarily uncocked, alternating with warm, perceptive geniality—the sign of a mild, brilliant schizophrenic, Ballard presumed. He recognized the narrow sensuous lips of a man who prided himself on being master of the entire shallow sea in which he waded supreme but, as one who had never learned to swim, was instinctively frightened of any uncharted depths. He saw a man who enjoyed being surrounded by other shallow water craft: movie stars, amateur artists, purveyors of cottage kitsch—but who was made uncomfortable by any troubling deep-water traits of philosophic or artistic genius.

Upon inspection of Ballard's face, Hitler's appraising smile hesitated. He found himself unable to work his clever knack of cold-reading a person's character, and making an appropriately smarmy little joke. Yet, as nervous as he was, Ballard tried to keep a relaxed expression on his face, an expression of appreciation, even willing servitude.

Without taking his eyes off Ballard, Hitler reached to the box held out to him by an aid, and picked up the German Order. They were cheaper than the gold or silver cigarette cases that were, previously awarded.

"For outstanding services to the Reich," he said in raised tones, "and by the highest recommendation of the Chief of the Abwehr, I present you with der deutsche Ordnung."

148

Hitler placed the ribbon around Ballard's neck. As he leaned forward, Ballard noticed that Hitler had an odd, not unpleasant smell—the sweet body odor of a vegetarian.

"The admiral tells me you want a fleet of my submarines for another adventure," Hitler whispered, straightening the medal.

"Six U-boats, mein Führer. To prevent the Americans from building an atomic . . . an uranium-burning bomb."

"And you know they are trying?"

"Jawohl. I have a photocopy of Herr Doktor Professor Albert Einstein's secret letter to Roosevelt proposing it," Ballard replied, trying to force a smile. "No one in all of Germany has seen it yet." He felt a sharp prickling sensation as Hitler's eyes suddenly riveted on his own. The abrupt power of the man's focused attention was overwhelming. Ballard felt as if Hitler had connected to him with a power cord, sucking energy out of him with his very presence and beaming it back in a glare of mad, psychic illumination. Ballard wilted under the assault.

"You have it with you, on your person, now?" Hitler asked suspiciously.

"I do, Jawohl, mein Führer."

"Remain in the hall," Hitler said softly, stepping past the American. Raising his voice slightly he announced to the assembled audience his pleasure at the honor of recognizing with these few men officially what the German people all know in their hearts: that the bravery and valor exemplified by the men gathered here is but the tip of the iceberg of the bravery and valor that exists in the heart of every German soldier.

His little speech was made not five feet from Ballard. It was a masterly monograph made by the consummate toastmaster. A hysterical round of applause burst out from the audience. Ballard unlocked his gaze from the Führer and looked at them. The expressions on their faces were like that of children at the circus—awe-struck, smiling, trembling. Some women, the young second wives of older, high officials and young women who, with the shortage of young men had finally married older men, had tears of joy running down their Nordic cheeks.

After acknowledging the applause, Hitler turned to leave the chamber. He stopped by an aide and muttered something. The man looked around and focused sharply on Ballard and nodded to Hitler in affirmation.

Ballard was still trembling under the mesmerizing shock of Hitler's attention. It was a phenomenon oft described but one that Ballard would not have believed as an intellectual, could affect him so strongly. He was wrong. Hitler's psychic assault left him emotionally prostrate.

As the ceiling-high interior portals shut on the commander-in-chief, the crowd moved in and set upon the newly decorated men with effusive congratulations. The Colonel who had blocked Ballard a few minutes ago practically leaped across the ballroom floor to get at him, greeting him loudly as if they had been lifelong friends.

"Our sincerest congratulations," the officer said, taking Ballard's hand and pumping it firmly. "And from my wife too, here, don't hang back, Ulrike, this is the famous Mr. Ballard."

The colonel was expertly blocking others who were trying to rush up to congratulate Ballard. But the crowd parted as if cleaved by an invisible force as a regal white-haired SS general strode vigorously toward the American.

"Herr Ballard would like to follow me to meet privately with the Führer," he said, speaking to the American in the royal third person. The crowd fell back, blanching at the aura of influence this message portended.

Through a door to the left of the great portal, Ballard was ushered quickly into an antechamber and motioned to sit. The SS general eyed him impassively. A light changed color above the door. "Los," he said tonelessly—go on.

Inside the small meeting room, Hitler was surrounded by functionaries and generals like a queen bee by her swarm. Martin Bormann was yanking generals away from the Führer as if they were errant children.

"The Ballard man is come," he heard Bormann mutter.

With his back to him, Hitler removed his spectacles and then turned around to face the American. "The others please leave," he said. At once they all filed out the door, except Bormann, skulking in the corner:

"You, too, Herr Bormann," Hitler chided. "Herr Ballard has something for my eyes only."

Bormann turned to Ballard and fixed him with a deliberately intimidating glare, then left the room.

"Not too long, mein Führer. Your plane is waiting." He clicked the door shut behind him.

"And it can wait, if I want it to, can't it Herr Ballard?"

Ballard laughed. "If you say so, mein Führer, I believe even the sun would stand still."

Hitler's eyes lit up in a twinkle of appreciation. "That's a power I didn't realize I had," he jibbed back.

"Well, perhaps better to test it only on a cloudy day," Ballard retorted.

Hitler's clucked appreciatively at Ballard's wit, a wit that was not over his head as so many of the so-called intellectual jokes that Goebbels often tried to make.

"You have the letter?"

Ballard reached into his jacket pocket and pulled out the photocopy Hitler fretted at the thought of having a stranger see him using his glasses.

"It is in English so I will translate it for you, mein Führer, if you will permit me," Ballard said, pretending he did not know that Hitler could speak and read English reasonably well. "Life" Magazine was one of his favorite periodicals. Relieved, Hitler nodded in acquiescence.

August 2, 1939: From Dr. Albert Einstein to FDR

In the course of the last four months it has been made probable—through the work of Joilet in France as well as Fermi and Szffard in America—that it may be possible to set up a nuclear chain reaction in a large mass of uranium, by which vast amounts of power and, large quantities of new radium-like elements would be generated. Now it appears almost certain that this could be achieved in the immediate future.

This new phenomena would also lead to the construction of bombs, and it is conceivable—though much less certain—that extremely powerful bombs of a new type, carried by boat and exploded in a port, might very well destroy the whole port together with some of the surrounding territory."

"Donnerwetter," Hitler said, a dreamy look crossing his face. Here was real power. "How did you get this letter? How far along are the Americans? We have a project along those lines as well, you know."

"Yes, I know, mein Führer," Ballard said, and then bit his tongue. Stupid slip.

"You seem to be extremely well informed about so many things, Herr Ballard," Hitler said, the air cooling noticeably. "Is the Gestapo aware of your sources?"

"I have been working very satisfactorily with the Abwehr, mein Führer," Ballard replied.

"Yes, but I asked . . ."

At that moment, Bormann entered the room. "Mein Führer. We must be on our way . . ."

"Yes, yes I'm coming. In just a moment." Hitler rubbed his jaw contemplatively, wondering as much about Ballard's request as about how an obscure foreigner had access to so much intelligence matter.

"I'm not yet convinced your little project is worth the price of six U-boats. U-boats don't just grow in cornfields you know, and we need everyone we can get to maintain the blockade of England."

Ballard's eyes fell in disappointment, but he remained silent. He knew pressuring Hitler would have the opposite effect.

"Perhaps you can consider it again later, mein Führer. The results would be of even greater value to the Reich than the Bletchley Park raid."

"You don't say," Hitler responded. By now his mind was already on to something else. He turned to pick up his glasses case laying on the table. "Well thank-you for this interesting letter. Bormann will certainly try, to find out how you got it."

"Perhaps I could say you expressly forbade me to give away that secret," Ballard replied, a smile of hope forming on his face.

Hitler laughed. "Try it. That would make him even more impossible."

"As you order, mein Führer. And have a good journey."

Hitler turned and raised his arm briefly in acknowledgment, then pushed open the door, entering an instantaneously arising buzz of activity.

Ballard left by the opposite door. There, in the antechamber, listening attentively on the telephone, was his escort, the SS general who had brought him to the meeting.

"Herr Bormann reminds you to be sure to contact him as soon as he gets back to his office, which he expects to be at 9 p.m. tonight," the officer said.

Ballard eyed him speculatively. Fight or flight, he thought. "You can tell Herr Bormann for me that the Führer has expressly forbidden me to discuss with any one this matter that took place under four eyes. He mentioned Herr Bormann's name in particular. I'm sure the Führer will tell the secretary everything he wants him to know.

"Thank you for your help. I know my way out. I believe the concierge has my pocket knife."

"That you can get at the top of the stairs," the General said dismissively. He checked that the door back to the meeting room was locked and then left the room and Ballard to himself.

Ballard sat down, realizing he was still trembling. Was it the effect of his disappointment at not getting Hitler's agreement on the U-boats, or a fear of having aroused in him a dangerous curiosity about where his information came from? Or was it the instant enmity he had earned of Martin Bormann? No, it was none of these, he realized slowly. It was Hitler himself: of simply being in the presence of such absolute, maniacal power. Like being locked in the cage of a momentarily passive lion, knowing it could change its mind at any moment and for no reason, instantaneously leap up and rip your guts out. Instead, the lion had licked his face.

Ballard left the antechamber and retrieved his knife. He descended the grand stairway and turned right at its bottom. There was the small service entrance Herr Hofmann had mentioned. He knocked gently and turned the handle. The door was pulled out of his grasp. Ballard looked up at the appraising stare of an SS sergeant.

"You are . . . ?" he asked curtly.

"Herr Robert Ballard," he answered.

153

"Ja, gut," the sergeant replied. "You're expected. Follow me." He led the way down a narrow corridor, made a right turn and then stopped.

"Third door on the right," he pointed. "You can let yourself out the way you came." He turned and disappeared down the dimly lit servants corridor.

Ballard counted the doors, expecting any moment to hear the chatter of men joking and bragging. He stopped at the third door and knocked. Hofmann opened it instantly.

"Aha, there you are. We had wondered how long you'd be. The party's in the next room."

Hofmann left by the door that Ballard was still holding open. Ballard crossed the small room—it seemed to be a self-contained apartment in the cellar of the Reichs Chancellery—to a sitting room. There, artfully seated on a couch was Eva Braun surrounded by a bevy of soldiers. Herta Schneider, her childhood girlfriend and confident, stood in a corner, flirting quietly with one of the new "Führer-decoration-holders." Her presence and Eva's sister Gretl, who was to soon marry the well know social climber and lady's man, SS Lieutenant General Hermann Fegelein, made this gathering of so many men and the unmarried Eva Braun socially acceptable.

Ballard saw that Eva Braun noticed his entrance, but quickly averted her glance and pretend to be jovially occupied with her admirers. As if on cue, Skorzeny turned, stood up and hailed his friend.

"Herr Ballard—so soon. We thought you'd be hours with the Führer. You didn't make him angry, did you?" The others stood up as well. Ballard was surprised to notice that Eva was only slightly taller than Sabina—about five foot-two. From all the pictures of her he had expected her to be taller: Each of them shook his hand and then resumed their seats.

"No, he's quite happy," Ballard replied. "But I don't know about Herr Bormann."

Eva Braun made a face of disgust. "Oh, that coarse man. I wish someone would teach him the minimal manners." She looked over at Skorzeny coyly, as if daring him to be the one.

"Fräulein Braun, such ungenerous thoughts," Skorzeny said with a hard smile that made it clear he couldn't agree more, but that he was nobody's fool, not even the pretty Eva Braun's, "about a very powerful man. Permit me to introduce to you, Fräulein Braun, another powerful man—this one with positive power—Herr Robert T. Ballard, an extraordinary friend of Germany. Herr Ballard, I present to you Fräulein Eva Braun." The absence of any explanation of title or verbal connection to Hitler always made her introduction to a stranger one of quickly overlooked impropriety.

Eva Braun held out her hand and Ballard shook it heartily and firmly, the convention of all German hand-shakes. He had been sternly lectured by Stumpfnagel that to shake a hand weakly or, perish the thought limply—was an affront, and invited speculation about possible deviant sexual inclination. Eva Braun gazed at him coolly, her blue eyes sweeping over him like a caress.

"I've heard quite a bit about our Mr. Ballard in the last few weeks," she said coquettishly, with a trace of South-German accent.

"All positive things, I hope," Ballard answered inanely.

"Positive, negative, I think it was more astonishment and great curiosity," she answered. "Even worry. And then your odd request . . ."

The others looked at Ballard, hoping to learn what his odd request to Hitler had been.

"A request about which the Führer has not yet made up his mind," Ballard said wryly.

"And will not," she answered, staring directly into his eyes. "without some very high level recommendations." She turned to Oberleutnant Gregor Michaels who had just been awarded the Oak leaves to his Knight's Cross, the 187th German soldier to receive that honor to date, according to Hitler's proclamation. "Maybe you need someone like Oberleutnant Michael to speak to the Führer on your behalf He certainly has the talent for convincing people against their will."

Her little speech completed, Eva Braun waltzed off coquettishly, deliberately Ballard thought, to converse with another group of soldiers.

155

Taking the oberleutenant's arm in hers, she pushed him along with her.

Skorzeny pulled his friend over by the shoulder. "A spirited little filly, isn't she?"

"For sure," Ballard answered. "Who is Michaels?"

"You don't know?" Skorzeny asked, astonished. "Today he got his Oak Leaves for unbelievable bravery while attached to the Sixth Army at Stalingrad. It was him and what was left of his division that stopped the Soviet encirclement."

"Oh, yes, now I remember that action," Ballard replied. "November 19th, M Corp., the 295th Infantry Division, sent in to bolster the Romanian third Army, wasn't it?"

Now it was Skorzeny's turn to be amazed. "You remember it that well . . . ?"

"It will be recognized as the decisive battle of the European war," Ballard replied, his voice rising in excitement. "But I didn't know who led the break-out." The rest of the gathering fell silent. "The order to take Stalingrad street-by-street was a terrible mistake. When it was tried for a few days, the combatants made mincemeat of each other fighting over a few meters a day. Thank God General von Paulus rejected the Führer's order as untenable and instead encircled the town with the Russian defenders inside. Even as it was, von Paulus was essentially cut off, but at least he didn't lose half his men. Göring promised to supply by air the five hundred tons a day the Sixth Army needed to continue fighting, but he never supplied more than three hundred tons, and much less than that as the weeks wore on. His promise was as reliable as the one he made about allied bombs getting to Berlin.

"If Michaels' unit had not succeeded in breaking out—and that was a spectacular success, catching the Russians completely off guard—they would have secured their encirclement of the Sixth Army. Hell, they did cut the Sixth completely off for a day or two, but von Manstein and the 295th broke through, Gott sei Dank. If it had not been for Michaels' action to rally the battalion-sized division that already felt itself beaten, to fight their way out in the middle of a bitter snowstorm, von Paulus would have lost half his 500,000 men in trying to break out weeks later, and then, failing that, would have had to surrender the rest. That loss would have represented Germany's most serious single defeat, and a change in the fortunes of war from which—frankly—it could never recover. Just now Guderian is wisely resisting Hitler's demands to reenter the city. Presumably he will succeed in cutting off its supplies."

Flushed at the memory and the spirited retelling, Ballard stood up and raised his wine glass toward Michaels. "It is whispered that the Führer didn't know whether to decorate Michaels for saving the Sixth Army, or to court martial him for disobeying his strict 'no retreat' order," he said. "Fighting the Russians at the same time you are disobeying Hitler, ladies and gentlemen, that requires courage and intelligence very much above and beyond the call of duty. A toast to Oberleutenant Gregor Michaels, for true heroism in thought and deed that saved the Sixth Army at Stalingrad. Zum Wohl!"

The astonished group pushed back their chairs and rose, holding their glasses high. "Zum Wohl," they echoed, their awestruck glances alternating between Ballard and Michaels.

Ballard looked around the room. The guests remained standing, open-mouthed at his commentary. Eva Braun had even let go of the handsome Oberleutenant Michaels' arm and was staring at Ballard wide-eyed. She quickly regained her composure. Michaels did not feign embarrassment at Ballard's speech. He looked at the American with an expression of fascination.

"Yes, what an interesting and frank military analysis, Herr Ballard," Eva Braun said, puncturing the awe-struck silence. "One hears so little of that around here." She turned her attention to the others. "I know all of you have other plans tonight, so I won't hold you up. You know the way out, right and then left. Hauptsturmfuhrer Skorzeny, if I may speak with you just for a minute after the others leave. I won't hold you up but a moment."

The men filed out of the strange little apartment and found their way back to the main hallway. Still under the spell of Ballard's speech, they milled around without talking—putting coats on, and lighting cigarettes until Skorzeny rejoined, then they all left the huge building together.

The usually taciturn SS Obersturmbanführer Fritz Vogt was the first to speak up. "That was a hell of speech, Herr Ballard. How did you get such detailed information?"

"He works for the Abwehr, Dummkopf," Skorzeny broke in. "Don't you know they know everything?"

"Ja, sometimes even before we in the field know it," Michaels said slowly. Some of the aura was beginning to wear off. He eyed Ballard with mild suspicion. "It's not 'von' Paulus, you know," he said to the American. "The noble lord may try to look like a Junker, but he's just an ordinary guy from Hesse."

"Hey, before you guys get too serious," Vogt piped up. "Let's go bar hopping. I know a lovely section of town where the women are all beautiful." Vogt had just received his Knights' Cross by capturing and holding the Swltocz bridge at Pochowiece, permitting Guderian's Panzers to cross. He was the fourth soldier of the Waffen SS to be so decorated.

"And the more you drink, the more beautiful they get," Michaels quipped. "In fact with most of them you can't even appreciate their beauty until you're nearly blotto. Let's ask the American where he wants to go."

"Downtown, of course," Ballard said. "For wine, women and song. But we can't all fit in my car, so we need to make other travel arrangements."

Ballard stepped out into the street and, by standing in front of it, brazenly flagged down a bus coming up the Charlottenburger Chausee, the grand east-west boulevard that passes by the Chancellery and through the Brandenburg Gate. Seeing so many Knights Crosses at once startled the bus driver long enough for the men to hop on board the open rear platform—to their astonishment and that of the bus passengers. An unscheduled stop—it was very un-German.

"For God's sake, Herr Ballard," Skorzeny said only half in jest. "Don't you ever stop working your miracles?"

The group trundled up the stairwell to the upper deck of the bus, stooping over to avoid hitting their heads on the low roof. They shooed three youngsters down stairs so they could have the upstairs to themselves.

"He worked a miracle on Fräulein Braun tonight, that I'll tell you," Michaels added.

"What are you talking about Michaels?" Skorzeny said. "We all thought you had her sewn up-at least until the Führer catches you and gives you a very special decoration."

"You mean he returns your own most prized family jewels in a 'presentation case'?" Vogt asked.

"Oh not so plain an award as that," paratrooper Hauptman Rudolf Witzig answered. "It's also decorated with a sword."

"Also your own," Ballard interjected, joining in the black humor. But he wanted to hear more. Could Eva Braun get him his U-boats?

"Rope burns and all," Skorzeny added, his face gleeful at the graphic direction their banter was taking.

"Arrgh," Michaels said disgustedly. "Skorzeny and Witzig, why are you paratroopers always so clinical?"

"You don't know why,?" Skorzeny responded, feigning a wide-eyed wonder that these young lads had never learned what was common knowledge. "It's because of our great experience with God's gift to manhood. If you youths wish to be initiated into the exotic wonders of the fairer sex . . ."

"We won't find any fair ones where you hang out," Michaels interrupted. "But it's true about the American. Fräulein Braun's bloomers dropped when she heard Ballard teaching the great Skorzeny what grand strategy is all about."

"Meaning I get invited to all the big state dinners?" Ballard asked expectantly.

"Meaning if you get asked to dinner again, bring a chaperon, old boy," Skorzeny said quietly. "She just asked me about you, too. But I'd keep my distance if I were you. Otherwise you'll end up as fish bait in the Spree River."

Chapter Thirty
FEBRUARY 28, 1943

Stumpfnagel called out to Ballard sitting in his 'office.' Ballard swiveled out from behind his desk in the large walk-in closet he had been awarded. A tiny window, heavily frost coated this last day of February, had been punched through the wall to distinguish his office from the far larger space Inge had in her reception area. But she had no window.

"Here's a piece of bad news," Stumpfnagel said wandering into Ballard's office. "Fifth columnists in Norway have sabotaged our deuterium-oxide heavy water plant in Vemork. All eighteen cells blown out. We lost 1,000 kilos of D_2O. Nearly our entire supply. At 150 kg a month, that'll take a long time to replace."

Ballard looked a Stumpfnagel without saying anything. Stumpfnagel read the dispatch out loud.

"General Rediess rounded up ten leading towns people and threatened to have them shot unless information about the saboteurs was forthcoming," Stumpfnagel read. He continued on, muttering and skipping sections of the report.

"However General von Falkenhorst arrived on the scene a few hours later and based on the evidence—hmmm, hmmm—of a British Tommy gun, etc.., etc., he decided that the job had been carried out as a British military operation, and released the hostages."

Ballard continued to look at Stumpfnagel impassively.

"That is going to set back our uranium bomb effort a long time, Herr Ballard," Stumpfnagel said. "Six months or a year. Do you know anything about this?"

"It'll probably save the German Reich a lot of money otherwise thrown down the drain, Herr Leutnant," Ballard replied. "If you can't

160

even get a jet fighter into the air to save yourself from the terrific bombing you're taking now, what chance do you think you have with a three billion—excuse me—three millarden-Reichsmark atomic bomb project that can't possibly be ready until 1948 or '49 at the earliest?"

"I don't know. What chance do we have, Herr Ballard?" Stumpfnagel asked, slightly peeved. He had learned to spot when the American was being evasive, and he didn't like it.

"None, my friend," Ballard replied. "The Brits did you a favor." He returned to his office with a cold smile of satisfaction.

Chapter Thirty-One

Ballard guided Sabina in front of him through the doors of the downstairs cabaret. The air was blue with cigarette smoke and the smell of stale beer. Public dancing was forbidden in Germany ever since the war had started, but some of the rougher dives in the nightclub section of town permitted it between shows. Ballard had read about the outré reputation of Berlin night life in Christopher Isherwood's 1939 stories Good-by To Berlin, and was anxious to experience it at least once firsthand.

"Darling, its so . . . low," Sabina said, looking back at him askance. Do you really want to do this, her eyes said. But she knew better than to appear to be blocking Ballard's wishes. He approached everything with such a schoolboy's enthusiasm, and he hated to be held back.

"Just five steps down," he tried to joke. The joke fell flat.

"May I help you?" a garishly dressed waiter asked, his battered eyes sizing them up as foreign guests and possible big spenders. His eyes lingered over Ballard, not certain if he was a soft touch or made of sterner stuff. An officer in civilian clothes, perhaps, the waiter calculated.

"We want to see the show, and we understand you have a dance floor," Ballard said. He pushed a five-mark note into the waiter's sweaty palm, and was waved to follow him. "And we don't want to sit where you're taking us," Ballard snorted.

"Oh, no, of course not," the waiter said, springing to life. His gambit of seating them among the hoi polloi had failed. "Let me take you to the back hall. You get a much closer seat to the stage and none of this riffraff will bother you."

The riffraff looked as if it had come out of a Hollywood production, except for the serious decrepitude of the clientele. Most were well above "a certain age," and heavily made up. Ballard noted the hard lines of many women's faces, suggesting that their sexual orientation was a recently acquired trait. These weren't university students brandishing their independence; this crowd was one of genuine cultural deviates streaked through with pain and despair. Theirs was a sub-cultural zoo, the cage being all of the outside world. Here, in this smoky pit they could be momentarily free to practice their officially banned lifestyles.

The waiter took them through a door into a short hall. At the other end was another door. The waiter held the second door open and ushered them into a smaller room on the opposite side of the stage. There was far less smoke, and Ballard noticed some of the audience was in uniform. Most of the people appeared normal. They were the zoo visitors.

"The dance floor is at the rear, but you are still closer to the stage here than anywhere in the other room." The waiter stood still, waiting for Ballard to speak. "You can sit where you like. Ute," he called out, grabbing a tall, thin, scantily clad waitress by the elbow. "Serve these honored guests immediately."

The waitress turned to Ballard and Sabina with a harried look. She quickly pasted a smile on her face. Ballard was shocked to discover she was topless, her tiny breasts jiggling as she maneuvered her tray to her other arm, and cleared a straggled mop of graying hair out of her eyes.

"Will the couple be seated?" the waitress asked. Her voice was so low Ballard realized "she" must be a he. Her pathetic "breasts" were nothing but painfully stretched flaps of skin.

They sat at the rear, as much for convenience to the dance floor as to avoid having the audience stare over them during the show.

"We'll sit here," Ballard announced. "Get us a bottle of Sekt, if you would—unopened. The real thing, please."

"Immediately," the waitress said, and disappeared into the gloom.

The five-piece band, which sat between the two rooms, began to play a haunting tango.

"Care to dance Madam?" Ballard said gallantly.

"Why Robert, we've just sat down," Sabina objected.

"But surely the Madam does wish to dance?" Ballard asked, just the slightest bit irked. Sabina had been dragging her feet all day. In fact, she had not really been herself since she had given up her apartment. He hated stick-in-the-muds, and lately Sabina had possessed none of the zip he once enjoyed so much. And their love making always seemed inconvenient, as if she had suddenly tired of it and was just going through the motions.

She stood up and the two swung onto the dance floor. Ballard squashed her in an embrace. "Aha," he whispered. "I notice the Madam is wearing a brassier."

"I . . . I'm a little bit tender today, Robert," she said. She turned her head so his kiss, aimed for her mouth, landed instead on her cheek.

Ballard did not know how to tango, so he just settled into his generic dance step, aping the tempo, so their movements at least did not totally violate the syncopated spirit of the music.

Two other couples began to dance, hunched over each other to extract maximum bodily contact. They had another rhythm in mind.

The band switched to an undanceable jazz piece. Ballard and Sabina were about to sit down when they noticed their table had been taken by another couple. Resigned to an evening that was not getting off on the right foot and probably never would, Ballard guided Sabina to a free table in the middle of the audience. He barked his shin trying to fit his legs under the table.

Their waitress came back, flushed from the effort of finding real Sekt.

"Oh, you've changed tables," she said frantically. "I thought maybe you'd walked out. Here is the Sekt. It's fifty marks. The house champagne is only twenty-two marks a bottle."

Ballard checked the label—Jakob & Riems. Fifteen marks at the wine shop. He clapped his hand around the bottle. "We'll take it. But I'll pay when you, serve it cold."

The waitress jerked back. Another special demand! Who do these foreigners think they are? She left in huff.

"Excuse me, mein Herr," Ballard vaguely heard someone saying. He looked up. A German officer—a captain was addressing him.

"Is this not Frau Sabina Pergolesi?" He was Leibstandarte Adolf Hitler SS—one of the palace guards.

Sabina was sitting back in her chair, her eyes sparkling silently. "Yes," Ballard said. The officer had already given his own name, but he had done so before Ballard was aware that he was being addressed.

"Frau Pergolesi and I met when I was attached to the Germany Embassy in Roma," the officer said politely. "May I ask her for a dance."

"Sure, why not," Ballard answered. He watched the pair weave their way to the tiny dance floor.

The band was playing a slow, forbidden tune-a Gershwin piece he could not place—'American in Paris'? "Jewish music" of any kind could not be performed anywhere in Germany. Gershwin, Mahler, Mendelsohn—their works were all pronounced "degenerate art," and therefore verboten. But the thrilling discordance of the piece was instantly recognized by this crowd. Idly, he watched Sabina and the officer dance. Both were excellent dancers. He bit his lip at the thought of how primitive his own shuffling about must have seemed. Sabina was as light as a feather in the officer's arms. He twirled her about and then let her fall nearly over backwards, before catching her close to the ground. It was a practiced step that caused a pang of jealousy to gnaw at his heart.

The young captain lifted Sabina up and was about to return her to Ballard, when the band continued playing, this time a melancholy waltz. Sabina was smiling broadly—the first time he did not see her without an anxious expression on her face since they had been together this evening.

Sabina pulled him back. He flashed her a broad grin of delight and they swooped about with all the grace and verve of two professionals. A loud clunk on his table ripped him out of his misery. It was the skinny transvestite waitress.

"There. Cold. Unopened. Echt. That'll be fifty marks," he/she said gracelessly. "Plus fifteen percent service."

"Here's fifty-five marks. Go stuff your service," Ballard growled. Before he could reach the bottle, a large waiter-cum-bouncer snapped the bottle up in his mammoth hands and began to wring its neck. The cork popped, but remained in the waiter's hand. He placed the bottle down delicately at Ballard's side. "Ten marks corkage fee, if you please," he said in a gravely voice that brooked no dissent.

Ballard reached wearily back into his wallet. So far this shindig had cost him about a week's workingman's wages. He poured his own glass and sipped the drink. It was cool, but not cold, and too sweet. He swilled the entire glass and poured himself another. He cast his eyes back to the dance floor. Sabina and the officer were gyrating like the two professional dancers they so obviously were. The other couples had sheepishly left the floor. The band had noticed, and was drawing the number out, to the delight of the audience—and the two dancers.

The dance tempo picked up and the couple were weaving skillfully around the floor. The management had turned up the spot lights over the dance floor and the entire room was watching the two spin and twirl. Ballard could see them sweating from the exertion. Both were beaming, staring into each other's eyes.

The music reached a finale. The officer stopped abruptly and spun his partner in a flourishing twirl, holding his hand up in the air so she spun about like a top. At the abrupt last note, he dropped to his knees, seized her waist, brought her to a complete stop, and let her fall lifelessly into his arms, a few centimeters off the floor. The audience clapped their hands raucously. Ballard could see people from the other room peering across the stage, trying to see what they were missing.

The officer escorted Sabina back. Both were breathless and sweating heavily in the stuffy atmosphere.

"Thank you. so very much Frau Pergolesi, and you, too, Herr Ballard." He bowed deeply and returned to his own table where an equally jealous date glowered. Ballard could not help himself from feeling foolish. She had told that silly dance instructor his name. Who would they 'bump into' next week-her tennis pro from Florence, or her ski instructor from Innsbruck?

"Oh, Robert, that was so enjoyable. Roland and I were in an Embassy dance show—a benefit for Italian war wounded and that was our number. It's remarkable how the band played the right tunes."

"And, of course he didn't pay them to do so," Ballard said sourly.

"Why Robert, you're upset," Sabina said, paying her first modicum of attention to him. "Yes of course he must have paid them. How thoughtful of him."

"Here have a drink, Sabina, before the champagne gets any warmer. Do you want to take off your jacket? You look very hot." Ballard filled up her glass. As she took off her jacket, her breasts pushed out her blouse so abruptly, Ballard felt a flush of arousal suffuse his body.

"Shall we leave, my darling," Ballard asked huskily.

"We just got here, Robert. And I have to drink my champagne. Hmmm. Delicious," she said gaily. "Don't you agree?"

"It was Disraeli, I think, who described yet another luncheon as `Everything was cold except the champagne.' Plus it's too sweet," he answered.

"You never like champagne to have any taste, Robert," she said. "You could just drink seltzer water and save a lot of money."

"I'll drink what I like, my darling. Especially when I'm paying for it." He felt like an idiot the moment the words escaped his lips.

Sabina sat there, silenced by his crude rebuke. She put her half-empty glass down and put her jacket back on. "Yes, Robert. I think we had better go." She pushed her chair back and stood up without his help.

Ballard got up, feeling foolish for being such a boor. His chair fell over backwards and he felt himself stumble as he stepped back to avoid tipping the table. Christ, he was drunk-from three glasses of champagne on an empty stomach. Sabina was already finding her way out.

He lurched after her, feeling dizzy from having risen so suddenly.

He came out on the Hohenzollerstrasse. Sabina had seen the streetcar coming and jumped expertly onto the back platform. "I am going home by myself, Robert," she said sternly. She pushed the curtain aside and disappeared inside the passenger compartment.

"But Sabina . . ." he shouted. Passersby barely looked up at him, staggering in the street. Another drunk, whose date had walked out on him. So what else is new?

Ballard walked unsteadily to where he had parked the car. Good God, what else could go wrong tonight, he asked. As he struggled to fit the key to the car lock, the air raid sirens went off. The shock of their shrill wail hit him like a cold slap in the face. The thought of spending the next few hours packed in with screaming babies in the fetid miasma of an air raid shelter was too much. He leaned over the curb and was sick.

Chapter Thirty-Two

Ballard left the office early. He learned from Major Hilflich that clearing the Gestapo wire tap found in his apartment would just result in another one being put up later—and probably more difficult to find. Use an outdoor telephone, he had been advised, but not the one nearest to his home, as that will probably be tapped, too.

Ballard got off the Number 71 streetcar two stops before his normal stop. There on the opposite corner was a telephone box. He, dialed Sabina at her apartment. They would have to have a talk.

"Darling, I'm sorry I barked at you last night. Can I make it up to you over diner tonight?"

"Oh, Robert," she answered. "I'm glad you called. I was going to tell you tonight, but I must break our date for tomorrow. Mama is very homesick, and I'm taking a week off from work to visit her and try to cheer her up."

"I could drive you," Ballard suggested.

"Robert, you know how much Mama disapproves of me seeing you. She is going to meet me at the train station. It would be much too awkward." Sabina stopped talking. Ballard could tell she was listening for his reaction, not what he said, but how he said it. He tried to control his rising anger.

"All right, Sabina. I'll miss you. But have a nice trip." Now it was his turn to listen.

"Thank you, Robert. I'll call when I get back. Auf Wiedersehen." She hung up.

"Goddamn it," Ballard cursed, slamming the telephone receiver back into its cup. He didn't like her cavalier 'auf Wiedersehen' one bit.

*   *   *

Ballard was still seething from Sabina's sudden departure to visit with her mother. He walked to his desk and grunted a greeting to the cheery Inge Schmidt. He had developed a sharp headache that aspirin would not cure.

The more he thought about it, the more aggravated he became. He even began to wonder if the meeting of Sabina and her officer/dance partner had been entirely accidental. He looked up to see Stumpfnagel walking over to him.

"Herr Ballard," Stumpfnagel asked. "Could you drive me the Stettiner Train Station? I have to make a quick trip to Pasewalk. I could take the U-Bahn to the station, but this way we could discuss the von Hoescht problem. Hilflich has come up with some interesting information."

Ballard's interest was immediately aroused. "Certainly Herr Leutnant. When to do you want to go?"

"At three-quarters to the hour," the lieutenant replied. "Frau Schmidt, I expect to be gone about two days."

As the two men motored up Friedrichstrasse, Stumpfnagel pulled out a file with Ballard's name on it.

"Here's something interesting Hilflich found out," Stumpfnagel said. "He reports that all travel checkpoints leaving Berlin have a secret tag on your name and description."

"But there aren't any checkpoints, Herr Leutnant. Anyone can come and go as he pleases."

"True. But if you buy a bus or a train ticket, especially if you go first class, they often write your name on the ticket receipt. Gasoline stations write down license plate numbers on ration coupons. It's an informal network, but it exists and it's used."

"Who's asking for the information?" Ballard asked.

"It's really odd, because its the RSD-the Reichssicherheitsdienst-our internal civilian security organization."

"I didn't think they got involved with foreigners."

"They don't. They're treating you as a German citizen which is clever because it keeps the whole thing on a lower official echelon.

170

Also, the RSD doesn't have nearly the awful reputation of the Gestapo, so a lot of the ticket agents will be cooperative."

Ballard though for a moment. "Do you know to whom the reports go?"

"Hiflich checked that out, too. They go to an office of animal import control. A Herman Meyerbeer."

"Who's he," Ballard asked.

"Nobody," Stumpfnagel answered blankly. "When I called pretending to be a long lost relative, the receptionist told me no one by that name works—or ever has worked—for RSD."

"So it's a front, and someone is trying to keep tabs on my coming and going, but without appearing to."

"Yep," Stumpfnagel agreed. "But there's more. Hilflich found an `H. Meyerbeer' working in Luftwaffe security, at the Potsdam Air Base."

"Only a short distance from the Lichterfelde Air Field and von Hoescht," Ballard chimed in.

Ballard helped Stumpfnagel carry his bags to the train. Stumpfnagel did not like to admit it, but he had not gotten back the strength of his arm since he was wounded during the Bletchley Park raid. As Ballard hoisted the leather suitcase up to the overhead carrying rack, he saw Sabina walking along the platform. He was about to cry out when he spotted her SS captain dance instructor following behind her, carrying their bags.

"God Dam!" Ballard spate out. The leather case tumbled out of his hands and fell roughly to the floor, bouncing first off the knee of an Army lieutenant.

"Aua, Mann!" he complained noisily. "Hey, clumsy, it's bad enough getting strafed by the Russkis."

"So sorry," Ballard exclaimed. "I should have sounded an air raid warning." He hefted the case back up, shook Stumpfnagel's hand much too quickly, and wished him a happy journey while racing down the aisle.

Ballard stepped out onto the platform just in time to see Sabina and her officer step into the train on the opposite track—Track 6.

He trotted back to the main hall and checked the schedule. Track 6 to Oranienburg, Gransee, Furstenberg, Neustrelitz, Greifswald, Stralsund and Bergen. So she was going to visit her homesick mother, was she? Ballard felt a cold fury rise in his belly. He considered his options: first, he had better make sure something innocent wasn't happening, as unlikely as that was. If Sabina's mother was meeting her at the station, this trip together can just be the harmless flirtation of two old friends. Let it not be said that Robert T. Ballard was so insanely jealous he wouldn't let his fiancée-to-be be seen in the company of other men. Ha, he thought. 'Fiancée-to-be.' Here she was making a complete fool out of him, and he still harbored illusions of marriage. What an idiot!

OK, he thought, trying to calm himself, I can board the train myself and see what happens at the other end, then take the next train back. Advantage: absolute, eye-witness proof, one way or the other. Disadvantage: I could be discovered and look like the world's dumbest green-eyed monster. Sabina would be furious.

Second, I could drive up. Advantage: same firsthand proof. Disadvantage: a three or four hour round trip, and if an air raid hits—almost a likelihood these days I could miss the train's arrival.

He thought some more. What about the Abwehr? Could they help? He drove back to Headquarters and located Major Hilflich.

"Herr Major Hilflich," Ballard said, letting himself into his office with only a quiet knock. "I've got a big favor to ask."

"Certainly, Herr Ballard," Hilflich replied cheerily. "What can I do for you?"

"I wonder if you can have someone meet the 11:21 train from the Stettiner Bahnhof, arriving at Furstenberg at 12:50?"

"No problem, Herr Ballard," Hilflich answered. "Who's he to meet?"

"I, ah, want to know if my . . . girlfriend, Frau Pergolesi, is meeting her mother at the train station. As she said she was." Ballard found himself blushing. Hilflich pretended not to notice. "And if possible, find out who the SS officer is she's traveling with."

Ballard looked up at Hilflich squarely, now completely unashamed of his own red face. Hilflich noticed the tears welling in the American's eyes. Another hapless lover led astray by the fairer sex, Hilflich thought. Surely if it can happen to Herr Ballard, there is no man immune to feminine treachery.

"I'll put someone on it right away. I'll have an answer for you thirty minutes after the train arrives. Don't worry. I'll handle everything. Now let me get right onto it."

Hilflich stood up and extended his hand. Ballard shook it again and left, slowly, returning to his office. Now he knew how Inge felt when she had first heard that Stumpfnagel would be taking another women to the Charlottenberger Chess Club. He felt like throwing up.

Chapter Thirty-Three

Later in the afternoon Major Hilflich handed Ballard the report of his man in Furstenberg.

Report of the activities of Case Nr. 421-067. The subject is identified as a petite, very attractive women, age circa thirty to thirty-five, Mediterranean complexion.

Berlin train arrived Furstenberg at 1345 hrs, an hour late due to enemy air raids. Subject seen leaving the station in the company of an SS captain, identified as Captain Adolf Hartnack, a local military resident.

No one else greeted the arriving woman. They boarded the autobus and disembarked at a small, pension—'Hotel Braunlage'—not of a class in keeping with the captain's status.

At the hotel, Captain Hartnack helped with the baggage and remained inside. He was then picked up by a staff car thirty-five minutes later. I remained behind at the hotel to watch the actions of the subject, rather than follow the captain to his destination, but that is likely to be the large resettlement complex on the outskirts of the city. I am checking Captain Hartnack's military occupation, which, from the looks of him, would not seem to be that of a combat officer. He may be a high level administrator or functionary.

Hilflich studied Ballard's face as he read the report.

"Is there anything more my man can do for you, Herr Ballard?"

Ballard let out a deep, bitter sigh. So this was Sabina's visit to her 'homesick mother'—a simple week-long tryst in a cheap hotel with her dazzling dancing partner. An acrid taste developed in his mouth. He took another deep breath.

"No, thank-you, Major Hilflich. You've been very kind to extend yourself this far." Ballard turned to go.

"Maybe I can find out what this Hartnack guy does, or what their plans are . . ." he called out.

"To tell you the truth, Herr Major," Ballard answered wearily. "I'd rather not know." He fished in his jacket pocket for his car keys. What a crushing confirmation. Sabina was the only woman he had ever really thought he might fall for—passionately so—and she seemed to love him with equal ardor. Then, for no reason he could fathom, she shoots off with someone else, an old 'dance partner.' What could have been the cause of it? Something had happened at Scharfenberg when she burst out in tears. He remembered it had to do with his citizenship.

Ballard fidgeted around at his desk to the point where even Inge Schmidt was about to remark on it. He got up and went for a walk down the street. He could think of nothing but Sabina in the arms of her precious dance instructor. Like a cinema screen, his overactive imagination threw up images of the two dancing together, naked, her erect breast squashing pleasurably into his slender body. No tender breasts for the instructor, no brassiere, either. In his replay she was gladly mashing herself into his probably hairless chest.

Ballard walked along the tree lined Bellevue Allee for nearly an hour, lost in recriminations over the perfidious Sabina Pergolesi—his lost love finding solace in the arms of another man. He stepped off the curb and was startled by the blast of an auto horn and the screech of brakes. A Daimler coupe swerved and slid sideways to a halt. A trim middle-aged man jumped out of the rear of the car and marched on Ballard.

"You Goddamned congenital idiot," he shouted, brandishing a fancy cane. "Are you completely blind or only completely stupid." He stormed toward Ballard, in a raging fury.

"Good Lord," Ballard said. "I wasn't looking where I was going, I'm sorry. Is this making you feel good, bellowing at me like a bull moose in heat?"

"I'll teach you who's going to feel good—and who'll be screaming like a bull moose," the man said. He threw off his cape and advanced

175

on Ballard with a roundhouse swing. A young driver emerged from behind the wheel of the car and followed timidly.

Ballard ducked easily and gave the man a sharp blow to the solar plexus. The man fell down pole-axed. He lay on the ground gasping for air. His driver left the side of the car, uncertain whether to leap into the fray or help his downed passenger.

"Help him to sit up. He'll be fine in few minutes," Ballard said. "In the excitement of our meeting, he's just lost his breath."

The man rolled over and sat up. Ballard gave him a hand to stand up. "Care to try that again?" he asked pleasantly. Upon closer examination, the man looked older than Ballard had thought perhaps a vigorous sixty. Half-heartedly, the man put up his dukes, a worried look of having got in over his head replacing some of the pugnacity.

"Stop," Ballard said, noticing his awkward stance. "It's not a fair fight. You don't know how to box, and I do." He seized the older man's, fist and spun him around, putting him in an easy half-Nelson.

"Let's call it a draw, and I apologize for not looking where I was going." He let the older man slip out of his grip. They both brushed themselves off and straightened their clothing.

"Permit me to introduce myself. I am Robert Ballard, an American," he said, extending his hand. The older man was shocked by this behavior; he did not know how to respond. People do not knock you down and then offer to become friends. At least not Germans.

"Look," Ballard said. "We both learned something. I learned I should look where I'm going, and you learned not to practice a sport at which you have no training. Those are valuable lessons. How about introducing yourself and giving me a lift back to Abwehr Headquarters?"

"You are from the Abwehr?" the man gasped. His breathing had not yet returned to normal. The scowl on his face turned to guarded respect. "I am SS General Alexander Bellhausen von Rittersdorf."

"Oh!" Ballard exclaimed. "Of the Fourth Panzer Army, von Manstein's relief column?"

"The very same. You know of it?" the older man asked, some of his anger replaced by a grudging interest.

"Who doesn't?" Ballard answered. "Your quick action prevented the Russians from regrouping after Oberleutenant Michaels miraculously broke out at Stalingrad. Michaels pushed through with just twenty two Panzers and a few hundred men. I don't think the breakout corridor was ever more than a kilometer or two across.

"Even so, if it hadn't been for your quick reactions, Lieutenant General Shurnilof of the 64th would have quickly pinched it off. Your quick, forceful reaction taken without asking either von Manstein or the Führer's permission was one of the finest examples of true combat leadership. One sees so little of that anymore. I was present when Michaels received his decoration from the Führer. You should have got one, too."

The older man drew himself up to his full height of five-foot, six-inches. He was a bantam, but with his slender figure he could be mistaken at a distance for someone six feet tall.

"I was at that ceremony, also," he said proudly. "And I was decorated for Stalingrad earlier. By Paulus himself. I had no idea our exploits were so well known and appreciated. Of course I would be delighted to give you a ride." All traces of anger had left. "I am on my way to a dinner party at the Reich's Chancellery. Perhaps you could expand your reasoning about the importance of Stalingrad. It is does not seem as obvious to me as you put it."

Ballard entered the rear door of the silver Daimler. He noticed they were hinged at the rear to swing open from the front, greatly easing access to the seat.

"Wait a moment," the older man said. "Aren't you the civilian who received the deutsche Ordnung medal from the Fuhrer a few months ago?"

"I am," Ballard replied.

"How remarkable. It was I who recommended Gregor for his Oak leaves. Perhaps I could induce our host for this evening's dinner to set an extra place for you. She enjoys hearing such frank talk about the progress of the war—much more so than most people give her credit for."

"She?" Ballard asked.

"Yes. Fräulein Eva Braun. The Führer's . . . consort. A delightful lady. Have you met her yet?"

"After the decoration ceremony," Ballard said. "And as you say, she's a delightful woman."

Chapter Thirty-Four

General von Rittersdorf brought Ballard to Abwehr headquarters where both men cleaned up. Von Rittersdorf telephoned Eva Braun and described his meeting of Ballard. Through the office door Inge and the American could hear von Rittersdorf laughing on the telephone. He was still beaming when he came out.

"It's all set. I'm off to change into uniform for a staff meeting at the Reich's Chancellery. Fräulein Braun asks that you arrive at 7:30, informal dress. A dark suit will be fine. She says you know the way in."

Still smiling, von Rittersdorf saluted and bowed at the same time in a theatrical gesture. He turned and left.

Inge Schmidt looked up at Ballard with big round eyes signifying her witnessing another of his inexplicable miracles. "How do you do it, Herr Ballard?" she asked. "You're always doing things differently, and yet they seem to work out so well."

"As with Frau Pergolesi, you mean," he asked archly.

"No. There you acted just like a German," Inge answered, flushing slightly at her boldness. But she knew Ballard expected such forthrightness.

"It just shows you how culturally bound we all are," Ballard said. He genuinely enjoyed Inge's innate intelligence. Being a good German girl, it would get her nowhere. He, at least, was determined to show his appreciation for it by challenging her mind whenever he could. "You can break out of your cultural limitations. Young kids are always trying to forge their own demeanor, but their explorations are awkward and then they are quickly disabused of them by strict enforcement of German cultural norms. Until you know exactly how to

179

do it, unconventional efforts all seem like youthful rebellion or simple avant-garde showmanship."

"Which yours don't," she said.

"But only because I have had lots of practice in a successful, looser cultural style that has evolved out of what the German style could become, but probably never will."

"But if your `American style' works so well, why won't we Germans discover it?

"You Germans might discover it," Ballard said. "But it will bump up against your national character, and who knows how much of that is learned behavior, and how much of it is bound up in the stock?"

"You mean, as Hitler says, our national character is a product of our Aryan race?" Inge wrinkled her nose.

"The Nazi Aryan race theory has never held still long enough to pass any rigorous muster. There are clearly different races—black, white, red, yellow, and so on, and many finer and finer subdivisions of each. Each race is the human evolutionary engine's long-term attempt to adapt itself genetically to its particular environment. But the culture of each race is the pushing and shoving of generations of people trying to lead 'natural selection' in a particular direction."

Inge paused. "Do you believe the Führer's claims of the superiority of some races?" Her eyes were troubled.

"The Führer's race claims are nothing but political propaganda. There is little evidence that Nordic racial types have any physical or mental superiority over other races. The 1936 Olympics in Berlin showed that blacks may be physically superior to whites—remember Jesse Owens' spectacular victories? Where was the Führer then? He could not bring himself to congratulate Jesse Owens' quadruple gold medals, because overnight a single black man demolished Hitler's Aryan fantasies.

"From what I've seen, intelligence tests consistently show that Orientals and Jews score higher in abstract reasoning, the bedrock of 'intelligence,' over European whites. So where is the great Aryan mental superiority?"

"I think the whole race business is disgusting, myself," Inge replied. "To me, there's more difference among a roomful of German school children than there could ever be between most races. But the Jews do seem to be a special case."

Stumpfnagel entered the office from the outside corridor. He looked at Inge and Robert and, realizing they were once again involved in one of their 'intellectual' conversations, darted past them without a greeting, and into his own office.

"The Jews have lots of problems," Ballard said, becoming suddenly very conscious of his comments on this inflammatory subject. "But none that deserve the treatment the Nazis are meting out to them—'Vernichtung'-utter annihilation."

Stumpfnagel reappeared at his doorway, listening, a half smile on his face. The conversation interested him.

"But the Jews have taken over the banks. They are robbing the German people . . ." Inge protested.

"Really?" Ballard said. "Then why break down the Jewish butcher shop down the block, or the Jewish haberdasher on the Kochstrasse? Why not go after those criminal Jewish bankers and prosecute them under German law—if you can still find any."

Inge Schmidt stared at Ballard with a frank look of adoration. Here was a genius, taking her fully into his intellectual confidence and conversing with her as an equal. And the man of her dreams was witnessing it all. She was proud fit to burst.

Stumpfnagel wore a face of rapt attention, a slack half smile, lips slightly parted. But his eyes had a liquid gleam such as Inge had never seen. The room was silent but the air still crackled from the corona of Ballard's lecture.

Ballard looked at each of them. He was enough of a show man not to disturb too abruptly the shimmering atmospherics. He sat down slowly. Stumpfnagel shifted his weight. Inge let out her breath in a long sigh. She walked over to Ballard and gave him a polite buss on his forehead.

"Thank you," she said simply, and returned to her desk. Stumpfnagel also recovered. "Remarkable what a spell you can cast, Robert," he said, using the American's first name, and walking toward the exit.

"You mean charming a young girl into giving me a kiss?" Ballard asked, getting up to join the lieutenant. "Nothing to it, really."

"I should say not," Stumpfnagel agreed loudly, leading Ballard out the office and into the corridor. "Especially with that brazen hussy. Do you know she once sent me a birthday card when she had been my secretary for less than a year . . ." Stumpfnagel's voice trailed off deliberately.

They heard a snort of laughter from the office.

As the two men strode wordlessly down the corridor, Ballard could sense in his friend a great sense of pride. She's the right woman for you, Ballard thought.

The two men felt such a spirit of manly camaraderie, Ballard realized, that neither needed to say a word. As for whether Sabina was the right woman for him, well, the hell with her, Ballard thought grimly. Maybe tonight will be my chance to get cut up into fish bait and tossed into the Spree River.

Chapter Thirty-Five

Ballard looked up sharply as he was being served dessert, a spectacularly fattening slice of layer cake comprised of a white cake with slivers of walnuts decking the pale taupe frosting, slathered over with whipped cream. It smelled delicious, moist and fresh. He caught Eva Braun staring at him with a forlorn hunger that frightened him. She quickly averted her stare, but he had caught her at it several times. He knew what that look meant.

Eva Braun had placed herself next to General von Rittersdorf. She had placed Ballard's seat across the table, diagonally opposite her own. They could look at each other without the signal intimacy of being seating next to one another, or directly across. Ballard believed Eva Braun had been mildly interested in him the first time they met. With this seating arrangement she would be able to safely revise her first impression upward or down, and act accordingly. As the evening wore on, it was becoming obvious to Ballard that her revision of him had taken a large leap for the better. At their first meeting she had mentioned the need for a "push" for his U-boat project. Was tonight the time to "earn" her help?

"Herr Ballard," Eva Braun said lightly. "The dispatches about Major Skorzeny's raid on the British decoding factory were so terse. And he is such an interesting fellow." She arched one eyebrow suggestively. And perhaps you are, too, the gesture implied. "He was invited here to tell us more about it, but I was not able to reach him. Couldn't you tell us a little bit more about what really happened?"

"I was not there, Fräulein Braun," Ballard replied.

"Yes but you were decorated by the Führer for planning it, for discovering the operation in the first place. You must know most of what happened."

The other guests had stopped talking and eating, and looked up at Ballard expectantly. Most were young, decorated officers and their girl friends or wives. The candlelight made them all look as if they were in their early twenties. With the exception of the general, he was nearly twice their ages. Yet he did not feel out of place.

"I could tell more," Ballard teased. "But it must remain secret . . ."

"Oh, of course it will," Eva Braun replied, her eyes sparkling in anticipation of a rousing tale. "Everyone here can be trusted."

"I was in England on the Abwehr's behalf a few months earlier," Ballard lied, following exactly the, script he and Stumpfnagel had worked out. "And unbeknownst to 'Arabel'—our former chief spy who we suspected had been turned by the British—I befriended one of the agents that he had supposedly recruited."

"A man or a woman?" one of the other guests asked excitedly.

"A Miss Catherine Landesdown, the personal secretary to the Chief Director of the Rolls Royce aircraft engine works," Ballard answered, to the squeals of delight of the women in his audience. "I was to check-up on her reported attempt to seduce the Chief Director. Her very expensive attempt."

"Ooh, we all know what 'checking-up' means, don't we," Fräulein Schneider cooed. "It's a good thing you're not married, Herr Ballard."

"Yes," he answered tersely. "A very good thing." He shot a direct look a Eva Braun. He saw her intense expression of interest in his story melt, her hand lifting to her breast, the fingers spreading out. It was an unconscious gesture of surrender. He felt a surge of arousal flood his loins, as insidious as alcohol hitting the blood stream on an empty stomach. His mind became splendidly alert, no longer restrained by rational thought of consequences.

"We met for an afternoon walk at which time I told her of my undying love. At first she said she could not meet me for dinner because she had a previous engagement. This worried me: perhaps

Arabel was telling the truth, and she really was going to seduce the director."

Ballard took a sip of wine to clear his palate. All in the group were leaning forward, entranced by his tale.

"So I fell on my knee and importuned her on the spot to, ah, marry me." A few soft "oohs" of wonder issued from the women. "She decided that further discussion of my proposition should take place at her summer cottage, to which we retired for the night, at which time I truly gave my all for the Fatherland. When I returned to my own safe house the next day at noon, they had already received a coded wireless message from Germany saying that Arabel had reported great success by Miss Landesdown who, he said, had seduced the great director that evening.

"Miss Landesdown, having gained the affection of the director, would now presumably have much freer access to the great man's life, and be able to obtain information about the production of aircraft engines—all for a heavy price in English pounds, of course, as Miss Landesdown was not the German patriot Arabel had thought: she was simply doing it for the money.

"So you discovered that Arabel was lying," General von Rittersdorf said. "Just as you did to Miss Landesdown." It was his return punch.

"Yes, Herr General," Ballard replied sharply, the travel of his wine glass to his lips halted in mid-air. "Except Arabel was doing it to line his pockets at the Reich's expense. I was doing it to save German lives and as a duty to the Fatherland."

A patter of applause circled the table. "Bravo! Well said, Herr Ballard," one of the farthest-seated younger officers said. "It's not every day that one hears of the rigors of being an indoor agent. Yet somehow I think I should prefer it to being outdoors on the front." His date glared at him, but a titter of laughter arose. Ballard joined in.

"I found it preferable duty as well," he said. He looked at Eva Braun again. "And I agree. Give me bedroom duty over battle field duty, anytime."

She returned his gaze levelly, a cool appraising look having replace the coy, schoolgirl cheeriness she so often affected. Ballard spotted the knowing look one of the women cast her husband across the table.

Just look at Eva going after the American, it said. Ballard suddenly grew sober. He knew if he did not handle this right, there would be dangerous gossip. A glance at Eva Braun told the story. She, too now had a randy look on her face that was shot-through with wariness. OK, Mr. Big-Shot American it seemed to say. How are you going to pull it off?

Delicious German coffee was served. Ballard quickly drank two cups. Most of the conversation had turned to small talk. What the weather was going to be. Good weather was bad, because it meant the Allies would try to bomb. Bad weather was good because they couldn't. Eva said nothing, her silence a signal that the party was drawing to a close.

Ballard looked at his watch. "Oh, for God's sake, already past eleven o'clock. I am terribly sorry, Fräulein Braun. We are expecting an important radio transmission at headquarters at midnight. I must be there . . ."

"Is that why your friend Skorzeny couldn't come tonight," Eva asked. Her icy tone brought him up short. He had been flirting madly, clearly leading her on, and now he was suddenly running out on her. Hell hath no fury, he realized.

The guests were shocked at his haste to leave. But the others took Ballard's cue and began to make getting-home noises.

"I can't speak about any ongoing operations," Ballard replied gravely. He shook Eva's hand. I'm leaving in such a rush, I hope I don't leave anything behind." It was his turn to arch an eyebrow. Eva Braun startled. She tried not to let a faint smile of acknowledgment alter her disgruntled expression.

"I'm so glad you could all come," she said sweetly. "It was such interesting conversation, especially from you General von Rittersdorf. I shall have you all back as soon as possible."

The general bowed deeply to Eva Braun, almost pitching completely forward. Ballard grabbed his arm and swooped him upright. "I'm a man of few words," the general acknowledged—indeed he had hardly said a word all evening—"but I measure them carefully." What he had measured carefully was six or eight glasses of claret.

Ballard steered the general to the door. "Shall we go out to your car together, Herr General?" The general's feet wobbled underneath him. "It's so dark down here, it's sometimes hard to see where to put ones' feet."

"I put them one ahead of the other," the general said, stumbling nevertheless.

Ballard helped the general outside and stuffed him into the rear seat of his Daimler, and clucked the door shut. His young driver winked in recognition and drove off.

Ballard got into his car and watched the Chancellery side entrance. There were eleven other guests plus Eva Braun. He had been the thirteenth. He had counted eight leaving. He and the general made ten. Two more remained behind. He waited five minutes, then ten. He was getting anxious. If he waited too long, he would look ridiculous returning to pick up his "lost" briefcase while one of the guests was still there. Fifteen minutes passed. Why did Era Braun not send them out? Was he making a big mistake? Or was this her signal to him—to forget any attempts to rejoin her? Were her longing gazes just frustrated dinner party flirtation? Would she be shocked to see him back? Angry?

He looked at his watch again. Out of the corner of his eye, he noticed the car next to his was moving slightly. He stared at it. It was jiggling on its springs, but there was no one in it. The driver had left the motor, running, and with petrol so difficult to get. He got out to turn it off when he heard a soft moaning sound. He looked inside. There, grappling in the back seat, lost to passion's delight, was the young blond lieutenant and his girlfriend—numbers twelve and thirteen!

Ballard walked hurriedly back to the Chancellery side entrance. An impassive SS lieutenant recognized him and wordlessly let him back in. Thank God he did not offer to get the briefcase himself. Ballard trotted down the narrow corridor and knocked on the apartment door. No answer. He felt a rush of heat cause him to burst out in a sweat of embarrassment. God, this was ridiculous. If he got caught . . .

The door opened slightly, a blue eye peering out. Then it was drawn open a few inches more. Eva Braun stood there, her dress buttoned incorrectly.

"Herr Ballard, I thought you were in such a rush to get back to the office . . . ?"

"I left something important here," he answered.

"And what would that be," she asked quietly, stepping back to let him in.

"You," he answered, and swept her into his arms.

Chapter Thirty-Six

Ballard was carefully edging his way up a precipitous mountain cliff, placing each foot delicately on the smallest of rock nubbins. He was climbing solo and unroped and the thrill of risk was exhilarating. A single slip would result in a fall to his death. He was clutching at each tiny handhold with furious strength, determined not to make a mistake, not to make any misstep. His next move was the crux, and his mind raced to decide what tiny clef to reach out to next. His grip was weakening on the tiny holds, he didn't have much time. Dammit, the annoying sound of a telephone ringing was disturbing his concentration. He reached out and lifted the receiver.

"Ballard here," he muttered, still agitated about the possibility of falling.

"Robert, it's me, Sabina. "I've just come back from visiting Mama." Her cheeriness sound forced.

"Oh, hello, Sabina," he said. "I'm glad you're back. I just woke up."

"You mean I just woke you up," she said with a chuckle. "But Robert, it's nearly nine o'clock. What is making you so tired?"

"Work," he answered dully.

"I thought we might have a picnic in the Frohnau forest," she said.

"What a nice idea, Sabina," he could not bring himself to say "darling"—but I must be back at work by noon . . .

"But it's Sunday, Robert."

"I know dearest," he answered. "But we have an operation coming up . . ." He stopped talking, aware of the Gestapo tap.

"Shall we meet for an early lunch?" Sabina asked.

Ballard felt a sense of revulsion rising in his gorge. He could not believe her gall, flitting from one meal ticket to the next, without skipping a beat. What had happened? Did the dance instructor have a wife?

"I've got to get some more sleep, Sabina. It's a nice idea, but I would make a poor partner."

Sabina did not miss his coolness. "Well, if you think so, Robert. I just wanted you to know I was back. I've got so much to tell you." Her voice trailed off.

"Good," Ballard answered. "I'll call you later, when I'm feeling better. Bye for now." He hung up the telephone and fell on his back in the bed. "SHIT, SHIT, SHIT," he screamed. He was furious at her for having the audacity to call him as if nothing had happened. He was furious at himself for not having the courage—the balls—to tell her he was furious with her for being such a brazen cheat.

His lovemaking with Eva Braun had been a disaster. In spite of a lot of whispered adolescent `kitchy-coo' endearments, she was almost completely passive, and had lain there with all the enthusiasm of a cow being artificial inseminated. It was the first time Ballard had made love that he was struck by the fear that he might not be able to bring himself to orgasm. He had saved the moment by recalling the time he was dinning at the Neva-Grill with Sabina imperturbably masturbating him under the tablecloth while the waiter refilled their wine glasses.

Even now, just by her telephone call, he found the hated woman had given him a throbbing erection. The fucking whore! He bolted out of bed and went over to the bathroom to take a cold shower. His story about having to work had been a lie. But now he was so agitated, he would go to the office out of spite. If she called him there at least she would discover he was not a liar like her.

At a few minutes past noon, Inge's telephone rang. He picked it up, curious to know who would be calling on a Sunday.

"Hello, Robert, It's me again."

"Oh, hi, Sabina," Ballard said weakly.

"Robert, you sound very angry with me. Can you tell me why?"

Ballard took a deep breath. He felt like slamming the receiver down. "I am angry at you because you lied to me about going to visit your mother at Furstenberg."

"But I did go there to visit her," she protested.

"And who did you go with?" Ballard shot back. "That dance instructor friend of yours who shacked up with you at a crummy hotel." He had the greatest trouble not shouting at her.

"So you had me watched, and that's what you think?" she asked, her voice suddenly very small. "Did your spies tell you anything else?"

"For Christ's sake, Sabina," he screamed. "What else is there to tell. Why don't you tell me what went on?"

"It's none of your business about my mother and me, Robert," she answered, her voice trembling. "But I can assure you I was not 'meeting' any dance instructor—or any other man. Roland, whom you met, took me to the station. And I was met at Furstenberg by SS Sturmbanfuhrer Hartnack, a friend of Roland's. But the only man I've 'shacked-up' with is you, Robert."

"I just don't believe you Sabina," Ballard answered flatly. "I saw you board the train with your SS dancing captain. You were seen at the Furstenberg Train station with him. You took a bus with him to a seedy hotel. And now you're trying to tell me you went on an innocent visit to console Mama. Shit, Sabina, my love may have been blind, but it's not idiotic."

There was a shocked silence at the other end. He waited for what seemed an age and then could take it no longer. He slammed the phone down in its cradle, his face white with anger. Christ, he thought. She's so surprised I found her out, she doesn't even deny it. The cleaning lady had not replaced his wooden trash basket under his desk. Well, he would show her. He booted it viciously across the room and felt enormous satisfaction as it splintered against the wall.

PART THREE

Chapter Thirty-Seven

Inge Schmidt was washing the four dishes of her evening meal—a small pot, a soup bowl—like dinner plate and a tea cup and saucer. Her Blaupunkt "people's receiver" a special, inexpensive radio with extremely limited reception range-was playing quietly in the background.

To get caught with a conventional radio, most of which contained at least several short-wave bands, was to risk being accused of espionage. Seven hundred and eighty Germans had been so accused last year, and most were serving long prison sentences. Some had been executed.

The woman announcer's voice droned on in the "theater German" affected by all radio announcers. It was the accent free German found naturally only in the Hannover region of the country, to which the excessively perfect diction had been added.

Inge was hardly paying attention as she washed the dishes, her mind roaming freely over any subject that happened to flit by without stopping to examine any of them. Then, sticking out in her memory was the odd recollection that the announcer had mentioned the word "swami." She recalled nothing else of the subject under discussion, but she was suddenly struck by a peculiar image. Unbidden, into her mind's eye popped the picture of the American Ballard with a towel wrapped around his head staring mysteriously into a large crystal ball. She chuckled at the silly sight, then paused.

She dried her hand on a wrinkled linen dish towel and made a few notes on a scrap of paper which she tucked it into her change purse. At work Inge forgot about her idea until just before "celebration evening"—quitting time. As she searched through her coin purse to be sure she had enough change for the streetcar, she came across her note. She got up from her desk and walked into the doorway of her boss's office.

"Herr Leutnant," Inge said, standing in the door way. Stumpfnagel looked up at her appreciatively.

"Doesn't it ever bother you how he knows so much, and how accurately he seems to be able to tell the future? It's unreal, as if he was a fortune teller complete with crystal ball."

Stumpfnagel turned in his chair to face his secretary. It was no longer necessary to say who "he" was.

"I've been trying not to think of it myself," he answered. "Because the logic of the answer doesn't make sense."

"What is illogical about having a crystal ball?" she asked.

"You don't mean literally being able to tell the future?" he parried.

"Yes I do. I know it sounds silly, but I do mean it. That's the only thing that does make sense."

"But Frau Schmidt," Stumpfnagel protested. "This is 1943. We live in a highly technological age. Radio beams, rockets, electronic vacuum tubes, even television. Crystal ball gazing has been claimed for centuries—and has always been proven totally fraudulent."

"I know, Herr Leutnant, but how else do you explain his accuracy on events that no amount of intelligence or calculation can possibly foretell?"

"Such as?" Stumpfnagel, felt an arousal of his appreciation of the intellectual powers of his secretary swell in his consciousness. This was what Ballard had repeatedly mentioned to him about her. His eyes glowed in appreciation.

"Well, when he first showed up here, he told us the exact date of the invasion of Russia—June 22. Even Hitler believed it would occur two days earlier."

"What else?" Stumpfnagel was on full alert now, an alarm bell clanging in his mind. It was not simply that he enjoyed the challenge of an intellectual puzzle, he loved it with the passion that most men reserve for sexual conquest. The alarm bell was a signal of his subconscious mind that she was onto something important. The very feeling he had when it began to strike him how the Norden bomb sight must work.

"A lot of things," Inge continued. She began to feel uncomfortable under her boss's acute stare. She did not like such strong confrontation. "There are a score of armies invading Russia. Why did he pick as an example the Sixth Army under General Paulus to convince General Guderian to strengthen its Winter capabilities—and no one else's?"

"I don't know. He was certainly right about it. The Sixth Army just made it out by the slenderest of margins. And look how their escape was turned around to Germany's advantage . . ."

"That's the point. From what I have seen, no one—not even the Führer—can tell what's going to happen in future battles that accurately. And how does he know about the upcoming great Panzer battle of Kursk?"

"Kursk? That's the first time I heard that," Stumpfnagel said, his smile turning to look of alarm. "He didn't mention Kursk to me or Guderian. When did he tell you that?" Stumpfnagel sat up, his mind piqued to full readiness.

"Maybe because it would give away his crystal ball," Inge answered quickly. "He mentioned it to me almost by accident over coffee. Several weeks ago. Let me see, it was the day you went to the dentist."

"The eighteenth of last month."

"Yes, that's it. He had been drinking at lunch, feeling sorry for himself over his breakup with the Italian woman. He brought it up briefly while we were discussing Guderian's Panzer strategy—how it would all come to a resolution on the plains of Kursk. The largest tank battle ever fought, he said, and he then quickly changed the subject when he realized what he was saying. I could tell he was hiding something. As much as I like him, I feel that he's always hiding something from us."

Stumpfnagel felt a buzzing in his ears. His mind had shifted into overdrive. A few other inexplicable facts about Ballard's "intelligence" dropped into place. A crystal ball was not a workable supposition, of course. But having been made, he could not shake off the aura of the possibilities it presaged. "We've all had that feeling, Frau Schmidt. But please, do go on." Stumpfnagel stood up and walked up to her. He

194

took her hand in his and bade her sit in one of the chairs in front of his desk.

Inge blushed at the tenderness of the act. He pulled the other chair out from behind the desk and sat facing her. Their knees touched. For the first time ever, he looked at her openly with eyes of adoration.

"There are many other things, too, Herr Leutnant," Inge said cautiously, unable for the first time to return his steady gaze. "Little things."

"Such as?"

"Well, doesn't it bother you how his tips always happen?"

"Meaning?"

"Even the Fuhrer's plans are sometimes changed by unforeseeable circumstances," she replied, her brow knotted quizzically. "The weather goes bad. An unforeseen mechanical failure. The operation is postponed or called off. Herr Ballard's operations are never canceled."

"Hmmm. That is exceptionally astute of you Frau Schmidt. A powerful internal logic I hadn't thought of." Stumpfnagel got up and began to pace back and forth. "Frankly I am amazed at your perceptiveness and I commend you for having the sense to bring this inspiration of yours to my attention." He felt he was being too official. "I really want to give it some serious thought. Hearing it from you like this does put an entirely new twist on his actions." Stumpfnagel returned to the chair behind his desk. He shifted his position, leaning back expansively. He was about to put his feet up on his desk—one of Ballard's relaxation tricks. He knew Inge would disapprove of such gypsy sloth.

"Listen, Frau Schmidt, you've been working late so often. Why don't you go home on time today? I want to think on your outstanding idea."

"Is the Herr Leutnant kicking me out?" she asked coyly.

"Exactly, dear lady. Your extraordinary feminine intuition has raised an extremely attractive possibility. I need to think about it undisturbed."

"And will you think about my crystal ball idea also, Herr Leutnant?" Inge said slyly, dashing out before he could see her red face.

"Why Frau Schmidt . . ." Stumpfnagel said, shocked. But that idea stirred him also.

195

Chapter Thirty-Eight

Stumpfnagel sat down on the small divan in the far side of his office. He could see out the large window onto the tree lined Tirpitz Canal, down which freight barges glided silently by, alternating every now and then with an occasional sailboat. Now that Inge was gone, he could put his feet up in the vile but comfortable habit he had learned from the American. He leaned back with his feet up and his hands behind his head.

Hers was more than a good idea, it was stroke of genius, but it was not quite right. Yet her imagination, unfettered by what was "impossible," had breached the self-inflicted barriers of his own thinking about Ballard's phenomenal intelligence successes. Stumpfnagel took the idea of Ballard's so-called crystal ball, and let his mind run freely, listening to the wisps of half formed impressions that were drifting, gathering, associating and re-associating into clumps of possibilities. He was good at this "free association," as that quack Viennese Professor called it. Of course as long as the ideas were not too outrageous. Maybe that was the problem. He was not being outrageous enough.

He thought about the entire collection of tips and information the American had given them. It was not any individual item, but the total selection of topics that burned into his mind. They seemed so—he couldn't formulate the thought adequately—so over-archingly all-encompassing. As if someone had been astute enough to skim the cream off the top ten of one hundred bottles of Germany's entire war effort and been able to unerringly separate the fresh from the sour by force of intellect alone. As if this person was looking back on the effort.

Aah, he felt the reverberation of that impossible idea again trying to wriggle its way to the surface. Too outrageous. He shut it off. Still, the subjects touched upon by the American evinced a discriminatory selection of such sure vision and intellectual perspicacity that Stumpfnagel was continually held in thrall, warmed by the heat of the intellect behind the selections. Blinded, perhaps. There was no dross, and the unerring "hanging-togetherness" of it all was continuously exciting. It was like playing chess with a grand master. Right in front of you, seeing just what you see, he blatantly out-thought you. Stumpfnagel could not help feeling so often that the American was just out-thinking him. But did that explain the incredible information he handed them? No. Out-thinking him was not enough.

He sat in his office, feet up and immobile, lost in a reverie of cerebration, trying to loosen his sense of intellectual propriety, which he could feel was holding him back from forming a judgment in the direction unfettered logic was gently pushing.

The pale afternoon light turned to a rich gold, illuminating the long white curtains of his tall office. The windows took on the glowing hues of a Rembrandt painting. As the evening approached the light suffused to the soft amber of ale and then momentarily to the blue mist of dusk. He sat up. It was dark. Had he been asleep?

The magnitude of the American's thinking continued to roil through his consciousness. When had he ever been wrong? No intelligence is always correct.

Unbidden, he felt his mind begin to formulate conclusions. No one could possibly have seized so confidently on such a precise combination of possibilities, unless . . .

The forbidden thought squirmed to be recognized. He began to fidget, resisting the direction it was propelling him, desperate to rechannel the impossible conclusion the pressure of logic was pushing. He seized at alternatives.

So the pen he used to write his original letter was "never before seen." A small bit, but the kind of hidden internal evidence that rings with the clear tone of veracity that cannot be ignored. Yet this was not a clue that pointed at a crystal ball. It pointed forward . . .

Stumpfnagel sensed himself cross involuntarily from the negative to the positive column of the ledger he was keeping on his "Friend of Germany," the switch from the impossible to the perhaps just possible. He was mildly shocked at where he was permitting logic to lead him like an alien succubus that had taken over his brain.

But he knew the workings of his creative thought process enough so that once fully engaged, it was his conscious mind's job to step aside, to halt his censorious impulses from automatically interfering with ideas that pushed and pulled in unconventional directions. He would not resist the siren call of the new idea spontaneously arising. Not now, anyway.

The more he let go of the barriers of logical rigor, the more Stumpfnagel felt the possibility he was trying to repress bubble forth.

His conscious mind began to panic at the realization that it was losing a battle with reality. And yet he felt excitement rising in his breast rather than dismay. Excitement the likes of which dwarfed the thrill of his discovery of the workings of the Norden bomb sight. In spites of the delight expressed by the High Command over that feat, he felt it had been a minor event in his life—it had been too easy. The answer to the mystery of Robert Ballard was different. The answer was "impossible," yet impossible was the only solution.

He had repeatedly to prevent his guard from rising to shut off his promiscuous examination of the possibilities. What had he said to Inge when she recounted her remark at the opera? "Mr. Ballard, you're something else." He had answered with "Is that ever the truth." At the instant he relaxed his mental grip to chuckle at that response, the idea which had been boiling beneath the surface burst forth fully formed into his consciousness. He felt the thrilling sense of its power washing over his body like a slow motion wave, lifting him to a higher realm of reality, a sensation more exciting than sex—the genesis of a vibrant idea, a new cerebral element so pregnant with possibilities that he felt dizzy until he exhaled his held-in breath. Possibilities that would have more impact on the fate of the nation than any generals or their armies.

It was already eight o'clock. Stumpfnagel picked up the telephone and dialed Ballard's apartment. The American answered lugubriously: "Ballard here."

"Herr Ballard, here is Lieutenant Stumpfnagel."

"Eh, Stumpfy," Ballard answered, brightening slightly. He had been drinking. "What gives at this hour?"

"Have you eaten dinner yet?" the lieutenant asked.

"Nope. I was just going to heat something up. What do you have in mind?"

"How about joining me for dinner? I've just had the most fantastic idea. I can't wait to tell it to you."

"Sounds good to me, Herr Leutnant. Is the Abwehr picking up the bill?"

"Of course."

"Ahh. Then let's do the Adlon Hotel for a change. On Pariser Platz. I could pick you up—no wait, you can walk and we can meet there in fifteen minutes. I'll make the reservation."

Stumpfnagel entered the low lit restaurant in a state of high tension. He spotted the American in a far corner table, chatting with the wine steward. Ballard had ordered a bottle of red wine and seemed to have drunk nearly half its contents already. He seemed to be discussing its merits with the sommelier, who had been importuned to take a sip with the small silver cup always at his side. As if sensing his presence, Ballard turned and saw the German officer approach.

"We're in luck, Herr Leutnant. They have several bottles of this great red: Musougny Chambolle Les Charmes, 1934. Much too early to drink, really, but the Musougny character is so noble, we will do so nevertheless. Here try some. Then tell me what your fantastic revelation is. Franz, here, won't seat anyone near us."

Stumpfnagel sat down carefully and took a tentative: sip. Ahhh, astounding and potent, but still quite tannic. And so distinctive. Odd how an American would be so well informed about French wines. Or maybe not, if what Stumpfnagel had divined was true.

"Let's order," Stumpfnagel said quickly. "Then if you faint with astonishment, at least I'll still, be served dinner."

199

"Ha-ha. You're a good one, talking about fainting from surprise, Herr Leutnant," Ballard retorted. "You must have completely forgot about your abysmal loss of control on witnessing Herr Hess's escape."

Stumpfnagel smiled. Ballard had clearly been drinking long before his telephone call. Now he was at the top of his ribald good humor.

The two ordered. Ballard asked for veal cutlets paprika; Stumpfnagel a Rinderfilet of beef. In spite of the war, the black market never failed those who could afford it. Already in 1939 the weekly ration of meat for a family was only five hundred grams a week. They would eat that tonight alone. After the head waiter left with their orders memorized, Ballard looked up expectantly.

"I have been going over your remarkable record of intelligence successes, Herr Ballard," Stumpfnagel began.

"And you're going to tell me you've finally discovered how I get my information," Ballard added.

"Why yes! How do you know that?"

"Stumpfnagel—think it through. If what you think is true, than my system really works. What do you think my secret is?"

The lieutenant was flabbergasted. Was the American going to admit everything? He expected denials and a fight. "Inge thought you had a crystal ball," Stumpfnagel said so lightly they both knew Stumpfnagel didn't believed it himself. "But, of course, I found that impossible."

"Impossible? Why so?" Ballard asked. Stumpfnagel could see he was enjoying himself immensely, but in that cagey manner of his, as if he was about to spring a gigantic prank. Was it a surprise party for someone, the young lieutenant wondered. Would the admiral come walking through the door singing "Happy birthday?"

"I'm almost embarrassed to say, it's so fantastic." Stumpfnagel said, smiling oddly, unfurling his linen napkin and draping it on his lap. "A crystal ball is too unlikely, because there is no sensible mechanism behind it. But what you must do is nearly the same thing, isn't it?"

"You tell me, Stumpfy. You invited me." Ballard said. He had stopped smiling, and was watching the lieutenant intently.

Stumpfnagel began his theory tentatively, alternately unable to look Ballard in the eye at one moment in desperate shyness at the outrageous line his argument was taking, and then scanning his face beseechingly, for clues to the correctness or falsity of what he was proposing. Ballard's face turned totally placid whether from too much drink or pity at the fool Stumpfnagel was making of himself, he could not be certain. In a few minutes that seemed like hours, the young lieutenant was finished. He looked up at his friend, not knowing what to expect.

"Why Herr Leutnant Werner Martin Stumpfnagel. You truly are a genius!" Ballard's eyes shone. "I really mean it." He wiped his lips to take another sip of wine. "Course I knew that all along. That you're very clever, I mean."

"Then you . . . you don't deny it?" Stumpfnagel asked, flabbergasted.

"How can I deny the product of such intellectual brilliance, Herr Leutnant? That's why I came to you in the first place. I needed someone who could follow logic wherever it leads—and take action based on his discoveries. You thought about it and followed the logic where it led. It all makes perfect sense."

"Yes, yes it's logical enough. But it can't really be true.

"Stumpf, you're faltering. You know enough to hold on to the reins of your convictions, no matter how rough the ride. You of all people . . ."

"Convictions be damned, Herr Ballard. Either deny or confirm my claims." The wine had hit Stumpfnagel's empty stomach, and he was becoming a bit hysterical.

"Calm down, my friend," Ballard hushed him and sat back in his chair. The waiter had been waiting for an interruption in the conversation. Quickly and efficiently, he served the meal, and curtly wished them "Gute Malzeit." He vanished as quickly as he had appeared.

Ballard dove right in.

"But . . . what are we going to do now?" Stumpfnagel hissed at his friend.

"We have to tell the admiral," Ballard said in-between bites. "Hmmm. This veal is outstanding. How's your beef?"

Stumpfnagel hadn't touched his food. His breath was coming out in short gasps of agitation. "It's too incredible. I . . . I can't believe it," he blubbered. "How can I believe it?"

"Oh, I wouldn't worry about that, my friend. You'll believe anything if you have enough irrefutable evidence."

"Like the evidence you've been giving us all along?" Stumpfnagel still had his fork halfway to his mouth with the first piece of his filet he had picked up minutes ago. "That's why we could never find any spy network?"

"Very good Dr. Watson," Ballard chimed in. He looked over at his friend, sitting morosely behind his fill plate.

"Look, this food is much too good to waste. If you're not going to eat your meat, let me have it." Ballard started to reach over with knife and fork to spear his friend's dish.

"Ha, the devil take you, you circus swindler," Stumpfnagel said, suddenly coming alive and parrying his friend's utensils with his own knife and fork. The rapacious American repulsed, Stumpfnagel attacked has food with sudden gusto. He looked up at Ballard disappointed. "It's gone cold."

"Herr Ober," Ballard waved. The head waiter appeared immediately. "My friend has been talking too long, and his plate has gone cold. Please re-heat it for him. And mine, too, while we indulge in a pause Normande."

"With Calvados, mein Herr?" the waiter asked.

"Perfect," Ballard agreed. He looked back at his friend who was staring at him morosely and in a state of profound shock. Slowly words came to his mouth. "How will I tell the admiral?"

"He's got to know, Stumpf," Ballard answered. "Because I've given you enough of these advance warnings of attacks and disasters to be avoided. That's not going to win the war. Stalingrad proved that. If we hadn't convinced Guderian to take active countermeasures, Germany would have lost a battle marking the beginning of the end. The Americans will soon produce more aircraft in a month than Germany can build in a year. From now on you guys are going to have to help me win with a lot more positive actions."

"This is the price you mentioned . . . ?"

"Oh don't look so worried, Stumpf. You'll enjoy paying for it even more than you'll enjoy paying for tonight's dinner."

Chapter Thirty-Nine

Stumpfnagel sat perched on the edge of a chair in the antechamber of Admiral Canaris' office. He had called for a formal meeting. It was the only way to keep the admiral seated for a complete presentation of his unbelievable revelation about Ballard. Otherwise the admiral would dart in and out of one meeting after another, hearing only ten percent of any subject.

Stumpfnagel felt a sense of panic mounting in his belly. What am I doing here? he asked himself. And then, this has got to be the craziest briefing anyone has ever bothered an admiral with. The massive door opened and Canaris himself came out to greet him.

"Herr Leutnant Werner Stumpfnagel, please do come in." The admiral extended his hand. Stumpfnagel jumped up, shook hands, clicked his heels and briefly bowed his head.

"So kind of you to see me Herr Admiral."

"I always have time to see my real workers, Herr Lieutenant," Canaris answered, sitting himself down in a small, red leather couch and gesturing to his guest to make himself comfortable in a matching armchair across a low cocktail table. "Especially when they request a formal audience. It's always so refreshing to hear objectively what's going on in the world of facts, free of all the politics."

"I'm not so sure the world of facts is what I have for you today, Herr Admiral," Stumpfnagel answered with a look of anxiety on his face. "In fact this is certainly the craziest thing I've ever come across."

"Really?" the admiral said. "How unlike you. But just like your fabulous Mr. Ballard. This should be good. Would you care for some coffee?" He buzzed his secretary, who entered immediately. She had been standing by for his signal.

"Frau Machter, coffee for the two of us please, and then see that we're not disturbed. This will take—what thirty minutes, Herr Leutnant?"

"It is about Herr Ballard, you are correct," Stumpfnagel answered. "The admiral will either throw me out in less than five minutes, or we'll surely spend the rest of the morning," Stumpfnagel replied.

"Ahh, at last, the wild revelations for which you are so justly famous. This sounds interesting. But before you start, if this is about our Mr. Ballard, I think I want to get Major Oster in on it. I use him as a sounding board for all . . . ah, unusual situations. You do know him?"

"Major Oster? Yes I know Professor Major Karl Oster rather well. He was a professor of mechanical engineering at Goettingen University and my advisor."

"Of course. I forgot. And we were up in the radio room together, listening to the clever lies of the former Arabel, too. Didn't the Herr Major have something to do with your coming into the Abwehr?"

"I graduated in physics from the University of Gottingen in 1936, worked at Siemensstadt as a researcher, got drafted into the Wehrmacht in 1939. Professor Oster—then Captain Oster—and I met by accident in 1940 and he managed to arrange my joining you."

They sat drinking coffee and making small talk. The admiral did not want to start until Oster arrived. At last they heard two quick buzzes from Frau Machter. The door opened and Major Oster entered.

"Karl, I think you two are acquainted," Canaris said. Stumpfnagel rose and shook hands. "He has a tale to tell us about our American master spy that is so remarkable, he is afraid I'll throw him out in less than five minutes. Well, let's see how accurate he is on that. Please begin.

Stumpfnagel could not endure the tension sitting down. He stood up and began to pace the room nervously.

"Gentlemen, I request only that you let me talk for a full five minutes, otherwise you really will throw me out. If I thought that, I would have to beat around the bush for an hour painting the picture slowly, as I learned it, until you arrive at the same conclusion that I have unwillingly come to." He looked at Canaris who waived his hand signaling agreement.

Stumpfnagel still did not know how to start—directly or indirectly. He decided on being direct. It would buy him a few minutes of time. "We all know the extraordinary intelligence information that we have been receiving from our American 'spy,'. Mr. Ballard. What has always puzzled us is where he gets his information. We've been looking for a massive organization."

"Which he's got to have to get the volume and quality of information he's been feeding us," Canaris added. "Especially the quality. It's the best I've ever seen."

"It's even better than just intelligence, Herr Admiral. First of all, in order to discover where his astonishingly valuable information comes from, I have had Herr Ballard watched over a five day period when he did not leave his apartment once."

"In spite of your promise not to do just that?" Canaris asked bemusedly.

"Jawohl, Herr Admiral. It was just too irregular to leave him alone. Anyway, this was just a single test."

Stumpfnagel seemed not at all contrite.

"If he stayed inside for five days, how did he eat?" Oster asked.

"He sent his girlfriend to the market," Stumpfnagel answered. "The pretty women who had married the Italian diplomat. She was followed closely by our men, and contacted no one. Nor was she herself contacted."

"It was a little honeymoon, I gather," Canaris said, tapping his pipe on the ashtray. "Recently gone to seed, one hears."

"Nor did he contact anyone by telephone," Stumpfnagel continued. "Every phone line to the entire apartment block was monitored, as were any radio transmissions. I put Herr Major Hilflich and six men on the job, Twenty-four hours a day for five days. I am certain he contacted no one."

"From what you say, we will believe that he was completely incommunicado, Herr Leutnant," Oster interjected pleasantly. "What is the point are you trying to make?"

"The day before he began this . . . ah, tryst, he gave us detailed information on British troop movements in Greece."

"I remember that," Canaris said. "Damned useful information. We gave the British a hell of a thumping."

"After the last day of his tryst, he left the apartment and came directly to Abwehr Head Quarters. Two of our men sat on the trolley with him. He arrived with a long list of new intelligence reports—reports of events that would transpire the following week." Stumpfnagel sat down abruptly.

"Well get on with it, man," Admiral Canaris said gruffly. "What's his secret? How does he contact his network?"

"There is no network, Herr Admiral," Stumpfnagel said softly.

"No network?" the admiral bellowed. "Did I miss something you said?" He glared at the lieutenant. A thought clicked in his brain, but he shook his head.

"You haven't been under too much of a strain, lately, have you, Herr Leutnant? What are you not telling us?"

"What I have not told you is the most recent information I have received from Herr Ballard, Herr Admiral. Because it so, so incredible."

"Go on." The admiral had a suspicious look forming on his face.

"Our Herr Ballard has given me a complete description of the war from beginning to end, down to the last hour in Berlin, on May 8th, 1945, when the Soviets over-run Hitler's Chancellery bunker."

Stumpfnagel, who was rubbing his chin in thought while he was talking, looked up at Canaris, who now sat bolt upright on the couch, all the fatherly geniality drained from his face. Stumpfnagel continued: "He has shown us copies of top secret orders of the recent past, and of orders that have yet to be issued. He has described completed weapons systems that are still on the drawing boards—and of course are not only top secret, but in such an infant state that not more than a dozen or so people know anything about them."

Canaris began to blurt out a question, but caught himself and turned the utterance into a clearing of his throat.

"He has described in great detail the great tank battle of Kursk—which has not happened yet, the top secret Type-XXI U-boat, and the assassination attempt by a certain nobleman on Adolf Hitler."

Stumpfnagel saw Major Oster's face go white. Admiral Canaris was breathing hard. He was containing himself with only the greatest of difficulty. Stumpfnagel gestured for him to speak.

"What are you saying; that this man is a circus gypsy who can read the future?" Canaris blurted out angrily, glancing quickly at Oster, expecting some supporting outrage from him as well.

"Nein, Herr Admiral. What he claims is to <u>be</u> from the future."

Stumpfnagel sat down, relieved to have got it out at last. The Admiral's face darkened like the sea in a summer squall.

"We cannot find any flaw in his claims," Stumpfnagel continued rapidly, unable to meet the admiral's blistering gaze. "I have put three men on the job of trying to punch holes in everything he has told us. Three good men. All the results of his predictions have come back positive."

"Positive?" Oster asked. "What is positive?"

"Well, for example, all four of the future Fuhrer orders that Herr Ballard provided me photocopies of last year have actually been issued."

This time it was Canaris who stood up. He also paced back and forth. "You're telling us he claims to be time-traveler from the future? This is more than utter lunacy, Herr Leutnant. You have lost all sense of judgment. Where is he right now, this magician? I want to question him. How quickly can he be brought here?"

Canaris looked up at Stumpfnagel with a furious glare. He said nothing, but his face spoke for him. This prank had better be a good one, or you, young man, will be on the first train for an indefinite stay on the Russian front. "Where is he right now?"

"Awaiting your call in my office, Herr Admiral."

Canaris bent over his intercom. "Frau Machter, send two guards to retrieve Herr Ballard sitting in the lieutenant's office." He looked up at Stumpfnagel, anxious to get this painful issue over with.

"But Herr Admiral, we have been getting along fabulously. There's no need to use force . . ."

"Frau Machter, you heard the lieutenant. You go yourself and bring him to me."

"Well, Karl, he's your baby," he said, shaking his head toward Oster, a look of bewilderment and disappointment on his face. "What do you say to this great intelligence coup? Is it better than the Norden sight analysis?"

Oster looked at Stumpfnagel benignly. "If this ami can fool Stumpfnagel and his men, he's going to be a pretty interesting fellow. How is the admiral going to find out anything the lieutenant didn't?"

Canaris snorted.

"A few questions will do it. I can smell fakers as soon as they open their mouths."

The three of them sat drinking coffee without talking, each lost in his own thoughts. It tasted bitter, Canaris thought. His face remained stony.

A knock at the door signaled the arrival of Ballard. He was shown in by Frau Machter.

Admiral Canaris stood up heartily. In an instant his face took on a charming smile. "Mr. Ballard," he said in passable English. "I've just heard such an amazing thing about your genius. I'm anxious to get to the bottom of your remarkable, ah, talent, so we can decide what the next steps will be. How is it that you come to speak German so well?"

"I studied it for two years expressly for this mission, Six months of that was here in Berlin," Ballard answered.

"And when was that?" Admiral Canaris raised his eyebrows, a disarmingly pleasant smile on his face. He looked like every young man's jolly grandfather.

"In 1988," Ballard replied guardedly. He looked over at Stumpfnagel.

"Ah, yes, Lieutenant Stumpfnagel has explained that part, You must admit it's rather difficult to believe."

"I think I would find it utterly impossible to believe, as you must. I don't think many people will believe it no matter what proof is offered. I can't help that. I have offered more proof than any reasonable man could want, and here I am." Ballard sat down in his large stuffed chair without asking, a move that, given the strained situation, sent a tiny ripple of shock around the room.

"What is the state of major warships in 1990? When did man get to Mars? And in what way is war conducted that is most noticeably different from today?" Canaris demanded.

Ballard smiled. "Excellent questions, Herr Admiral. He looked around as if missing something.

"Oster," Canaris, said, spotting the look. "Ask our guest if he might not like something refreshing."

Oster rose and walked to the liquor cabinet.

"Major warships changed slowly, with few new battleships being built. Aircraft carriers, however, got very large—ninety thousand tons with a crew of five thousand men. They carry about one hundred fighter and fighter bombers—jet aircraft that can fly at twice the speed of sound and carry as much ordinance as one of your bombers. Submarines also grew much larger—more than one hundred meters long, nineteen thousand tons and a crew of over one hundred men. Both were given nuclear power, that is, 'uranium burning' power—so they could cruise for months without refueling at about thirty knots."

Ballard poured himself the schnapps from a tray offered by Oster, and sniffed it appreciatively.

"As far as Mars is concerned, man has not got there yet in 1990, and probably won't for another twenty-five years or so. The human body does not tolerate extended periods of the weightlessness of space well—the round trip would take two years—and space is filled with dangerous radiation from the sun that is difficult to shield against."

"But the moon?" Canaris interrupted.

"The Americans put two men on the moon in 1969. They walked around for a few days and returned safely. It was on worldwide television. A total of a dozen men got to the moon shortly thereafter, and then the effort was dropped as too expensive. It was a great personal triumph for Werner von Braun."

"Who is . . . ?"

"Currently the technical director in charge of the German A-4 rocket project at Peenermünde."

Canaris arched his eyebrows. "How did he end up with the Americans?"

209

"At the end of the war, both the Americans and the Russians converged on Peenemunde to capture as many rocket scientists as possible. The A-4 ballistic rocket, what Hitler will later name the V-2 'Vergaltung' or 'revenge weapon'—was the great German 'secret weapon' of the Second World War. Von Braun got most of his team to Bavaria, with several truckloads of documents. There they negotiated a surrender to the Americans. That was in May of 1945. By October, von Braun arrived in Boston to begin working on the American rocket campaign. Eventually over four hundred German A-4 engineers joined the Americans in their 'rocket race to the moon' against the Russians. But, of course, as incredible as it is from a scientific point of view, the V-2 is a great waste of effort for this war, militarily speaking.

"Your last question, on how war changed the most," Ballard said, thinking of what the answer might be. "Mechanically everything got a little better, but not enormously so. The infantryman's rifle and his ammunition got lighter so he could carry more. His lightweight body armor cut injuries by 60%. Explosives became more powerful, artillery more accurate. There are now many, many missiles for all sorts of missions—but all are a variation of the V-1, the A-4 and Hs-296. German rocket science was one of the most seminal engineering efforts of this century."

Ballard paused to take another sip. Like all academics, he enjoyed nothing more than holding a lecture.

"Certainly the most noticeable change is in the tremendous strides made in electronics, both in complexity and miniaturization—is that the right German word?—to make smaller—of electronics. An entire calculating machine like the Enigma can be as small and nearly as thin as a business card. A television receiver that shows pictures in color is as small as a pack of cigarettes. This incredible miniaturization permits enormous increase in the use of electronics in warfare, especially reckoning machine—we call them 'computers'—which take over many tasks such as guiding aircraft and missiles, intercepting missiles, helping to fly and navigate aircraft. A single modern fighter aircraft in 1990 has more mathematical computing power than all the university graduates in all of Germany and is all but invisible to radar. Its missiles can be fired at targets beyond visual range. About a third of aircraft costs are for electronics alone.

"Helicopters became very important, essentially joining with tanks as shock-effect offensive weapons platforms. But electronics played the biggest role. Many types of sensors were developed that can detect the enemy at great distance, through smoke, fog, and darkness. There are electronic goggles that let you see in total darkness.

"But the single most important military invention was certainly atomic power, as a weapon in the form of an enormous bomb, and later as a power supply. The atomic bomb was only used twice, both times against civilian targets in Japan in order to stop the war. By the Americans."

"You are certainly very anxious to help Germany win the war. Why?"

"It's quite simple, gentlemen. Although the process of doing so may not be. In my time, shortly after Germany surrendered, the Americans completed the construction of four atomic bombs. They tested one successfully at Los Alamos in the state of New Mexico, and then dropped two of them on Japan, destroying in a few seconds 200,000 lives. Nearly all the people killed were innocent civilians. Another 100,000 more suffered unimaginable injuries—flash-blinded, much of their flesh burned off, broken bones, bodies and minds. Then came the after effects—leukemia—white blood cell destruction—and other subsequent cancers, sterility, the still-birth of malformed children, or worse—their live birth.

Ballard's chin began to tremble. "The atomic bomb marks the first invention of mankind that annihilates civilians in order to stop soldiers. Its use was a violation of every human norm on this planet. In two clashes of hellish light, science—American science—threw the human race back into the dark ages of brutality, bestiality and uncontrolled horror. I have dedicated my life to stopping the use of the atomic bomb. By coming here, I intend to prevent its use, and you, you Germans are going to help me do it. It will be a small price to pay, and may make up partially for your—own war, crimes. But in the long run, stopping the use of nuclear weapons will prove to be one of the greatest gifts sane men can give to mankind."

211

"Our war crimes, Herr Ballard?" It was Colonel Oster speaking, and only after a long silence.

"Your treatment of the Jews, gypsies and other so called undesirables is criminal beyond all human measure. For the rest of the century, what Germany has done to these people—and especially to the Jews—will tarnish the soul of anyone born a German. It is an event of such incredible insanity that this 'holocaust,' as it becomes called—will enter as a landmark element of the Jewish religion, a near supernatural event that focuses and alters Jewish religious thought for centuries to come.

"The holocaust will become to Jews nearly what the crucifixion of Christ became to the Christians—a defining event that will live in their religion forever."

Major Oster rose from his seat and refilled his glass to the top with schnapps. His hand was trembling visibly. Admiral Canaris looked hard at his friend, yet could not bring himself to speak. It was as if an invisible communication was passing between the two men. Lieutenant Stumpfnagel finally broke the awesome silence.

"But Herr Ballard," Stumpfnagel interjected. "If you wish, to stop the use of the nuclear bomb, and you can travel through time, why not just kill off the inventor?"

"Ballard looked over to the lieutenant with hooded eyes. He took a long pull on his drink. "Because as trite as it sounds, you really can't kill ideas, Herr Leutnant. And too many people have independently arrived at the same idea—that splitting atoms will release incredible energy. So I can't stop atomic bombs from being built. The only practical thing I can do is to prevent their use against humans. They will only be used during war time, and only if the people against whom they are used can't retaliate in kind. Once this war is over, many others will build atomic bombs but, because of fear of their vast power, will be hesitant to use them precisely because retaliation in kind would quickly follow. Right now, no one has the power to retaliate and the sole possessor of an atomic bomb—the Americans—are free to use it as they see fit."

"Mr. Ballard, Herr Ballard, I am sure that I cannot discover in a few minutes what our very capable Lieutenant Stumpfnagel has been puzzling over for several months. I'll leave that to him." Canaris said.

Stumpfnagel could not help himself from releasing a deep sigh of relief. Canaris was buying the story. Or at least wanted to appear to be.

This time Canaris stood up to refill his drink. He walked over and stopped in front of Ballard, looking him straight in the eye. "So after you get us to stop the American uranium bomb effort, what do you care whether or not we Germans win the war?"

Ballard's expression tightened. "I would like to answer that question in your presence alone, Herr Admiral." Ballard gave the admiral a hard look and then glanced over at Colonel Oster with an appraising stare. The Colonel shuddered.

Canaris reflected on Ballard's answer. He was about to ask the others to leave when the American raised his hand. "Herr Admiral," he said, "I suggest we go for a little walk outside. There is no telling how secure your office is from prying ears."

Canaris raised his eyebrows. Was this entire story getting just a bit too crazy? Ballard had shown he was a time traveler, was he also a madman? The admiral was used to dealing with highly unusual situations. But this time travel business was . . . supernatural. It defied all logic and common sense.'

"Ja, gut." The admiral said. "Let's go for a walk." He hoisted himself out of his chair and without turning to Ballard or Oster, ambled out the office. Ballard jumped to and followed, as did the two dachshunds. They had heard the word "walk." The two remaining officers looked at each other blankly.

` "What in heaven's name can they be talking about?" Stumpfnagel finally asked.

"I'm afraid I know," Oster answered, his face ashen. "I mean, I'm afraid I don't know. Don't have any idea." He was staring intently at the rug.

Chapter Forty

Stumpfnagel and Ballard spent the entire week holed-up in their command post on the top floor of the Abwehr, scouring dispatches of aerial battles over Germany and from the Eastern front for news of battles won and towns gained. Stumpfnagel finally realized what Ballard had been doing with his detailed lists of conquests: he had been comparing the current East Front advances to those of the 'previous' World War II.

Entry into their room was restricted to just four people: Canaris, Stumpfnagel, Ballard and Inge Schmidt. On one wall, Ballard had posted a large chart. Showing the names of towns captured by date in the first Second World War, titled "Planned Date," he had left blank spaces alongside each entry to enter the "Actual Date" of capture during this, to him, the second Second World War.

Except for Stalingrad, the differences between "planned" and "actual" battle results on Ballard's Board had been too close to call. But Stalingrad had been a specific warning. The real question was, had the narrow escape there been bought at the price of another terrible loss somewhere else? Were Ballard's warnings a zero-sum game, a mere robbing of Peter to pay Paul? What they were hoping to see was a general tide of improvement. That would indicate that due to Ballard's advice, Germany had gained a genuine battlefield advantage. While there were differences in the Russian campaign due to the successful escape at Stalingrad, it was still damnably difficult to tell if these differences were overall advantages.

Anotherr reason the map data was unclear had to do with the refining and smoothing effects of history. When a town is taken can depend very much on who reports it. A tank commander believes he has "taken" a town if he can race through it without encountering any antitank fire. An infantry commander might still find the buildings filled with armed partisans and be in for a long struggle. Pressure from rear echelon commanders, anxious to pass back good news to the Führer, often reported a town was taken as soon as troops reached its outskirts. There was often no way to tell if the history books on which Ballard was relying were based on front-line dispatches or subsequent ground truth.

It was a gorgeous spring-like day and the command post room was overheated. Inge opened the window to let in some fresh air. As she struggled to swing the windows—out they had obviously not been opened for years—Lieutenant Stumpfnagel rushed to her side,

"Permit me, Frau Schmidt," he said, smiling broadly to be able to come to her aid. The window frames grunted strongly from his repeated blows but finally yielded. As Inge stood by the window staring out, she noticed a group of people filing out of a distant building.

"Which building is that?" she exclaimed.

Stumpfnagel looked out. "Which one?"

"The one with all the people leaving that back door."

"Oh, that," Stumpfnagel answered. "Those are the buildings on the Prinz Albrechtstrasse. That's the back of the Gestapo Headquarters. They've got a shortcut to the cafeteria by crossing through the backyard."

"Ooh, look, isn't that General Reinhard Heydrich," she exclaimed.

"What? Let me see," Stumpfnagel said. He strained his eyes but could not make out the identity of the men lolling about. "Can you really see them that well, Frau Schmidt?" Stumpfnagel asked, half in disbelief, half in envy . . .

"Yes, I think so," Inge replied. "I'm sure that's General Heydrich."

Stumpfnagel rooted around in a file cabinet and came up with a pair of submariner's binoculars. The lenses had the new purple anti-reflective coating. He peered through the giant lenses, focusing each one.

"Well I'll be damned," he muttered. "It's Heyrich alright.. And look, there sucking up next to him is that horror, Faulheim."

215

Ballard cleared his throat. "While you two are admiring the view, I say it's too early to tell anything yet," Ballard fussed, erasing another date on their blackboard and replacing it with a later date. "And it's not just a question of being a day or two earlier or later. That could just be miscommunication. What we're looking for are battlefield results that are different in kind, not just in time."

"What do you mean Herr Ballard?" Frau Schmidt asked. She replaced the binoculars in the cabinet.

"He means the order of battle has to change," Stumpfnagel answered. "Instead of an advance in the south that is slower than expected, say, we see a breakthrough in the north. That will mean, if Herr Ballard is correct, that the work Herr Ballard and I have been doing to change the behavior of our generals has worked and our efforts have changed the expected course of the war . . ."

"But change it compared to what?" she asked blankly. She used not to ask questions when she didn't understand something. Now she felt confident enough to ask.

Ballard and Stumpfnagel looked at each other. They had agreed to tell as few people as possible about Ballard's secret. Neither had expected Inge Schmidt to notice anything unusual in the welter of battlefield information streaming back to Abwehr Headquarters. She was only a secretary. Yet on several occasions now she had shown unexpected resources.

"Ah . . . this is the schedule the High Command expects the war to follow," Ballard started to explain. "If it doesn't and we pull ahead earlier than planned, we believe it will have been due to our efforts."

"And if they fall behind?" Inge persisted. There was an awkward silence. Stumpfnagel was staring at his secretary as if seeing her for the first time.

"I will explain that to you this evening, Frau Schmidt," Stumpfnagel finally said. "That is, if you would care to have dinner with me."

Inge Schmidt turned wordlessly to the lieutenant, her eyes grown suddenly very large. There was a long, embarrassed pause.

"But Herr Leutnant, you are in mourning . . ." Inge finally muttered. She was not saying no. But with Ballard there, appearances had to be maintained.

"F-F-Frau Schmidt—Inge, dearest, my thoughts every day for the last few weeks have not been of her, but of you." Acutely embarrassed, Stumpfnagel choked out the declaration with great difficulty, his head bowed.

In the thrilling recognition of love requited, Inge gently grasped Stumpfnagel's hand. Ballard snapped his fingers, remembering at that instant an urgent matter to attend to on the second floor. As he swung closed the door behind him, he saw Inge move up against the stunned lieutenant, her eyes closed, her head tilted back.

Ballard halted his closing swing of the door. Through the open slit he watched Stumpfnagel encircle the young woman in a tender embrace. She raised her arms slowly, her fingers tracing up the sleeves of his uniform. Her hand stopped at his black armband. Nimbly, her finger tips found the thread holding it in place and slipped it free. It was she who had sewn it on. Stumpfnagel kissed Inge gently, tentatively, holding her slumping body in his arms. At last the lightly sewn thread was free. The black armband dropped silently to the floor and Inge returned the kiss with deep passion.

"About time," Ballard muttered as he quietly pushed the door shut.

Chapter Forty-One

Admiral Canaris pulled gently on the reins and his horse instantly broke from its spirited canter into a slow walk. Colonel Oster brought his steed alongside. The horses made a shuddering sound with breath passing between their lips—a sign of pleasure at being exercised together. Their heads bobbed up and down, hinting at their readiness to gallop farther.

"He knows everything about our plans," Canaris said tersely.

"Our plans?" Oster said uneasily.

"To kill Hitler."

"But that's impossible . . ." Oster said angrily.

"Unless he did read about it in his history book," Canaris answered testily. "Look, use your head. There's no longer any question about it. He reads our future like a book, God-in-heaven, it is a book in his time. The important thing is he wants to help us. Insists on helping us. He says we failed. And paid the price."

Colonel Oster swallowed hard. "So what's he suggest?"

"He says he'll help us kill the monster as soon as he gets back from his mission to stop the American atomic bomb effort. Until then we wait. He's not going to do anything, and we're not to do anything or talk to anyone until the time is ripe. If we continue plotting, all we can do is somehow tip off the Gestapo. And then we really will end up paying the price."

Canaris pressed his heels lightly into his horse. The animal leaped forward into an exuberant run. Without being bade, Oster's horse bolted forward to keep up.

"And the maniac will still be alive," Oster shouted. "Doesn't sound like much of a choice to me."

"He also repeated his warning that this Jewish business is much worse than we can imagine. 'Clean your hands,' he said." Canaris spoke at Oster without taking his eyes off the path ahead. They were going at a fast canter. "Otherwise surviving this war won't do us much good."

"Much worse? Jesus Maria, have you ever been to one of the camps," Oster asked in horror. "It's unbelievable what those animals are doing. Heydrich is your neighbor. You play tennis with him. Can't you do something?"

"Colonel Heydrich and I have made our truce with each other," Canaris answered sourly. "And that was difficult enough. If I start sticking my nose in his business, he'll call the whole thing off. And I don't think I could bring a confrontation with him to a stalemate this time. He could make a snack out of us this time around. And then we'd never get to the root of the problem."

"You mean `Plan A,'" Oster said. "To execute that Schweinehund."

While Oster spoke, Canaris had spurred his horse to a full gallop. Wordlessly he had thrown down the gauntlet—a race home. Oster forced a smile to his grim face and kicked his mount harshly in the ribs. The steed exploded into a run that nearly left the colonel behind. Standing in the stirrups, Oster leaned forward and stroked his mount's neck. Grabbing a sneaky head start like that, he'd show the old man . . .

Chapter Forty-Two

Göring was pacing back and forth—mincing would be a better word, Ballard thought his corpulent bulk shaking with agitation atop his slender legs.

"But mein Fuhrer, the V-2 program is the wave of the future. Already we can strike out at the British and Soviets from German soil, delivering a ton of explosives at one-third the cost of a Bf-109 fighter!"

"All at a cost of forty-five times as much per ton of explosives delivered as by using the V-1," Ballard intoned. "And offering no greater range. But the exotic resources demand liquid oxygen, special metal working, 20,000 individual parts per rocket, thousands of highly skilled engineers—all of these demands will only take away resources from the defense of Germany which is only possible with superior fighters—the manned V-1b and the Me-262."

"And who is this so-called strategic expert, I'd like to know?" Göring shouted, standing directly in front of Ballard, looming over him as if threatening to fall on him and so end the matter once and for all. "Coming here out of nowhere with what testimony to his expertise? We are talking here about the future salvation of Germany. What credentials . . . ?"

"Now, now Herr Reichsmarshall," Hitler tutt-tutted. "The arguments Herr Ballard is making seem to make sense no matter why he's making them. Perhaps you have some factual objections . . ." Hitler was enjoying himself enormously. He made a habit of pitting his lieutenants at each other, hoping to see which one came out on top. It drove them all crazy, he knew, but it often forced them into reluctant forms of collaboration and lessened his need to make every single decision for them.

"Factual objections?" Göring bellowed. "Yes, I have very serious factual objections. I object that an enemy alien is privy to our innermost state secrets. I object that this mysterious person, whose motives are entirely unknown—as well as his background—is held up as someone I—Chief of the Luftwaffe, a pilot decorated for bravery—have to submit my plans to. I object . . ."

"Hermann," Hitler interrupted. "What is wrong with canceling the V-2 project if it offers no military advantages over the V-1?

"No advantage, mein Führer? You don't consider a rocket bomb that arrives at 5700 km/hr—four-and-a-half times faster than the speed of sound—a technical performance of the highest order? A demonstration of superior German science that will strike fear into the hearts of the British military and demoralize the populace?"

Hitler turned to Ballard with a twinkle in his eye, nodded to him to voice his objections.

"Herr Reichsmarshall," Ballard replied, trying to keep his voice level. He knew that every word out of his mouth was being memorized by the Reichsmarshall, to be held against him forever. But his benefactor was Hitler, and he must convince him now so that his future request would have the ring of truth to it. "Whether the ton of explosives each of the two missiles is each capable of delivering takes forty-five minutes or five minutes to reach its target makes little difference on the ground. What does make a difference is that with its very high arrival speed, the V-2 will bury itself so deeply that its explosive effect will actually be less than that of the V-1. Except perhaps to destroy reinforced bunkers. Also, with the new electrical eye terminal guidance system that Dr. Lusser has worked out, the V-1 is far more accurate now than the V-2 will be. Because of the V-2's very high arrival speed, there is too little time to redirect its final aim."

"Herr Ballard," Göring screamed. "I forbid you to continue to contradict me like this in front of the Führer at the same time you are demanding money for your own crazy scheme. This is absolutely ridiculous. If you don't stop, I will be required to settle the matter in the old-fashioned way, by calling out my seconds. Please don't make me take that irrevocable step."

"Hermann, when was the last time you parried someone with a sword?" Hitler asked, still smirking at the heated exchange between the two men. "Mr. Ballard, I will take the matter of redirecting funds from the V-2 project for your six U-boats under advisement and let you know." He turned to the glowering Göring. "In the mean time, Herman, let us talk about other things. Under four eyes. Thank-you Mr. Ballard."

Ballard realized he was sweating profusely. He rose from his chair and nodded to both men. Hitler watched them with a bemused smile. Göring was taut with anger. "You have not heard the last from me on this subject, Herr Ballard," Göring shouted, and then pointedly turned his back. Hitler looked at Ballard over Göring 's shoulder and twinkled his fingers to indicate a friendly good-by. Then his expression turned blank. Ballard was already out of his mind.

Chapter Forty-Three

The flow chart of battles in Ballard's command post on the top floor of the warren of Abwehr buildings began to show without a doubt a trend of German victory that could no longer be attributed to chance. Fed false Enigma reports purporting to come from Hitler furiously demanding Moscow be vanquished to the last German soldier if necessary, Stalin reinforced Moscow heavily enough to repel the German army twice over. Four rings of Maginot line-like fortifications were built to prepare for these reported major assaults that would never come.

While much of the Soviet army bottled itself up in huge defensive installations, the Wehrmacht—the German army—remained completely mobile: It refused to let itself get drawn into any major battles not of its own choosing. It was the route of Kursk that finally offered von Manstein the opportunity to push his 9th Panzer Army in one thunderous charge within sight of the Ural Mountains. Kursk, Vornezh, Saratov, and finally, on December 1, 1944, Kuybyshev fell, and with it the morale of the Soviet Army. Stalin's hysterical second purge of Soviet officers resulted in battle-hardened senior commanders being replaced by political hacks. The result was chaos and rampant mutinies among the ranks and the remaining junior officers. Outside "Fortress Moscow," the Soviet army began to disintegrate.

With all attention focused on southern Russia and the Caucasus, German troops from Norway joined Finnish Troops and took Leningrad by a mere show of force, declaring it, like Paris, an "open city." Relieved of the overhead of occupying a major city, the northern armies hurtled past Moscow, overran Gorkiy, weakly defended Kirov and, in less than two months, supplied the northern anchor to the Archangel-Kuybychev

Line. With Red Army headquarters pushed back to Sverdlosk, Moscow was now impregnably isolated 1000 km behind enemy lines.

The fiercest fighting occurred at the port of Archangel. Murmansk had long been cut off by the Finns, leaving Archangel the last deep water port available to the Allies to supply the Soviets. After several ferocious ground battles, the Germans pulled back and encircled the city. The first of the new Type-XXI U-Boats patrolled the Vardo-Spitsbergen line in large packs. Four times faster underwater than the older Type VII submarines they replaced, the sleek new U-boats were virtually unstoppable. The White Sea of Archangel was mined so heavily, even German U-boats no longer dared enter.

Thus began the siege of Fortress Moscow. The first reports showed evidence of an indomitable spirit. Grand parades were held across Red Square displaying masses of defensive weaponry. Russian propaganda outdid even German exaggeration of how spirited the defenders were. But later eyewitness reports of an acute shortage of sewer rats soon told the real story. As with the ill-fated attempt to supply Stalingrad by air, Moscow too could not receive nearly enough material to keep going. With Archangel strangled, the Allies could no longer supply Moscow except by the most carefully planned and largely symbolic long-range flights. Able to carry only a token quantity of supplies, these flights quickly dropped off as soon as fuel supplies for return trips was exhausted. Worse, many of the heavy-laden supply aircraft were shot down. Often their freight was salvageable by the thinly-stretched German army. Ignored by Allies and cordoned off by Hitler, the city slowly fell of its own weight.

Churchill and Roosevelt soon realized that their costly efforts to supply the defenders of Moscow were resupplying the German occupation force nearly as effectively as the Soviet troops expected to break out of Moscow. Stalin sank into raging fits of paranoia. "Where are the Allied invasion forces to take pressure off Fortress Moscow?" he screamed. Receiving no answer, he refused to risk his troops in breakout attempts to nowhere. Soon, even the symbolic flights were cut off. When told that no relief flights had been sighted in the last three days, Hitler, in his Rastenburg forward headquarters, danced another jig. With the Russians out of the way at last, and the British nearly cut off, perhaps now was the time to strike the crushing blow at the Americans.

Chapter Forty-Four

Korvettinlieutenant Wolfgang Luth carefully placed his half full bottle of Beck's beer on top of his bald head. He pushed his chair back and, balancing the bottle on his head, disappeared beneath the dining room table. Slowly, the very top of the bottle appeared just above the level of the table. It began to move forward.

"Just like that, mein Führer," Luth said from beneath the table. "We stick the periscope up only a few centimeters above the water's surface and search for enemy ships. Any more and they see us first."

"And when you do see them Herr Kaleunt?" Hitler asked, displaying a huge grin of appreciation. 'Kaleunt' was short for Kapitenleutentnant, the usual rank and universal address of U-boat commanders. This was what Hitler liked. Two real soldiers talking shop, man-to-man, about real problems of fighting. None of the this foggy strategic issues business; just nail-hard, front-line facts.

Luth popped up from his crouch. He grabbed the bottle before it could fall off. A wet ring glistened on his pate. "Why, we set up the firing solution, mein Führer. And then, 'basta,' we shoot. Two or three minutes later—sometimes five minutes on a long shot—we see the result." The U-boat commander raised both hands in a gesture of a column of water raising in the air. "A few seconds later we hear the crunch of a direct hit, then metal twisting and breaking."

"The torpedo hits the ship how far below the waterline?" Hitler asked excitedly. The assembled guests were awestruck by the conversation of the two men. First they all looked at Captain Luth when he spoke. Then they all shifted their gaze to the Führer. Back and forth, Like spectators at a tennis match.

"Ideally, it passes just below the ship by a few meters, and then blows up. That breaks the ship in half and is a guaranteed kill," the Navy officer replied. He took a quick swig from his bottle.

"But how does the torpedo know?" Hitler asked.

"It's magnetic," Luth replied. As soon as it detects the iron of the ship, the detector sets the detonation pistol off."

"And that works reliably"? Hitler asked, incredulously.

"No," Luth answered. His genially grin becoming tight. "I said 'ideally.' When it works, the effect is miraculous. The ship sinks in minutes. But not only have the Allies recently installed anti-magnetic degaussing equipment, but the reliability of our advanced torpedoes is always suspect. So we're back to using the older versions with contact fuses. You hit the ship a few meters below the water line. A lot of the explosive energy goes into sending a beautiful water plume twenty meters in the air. You can put them out of action, but it's a rare merchant ship that sinks with a single torpedo hit any more."

"Hmmm," Hitler responded. He had listened to complaints of malfunctioning torpedoes for years. The Americans had terrible problems too, he was told. God in heaven, who appreciated the thousands of problems of running a simple war? Certainly none of the dandified generals and admirals he had to carry out his plans. Sometimes he wondered if it was worth it all. He quickly straightened up from his momentary slump of resignation. He looked over at his guest of honor affectionately.

"You know I can't send you back into combat anymore. Not as the only living U-boat Diamond holder."

Luth's face fell. He knew the two other holders of diamonds and oak leaves of the Knight's Cross. Prien of U-147 and Schepke of U-100 both had found their end in Neptune's icy grip. Kretschmer of U-99, the highest scorer of Allied tonnage sunk had been captured when his boat was disabled and he could not scuttle or escape.

"I understand, mein Führer," Luth muttered. But the disappointment was writ large upon his face. He knew where he would be sent—to head up the Kriegsmarinschule, the Naval U-boat Academy at Memel Werft near Flensburg. It was an honorable promotion, but a retirement just the same.

"Well, don't look so disappointed, Herr Fregattinkaptitan," Hitler said archly. He spotted the look of concern on the thirty year old commander's face. "No, I have not made a mistake. I've made a promotion."

A light ripple of applause ran through the silent dinner guests. None had dared interrupt the Führer's on-going conversation. Even the usually serious Luth himself had to repress a chuckle at the memory of the protocol officer's frantic briefing prior to meeting Hitler:

"Whatever you do, don't address the Führer unless spoke to. Keep your answers short. And in God's Will, don't bring up any problems."

"But I'd like you to head-up just one mission more," Hitler said, wiping his mouth with a napkin. Luth noticed a sleight-of-hand gesture. Had Hitler just quickly put something in his mouth? An anti-gas pill for his chronic flatulence, maybe?

"Not combat in the true sense. In fact you're specifically, ordered to avoid any fighting, except in self-defense. But you'll have the opportunity to strike a blow for the Fatherland unlike any that have gone before." A murmur of interest circled the table. Hitler eyed his honored guest slyly, deliberately refraining from saying any more.

"Mein Führer. Anything I can do . . ." Luth murmured. ,

"Excellent. I knew you'd accept. Admiral Doenitz will give you the complete details." Hitler guiltily popped another pastry into his mouth. So that was it, he was sneak-eating those delicious Viennese pastries. And he knew if Eva Braun found out she would scold him, but they were irresistible.

"Now then," Hitler continued. "Before we get back to our guests, is it true the Schnorchels have a coating that is invisible to the radio direction finding beams of the Allies . . . ?"

Chapter Forty-Five

Ballard pressed his hands and feet against the cold steel sides of his bunk. The bunk heaved left, pitched downward and counterclockwise. While his body was prisoner to this corkscrew motion, his stomach remained always two nauseating steps out of sync. A scrubbed young face knocked on the wall outside his alcove and slipped the curtain open.

"Herr Ballard, The kaleunt requests your presence for dinner in five minutes."

"Arrrgh, dinner," Ballard replied. "Surely you're not serious?"

"Quite serious, Herr Ballard," the ensign said officiously. "If you do not wish to come, your illness will be judged to be such that I am to put you in irons and feed your bread and water until we sight land."

"Oh, so dinner is quite voluntary, then," Ballard said disgustedly.

"Always with the Kaleunt," The youth replied instantly, and without the slightest trace of humor.

Ballard swung his feet over the edge of his bunk. The motion of sitting up made his head swim and his stomach heave. He breathed deeply three times and slid queasily to his feet. "Lead on MacDuff," he groaned through clenched teeth. After this fresh-faced recruit, all Ballard needed was to have someone lecture him on how mal-de-mer was "all psychological." He grinned evilly at his plan to eject a stream of "psychological" vomit in the miscreant's direction.

"Aha, Herr Ballard," Captain Luth exclaimed as the pasty-faced American staggered to the officers' table. "How kind of you to join us after all. We haven't seen much of you so far."

"Oh, I wouldn't have missed this dinner for all the world," Ballard replied coolly. "Especially when the invitation was so unmistakably presented."

"Yes, we do tend to be rather formal, we German people," the captain said, enjoying enormously the American's look of discomfort. Influential friend of Canaris, Hitler, Göring and Eva Braun, if rumors were correct, yet what did that buy him once they were under way? Nothing but a greening about the gills. Oh how this mighty big shot has fallen, Captain Luth though with great satisfaction. For once, justice triumphs over politics.

Ballard swiveled into the remaining stool behind the eight-man table. He eyed the officers warily. They looked back at him with considerable amusement. He could read their thoughts on their faces: was this really the great American spy who seemed to know everything? Funny how pathetic he looked on the high seas.

"Herr Ballard," the Kaleunt said genially. "Now that we're under way, how about telling us just exactly what we're doing and why?"

Ballard realized the question, like the invitation to dinner, was not a request "Herr Kaleunt, You are aware that I am required to answer to no one on this mission, and, in fact, that I am its nominal leader." Ballard watched the look of shock spreading on the captain's face. He figured he had less than ten seconds left to make his point. "However, everyone knows—and I certainly know—that once we left port, the real authority can only be the U-boat fleet commander, that is, you, Herr Kaleunt."

Ballard shifted his position on the stool. "That is an arrangement I subscribe to fully. I place myself completely under your command."

The captain leaned back slowly from the hunched oven position he had taken. "Ja, natürlich," he said with a sigh of relief. "That was always clear to everyone except those remaining behind."

"The chain of command being completely clear," Ballard continued. "Ask me anything. I'll be delighted to answer almost any of your questions."

"Almost any of them?" the captain said. "Which questions do you wish not to answer?"

"I will not answer any questions about how I get my intelligence information," Ballard said levelly. "Or from whom. Otherwise, ask away."

Wolfgang Luth stood up from his stool and propped himself against the galley wall to consider the situation. The American was a combination of disarming openness—an openness that struck a resonant chord in the

German military code of instant, unquestioning honesty. Yet coupled, with that admirable trait was a habit of stubbornness that would be considered rank insubordination. As a German officer he would not last a month. Yet he was undeniably an Abwehr big shot. For the first time in his career, Luth understood why someone as different as this American could be trusted. Nothing he did was for personal gain. When he was "insubordinate" it was not to advance himself at someone else's expense. Nor did he ever try to put his own program ahead of anyone else's without thoroughly and openly explaining his reasoning. When you came down to it, Luth recognized, the guy was not simply brilliant, much more importantly he was honest and aboveboard. Intellectual or not, that's all one could ask. The stubbornness became a mere detail, like a case of smelly feet. Luth had commanded enough men to be able to distinguish the wheat from the chaff.

"That sounds like a fair bargain to me, Herr Ballard," the Kaleunt said easily. A knot of tension among the officers evaporated wordlessly.

"Hey, Arni. How about a beer," the chief engineer said, breaking the ice.

"Beer?" Ballard asked, his eyes lighting up. "I thought official policy prohibited the consumption of alcoholic beverages on board a U-boat."

"And so it does, my friend," the engineer said, pulling a brace of Löwenbrau bottles from under the table. "But this is an Abwehr mission we're on, is it not? And we have a well-known saying in the Navy: 'Abwehr business always takes precedence over non-Abwehr business'—isn't that right, men? Surely the good Admiral Canaris would not disagree?"

"Absolutely not, I'm sure of that, too, gentlemen," Ballard said, the enthusiasm returning a little color to his face. He opened the wire-captured ceramic top of the beer bottle. The 'psssst' of the carbonation released sent a nostalgic whiff of German hops and barley throughout the galley that augured well for the evening ahead. And the questions.

* * *

"DIVE, DIVE, DIVE!" the lookout screamed into the speaking tube. The four others instantly put down their huge binoculars and dropped down the conning tower hatch sequentially, in smooth, practiced motions. "Get down immediately, Herr Ballard," The lookout barked, pushing Ballard roughly toward the hatch.

"I didn't see anything . . ." Ballard muttered, protesting.

"If we had to wait for you to see the aircraft, we'd probably have to wait for it to make a second pass," the lookout said angrily. "Nun Los, get down!"

Ballard half-slid, half-fell down the ladder into the Command room. Slamming the hatch shut and spinning the wheel to seal it, the bosun's mate nearly landed on top of him. Wolfgang Luth's head poked up through the hatch below.

"What is it?" He asked worriedly.

"Two engines, coming right at us," the lookout re plied. "I couldn't tell whose."

"Dive to sixty meters," Luth said to no one in particular. A voice echoed the command: "Dive to sixty meters." Ballard heard it repeated once more from deeper still within the submarine. The craft tipped suddenly, throwing Ballard against the conning tower wall. Everyone else had instinctively grabbed a hold to remain in place. Luth looked at the crumpled American with a face of pity.

"Good Lord, men, will we ever make a submariner out of him?"

As Ballard sat up, he noticed something was very wrong. In the frenzy of the activity around him, each crewman leaping to his battle stations, it took a moment for him to realize what it was, the rumbling sound was gone—that basso profundo of background noise that had

231

permeated every instant of the trip—had disappeared, shut off with the unexpected finality of a concert silenced by switching off the radio. The deep rumble was a pleasant sound signifying the health and modulated two thousand horse-power of the U-boat. Like a heartbeat, he had long ago ignored it as such a normal part of his underwater existence that it became a reassuring—a necessary—part of that existence. Now he heard only the rushing of water and an occasionally creaking sound of metal rending.

The U-boat leveled out. A signal light flashed above Luth's head. "Sixty meters," his second in command said.

Luth nodded in acknowledgment. "Twenty degrees to Steuerbord," he said. The pilots sitting in the command room spun their rudder wheels to the right. Another groan of metal in pain filled the cabin. The silence was eerie.

"Why is it so quiet?" Ballard whispered.

"Quiet?" Luth asked. We don't want to be heard."

"Yes, but the engines . . . ?" Ballard said, still puzzled.

"Ah, the engines. The engines are shut off," Luth said quietly. "We're running on electric motors now."

Luth's dreamy face became suddenly taut. "Dive to two hundred meters. Brace for mine attack!"

In the distance Ballard heard a gentle 'crump,' and then another, and then louder yet another, like distant footsteps in a haunted house. Ballard realized the footsteps were getting closer. The floor of the boat pitched forward again. This time he was clutching a map drawer handle. The drawer pulled open and then stopped, arresting Ballard's fall A crewman smirked at the disarray of the lanky American.

The boat creaked some more, with horrible 'sprongs' and other sounds of metal in agony issuing forth loudly but from no identifiable spot. Surely water would burst through the next such horrible clang.

The first mate looked over at Ballard, pityingly. "It's normal," he said. "The sound. It's just the pressure hull compressing. Nothing to worry about."

Chapter Forty-six

Admiral Canaris showed the one-page report to Oster. "This is what Major Hilflich has come up with on the Pergolesi woman. The father was German—Herr Professor Gunther Stellmann—on the electrical engineering faculty at the Humbolt University. He died a few years ago. The mother, born in Neustrelitz, nee Anna Freund."

"Ahhh," Oster said. "so that's it . . ."

"Ja," Canaris said sadly. "Should we tell Herr Ballard?"

"You think he doesn't know . . . ?"

"American's don't seem to be able to tell—and this one doesn't seem to care."

"We should all not care," Oster agreed. "But nowadays, that's not enough. But it is his personal business, isn't it," Oster said after some thought. "One reason we get along so well with him, I am absolutely certain, is because we've respected his privacy. Stumpfnagel believes it strongly, too. He is really a very private person, our Mr. Ballard."

Canaris pursed his lips. "Wait. This is what the Pergolesi woman is afraid of—that she'll be picked up. God, how has she avoided Goebbels' dragnet so far? No wonder she came apart when Ballard said he would have to drop his American citizenship."

"Jesus Christ, of course. How could we have missed it? This is awful. What should we do? He won't be back from. his mission for another month."

Colonel Oster got up and started pacing the office. "Should we try to check up an her and the mother? Offer them protection?" Oster stopped his pacing. There was a long silence as the two men looked to each other for suggestions.

"His girlfriend is not going to be picked up," Canaris said, finally. "As long as Faulheim thinks he can still squeeze her for information . . ."

Oster looked at his boss. "Of course: through the mother . . ."

"Idiots!" Canaris shouted. "We've been total idiots." He picked up the telephone and asked for a number.

"Hilflich, Canaris here. Where was it that Herr Ballard's girlfriend went on her so-called visit to see her mother—the one he asked you check up on?" A pause. "Furstenberg? Thank-you."

Major Oster sat down in a state of mild shock. "Furstenberg isn't that near . . . Ravensbruck? The women's concentration camp. That's where the mother is visiting 'old friends.'"

"Making sure the daughter didn't have a change of heart. God, it makes me want to puke," Oster said angrily.

Canaris wore a blank mask on his face. "Faulheim's got the mother up there as his trump card. Hilflich thinks Faulheim probably put the old woman up at the local hotel. Hell, the Gestapo is probably putting the old lady up at that sleazy hotel to make it seem like they're really concerned, but making sure they both get a tour of the camp during their visit to see what will happen if the daughter doesn't cooperate. Faulheim is going to a lot of trouble on this one. Whenever he's this clever, I worry. This is not going to be easy."

"But we've' got to help them," Oster interjected fiercely. "We owe it to Ballard."

"So we pull her out," Canaris said. "I'm not at all sure we can do it. But then what?"

"The three of them are going to have to leave. Switzerland, Brazil . . ."

"And we lose Ballard in the process? And all his help? According to him, without it, Germany will lose the war . . ."

Finally Canaris spoke up. "That's what this Nazi shit has come to. The usual choice between honor and country."

"So once again the monster leaves us no choice," Oster said in hollow tones. The two men looked at each other hopelessly.

Chapter Forty-Seven

As the faint glow of evening turned to black night, U-114 surfaced. On the conning tower, Ballard could just make out the faint outline of the four other U-Boats that had each towed their submerged barges across the Atlantic. Although they had been two weeks underway, Ballard had not yet fully acquired his sea legs and the rolling pitching of the surfaced U-boat required him repeatedly to focus intently on the unwavering horizon.

Rowed over in small boats, the captain of each boat assembled in the control room of the command ship, the new Type-XXI. Luth unrolled an American government nautical chart.

"Well, good," Luth said pressing his finger to the chart. "We're exactly here, twenty-five miles southeast of Fripp Island. This will be our daylight location for the duration of the operation. The depth here is uniformly eleven fathoms, so we can still all submerge and escape, if necessary. But just barely."

Most of the commanders had brought their navigators with them, and the crowd of men hunched over the chart table was tightly packed.

"You navigators, notice the little channel that remains at eleven fathoms for another seven miles and points us at Port Royal Sound. We'll follow that and when it runs out, head due north until we get to the three fathom contour. That's as close as I can go, but that should get me to less than a mile offshore—about 1600 meters.

"The rest of you, can bring your Type-VIIs in to two fathoms depth-right up to shore. Our landing point is this small scrub island next to Fripp Island. Port Royal Sound at port, and St. Helena Sound at starboard are both surface-navigable at six and five fathoms, but don't get bottled up. Port Royal Sound especially has a small coast guard station out of the city of Beaufort.

"All right, let's get at it. Put some men ashore with gas powered winches and tow your barges up to shore. I'll play the lookout." The meeting broken up, the crews filed up the ladder and to their waiting tenders.

The four type-VII U-boats eased slowly to within one hundred meters of the scrub-covered island. Kaleunts Luth and Wohlfarth pulled out north and south to the eleven fathom contour and submerged up to the tops of their conning towers to minimize accidental radar or visual contacts. When the coast was clear, the boats surfaced.

Silently, the crews scrambled onto the deck and hauled the trailing submerged barges up along side their boats. The U-boat compressors grumbled and pumped air through connecting hoses to displace the water ballast. Slowly the containers rose above water. Soon they were a full two meters high, with only a shallow draft remaining. With his red lamp, the Bosun's mate flashed a single blip of light to the island shore.

Four men had rowed to the island and mounted a motorized pulley, cabled firmly to a half-dozen of the stunted, tenacious rooted pine growths. A few jerks on the starter made it putter into action. The line to the submersibles became taut and gently pulled them forward. A hissing sound soon signaled the beaching of the first container craft on the sandy shore. In less than an hour, three more containers slipped up onto the beach.

Their cargoes safely delivered, each of the four tugboat U-boats backed out and picked a spot off the three kilometer-long island to submerge and keep watch.

While the Type-VIIs were delivering their barges, the crew of the U-1143 began to bolt a flimsy iron framework over the top of the surfaced submarine. Once erected, large painted canvas panels were unfurled and stretched in place. It was too dark to see the result. They would wait until morning to get a report from island spotters.

On the island the men worked all night. Occasionally clangs of hammers were heard pounding recalcitrant bolts into place, followed by curses and angry hushing sounds. Ballard had been up for thirty-six hours, unable to sleep because of the high drama that was unfolding. His life's ambition was being put to the test. Would his plan succeed? A half-dozen times he lay down and tried to sleep. Each time his mind whirled furiously, preventing it. He jerked his head up from the mess table where he had rested it in his hands for a moment. Some of the officers were sitting down to eat.

"Dinner already?" he asked. "Aren't you going to wait until you're finished?"

"We're finished working," a voice growled back. "Not snoozing, like certain people."

"Snoozing? I was just resting my eyes," Ballard protested: "For less than a minute."

"Oh yeah?," the young man replied. "What time is it, then?"

"Around two a.m.," Ballard said, looking reflexively at his watch. The hands refused to make sense.

"It's half before seven, mein Lieber," the young man said, sitting down next to Ballard. "And too light for most of us to work anymore."

As soon as the words were out, Ballard felt his mind modulate the view of the watch hands into a recognizable image. Ah, yes—6:30.

Ballard made his way up to the bridge. It was bright outside and only a few men were scampering around the deck. Loth was directing them after getting comments from island by semaphore.

"The third panel after the deck gun has a noticeable crack," he hissed. Crouching down, two crewmen scampered over the false deck and hammered the panel into position.

"Good. Perfect. That's it. Come below," Luth said. He turned to Ballard. "Well, I hope this theatrical brain wave of yours is worth all the trouble."

"I hope so too," Ballard said. "The coast guard patrols the coast very regularly. I'm only worried if we get spotted by aircraft. But that's less likely. The illusion is not nearly as good from above because they can see the shape of the boat is not that of a ship."

Ballard picked up a spotter's binoculars and focused on the island. A single, long V-1 launch ramp was being assembled. Pulled back into the scrub pine, the camouflage of the submersible tow barges was near-perfect. Ballard knew that inside each tank, a half-dozen

237

technicians were cleaning, assembling and arming their missiles. At night they would be pulled out of their tow barges, the wings attached and the first one hoisted onto the ramp. At the right moment, each would be fired off, one by one. Ballard felt a renewed tingle of anticipation. This is it, he kept repeating to himself. Every thing you've worked for. The abortion of nuclear weapon use. Be cool, don't blow it now.

"It's 1700 hours, Herr Ballard," a voice next to his bunk said. "The Kaleunt requests your presence in the radio room."

Ballard swung his lanky frame out from his narrow bunk. He felt dazed, having fallen into a deep, sweaty sleep. As he slowly awoke, he realize how refreshed he was.

"According to your information, we can expect the patrol any minute now," Luth said tersely. "USN-365, a small cutter. I hope this works."

"You and me," Ballard muttered. He felt a sharp stab in his stomach.

Luth hung over the periscope, swinging back and forth over a twenty degree arc. Suddenly, he stopped swinging. "Achtung!" he said conversationally. All talking in the room ceased instantly.

"There he is, right on schedule," Luth said. "Good. Send him the first message."

The radioman tapped out a light blinker message:

> SHIP AHOY/STOP/THIS IS DE
> STROYER USN-211 TO COAST
> GUARD CUTTER 365/STOP/YOU
> ARE APPROACHING A RESTRICTED
> NAVAL OPERATION/STOP/ STEER
> TO PORT IMMEDIATELY/STOP/
> MAINTAIN THREE MILE DISTANCE
> AND PROCEED/END

"They've slowed," Luth said. "Their bow wake has dropped." He turned to Ballard. "All right my friend. Let's see if this idea of yours

238

works. The radio man tapped a Morse key sending flashes of light toward, the cutter.

> HARRY/SORRY FOR THE ABRUPT ARRIVAL/STOP/
> CLASSIFIED MISSION/STOP/CHECK YOUR HQ
> BUT NOT BY RADIO/STOP/DISCUSS ALL AT O-CLUB
> SATURDAY DINNER/STOP/BANKS/END

The cutter came to a complete stop. Luth saw its light blinking a response.

> 365 TO 211/STOP/HARRY TDY/
> STOP/O-CLUB SATURDAY NIGHT
> SOUNDS GOOD/STOP/CAPT WLLM
> CLEAGLE/END

Luth stood up from the periscope with a broad grin. "It seems to have worked. They're moving off. What does TDY mean?"

"Temporary Duty—it means he's away on a trip, other duty—it can even mean vacation."

"You're lucky your friend Harry wasn't on board. He might have recognized you aren't who you say your are."

"There was no chance of that," Ballard retorted.

"Really?" Luth asked. "How do you know so much, Herr Ballard? We all wonder—even Grossadmiral Doenitz commented on it."

The other crew men turned to listen to Ballard's answer.

"Ah . . . remember our agreement, Herr Kaleunt," Ballard smiled nervously.

"Ach, ja. I almost forgot. Any questions except how you get your information." Luth had a fixed grin on his face, Ballard was not sure whether it was meant as a joke, or whether his welcome had worn out. "Well, it's working so far. Let me buy you a beer, Herr Ballard." He slapped the American on the back. "Jurgen, keep an eye out on the cutter. Make sure it circles us and keeps on going."

Chapter Forty-Eight

Captain Banks stood looking at the destroyer from the Bridge. "What did you say his range is?" he asked.

"Must be about six thousand yards," the first mate replied. He was looking through range-finder binoculars that measured distance by lining-an object of known size up against internal stadia. He turned to the navigator standing just inside the Bridge for confirmation.

"About three thousand yards, Sir," the navigator said nervously.

"Three thousand yards? What are you talking about, Corners? Take a look at the size of it—that ship is at least three miles away!"

The young navigator was sweating. This was his second active-duty mission, and he had made a critical mistake only a few days earlier.

"I'll check it again, Sir," he said, his face turning red with embarrassment. Christ, at this rate he'd never make promotion. He'd end up shoveling coal. He looked down at the map. Sandy Hook was definitely off the starboard beam, and the little island, Fripp, was ninety degrees off the bow. They'd have to be on land to be six thousand yards away.

"Can the island have shifted?" he asked. "No, wait. Let, me check the date of this chart." He scanned the bottom legend. "Nineteen twenty-one, Sir. The chart is over twenty years old." He looked up at the first mate hopefully.

"Goddammit Corners, islands don't move three thousand yards in twenty-three years, and then suddenly stop and grow trees." The first mate was not absolutely certain that didn't happen. But he wanted to assert himself in front of the Old Man. "Check it again."

"We're already drifting too close to them. They'll probably report us for interfering with a military operation."

"Yes sir. Shall we radio Operations, Sir?"

"And give their entire mission away to any German spy happening to be listening?" the first mate said sarcastically. This was only his second mission, too, but at age: twenty-three, he felt infinitely superior to the young recruit. "You figure it out."

"Yes, Sir," the navigator replied. "I mean, No, Sir, we won't need to call." He picked up his parallel rulers and compass rose and pretended to recalculate the distance.

The first mate walked out to the flying bridge and sidled up to the captain. "Looks odd, though doesn't it, Captain, how sharply we can see it just sitting there in the light, and yet it's well over three miles away."

"The beauty and mystery of the sea, Hamilton," the Captain replied, hoping he sounded appropriately wise. It was a type of battleship he could not exactly place. But there were so many of them. And the camouflage treatment of mottled squares—it worked-sort of. He preferred the clean lines of his pin-neat coast guard cutter himself. He was conscious of the fact that it was only his fourth week of command. He had been an accountant when he joined up. No need to appear too inexperienced in front of the men.

Chapter Forty-Nine

The V-lb assembly crews worked all Thursday night in a heavy cloaking fog. Luth had sent out a four-man patrol to hide among the dunes of the mainland beach and report on noise and light coming from the islands, or to warn of any approach of military force.

Inside the tow barges which served as portable workshops, the engineers and technicians were working at a furious pace. They reported difficulty getting the pulse-jet shutter linkages to function smoothly. They would work fine at the high pressure of cruise speed but in order to start at the lower speed of the take-off ramp, they needed to work perfectly. Three weeks in a rubber tank had nevertheless caused some small amount of corrosion of the critical bearings, and they were not sufficiently free wheeling. The engineers had borrowed as many men as would fit inside the stuffy tow barges and had disassembled every pulse jet shutter. Parts were carefully spread out on bedding-blankets that had now become oil-soaked. Engine fuel was being used to wash off the bearing surfaces. The spring-loaded shutter link ages had the annoying habit of bursting out of an assembler's hand at the critical moment of trying to remount it in its fixture, sending the parts scattering throughout the tank. This would be followed by a low and lengthy growl of curses, to which the German language was particularly well-suited. Then the parts had to be hunted down, cleaned of sand and grit, and the assembly attempt begun over again.

"We will only have half the missiles ready by morning, Herr Kaleunt," Chief Engineer Lorenz Beckmesser reported. "Eight, maybe ten."

"Shit," Luth replied. "That's not enough. We must make at least twelve hits—four per factory." He looked long and hard at Ballard sitting at the mess table with the navigator. They were studying the US topographic survey map of the target area.

"We will lose a day and strike on Saturday," Luth said. "Make sure the men get enough rest. I don't want them to do a poor job so we launch the jets only to watch half of them lob into the sea."

"Jawohl, Herr Kaleunt," Beckmesser replied. "The first shift is resting now."

"ACHTUNG-AIRCRAFT SIGHTED!" the loud speaker blurted out. The first mate sprang up the ladder to the conning tower. At its top, the hatch was open only slightly, disguised to look like the superstructure of the battleship. The disguise passed muster if it was not examined too closely. But it would not fool an experienced observer. Not up close.

The first man felt the tug of his commander on his ankle. "It's a blinker alert from the shore patrol, Herr Kaleunt," the mate said. "But I can't see any aircraft yet because the island is in the way-oha-there it is, a PBS coast guard markings, Gott sei Dank. It's flying outside our three-mile zone."

"See if you can tell whether it's just passing by, or whether it's circling outside the zone," Luth whispered.

Even though there was no chance the pilot could hear them speaking, like all submariners, Luth was pathologically afraid of giving his position away by excessive noise.

Luth watched his first mate turning on the ladder. He changed his position from facing the ladder, to facing out.

"Yep, he's circling outside the zone."

"Can he see anything on the island?"

"Just the launch ramp," the first mate replied. "But it's pointing north and south. And who knows what it looks like lying on its side—a railroad track, perhaps."

"Good. That means they're nosy, but not yet alarmed. We've got to get them off our track. This battleship disguise is not going to last forever. What do you think, Herr Ballard?"

"I think the disguise has already served its purpose," Ballard answered. "It's bought us today. But with every hour of being unable to get a confirmation of who we are, the next pair of eyes they send are going to be experienced and very inquisitive." He stopped to stroke his chin. "We need a diversion."

"Ja, a diversion is right." Luth walked over to the map. "That cutter, yesterday—where did it come from?"

"Right from Beaufort, Herr Kaleunt," the navigator answered, pointing to a location twenty-five kilometers up the Beaufort River. "But there is a large US Navy base at Charleston, forty-five miles north of us. They might send a destroyer from there."

"In fact it's almost a certainty," Luth said tersely.

"Once the Navy gets its suspicions raised, it's not going to let a junior partner get any of the glory. Sparks," Luth called out. "Send a blinker message to Kaleunt Wohlfarth. Tell him to station himself just north of Charleston harbor, and fire on any military vessel that leaves port and turns south toward us. Tell him to draw the Amis off toward the north. Tell Kaleunt Stolzing to continue to maintain his position outside of Port Savannah, and be prepared to draw the Amis south. Tell the men on the island we'll be back this evening. They should post guards and shoot only if the island is landed upon. And tell the men onshore what we're doing."

Luth turned to his crew chief. "Head out to sea, ten knots," Luth said causally. The crew sprang to immediately. "Take it out ten kilometers and we'll dump this Hollywood excrescence and turn ourselves back into a real U-boat."

By late afternoon, the crew had dissembled the steel-work and rolled up the canvas panels disguising the submarine as a half-scale destroyer and wrapped them in a chain. An anchor was attached to the bundle, which would not sink, and left moored in the water.

"Let's sit outside of Port Royal Sound," Luth said. "And wait to see what pops out of the coast guard station."

As Friday turned into Saturday, Luth nosed the U-1143 as close to Fripp's Island as it could get, about one thousand meters away. In case of a premature discovery, he could conceivably take all the men off the island, packing them into every nook and cranny of the submarine, and make good an escape.

Luth was watching the island in the moon light. A signal winked: "All clear, ready."

Ballard climbed out onto the bridge and took up a position next to Captain Luth. To him, the trickiest part of the operation came now. He felt a shudder and was pitched forward as the submarine ran gently aground in the shallow water. Although he could not see it clearly in the blackness of the night, he knew that on the island, the first piloted V-1b was being readied to be placed on a ramp that was still lying collapsed on the ground and was just now being lifted upright. The ramp was nearly one hundred meters long.

"Tell me again why the conventional shorter V-1 ramps can't be used?" Luth whispered to Ballard. "This dammed contraption has been hellishly difficult to set up correctly on the uneven ground."

"The conventional ramps use a very powerful steam catapult to launch the jets," Ballard said softly. "Normally the V-1 missile is accelerated at seventeen Gs to get up to a speed fast enough to make the pulse jet work. At a seventeen-G acceleration, the ramp need only be twenty-five meters long. But no pilot could stand that; he'd black out, faint and crash. The rocket boosters we have are less powerful but more portable than the steam generators."

"So we're using a rocket to start the take-off to avoid the use of steam generators, and to keep the G-force down we need to use a longer launch ramp so the jet gets up enough speed for its engine to start?"

"Exactly," Ballard said. "The pulse-jet—its called a 'ram jet' in English—depends on forward speed to ram air into the engine in order to operate. And once the ramp is up for the two scout jets, we might as well launch the other missiles on it as well.

"How much time do the scouts need to drop their beacons?"

"Only a few minutes. Flight time is about an hour. We're giving them a quarter of an hour head start because they fly slightly slower than the missiles . . ."

"But I thought without the explosives they were lighter," Luth protested. "They are, but the cockpit windscreen adds some air resistance—and they're not that much lighter—they need to carry almost twice the fuel."

245

"Because they're making a round-trip," Luth finished the sentence. He saw a blinking light from the island. "I think they're ready."

"Are the pilots dressed in German uniforms?" Ballard said, suddenly realizing a detail he had entirely overlooked.

"Of course," Luth said. "Navy uniforms, though. Not Luftwaffe."

Ballard smiled to himself. Turf. Even now, in the most unconventional battle of the war, Captain Luth was making sure that the Navy got as much credit as possible, and shared as little as possible with any other service.

Suddenly the night air was split with a loud roar. A blaze of light traversed the island from right to left, and lifted off awkwardly. A second point of light appeared, a droning sound was heard and the trajectory of the twin points of light seemed to stabilize. The spent rocket booster separated from the new bright torch and tumbled down, glowing, into the sea. Piloted by Lieut. Johnnes Richter, the V-lb turned toward the mainland and then northwest, steadily gaining altitude and buzzing off into the night.

Ballard felt his heart pumping with loud thumps. He felt sure Luth could hear it. The first scout was off, his ultimate mission was starting. As the drone of the jet died down, he heard the faint clatter of a chain winch. The second scout jet was being hoisted into place.

"What is the marker they use?" Luth asked. "How does it work?"

"As you know there are three main refinery buildings, Herr Kaleunt. One in each of three valleys. They are huge beyond imaging. Each is to receive four markers on its roof spaced about one hundred meters apart. The scout is to drop them from only ten meters above the roof. He can't miss, but we're using two scouts, each with the same mission just to be sure."

"And the markers, how do they work?"

"What they are is a heat source—like a barely-glowing coal. You can feel the light they emit as heat, but you can't see it. Each one has a top that revolves slowly, with different sized slots, creating a Morse code blinking at a certain rate."

"And the missiles can see that?" Luth asked.

"Yes. They use crude electric eyes that are more sensitive than human eyesight to infrared light, which is what heat is—light a color, or frequency 'infra'—below—red. The big eye has a wide angle view and just looks for anything that's hot and has the correct blink rate. In the center of that sensor is a smaller, narrow-angle eye. The trick is once the wide angle eye sees the correct target blinker, to turn the missile to point so that the center eye sees it. Once that's done, the missile will hit its blinker within a few meters."

"Ahhh," Luth sighed. Ballard could sense the captain was trying to think how this arrangement might be used to guide torpedoes with the same accuracy. "But how does the missile know which way to turn once the blinker has been detected?"

"The wide angle eye actually consists of several concentric rings, Herr Kaleunt, initially working together as one. The missile is always flying with a slight back and forth wedel, both to discourage flak and ambitious fighter interceptors, and to scan as wide a view as possible. Once the correct blinker code is first detected, the rings are switched over so each ring senses the blinker individually. Because of the wedeling, the blinker is seen first by one ring and then another.

"After the correct blinker code is detected, each time the image of the blinker moves from an inner ring to an outer ring, the missile changes course in the opposite direction. When the blinker moves to an inner ring of the electric eye, the missile sets the flight in that direction. In just a few moments-thirty seconds usually—the missile is oriented so that the blinker only moves between the center electric eye and the first inner ring. That's where the slight error of a few meters enters the picture. And at that point the wedeln stops, they explosive is armed and the missile heads home."

"If we are successful will this mission really stop the American uranium bomb project?" Luth asked.

"Aaah, well, it's still top secret, Herr Kaleunt." Ballard eyed the captain for a moment before deciding to continue. "But the Americans have a duplicate facility in the state of Oregon—the Haniford plant . . ."

"And that's also being sabotaged? By whom?"

"By our allies, the Japanese," Ballard said. "We sent them sixteen V-1bs in exchange for fifty of their torpedoes."

"So that's how we came to those unusual fish! We fired forty-five of them in the Atlantic. Forty-two hit their targets and blew up."

"Yes. Japanese quality is hard to beat," Ballard agreed.

A second roar and blaze of light signaled the launch of she second scout piloted by Lieut. Armin Zeisler. He turned southwest. His mission was to approach the Oak Ridge plant from the south. Both pilots would lay their markers down over the same three buildings and then head back to a rendezvous point five miles south of Fripp's Island. The drop of two blinkers for each missile assured that even if one blinker malfunctioned, another would be there to take its place, Or if one of the two scout plans malfunctioned. Once back to sea, a water landing was to be made, and the lucky pilots would be recovered by awaiting submarine. Admiral Doenitz had discussed with Luth whether or not he wished to risk his entire crew to wait for the returning pilots.

"It has nothing to do with wishing, Herr Grossadmiral," Luth had said simply. The formal Doenitz had unbent momentarily, eyed his fleet commander, and uncharacteristically patted Luth on the back. "A sentiment that expresses precisely the spirit of the German fighting man," the admiral said quietly.

Luth had ignored the compliment. "I give those poor sods less than a thirty per cent chance of getting back alive," he is said to have muttered. "I hope this is worth it."

Chapter Fifty

The launching of the two scout planes, was timed to precede the dawning of First light by one hour, and fifteen minutes—the time necessary to reach the target. Although the atomic refineries were working three shifts and would certainly not be blacked out, the roof of the plaints would not be illuminated, the roofs were so large that at night their large dark expanse could easily be mistaken for a runway or an open field. Ballard wanted to take no chances on the scout pilots missing the target.

Although the unmanned missiles would fly at one thousand meter altitude for optimum route-finding, Ballard had suggested the scout pilots fly only as high off the ground as comfortable for safe flight—a few hundred meters or so. This would reduce exposure en route.

The engine drone was unmistakable to those who had heard it but that would not include any Americans. By the time anyone up that early heard anything odd and recognized it as a possible aircraft, the jet would already have flashed by.

Try as he might, Ballard had not been able to find out what air defenses the Clinton Engineer Works possessed. He suspected there were none. The only remaining unknown was whether the scouts could drop their target blinkers the fifty feet or so to the roofs unnoticed.

Each was the size of a soccer ball. Although the devices had small parachutes, they fell rapidly to avoid drifting off course, and they would hit the roof with a loud "clunk"—a noise Ballard hoped would be drowned out by the background noise of the refinery equipment.

The first scout, piloted by Lieut. Richter flew north west towards the town of Columbia which he found easily, by following Lake Moultrie and then the narrow Lake Marion and the Congaree River. He checked off his course by means of a map folded on his lap. He continued an to Greenville, marveling at how responsively his jet aircraft handled. The fancy wings with their odd vertical tips had turned a fast but rough handling 'flying bomb' into a smooth, lithe performer. Oops, a stutter from the jet engine, but it passed instantly. The young pilot was ecstatic: a secret mission far behind enemy lines, to strike a crippling blow at the enemy's secret weapons program by using Germany's own secret weapon—the V-Ib. And he, a twenty-two year old pilot, not even out of the university before he was drafted into the Navy. The Führer was absolutely right: only in Germany could one rise so rapidly to such great opportunities.

He checked his magnetic compass. His course was 315 degrees less eight degrees for magnetic inclination, he remembered. Nudging the stick ever so slightly, he corrected his course by two degrees. Below him the faintly visible gray sea of Smoky Mountain forest sped silently by, punctuated by an occasional homestead clawed out of the woods. Do they still all wear cowboy boots? the pilot wondered.

The police chief heard the ringing of a hand crank telephone. She put her feet down from the desk one at a time and lay down the Life magazine that was covering her eyes. Reluctantly opening one eye, she peered at the switchboard. The little light was blinking over the RCA jack in the far corner. Woody Arsenault, up in the Clingman's Dome tower, reporting another forest fire, she realized. Damn! Why did he have to call so early in the morning? She plugged him in and lifted the operator's headset.

"Yeah, Woody. What d'ya got?"

"Thelma, I just saw some kind of funny airplane come shooting by, heading over to Oak Ridge." Woody's voice was excited and earnest. Not like him at all. Thelma sat, up and started to take notes. "I couldn't see any propeller and it made a funny droning sound. Flames came out the back. Had a funny shape, too. I've never seen anything like it."

"So what to you want me to do?" Thelma asked, peeved to have sleep awakened for such a incongruous event.

"Call the military, Thelma, for god's sake. It could be an attack."

250

"From a single funny-looking airplane?" she asked. Maybe Woody had just woke from a bad dream.

"Come on Thelma, I ain't kidding."

"Well who do you want me to call, Woody?" she asked crankily. She wasn't even sure the military was listed in the phone book. What would she look under? Army Air Corps? US Army Air Corps?

"The G-men, or somebody, Thelma. Hell I don't know who to call. But what if it's a sneak attack on that secret factory town, like Pearl Harbor?"

Woody had a point there, Thelma recognized. And she was the law in these parts. "O.K., Woody, 'I'll call somebody right away. You hang around in case they need to talk to you." As if he had any place to go, she chuckled. She pulled her plug out of his jack. Thelma knew the local telephone directory wouldn't have anything. It was twelve pages long and she knew every number in it by heart. She plugged into their one long distance line and rang the operator in Knoxville. "Who was going to pay for this call?" she wondered.

Chapter Fifty-One

The McGee-Tyson air field south of Knoxville had only three operation military fighters—all terribly beat-up Curtis SB2C "Helldivers." They had been used as trainers for strafing attacks, and other close air support duties to the tank crews training at Fort Knox in Kentucky. The entire rest of the squadron had been long shipped out for active duty. Why these three tired aircraft remained here was any body's guess.

First Lieutenant Charles E. Bell was Officer of the Day when he took an urgent telephone call from Washington: take off with all available forces and shoot down suspected incoming German fighters attacking the secret Oak Ridge refinery. Holy shit! Lieut. Bell needed no further urging. A chance to see some combat action at last. Just as he was certain he would be sitting out the war in this godforsaken hole with not one whit of action, in comes this emergency call to arms. It was like a miracle from heaven. He raced out to the flight deck, snagging his wing man Warrant Office Justin Youngblood, and took off in less than eight minutes. No rear gunners were available and the third aircraft would not start.

"All right, Justin," Bell said over the radio. "The fire ranger said the unidentified aircraft was coming in low, so let's keep our altitude to one thousand feet and go in on full military power."

"Aaah, Lieutenant," Justin wailed back. "If I go to full power, I'll never make it. She's heatin' up already."

"OK, Justin, I'll go in at full military power and you just mosey along after me. I'll see you when you get there."

Disgusted, Lieutenant Bell pushed the throttle to the firewall.

The distance to the huge Oak Ridge installation was only twenty miles. It would take less than five minutes to get there. The call from the ranger station had been logged in at 6:05 a.m. Washington had called twenty minutes later and they were in the air eight minutes after that. Not a bad reaction time for a back-water training base. Thank God he had been the Officer-In-Charge, working the graveyard shift. Finally something to break the monotony. With the war going the way it was, he would be unlikely to see any real combat. Maybe this would be his lucky day.

In the morning haze he saw the distant glimmer of the huge Oak Ridge processing plant. Flying over it was strictly off-limits, but this was an official military emergency. Back and forth he made his eyes systematically scan the valley in front of him. What the hell were they making down there, anyway?

Some movement caught his eye. He saw a single line of fish-like objects racing toward him at three hundred feet high, separated from each other by a mile or so, Each waggling back and forth as if they all had loose rudders. Jesus Christ, a squadron of enemy aircraft slipping in like a single file of Indians creeping up to the unsuspecting settlers. He had never seen anything like it. Suddenly one of the planes stopped wagging and tipped into a shallow dive straight for the Clinton Engineering Works.

"Mayday, Mayday," he yelled into his throat micro phone. "This is Alfa Bravo Two-Six-Niner over Oak Ridge. Have spotted a squadron of unidentified aircraft—fighter-bombers or something—making for the Clinton Engineering Works. I'm going in!"

He felt an enormous chill of excitement ripple down his spine. Combat! Time slowed down almost to stop. His mind was able to analyze the situation clearly and with plenty of time to make decisions. He was ahead of the column he had turned north to intercept. Holy Mackerel, they were moving fast. He realized in an instant that, with them flying low and fast, he had no chance of catching them once they got past him. And he had no time to drop down to their altitude. He could only nose down at them and fire as they crossed his path.

That maneuver would give him multiple opportunities, and, maybe make them break formation, too. Here came the first one about to cross low and in front of him. He pushed the stick forward, pointed the nose of his Helldiver down, aiming for an intercept point well ahead of

253

what an ordinary aircraft would require. He fired a burst and missed. "Dammit," he cursed. He spun the aircraft around for another pass.

"Lieutenant Bell," A voice spit into his ear. "I see you. I'm two miles behind. What's the situation?" It was Justin coming on to the scene.

"Justin," Bell answered. "Unidentifides at 6 o'clock from my position. Single line. Some of them seem to be going into an attack dive. They're very fast. You can't catch them. Look east to see if any more are coming. Shoot those down as they pass by," Bell ordered.

Bell saw another aircraft out his left window. It had stopped wiggling, and had entered a shallow dive. The idiot! Right into his line of fire. Bell easily lined up and fired just before the object passed in front of him. A tremendous explosion shook the air. Debris clattered on his windscreen. "Got one!" he shouted into his mike. He pulled up hard to avoid the approaching hill. Jeez, it was just like the training manuals said: the enemy pilot had been so intent on his attack he hadn't even tried to evade . . .

He turned right to reverse his cross-ways approach. Out of the corner of his eye he saw a gout of flame bursting out of the top of a long building. God, they were diving right in to the roof of the Clinton Works. Of course—they were suicide planes! The roof of the building was bigger than an aircraft-carrier landing deck. Another explosion billowed up farther away. He turned back to intercept the next attackers. Where were they? All this twisting and turning—he was monetarily disoriented.

Lieut. Bell heard a terrific whooshing sound and looked up as an enemy aircraft roared a few feet over his cockpit. "Holy shit . . ." he screamed and spun the aircraft down. He looked to the right and behind. He could see at least three more planes approaching, one after the other, imperturbable lined up like mechanical men. Other than their jinking movement, they were taking no evasive action whatever. Nor attacking him. This is not what the training manuals said was supposed to happen. It was eerie.

"Justin," he screamed into his mike. "Where the hell are you?"

"Lieutenant, sir," the voice came back. It was almost a sob. "You're not going to believe this. I had about twenty rounds on board. One pass and now I'm out of ammo."

Lieutenant Bell almost fainted at the thought. Christ that would be a court martial for sure.

"Justin," he warned. "You better do something if, you intend to make a career out of the Army."

There was a pause. "I catch your drift, sir," the voice said laconically.

Lieutenant Bell turned his aircraft around to the south, to cross the path of the next incoming aircraft. It was coming at him much faster than he expected. He saw no propeller. There was no cockpit, either! No wonder they weren't counterattacking him—they were winged missiles! Smaller than he thought, too. The planes that had passed him had a torch-like exhaust flare, visible even in the brightening morning sky. An explosive burst of light flared into view a mile east. Justin had got one after all.

"Justine," Bell said. "Did you get one?" There was no answer.

Bell's plane shook violently and began to buck. Another mystery aircraft roared by him, passing just a few yards above, but this one came from behind. God Damn-it, one of the mystery missiles was attacking him! It flashed past him overhead. God, the flame coming out of the giant tube on its back was incredible. It was a rocket plane of some kind. Something was wrong with his stick—the air craft was bucking, not responding. He looked down at his instruments just as his engine gasped and froze. His plane had been hit! The tachometer needle had swung to zero. His leg was splattered with oil. No, it was blood.

The Helldiver pitched over forward, losing speed rapidly. The ground began to come up in spite of his full back elevator control. He was only a few hundred feet above the forest. Too low to bail out. He tipped the nose further down, hoping to pick up enough speed to pull out and crash land. In seconds he dove into the forest.

After the last V-lb was launched, an enormous sense of suspended animation set in. Everything that could be done had been done.

255

Everyone was evacuated off the island and the mainland. There was nothing more to do except sit around and wait: Wait to learn whether or not Dr. Steif's engineers had done their job in building the missile as well as Frigatinkapitan Luth's men had in launching them.

The ship's crew settled into an alert watchfulness. The men moved about causally, yet not speaking. Some lit up cigarettes. Others did their laundry or repaired clothing with needle and thread. A full watch was kept for aircraft and other ships, of course, but in the absence of any identifiable threat, the atmosphere of the boat became a little dreamlike.

Ballard sat with the officers, but he found he could not enter into their mood of relaxed vigilance. A disjointed series of thoughts kept intruding into his mind, dreams almost, although he was fully awake. Yet these waking dreams interfered with his attempts to enter into the mood of the men.

Confused, Ballard retired to his cabin to sort his sentiments out. He lay down and tried to untangle the conflicting emotions roiling through his mind. They all had to do with Sabina and some great sense of failure. Failure of what, he asked himself. Failure to ask her to marry him? That was her fault. She was the one who had turned her attention to the SS fairy. And did he give a damn? He thought back to the night they met at the opera in Berlin. He had one thought in mind then—to get her into his bed. And he had done it, and the sex had been astoundingly good. And that was it. What was the sense of indefinable guilt that now plagued him?

He knew his thought processes well enough to realize that his conscious mind was trying to avoid coming to grips, with some fundamental problem. It was simply a matter of sitting down and sorting things out. What did he feel? He felt guilt over his behavior toward Sabina, shame that he had used her so cold-heartedly. But she clearly was using him, too. After all, that was what all that nonsense on Scharfenberg was about, wasn't it? She wanted the status of his foreign citizenship to elevate her station in life, didn't she? And when those plans wouldn't work, she slid into the arms of a glamorous military type, although Ballard had trouble picturing Sabina as a spit-and-polish SS wife.

Ballard snickered at the image of Sabina kissing an SS captain off to work each day and keeping an immaculate home for him to return to. It just didn't compute. But he realized at the same moment that it was not the thought of Sabina leaving him that rankled, it was the other way around; he had left her—left her in tears on Scharfenberg for reasons he could not figure out. If she was dumping him, why did she cry so in such despair? Was he being willfully blind—using the Scharfenberg incident as a convenient excuse to drop her? Now that made sense, even if he could not comprehend the logic of it.

Maybe it was her complete vulnerability that made him feel so guilty. He was taking advantage of someone who couldn't fight back. Hell, of course she could fight back! She was an expert at putting men down—he had witnessed it himself on a number of occasions.

The thought struck him that maybe—just maybe—with him, she didn't want to fight back. He flushed deeply at the realization that this was exactly what his macho pride could not acknowledge. Sabina had been in love with him and had refused to play any more games. And he was too selfish to recognize it. Or rather, he did recognize it and was too stupid to be able to respond in kind. Too immature.

His hip ached on the thin mattress. He turned over in his bunk to lay on his other side. The thought of his failure to respond to Sabina's love burned in his gut, giving him a sour taste in his mouth. But a sense of relief washed over him that he had indeed finally recognized this troubling reality. Was he really in love, too? As he always claimed to be? Lord knows he had told her often enough but was that just to turn her on for sex?

He was lying on his back, his fingers intertwined as if in prayer. Their joints ached with the pressure he had been applying. Shit, let's face it, he was like nothing less than a horny teenager leading a young, impressionable girl on. As soon as she fell for him, he got cold feet. So he subtly rebuffed her and she fell into the arms of someone more sympathetic. Could he blame her? Was she too proud to admit she was acting as vainly as he?

That idea sounded good, but the more he rolled it around in his mind, the more he realized that it didn't wash. It was pure selfishness that was to blame. He thought of no one but himself. When he acted solicitously, it was for some future gain for himself. When had he done anything in his life on someone else's behalf with no thought for himself?

His eyelids faltered. It had all been such a twisted, impossible-to-sort-out game between the two of them. He became confused again as all the chess pieces seemed to lose their bearings. Devious knights moved in straight lines, and rooks could circle their opponents and pounce from behind. Who was changing the rules?

Nothing made sense anymore. He fell into a troubled sleep, as all his powers of logic could not seem to straighten out the confusion.

PART FOUR

Chapter Fifty-Two

The exhilaration Lieutenant Richter felt was followed quickly by a sense of letdown. Dropping his twelve blinkers, four on each building complex, had been, well, too easy. His targets—the roofs of the three Oak Ridge atomic bomb refinery buildings—were huge and impossible to miss. In spite of the 85,000 employees working the plants around the clock, he felt certain no one had noticed the predawn operation. But all that preparation and training for just two minutes of work—Donnerwetter it hadn't been difficult or dangerous! He felt that secret missions behind enemy lines should at least be a little more perilous.

The lieutenant cut the throttle of the pulse jet to barely an idle. He found that by keeping the V-lb flying along the ridge lines of the foothills separating the three valleys, the rising morning thermals were keeping him aloft with minimum power. The plan was for Lieutenant Zeisler and him to drop their blinker buckets and head back to sea. But he still had slightly more than half a tank of fuel left. The job had been so easy—and yet so exciting—he couldn't bring himself to leave after just two minutes of work. He decided instead to circle in order to photograph Lieutenant Zeisler making his blinker drop. What pictures those would make! If he continued to be as economical in his flying, maybe he could even remain until the first wave of incoming missiles struck home.

Off his left shoulder he saw a puff of smoke blow out windows on the northernmost factory. The first missile had slipped in right on target; he hadn't even noticed! Where was Lieutenant Zeisler? He looked up the valley. He saw the next missile exploded in a blaze of white light. A kilometer short! It had exploded in mid-air. No—it was being attacked by an aircraft! He shoved the stick hard to the left and jammed the throttle slide forward. The engine changed from a drone to a snarling roar as the piloted missile leaped forward.

He scanned the valley in front of him. There they were—a long column of V-1bs lining up for the attack. What a glorious sight How disciplined they looked, and how graceful, wedeling back and forth in a long, sinuous file. The nearest missile suddenly straightened and pitched into a shallow dive. Its electrical eye had spotted its target—the target he had dropped in place! And there below was an American intruder—a Navy Helldiver. Richter pushed the stick forward and began a short dive.

The American was smart, Richter realized. Unable to catch up to the V-1s, he was flying back and forth across their single-file path, shooting at them as they passed by. He saw the smoke of one hit drifting out from among the trees. Then, God in heaven, the dumb fool almost ran into a missile. An explosion a few kilometers farther away indicated another flyer. Jesus Maria, how many of them were there, and how many V-1bs had they shot down?

Richter saw the Helldiver turn south, completely absorbed in his attack. He did not even have a rear gunner! Richter swung his V-1b over easily to line him up. A short burst of his twin 30 mm canon was all it took. But what quick reactions were needed to keep the target in the sights. In an instant he flared over the enemy aircraft and slowed the throttle, making a looping turn. Yes, the Navy pilot had been hit, his propeller already seized. No need to finish him off. Lieutenant Richter pushed the throttle forward again and lifted up to find the other intruder.

The German lieutenant saw a billow of flame arising out of the forest down the valley along the Clinch River. A gasoline explosion, but far too much fuel for a V-1, which would have been nearly empty. Had a missile perhaps gone after the second American's engine exhaust heat and brought him down? He seemed to remember the American advisor, Ballard, mentioning that possibility.

He checked his own fuel gauge. It was just trembling below the half-full mark. As he passed the explosion, he saw the burning wreckage of another American fighter. So this was the vaunted American Army

Air Corps defense—two aging and half-manned fighter-bombers. Ha! What a joke.

It was time to leave. Richter made a last lazy climbing turn and, looking back at the Oak Ridge complex, pulled the throttle slide back to an idle. In the central valley where "K-25," the gaseous diffusion plant lay he could clearly see three burning hits of the huge refinery. He held his Leica camera and snapped a picture with one hand. Then he put the V-1b into a straight flight attitude, maintaining course by holding the stick with his knees. The little camera required two hands to wind the film knob. He gained altitude quickly to view the southernmost valley, already filling with smoke in the clear air. It was "S-50", the plutonium factory. He took a second picture and noticed one hole in the roof with no sign of explosion. He turned briefly north to take his last photograph of the third valley complex, "Y-12," the electromagnetic separation plant. At least two hits were visible in the roof and the building was burning furiously.

Lieutenant Richter took a last satisfying look at the smoking wreckage. Except for the two that had been shot down (who could have expected that?) the jet missiles had all done their jobs perfectly. So had he in guiding them. He wheeled his craft southeastward. He had accomplished his mission and he had added another enemy aircraft to his credit. He could head back with pride and a clear conscience. Once again he had served the Führer well.

Chapter Fifty-Three

"TORPEDO ON THE PORT BOW!" the lookout yelled. The pilot slammed the engine room signal handle backwards, calling for All Engines Emergency Full Stop. The lookout saw the wake of a torpedo racing toward them. Traveling twenty feet below the surface at forty knots, the air bubbles rose at one foot per second. By the time the bubbles reached the surface, the deadly under water missile had already traveled 1300 feet closer. He saw it at 1500 feet distance. It was already too late.

The ship shuddered like a locomotive that had run off its rails. A geyser of water rose at the bow railing followed by a concussive blast. Alarm bells began clang raucously. Fire fighters raced below deck to ascertain, control and repair the damage.

"TORPEDO AMIDSHIP PORT BEAM!" the lookout cried.

"Oh shit, brace yourselves," the captain said, picking himself off the floor of the bridge. A thud jarred the ship.

"Thank God, a dud," the pilot cried.

"Hard to Port, all engines forward, flank speed," the captain shouted. "We're going after that son of a bitch. Lookout can you see anything?"

"No sir," the lookout replied without taking his eyes from the binoculars. He was on his knees with just his head above the armored railing. "Oh, wait. Periscope. Forty-five degrees off the port bow, range four thousand yards."

The captain stopped in mid-stride. "Lookout, can you still see him?"

"Yes sir. I can even see his snorkel every now and then, sir."

The captain pursed his lips in puzzlement. "Lieutenant, send a message to headquarters:"

BOW HIT BY SINGLE TORPEDO/
STOP/DAMAGE NOT YET KNOWN/
STOP/ U-BOAT SIGHTED ONE MILE
NORTH OF CHARLESTOWN HARBOR
LURING US NORTH/ STOP/WHY?/STOP/
IN PURSUIT/ STOP/CARTWRIGHT

A young ensign entered with the damage report. The captain perused it, muttering out loud. "Forward bulkhead filling with water, but compartment doors undamaged." That means we can pursue and we'll be a little slower and a little bow heavy he thought to himself. He turned to his second.

"Mr. Henderson, rig for hedgehog attack, standard pattern."

"I don't get it sir," the lieutenant said after relaying the command. "What makes you think the Kraut is trying to draw us north?"

"No U-boat I've ever seen hangs around and lets itself be seen after an attack, Henderson. Not against a destroyer. All they've got is the surprise of their first shot. After that the advantage swings heavily in our favor. We can hear him and we're much faster and better armed. All he can try to do is keep out of sonar range, duck down and find a new shooting position. Hell, we should have been hit by four torpedoes by now. That means he's shooting out of his stern tubes so he can be in position to make a run for it. He's trying to drag us up north, for sure. He's covering for something going on further south."

"But what? We don't have any report of activity . . ."

"Son of a bitch," the captain said, slapping his fist into his hand. "The missile attack on Oak Ridge—these must be the Heinies that are firing some kind of missiles at Oak Ridge, but not from hidden inland caves. They're firing them from submarines. That's it, God dammit. And they're doing it from south of here probably the closest they can get to Oak Ridge. Pilot, change course to south, south west. Mr. Henderson, you have the bridge." The captain walked into the navigation room just off the bridge. "Beaverton, let me see a chart that shows the coastline between Charlestown and Savannah."

The captain scanned the unrolled chart. St. Helena Island was midway between the two port cities, and was also the closest saltwater point to Oak Ridge, Tennessee. St. Helena consisted of desolate shoreline with four smaller islands pushing out into the Atlantic. Fripp Island stuck out the farthest and was therefore the closest to water deep enough for U-boats to operate.

"O.K. The Kraut bastards are launching their missiles, probably somewhere around Fripp's isle, and probably doing it off their subs like they did back in '42 off the coast of England."

"But sir, those were just small, unguided antiaircraft rockets," the navigator protested. "And they scared air craft away, but nothing more. They couldn't hit a thing."

"Yeah, and that was three years ago, too. But the idea is a great one Henderson. And the Krauts never leave a great idea alone. Here, give me a pad." The captain wrote out:

> CAPTAIN ANDREW CARTWRIGHT
> USN21 1. TO SHAFECOM/STOP/
> SUSPECT OAK RIDGE MISSILE
> RAID LAUNCHED NOT INLAND BUT
> FROM GERMAN SUBS OFF FRIPP
> ISLAND/STOP/CLINGMANS DOME
> REPORT OF MANNED DOGFIGHT
> SUGGESTS POSSIBLE RETRIEVAL
> ATTEMPT OF PILOT/STOP/ESTI
> MATE RENDEZVOUS 0730/STOP/
> UBOAT ATTEMPTING TO LURE
> THIS SHIP NORTHWARDS/STOP/
> AM BREAKING OFF CHASE AND
> HEADING SOUTH/STOP/REQUEST
> ALL POSSIBLE AID ESPECIALLY AIR
> CRAFT TO INTERCEPT POSSIBLE
> SECRET GERMAN MISSILE
> LAUNCHING U-BOATS VICINITY
> FRIPP ISLAND/END

"Send this off immediately, Mac Andrews," the Captain said, handing him his note.

"It will take ten minutes to encode, Sir"

"Forget the encoding," he snapped. "What are we afraid of? That Germans spies might signal Berlin what their submarines are doing?" He trod through the navigation room door and back to the bridge. "Henderson, I have the bridge. O.K., now. What's the latest word on the forward damage, and how fast are we going?"

Kaleunt Herbert "Parsifal" Wohlfarth of U-556 peered through the periscope at the retreating destroyer. "Scheisse, the Ami is not taking the bait!" He slammed the periscope down. "All right, we'll play his game. Let's get far enough away to surface. Navigator, plot a course to put us alongside Fripp Island, and get us there as fast as possible. With the hole in his bow, we might just get there before him. Next time we won't send just two fish."

Chapter Fifty-Four

Lieutenant Richter was approaching Clingman's Dome, the two thousand meter-high checkpoint in the Smoky Mountains and the highest landmark of his journey back to the sea. His pulse jet engine was purring contentedly at a near idle as the young pilot sought out one rising thermal after another. His course was to pass between it and Thunderhead Mountain to the south. Richter couldn't contain his elation at the incredible success of his mission; whether he returned alive now was incidental. He saw the fire tower on top of the mountain and turned slightly toward it, rocking his wings. He could see two large glass eyes staring back at him. Ha—the fire watch with his binoculars. Well let him gape at the latest secret German wonder weapon. When he learns what happened, he'll have something to tell his friends at the pub. Richter eased back on the stick. He was losing altitude at this throttle setting and he needed to find another updraft. His fuel supply was getting precarious, but if he continued to fly high and slow, taking maximum advantage of the morning thermals, he felt sure he would make it.

Chapter Fifty-Five

Captain Luth picked up the telephone. It was from the auto gyro they were towing, an unpowered, insect-like helicopter, whose free-wheeling rotors obtained lift by being dragged behind the submarine.

"Herr Kaleunt," the voice said fluttering fifty meters above the U-boat. "A destroyer approaching from the north at half speed. The bow is low as if they're taking on water."

"Good work, Jurgen. Let's reel you in and give him a proper U-boat greeting." Luth ordered the helicopter retrieved. The skeletal craft was quickly folded and stowed

Captain Cartwright had every available man stationed about the perimeter of his ship on the lookout for signs of submarines. He knew that this time the Germans would be much more cautious about letting their periscopes be spotted. They would pop up, take a brief look and submerge-all in a few seconds. If you weren't looking almost directly at one, you missed it. He also knew that if his hunch was correct, he was running into a certain U-boat attack. The only question was whether he could sink some of them before he himself was put out of action. A destroyer is a fearsome weapon against submarines, but only if they can be located. Otherwise it becomes prey. But if the Germans really did have long-range submarine-launched missiles, Cartwright wanted to be the first to find out about them.

Shouts from the extra men stationed to keep watch occurred regularly. Fully aware of the danger they were steaming into, and inexperienced at watch duty, they called out at nearly every distant wave crest that remained frothing in view for more than a few seconds.

"Captain, I just caught a glimpse of a periscope going down, two thousand yards, thirty degrees off the Port stern."

"You sure Scottie?" the captain asked. Everyone was getting twitchy.

"Yessir."

The captain ordered a turn to port. "Prepare to fire hedgehogs," he ordered. "Commence firing on my command." He turned to the navigator's chart and pointed to the estimated path of the U-boat. "Let me know when we've come 1500 yards on this line from our current position." He wheeled from his chair on the bridge and stepped outside to the lookout balcony.

"See it again, Scottie?" he asked.

"No sir."

"Then it's really a sub," the captain said bleakly. "Afraid they're not trying to suck us up north anymore. They're probably targeting us right now."

Kaleunt Wohlfarth swore under his breath. He was certain the destroyer would have started a Hedgehog run on the last sighting—that was American S.O.P.—a straight-line attack at any suspected U-boat, followed by another in the opposite direction. But the American had broken off this attack in order to turn south. Their attempt to lure him by showing part of the superstructure had been too obvious. Now the American suspected their motives. Wohlfarth knew he had made another mistake. He had misjudged where the destroyer was heading and had been too close when the periscope went up, An alert destroyer crew could have spotted them.

"Destroyer is turning toward us, Kaleunt," the sonar operator said. "Range 1850 meters."

"Shit. They've seen us." The captain stopped to think. The situation was suddenly getting awkward. A shot at the bow of a directly-approaching ship was damned difficult. A torpedo contact fuse was designed to hit at no more than a sixty degree glancing off-angle. And with the luck they'd been experiencing with dud fuses, a direct bow shot was a five to one chance against best. But you gave the enemy a one hundred per cent chance of learning your position, and do so staring at a destroyer's strongest offensive capability—the high-speed frontal attack.

"Navigator, plot a course to bring us alongside the north side of his approach. We'll have to shoot quickly." Shit—they would have to use the aft tubes again. He leaned over the navigation charts to see the course being plotted. They heard the distant ping of sonar bouncing off their hull. Too faint to have been detected. A distant rumble echoed through the steel hull. "Launching hedgehogs," the sound operator said, abstractly. "A thousand meters."

"PING"—a burst of submarine-seeking sonar clanged off the hull. Very loud this time. They were surely spotted.

"Come to zero degrees, flank speed," Wohlfarth said. "Depth 150 meters."

"They'll hear us at flank speed, Herr Kaleunt," the sonar man volunteered.

"They've already heard us. At least we can still try to draw him up north some more."

"He should have got here by now," Luth said tersely to his sonar man. The young man froze in place, raising his hand, index finger pointing up, to signify an intelligible sound.

"Underwater explosions, about ten kilometers north," he said.

"The destroyer is after Wohlfarth," Luth said. "Good man. He's probably sucking him back north."

"I don't think so, Herr Kaleunt," the navigator said. "Kaleunt Wohlfarth was waiting outside Charlestown. That's fifty kilometers away. These are Hedgehogs at ten thousand meters. It means a hit or near hit."

"Which means the American didn't snap at the bait, and now Wohlfarth is following him or fighting him off. This destroyer commander does not travel in the same circle as his coast guard colleague. It sounds like we'd better give Parsifal a hand."

Luth gave the order to head north at thirty meters depth. In any other U-boat, he would have surfaced to make better time. But the XXI-Type could cruise one knot faster under water—seventeen knots—than above. It could outrun underwater any surface cargo ship. And they had all heard the American's radio call for aircraft.

There was not much time left. Alone, the destroyer had a seventy-five percent chance of catching a single Type-VIIC underwater attacker. Being moderately disabled reduced those odds to fifty-fifty. But if aircraft entered the fray, that would seriously complicate matters, putting the U-boats at a fearsome disadvantage.

"Captain, U-boat contact at west eighty-five degrees, 4500 yards." It was the disembodied voice of a sonar operator.

"Got it. Henderson, steer west to eighty-five degrees," Captain Cartwright ordered.

"Yessir, west to eighty-five degrees," the first mate acknowledged. "We haven't finished the hedgehog run, sir."

"Cancel it. The Kraut is not running away from us out of fright, Henderson. He's trying to get a better angle on us. As soon as we turn towards him, he loses his chance again. He's got a choice of heading north or south to get a side shot. He doesn't want us going south, so he's probably turning north. So will we. When he pops his scope, he'll be hoping to see as abeam."

"Instead he's going to see us barreling down his throat again," Henderson replied, a grim smile on his face. The captain had more experience in chasing subs then any commander he had ever served under, Henderson thought. He would still be providing escorts for the Murmansk run, had he not been recalled due to what was politely called "taking excessive initiative." Well, they'd see whether that trait was cowboy bravado or tactical brilliance.

The navigator plotted the possible area the U-boat could be at any minute, assuming it was the standard Type VIIc with an underwater speed of four knots. Three lookouts were called to duty to scour the expected location. The hedgehogs were all aimed forward to produce the widest swath of destruction. The entire crew was poised at a hair-trigger alert.

"Periscope at two thousand yards ten degrees off the starboard bow," a voice cried out. "Confirmed periscope," a second voice shouted an instant later. Then the scope was gone. The captain waited several agonizing minutes. The silence on the bridge waiting for his command was intense.

"Hedgehogs, range one thousand. Fire at will," the captain shouted. The ship trembled with the repeated mortar-like launchings of the small magnetic-sensor mines. Ten rounds fired in a forward arc. Once armed by their short flight, they plunged into the water and sank silently. Only contact or the presence of nearby metal caused them to explode.

"A hit!" screamed one of the lookouts "Eight hundred yards directly off the bow." A small burst of water bubbled up. Hedgehogs were much smaller than conventional depth charges, and they did not explode unless set off. Water was too good a shock absorber making near misses ineffective, even with large depth charges. And with all the explosive power of conventional depth charges, sonar operators lost track of their quarry among the air and water they churned up. The silent hedgehogs let the sonar crew continue to listen for evasive action. Much smaller explosives were used and many more rounds fired. A hit meant the hedgehog had struck or passed within five yards of a U-boat, thus possibly damaging it, and certainly giving away its position.

A messenger handed the captain a report from the damage control party. The temporary repairs on the torpedo bow damage were on the verge of letting go. If the vessel continued to try to operate at full speed, it would cause the lost of the next compartment and would seriously disable the ship. Even at half speed, the repairs would not hold up for more than an hour.

The Hedgehog crew chief ordered the launchers re-aimed to circle the bubbling wake of the first hit. The small mortar rounds were lobbed into the air as fast as they could be reloaded. Occasionally, a crew would fire off another round of mines before the previous round had hit the water. At this rate they would quickly run out. But if the U-boat got them first, all the unfired hedgehogs in the world would do them no good.

The crew instantly sensed they were turning the tables on their feared and hated enemy, a feeling that quickly engendered a feeding frenzy, a lust to kill that made their spirits soar.

271

"Hit off the port bow five hundred yards," a lookout shouted. "Another hit. Wreckage sighted."

"Message from the sonar room, captain," the first mate said. "The sub is coming up."

The captain moved out onto the balcony to view the scene. It never failed to thrill him to watch a crippled U-boat surface—if it could. Most just disappeared with their crew, never to be heard from again.

Dozens of the destroyer crew crowded up to the port rail, watching the incredible scene.

"Lookouts return to posts," the captain ordered. "This Heinie is not alone. Keep a sharp watch."

U-556 was barely able to get its conning tower above the water line before men began streaming out and jumping into the sea. The stricken boat rolled heavily as sea water sloshed uncontrollably within its compartments.

Men were hurled off the conning tower as it wallowed in the ocean. Groaning as if in great pain, the boat began to settle. At the moment the conning tower hatch slipped beneath the surface, an inflatable raft was heaved into the water. A white-capped figure grabbed on and was washed into the sea as the mortally wounded craft gave a horrible sigh of exhaustion and bubbled under the surface.

"Jesus Christ, talk about getting out just in the nick of time," the captain said. "Pick the men up. Have the captain brought to me," he ordered. He stepped out on the starboard bridge balcony, now facing south. Only a single lookout was on duty on the far side.

"Goddammit," the captain, shouted. "Where are the others? These Kraut subs don't hunt solo." The lookout continued his watch without flinching. Two men came scrambling around the rail.

"Sorry sir," one of them said breathlessly. "We've never seen a German sub up close."

"Or sink," the other added, hoping to strike a note of ingratiation.

"Well now you have," the captain said sourly, "and you're both on report for leaving your posts."

"Captain," the first mate called. "The German sub commander is here."

272

Captain Cartwright returned to the bridge. He saw the white cap of the grimy young U-boat commander who gave him a respectful salute. "Captain Wohlfarth of ze U-556," he said amicably. "You fooled me."

"Are any other subs out there?" the captain asked, his expression unyielding.

"Ja, many," the commander answered: "Maybe you can signal viss—how do you say 'Fahnen'?—flegs—zat German U-boat crew goes on board zis ship."

"Good idea," the captain said. He ordered semaphore signals to be repeated every five minutes off both sides of the ship: "U-556 crew on board." He was far from giving up. In fact he was free to fire at will. But maybe the prowling wolf pack would go back to their business at hand, and he could get another chance to take some "excessive initiative." He sat down in his command chair. God, he loved battle. What would he ever do when the war was over?

"Range 2500 meters, Herr Kaleunt. He's signaling with flag . . . something 556."

Luth took the periscope in his arms. "They claim they've picked up the crew. Smart move. He's partially disabled himself, which means Parsifal probably got off a shot. Good for him. Sonar—are you sure about the hedgehog hits"?

"Jawohl, Herr Kaleunt. Three of them," the young man nodded. "And no more screw noise."

"All right, he's got our boys, or claims too. Does he want to give them back to us? What do you think, Ballard?"

"I doubt he'll do that voluntarily, Herr Kaleunt," Ballard said. "He probably doesn't want you to sink him."

"And can't do anything about it, you mean," the captain smiled. "He's a clever one this Ami. Just like you Herr Ballard. He's trying to talk us out of doing our job."

"Well, you've done it, Herr Kaleunt. If he's disabled, he can't interfere with the remainder of our mission the pickup of the returning pilots. And he has rescued the crew of the U-556. Sink him and you gain no further advantage, but you may lose the crew."

273

"Ja," Luth agreed, eyeing Ballard warily. Always the fast answer that was disconcertingly right. "But let's make sure he really is disabled." He turned to his speech tube. "Torpedo room, Make ready a T5."

"A T5?" Ballard asked.

"An acoustic homing torpedo, Herr Ballard," the first mate answered. "With short range. But it never misses a ship's screws."

Captain Cartwright gave the order to limp in as close to shore as possible and make a return at quarter speed to Charlestown Navy Yard.

"Torpedo off the aft quarter." The captain looked out the window. The pilot glanced at him desperately.

"All ahead full, sir?"

"No," the captain said picking up a speaking tube. "Evacuate the engine room immediately." He turned to his first mate. The wake of the torpedo was slithering through the water at them at a terrifying speed. "If he misses, he'll just fire another." A gout of water burst into the air and a roar shook the ship. The pilot's wheel spun uselessly.

"You can tell the semaphores to stop signaling," the captain said. "The intended party got our message." He turned to radio his location to Headquarters:

> USN211 TO SHAFECOM/STOP/
> POSITION TWO MILES NE FRIPPS
> ISLAND/STOP/SUNK U556 AND
> PICKED UP CREW/STOP/ RUDDER
> AND SCREWS DAMAGED BY SEC
> OND TORPEDO/STOP/NO IMME
> DIATE DANGER OF SINKING/
> STOP/REQUEST TOW/STOP/
> URGENTLY SUGGEST AGAIN
> ARMED PATROLS VICINITY
> FRIPPS ISLAND PARTICU
> LARLY AIRCRAFT/END

"Send this, but have it coded," he said to the messenger. He turned to the white-capped young man standing slackly at attention. "Well now Captain Wohlfarth," he said with a genial smile. "Since we're now both out of action, perhaps you'd care to tell me what you're doing here . . ."

Luth pulled his boat to five kilometers north of the V-1B pickup point. They could barely make out Steglitz in U-96, which had just surfaced to provide a target for the returning scouts.

"How much longer, Herman," Luth called to his navigator.

"The first one—Richter—should arrive momentarily, Herr Kaleunt," the navigator replied.

"Have your heard their signals, yet?" he asked.

"Twice, faintly, twenty minutes ago," the radioman answered. "But I couldn't tell if it was the same pilot twice, or each one once. They were probably on the far side of the Smoky Mountains still."

"Man the Flak gun," Luth said conversationally. "If they get here on time, the only thing that can hurt us now are aircraft." His command was shouted down the line, and three gun crews rushed through the command room to the conning tower.

"What caliber are the guns?" Ballard asked idly.

"Two are two-centimeter, one is three-point-seven," Luth answered, looking up at Ballard quizzically.

"Two centimeter is barely effective," the American answered. "By the time you do any damage, they've already dropped their load on you."

"That's true," Luth replied. "So we rely on the three point-seven for effect, and the little ones to frighten the air crews. We couldn't get everything we wanted. Maybe the coast guard will send an aircraft manned by friends of Captain Banks."

Ballard snorted.

The men stood around, keeping watch, but with little else to do. It was now 8:05, thirty-five minutes past the estimated rendezvous time of the first pilot.

"Strong signal from the scout plane, Herr Kaleunt," the radio blurted out. "If he's first pilot, Lieutenant Richter is about fifty kilometers away."

"That puts him ten minutes from here, plus five or minus two minutes—depending on how fast he's flying," the navigator said. "That means Lieutenant Zeisler is twenty-five minutes behind schedule."

Ballard marveled at how the crew instinctively supplied their captain with the answers to his unasked questions. It was a sign of near perfect teamwork. Willing and able to jump right in without the slightest self-consciousness of omitting the normal military etiquette.

"He wouldn't be returning at top speed?" Luth asked.

"Not if he's low on fuel, Herr Kaleunt," the navigator answered. "Which he must be to be out this long. In fact he's already exceeded his maximum time-in-air fuel supply. He must have done a lot of gliding."

"Richter sighted, Herr Kaleunt," the shout came from outside the conning tower.

"ENEMY AIRCRAFT!" the First Mate screamed. The crew jumped-to, ready to dive at the instant of the command.

"Take it easy men," Luth said, and then called up to the tower: "How many aircraft?"

"One patrol craft—its a PBY-4—and that's it. Oh, wait. Two more. Far away-forty kilometers. Low. Multiengine. I can't make out the type."

The radioman blurted out. "They see us, Herr Kaleunt. The patrol craft is signaling our position."

Luth clambered up the conning tower ladder and scanned the sky.

"Don't fire on the observation plane until you can't miss with the two centimeter. He can't harm us anymore, and no sense in letting them know we've got a big gun." Luth picked up a set of binoculars and scanned the horizon. "I can't see the others," he said. "Do you still have them?"

"Jawohl," both lookouts said simultaneously. "It might be a Douglas Dauntless, the one on the left, just beyond the bump on the horizon, to the left of the smoke stack."

Luth swung his binoculars around to the northwest. Where were the damned V-1 pilots? If they had only heard from the first one, it meant the second one had probably gone down. Ah, he saw him: two black dots, one on top of each other—the fuselage and the jet engine, the wings too thin to see. He was making toward Steglitz's position just ten kilometers south of them.

"Signal in the clear to land with caution, we are under enemy air attack," Luth spoke into the tube. He waited a moment and saw the V-1 turn eastward toward them.

"Look, he's spotted the PBY," Luth said. "Tell him to leave the observation plane alone. It's the ones following that we're afraid of."

But the message went out too late. Luth was astonished at how rapidly the V-1 approached the observation plane warily circling the submarine just outside of cannon fire. He saw a stutter of smoke from the V-1 and suddenly the PBY bucked and lost altitude. Smoke arose from the port side. Two parachutes emerged and billowed open just before the men hit the water. The aircraft went into a steep dive and then began to pull out. Smoke was pouring out now and an instant before it landed, a huge yellow gasoline fireball colored the air. The sea was pocked by a rain of metal parts and then exploded in a geyser of water as the fuselage hit the surface.

The V-1 passed put to sea beyond the U-boat, and began a silent diving turn.

"He's out of gas," Luth said. "Shit, he's going to land by us instead of Stolzing. Lookouts, keep a watch out for the other V-1, but don't lose sight of the two attackers you've already spotted."

Luth watched the V-1 carve a sharp descending arc around the U-boat. For a moment its wings stood exactly vertical. How it kept itself in the air, Luth wondered. The small craft flipped upright a half kilometer south of the boat. It dove steeply down and then leveled out. The craft sped silently toward the side of the U-boat, flying exactly two meters above the sea surface, its nose rising gradually, as airspeed dropped. When the nose of the small craft pointed up fifteen degrees, the pilot tipped it down and flared out. The tail of the V-1b touched first, rocking the plane forward. The nose touched the sea surface and skipped the plane back into the air. It skimmed the surface and then a huge rooster tail, of water sprayed into the air, bringing the craft to a halt in a few dozen meters. The winged missile bobbed in the water, steaming. The cockpit windscreen popped open and the pilot rolled onto the wing.

"Send a dingy out to get him," Luth ordered. "Gunners, hold your fire against the incoming fighters until I give the word. We don't want these guys to know about our artillery."

Richter waved wearily to the U-boat, the white teeth of his broad smile visible three hundred meters away in the morning light. He inflated his yellow life vest. Holding onto the open cockpit, he stood on the wing of the slowly sinking craft as the water reached up to his knees, and then his waist. A screaming bellow of steam signaled the flooding of the still red-hot pulse jet engine. The pilot pushed off the sinking craft and began paddling ineffectually toward the U-boat.

The first fighter bomber veered slightly off course, making directly for the downed V-1. Sparking from its wings was quickly followed by spouts of canon rounds hitting the water between the rescue dingy and the pilot,

"The bastard is trying to prevent us from picking up Richter," Luth shouted. "Gunners open fire."

The twin barrel two centimeter flak guns began to spit out their rounds in a high-pitched "ack-ack" sound. Instantly the, plane veered back toward the sub. Then the three point seven cm canon joined in the chorus, it's deeper, slower bark eminently satisfying.

Luth watched the tracer rounds arc up toward the Dauntless. The American plane immediately tipped on its side and broke away. Agonizingly, the tracer rounds edged toward the plane, but the gunner could not keep up with the sharp maneuver. Then Luth saw a slight wriggle of the plane followed by a burst of metal. "A hit," he shouted.

The big gun fell silent, both barrels steaming hot oil as the crew changed magazines. Luth lifted his glasses. The Dauntless had had its wing; tip shredded. To little effect. He watched the plane swing around, ready to make another pass, it's bomb bay doors opening with lethal grace.

"You nicked his wing, but he's coming around for a bomb run. Where's the other one?"

The gunners had swung around to face the new threat. The second fighter-bomber had ducked below tree-level of the shore line and completely disappeared.

They waited anxiously, every second stretching out to a minute of high tension. Suddenly it popped over the tree line of the shore and began a straight and level run broadside to the U-boat. A large tube dropped lazily from the bottom of the craft. Instantly the aircraft soared up and Turned away.

"TORPEDO BROADSIDE TO PORT!" a lookout screamed.

"All ahead full!" Luth shouted into the voice tube.

"Brace for torpedo hit." The idling diesels burst into a growling roar sending a shower of useless spray from the cavitating screws as the fighter bomber roared overhead. Black smoke fumed out of the U-boat exhaust ports. The boat began to surge forward. Luth estimated the vector of the incoming torpedo. They weren't going to make it. The torpedo hissed through the water, seeming to arc toward the rear of the now accelerating U-boat. Luth saw the lethal tube planing on top of the water. A surface runner! It struck the curved deck of the boat and bounced upward, leaping into the air with a furious whizzing of its propellers spinning uselessly in the air.

"Jesus Maria," Luth said at the astonishing sight. The torpedo had jumped fifteen meters in the air, sailing over the U-boat and plunging into the water at a steep angle. Once back in its element it tried to attain its designated depth—the surface, but it could not turn rapidly enough. It struck bottom. A rumble of water bubbled out of the sea, rocking the U-boat, and disturbing the gunners' aim.

The two men in the dingy seized Richter and plucked him out of the water. Even as he sped away, Luth waved his congratulations. He signaled by pointing to his wrist watch: we'll be back. The men looked forlorn in their tiny, crowded dingy, pitching in the vast sea. Luth turned back to the approaching first fighter-bomber. It was banking just out of range, lining up for a similar broadside. By now the U-1143 was up to full surface speed, sixteen knots.

"Hard to starboard," Luth ordered into the tube. If he was going to be torpedoed from the air, he would give the approaching aircraft the narrowest target. "Gunners, fire at will." The cannon responded instantly, pouring out three streams of explosive rounds.

The streams seemed to coalesce into a single hot arc, streaming directly into the approaching aircraft, yet nothing was happening. Dam, that puny caliber, Luth thought. It was like a nightmare—shooting the enemy at point blank range, and yet he keeps on coming.

In a momentary lull in shelling, Luth thought he saw the completely destroyed windscreen, yet the plane continued directly toward them, not flying overhead but dropping down.

"Brace yourselves, he's going to ram," Luth shouted. "All men take cover."

The gun crews raced for the opposite side of the conning tower as the second Dauntless roared directly at them. Luth could see the propeller had been shot away, as had the entire cockpit. In seeming slow motion the plane finally lost its grip on the air and plunged abruptly into the sea, sending up a geyser of water less than fifty meters from their bow, followed immediately by a series of sharp explosions. The conning tower crew was showered with water. Aircraft parts clanged on the bridge.

"Back to the guns. Fighter attack from the port side," Luth shouted. It was the plane whose wing tip had been frayed.

The gun crew had found their sighting lead and fired well ahead of the fighter. In desperate evasion, the plane dove directly into the stream of fire. A black plume of burning oil streaked from the craft as it roared overhead, its bomb bay doors still open. The guns fell momentarily silent as the fighter passed directly behind the conning tower, blocking fire. As it began to turn, it spotted the dingy and opened fired. A series of rapid step-like spouts in the water shuffled toward the bobbing raft. Luth was outraged. He could see two men diving from it. Then the heaving sea intercepted his view. He continued to stare in that direction. Tie dingy was still afloat, but only one man was in it, laying motionless. The fighter's engine, still smoking furiously, began to sputter. Abruptly the attacker turned inland, lining up on the beach. The pilot was to low to eject and could no longer gain altitude.

Flying at less than one hundred meters altitude, the aircraft, disappeared in the haze of the incoming surf.

"Enemy aircraft to the north, Herr Kaleunt. Six, maybe eight. Range thirty-five kilometers. Four engines, some of them."

` "Damned shit," Luth answered. "All right, let's pick up the men in the water, and then get the hell out of here. Zeisler isn't coming. Get below gentlemen. Hurry."

Luth jumped down the hatch in front of his men and walked over to the radio man. Send a signal to Stolzing. Tell him we're on our way out of here and he should follow. We'll meet at the prearranged point `Gerda' and contact Headquarters from there."

Chapter Fifty-Six

Ballard hovered around outside the circle of men at tending to the injured scout pilot. Completely exhausted from his flight, the hard water landing and his swim to the dingy, Richter had passed out as soon as he was hauled aboard. He knew nothing about what had happened to the two crewmen who had dived out of the dingy during the strafing attack, nor were they found by Luth's brief search. But he had taken some canon splinters in the thigh. The wound had been dressed eighteen hours ago, but now was turning ugly. The surgeon looked at Luth with downcast eyes.

"High fever, deep-set infection, Herr Kaleunt. Even if we take, off the leg, I can't guarantee he'll live."

The second V-lb pilot, Lieut. Zeisler, had not been heard from since his takeoff. Lieut. Richter had seen no signs of him or any of the blinkers he should have dropped fifteen minutes before the first missile strike.

Both garbled radio signals had been his own, the second one sent after he was not certain if he had keyed his transmitter correctly on the first signal attempt.

Captain Stolzing had waited, submerged, but with the radio antenna above water for an additional half-hour long after Lieut. Zeisler could possibly have remained aloft, even using all the fuel economy tricks that Lieu. Richter had employed. They assumed he had run into engine trouble and crashed shortly after take-off. He had gone down wordlessly, maintaining radio silence on the outward leg.

With Lieut. Richter lying in the dispensary bunk moaning in pain, Luth noticed that Ballard was in a state of high agitation. He paced back and forth in the small confines of the control room. His hands fumbled around in his pockets. He sat down. He stood up. Finally he reached into his pocket and pulled out two glass vials. "Here," he said brusquely to the ship's doctor. "Inject, him with this."

"Was?" the older man said. "What is that?"

"Penicillin," Ballard answered. "My entire supply."

"How do you get such a shiny, nail-new American wonder drug?" the doctor asked, astonished.

"You better not waste any time Herr Doktor," Ballard said evasively. "He'll need every bit of it, and that's really all I have."

Ballard found Luth staring at him with troubled eyes. "I won't ask you how you came to such a precious commodity," the captain said. "But having that miracle medicine, what brings you to make such a personal sacrifice for Lieutenant Richter whom you hardly know?"

"I'm just beginning to learn that I've got to stop thinking only of myself," Ballard said bitterly. "At my age it's a hard lesson to learn."

Chapter Fifty-Seven

Ballard escaped from the festivities of the Abwehr reception as quickly as manners would permit. The Führer had called to inform the Admiral that the strange Mr. Ballard would be publicly decorated once again for his outstanding services to the Reich. Grossadmiral Doenitz would personally decorate Frigattankapitan Luth. Ballard had hardly been able to keep a pleasant outward, appearance at the Abwehr reception. Even Inge was surprised at his rapid departure.

As soon as Ballard closed the door of his apartment, he threw himself spread eagle on his bed. Thank God, no more sleeping huddled in that tiny bunk, pressed in on three sides by cold metal. No more weeks-old stench of fifty-seven sweating men; no more eating wurst and cheese with dense commissary bread day after day. He would have his next meal at the Neva Grill with . . .

The image of Sabina sprang into his mind's eye like a Broadway billboard. He squirmed and tried to shut it out. But it only illuminated all the brighter.

"She doesn't love me," he shouted. "She's hot for her SS dance instructor."

He rolled off the bed and went to the cupboard to pour himself a drink. He slugged it down but Sabina did not disappear.

As the alcohol in his empty stomach rushed to his brain, it brought along the stunningly simple resolution to the problem: he loved her desperately. Why could he not just admit it? She was not just the world's greatest lay, which is how he treated her in the past. Angry at her only for cutting him off. He wanted her more than anything else in the world. Say it out loud, for Christ's sake. "Sabina, I love you!" he blurted out to his pillow. Tears of shame welled into his eyes at the realization of how desperately stubborn he had been in refusing to admit he was not in complete control. That he could not just take her or leave her. And the excuses he used to prop up his adolescent machismo. And all the while I've been using her: using her for sex; using her for companionship. Even beating around the bush about marrying her just to get her heated up.

He sloshed down the rest of his drink. "I want her more than anything else in the world," he said aloud, realizing the truth of the matter with a precision that cleared away all impediments to action. He grabbed his jacket and bolted down the stairs.

Ballard drove past the dowdy apartment buildings slowly, looking for number fifty-two. He was thankful for the fact that in Germany, all buildings must be clearly numbered with the official blue porcelain metal shields with white numbers and hung so as to be easily visible from the street. But this neighborhood was rather decrepit, and the numbering scheme seemed mired up. Then he saw the problem—because of a center island, the street numbers ran down one side of the street and up the other side! More great German logic!

Apartment 2B, he recalled. 2B or not 2B. In Europe the second floor meant two flights up, the "first" story being the first one above ground level. He rang the bell. No answer. He rang the bell again and waited. He felt nervous, What was he going to say? That he had been an idiot? Could he joke about it? Would Mrs. Pergolesi be so kind as to accept the humble apologies from a foreigner too backward to know the proper social graces? Would she even care? What if the mother answered? She would resist letting him in. Or even telling Sabina he had called! He rang the bell again. It was certainly loud enough.

"You can ring the bell all day long, buddy," a voice slurred out from a door across the hall. "But that's not going to open the door, especially for them."

"What? Why not?" Ballard asked. The door across the hall was open by a slit.

"She got taken away. Last month."

"Taken away?"

"Yeah," the voice slurred. "You know—resettled."

"Resettled?" Ballard said, puzzled. "But that's only for Jews."

285

"No shit," the voice said. "Say, you wouldn't have a drink on you, would you?"

Ballard felt his stomach churn into a maelstrom of pain. "You mean Pergolesi, the Italian lady, is Jewish?"

"How about a Reichsmark for a drink," the voice said plaintively. "It might be an aid to my memory."

Ballard fished into his wallet. He pulled out a five-mark coin and held it up between thumb and forefinger.

"Five marks if you tell me all."

"First the money," the voice whimpered.

"First the information," Ballard said firmly.

"Are you Gestapo?" the man said, moving partly out from behind the large oaken door.

"Do I look like one of those animals?" Ballard asked wearily. "I'm a friend of the family, trying to find out what happened to them."

"Well then, you know, the old lady was born 'Freund,'" the fat man said. "As Jewish as they come. She married a German, Stellmann, so the young one is a half-breed. Then the old man died. His body wasn't cold when the daughter married that Italian count, or whatever he was, and both of them took on his name—Pergolesi. Thought that would keep the Gestapo off their backs. Fat chance of that."

"Where did they go?" Ballard asked, twirling the large coin.

"I know," the fat man said, his eyes piggish with greed. "But first give me the coin."

Ballard flipped it expertly, but the man made no move to catch it. Unlike Americans who had grown up throwing and catching baseballs by the millions and who took for granted the extraordinary eye-hand coordination that nationwide activity developed, the Germans only played soccer. The man shielded his face and the coin clanged to the floor. He darted out of the doorway to fetch it.

"Hey, you don't have to throw it . . ."

Ballard grabbed him and spun him around shoving his back against the wall. Ballard smiled at him expectantly.

"They got taken to Ravensbruck, far's I know. You know, the 'resettlement camp' north of here. First the old lady, four or five months ago. Then the daughter last month. That's it. That's all I know. Really," he snuffled.

"Damned shit," Ballard said grimly. He bounded down the two flights, but quickly came to a halt. I'm racing off. But what can I do now? he walked back to his car slowly, lost in thought.

Chapter Fifty-Eight

Once again Ballard found himself standing slackly at attention among a line of soldiers to receive a decoration from the Führer. There had been much discussion of what medal it would be possible to give him. The previous deutsche Ordnung was already the highest civilian medal available. The Office of Aryan Heraldry was summoned, quickly conjured up a new award—the Zum Ehrendienst medal—a medal of honor, to be made available in several versions. Ballard's was to be of bronze, thus leaving room for two more grand feats in versions of silver and gold. Should Ballard in a single stroke vanquish the Americans and the Russians, and save Hitler's life at the same time, the gold version of the medal could always be additionally bejeweled (as was the Knight's Cross) with oak leaves, swords and then diamonds.

Hitler sidled up to Ballard with a slight limp. He had stumbled during an inspection tour and his knee was still sore. Ballard was astonished at how rotund the Fuhrer had become.

"So Herr Ballard," Hitler said softly. "Do you have any more fantastic schemes up your sleeves?"

"The most fantastic scheme of all, mein Fuhrer. I hope to get married soon," Ballard said with some hesitation. "It's just that I have a small problem."

"Which is?" Hitler asked, peering at the tall American with good-humored puzzlement. Marriage was good. Having lots of children was good.

"My wife-to-be and her mother are currently guests of Herr General Heydrich's . . . ah . . . establishment at Ravensbruck. If there was any way they could be released into my personal custody; I would do my utmost to assure that another great event could occur to help bring the war to a speedy and successful conclusion."

"You don't say," Hitler said with chilling lack of enthusiasm. He was sorry he had asked. Everyone always wanted something. Ravensbruck was Gestapo territory. They didn't make many mistakes. Now he would risk going against the wishes of one of his most loyal and efficient generals. Why didn't these underlings get along, see eye-to-eye? Work things out amongst themselves. Why did everything always have to be decided by him? "I suppose you've talked to Secretary Bormann about it?"

"Herr Bormann accepts General's Heydrich's arrangements until ordered otherwise by you, mein Führer."

"Yes. As he should," Hitler said, pinning the new medal on Ballard's chest, at arm's length, remaining back so as to be able to see more clearly. "Well, I don't know . . ."

A thought struck Ballard. "I have another small miracle that you might make personal use of, mein Führer," Ballard volunteered. "If you could spare a few minutes after the ceremony, I'd like to show it to you."

"You've always got something up your sleeve, don't you, Herr Ballard," Hitler said disgruntled. But the idea of another "miracle" was not unattractive. Particularly coming from this American. He had a good track record. Wars were won and lost on miracles, Hitler realized. And one for him personally, hmmm. Well, it might be worth a few minutes. If it didn't pan out, he would send the skinny foreigner back to Canaris and let him dream up another scheme. His record was pretty good so far, in spite of Bormann's obvious attempts to discredit him. In fact that made his feats even more believable.

"Remain here after the ceremony, Herr Ballard," Hitler said as he decorated the soldier next to him. "And we'll see about your 'little miracle.'"

Ballard was ushered into the same meeting room as before, when he had shown Hitler Einstein's letter to President Roosevelt concerning the atomic bomb. This time Bormann was not present.

"Well, what is it this time, Herr Ballard," Hitler asked impatiently.

"Mein Führer," Ballard said. "My arms can no longer hold a newspaper far enough away to read it. Yet I am wearing a pair of invisible glasses that let me read perfectly. I'd like to show them to you, and you may try them on. If they fit, you too could read any print easily. And no one could possibly know you are easing the slight eyestrain that becomes inevitable with age."

Hitler moved directly in front of Ballard and peered into his eyes. Ballard recognized his sweet smell. "I don't see anything in your eyes," Hitler said skeptically.

"They're difficult to see," Ballard replied. "And no one will possibly suspect you're wearing anything. But watch closely."

Ballard carefully pinched his eyeball with thumb and fore finger and lifted a clear, soggy flake from its surface smaller than a Pfenning coin.

"This is tiny piece of artificial material"—there was no German word for 'plastic' yet—"that lays imperceptibly on the eyeball and acts as a tiny lens. Tear fluids can pass though it. After a few days of practice, you don't even realize you're wearing it." Ballard lay the tiny object on his palm and poked at it. It unfolded and assumed a clear, hemispherical shape.

"It's called a contact shell," Ballard continued smoothly, using German words that most closely corresponded to what he knew Hitler would be thinking of at the sight of the tiny hemisphere. "I'm not sure whether this one has precisely the corrective power you would be most happy with, mein Führer. But like you, I'm slightly far-sighted, so it should be close. If you'd like to try it now, you could see."

"And if they work as you claim, what then?" Hitler asked, not sure of the value of this particular miracle.

"Why you would be welcome to have these, mein Führer," Ballard replied. "They, and a spare set I will also give you are the only ones in the world. And I would have to go back to wearing glasses. Which I would do gladly," he added.

"How do I do it?" Hitler asked, uncertain about letting the odd foreigner get so intimate with him as putting something in his eye. He knew there were plenty of quacks around. Every time his own Doktor

Morell gave him an injection to increase his vigor, or to let him sleep, he had warned him about falling into their clutches.

"If you could send for a glass of water, I could rinse this off and lay it on your eye. In a few seconds you could tell if they fit you." Ballard stepped back slightly so as not to give the impression he was pressuring Hitler.

Hitler lifted the telephone and ordered a glass of water. Within a minute, Bormann was at the door.

"Ah, thank you, Herr Bormann. My throat is so dry. The American and I will finish our conversation shortly, and. I will join you then." It was a polite dismissal.

"Mein Führer, it will feel a bit odd, even slightly uncomfortable to have something put, in your eye, but I assure you that if you wait just a minute or two, your eye will get adjusted to it." Ballard sloshed the tiny lens in the water and bade Hitler to sit down and hold his head back.

"Stare at the ceiling, mein Fuhrer," Ballard crooned. He leaned over Hitler and held his eyelids apart with thumb and forefinger. Gently he lay the contact lens on the exposed eye ball: Hitler blinked once reflexively, and then kept his eye open.

"OK, blink once again, please," Ballard said, seeing that the lens was not centered on Hitler's cornea. Hitler blinked and the lens centered itself. He looked around the room.

"Nothing," he said, staring hard at Ballard.

"Just look at this," Ballard said. He pulled out a photograph of him and Sabina at the Teglersee. On the back, written in her tiny script, was a caption: "Robert and me on a sunny day in August, 1942."

"Donnerwetter," Hitler muttered, closing one eye. "I can read it. Easily, even. But with one eye only."

"Let's try the other shell," Ballard said, plucking out his other contact lens.

Hitler pushed Ballard's hand away when he tried to hold his eyelid open. "Just put it in," Hitler bade him.

Ballard looked at Hitler's bobbing Adam's apple. If he had a razor in his hand, would he have the courage—right now—to slit the man's throat? No, he would not, he realized. Not without any chance of escape. As Ballard dropped in the other lens, Hitler's eye twitched slightly, but did not blink. Then he blinked twice, slowly, deliberately. He lifted the photograph to his view.

"Sabina," he said. "Is that your fiancée?"

"Yes, mein Führer. Pergolesi is her name. Stellmann is the family name. And her mother Anna Stellmann, was born 'Freund.'"

"Jewish, of course," Hitler said, eyeing the photo. "Some of their women are quite attractive . . ."

"And only a half-breed for the daughter, mein Führer, according to Standisampt records," Ballard added quickly. God, it was mortifying to beg for her life like this and at the same time pretend to be genteel. As if she was a pet being put out for slaughter because of a question of the pedigree. "And by marriage she would become an American. I'll gladly remove them both from the Reich." He moved away from the sitting dictator.

"You must take the shells out every night and let them soak in a cleaning solution, mein Führer," Ballard continued. "Otherwise your eyes will become irritated. And the shells must never dry out. This is very important. If you could have Herr Doktor Morell get in touch with me, I will gave him the formula for the cleaning solution. They are rather delicate. If anyone tries to analyze them, they will be destroyed, I'm sorry to say."

Hitler walked around the room, blinking his eyes methodically. "I can feel them, like an eyelash in my eye," Hitler said. "But not at all bad." He moved to the door. Opening it, he called to Bormann. "Get me a newspaper and bring a pad."

Hitler held his hands out in front of him, examining his fingernails as if he was seeing them for the first time.

"Wear them only for an hour or two today, mein Führer. Then each day an hour longer. If they bother you, or sting, take them out and give your eyes a rest. After a few weeks, you should be able to wear them for extended periods of time—even all day. As long as you always clean them over night."

Bormann entered with a worried expression. "The paper is only from yesterday, mein Führer . . ."

"That doesn't matter. Here watch this." Hitler held the paper at a normal distance and began to read rapidly.

"'Reichminister Göring announced today that a new secret 'vengeance weapon' had been used against the American aggressor, catching him completely unawares and striking a mortal blow to their own secret weapons program, a form of radiation poisoning, which is in direct violation of the Geneva Convention. Foreign experts—that means you, Herr Ballard—have estimated the damages done to the Oak Ridge weapons complex in the states of Tennessee and Oregon to have exceeded ten millarden Reichsmarks.'"

Hitler looked up at Bormann. "So, what do you say to that, Herr Deputy Secretary?"

"I..I don't understand, mein Führer. How . . ."

"Mesmerism," Ballard, volunteered. "I have the power to make people see what's there, or what isn't."

"Hah!" Hitler barked out in a single laugh. "Ja, that's it, Herr Ballard. You have hypnotized the Führer to see with the eyes of an eagle. Now then, Herr Bormann, see that the two women that Mr. Ballard says have been guests of the Reich are allowed to complete their stay at the Ravensbruck facility. He wishes to be allowed to marry the daughter and send her immediately out of the Reich as an American citizen by marriage, along with her mother. Is that correct Herr Ballard?"

"Oh, yes, thank-you, mein Führer. That is absolutely correct. Thank-you so much. You won't regret it, I promise you." Ballard felt faint with elation. He had made his sale. He knew he needed to exit gracefully, and as quickly as possible.

"What are you making such a face for, Herr Bormann?" Hitler asked, blinking his eyes. "This simple request of mine doesn't please you?"

"Oh, no mein Führer. Whatever you wish. I'm sure it will be fine with Herr General Heydrich. But . . . ah, I'm afraid one of the women—I don't know which one—was shot while trying to escape. The other is very weak."

Ballard was not sure he had heard correctly. He felt his spirits crash into an abyss of helplessness. A squirt of urine passed into his pants. Good God, no, not too late! He had abandoned Sabina and she had been killed trying to get back to him. Ballard felt the room begin to spin. He sat down, his head bowed, fighting to keep from bursting out into tears.

Ballard could not concentrate on what was going on around him. He felt the room spin. A stiff hand pawed his shoulder, awkwardly trying to console him. He heard Hitler tut-tutting something, " . . . everything in our power, to discover the fate of the remaining person and turn her over to you by . . . tomorrow—is that possible, Herr Bormann? Yes, by tomorrow, or Wednesday at the absolute latest. Well, I'm sorry to hear of this tragic news, Herr Ballard, but, ah, thank you for the, ah, hypnosis, and Herr Bormann will show you out."

Hitler turned and left, followed by his faithful secretary, When the door clicked shut, Ballard could no longer contain himself and burst out into uncontrollable sobbing. He felt a yawning sense of revulsion at himself, a recognition that he had failed the simplest test of a human being—that of being loyal to his friends—and especially to the one who loved him. He had been blinded, blinded by the thrill of exercising power, as blinded by the lust to control events in the world as the worst Nazi war criminal. It was this damned time travel business, the apotheosis of his genius, that had seduced him from all vestiges of humanity. He felt like wailing for forgiveness but the only one who could forgive him was dead. He had failed all by himself. He realized he was nothing but a shameless braggart, the lowest of creatures, unworthy of Sabina's love or anyone else's.

Ballard picked himself up and left by the rear door. The SS sergeant on duty looked up from his book for a split second, and, recognizing Ballard, paid him no heed.

Ballard climbed the stairs to retrieve his Swiss Army Knife. It was made of carbon not stainless steel he had discovered, and needed to be kept lightly oiled to prevent rust. That meant it needed to be wiped clean before being used to cut fruit, and the oil stained his pants pocket. Convenience, he realized. That was single most telling difference between the 1940's and the 1990's. Nothing was convenient in the 1940's; everything was such an effort.

His thoughts returned to Sabina and her mother. What was he going to do with an old Jewess in Berlin—one who would to her dying day blame him for the death of her daughter? What, in fact, was he going to do with himself?

Chapter Fifty-Nine
JULY 20, 1944

Claus Philipp Maria Schenk Count von Stauffenberg entered the bathroom of Lieutenant Colonel von Freyend, a member of the staff at Hitler's Wolfschanze command post in east Prussia. With his aide, Lieut. von Haeften, Stauffenberg had asked to change his shirt and freshen up before entering Hitler's briefing. He limped in, carrying; his heavy briefcase stuffed with maps and situation reports, his aide following behind.

As soon as they entered, the aide made sure that no one had followed them and then secured the door.

While Stauffenberg struggled to change his shirt and wash up—his right arm was no longer functional due to a recent war wound which also left him blind in one eye and with a damaged leg—the lieutenant ferreted out one of two powerful bombs and repacked it in the count's briefcase—removing a number of superfluous papers to make room. Around the bomb had been taped a series of small glass flasks. The flasks were a last minute addition suggested by their Abwehr contact, Colonel Oster.

Standing up, he helped the count get into his uniform and buttoned him up. He straightened his black eye patch and looked straight into his remaining good eye.

"Everything's set to go. What's the schedule?"

The count looked at his wristwatch. "It's now or never," he replied. "Los."

Lieutenant Haeften placed the metal vial between the jaws of a pliers and squeezed, breaking a lead foil seal separating a small amount of concentrated sulfuric acid from a metal band restraining the spring-loaded firing pin of the bomb's detonator. Silently, the acid began to attack the metal band. It would take ten to fifteen minutes.

There was no turning back; Stauffenberg had to work fast. He strode vigorously across the yard to the briefing hut. Several junior officers offered to carry the obviously cumbersome briefcase, but the count curtly refused their help. The daily briefings were generally held in the map room, and today was no exception.

As Stauffenberg entered, the briefing was already in progress. Various staff personnel were coming and going, as their presence demanded. General Keitel murmured to Hitler that Stauffenberg had arrived to give his report, and Hitler greeted him perfunctorily.

Standing next to Hitler, General Heusinger was in the middle of his briefing of the situation on the eastern front. Stauffenberg attempted to push his way, to the table, to get as close to Hitler as possible, but Colonel Brandt, Heusinger's staff officer, stood in the way. After some minor jostling, Stauffenberg managed to place his briefcase under the right half of the map table less than two meters from Hitler. He withdrew unobtrusively.

Hitler interrupted Heusinger's monologue with a question about the status of an actual fighting unit. General Heusinger could not see the location on the map spread out on the table that Hitler was so adamant about. Ever since the Fuhrer's eye sight had been magically transformed—some say it had something to do with the American magician the Abwehr owned—he seemed to be making a point of proving he could see details with the eyesight of a thirteen year old virgin. Heusinger was damned if he was going to give Hitler the satisfaction of having to put on his reading glasses. He attempted to lean forward over the map. A briefcase blocked his footing. He pushed it sideways, up against the massive partition that acted as a table-leg.

Back outside Count von Stauffenberg walked rapidly to meet with General Fellgiebel at a nearby shelter. Both men tried to look nonchalant as they waited for the acid to etch its way through the detonator restraint.

Minutes later, at 12:45, a powerful explosion rocked the compound. Next to them; someone joked about the propriety of setting off a mine so close to the Fuhrer's compound. At that moment Colonel Haeften's car arrived as ordered. Stauffenberg entered it and the men drove off, passing within fifty meters of the briefing room.

The entire front half of the building had caved in. A greenish mist was seething round the blown-out windows.

"Slow down," he said. He saw two adjutants stagger out of the wreckage. They held out their hands in front of them as those of blind men hoping to avoid walking into a wall.

"The mustard gas seems to have worked," Haeften said, smiling grimly. He pulled the car away sharply.

At the south gate, a sentry stopped the car. "I am sorry Herr Graf von Stauffenberg. The compound is sealed off by orders of the commandant. No one is to enter or leave."

"I have a flight that is scheduled to leave Rastenburg Airport at 1:15," von Stauffenberg retorted angrily. "The commandant has given me specific permission to leave. Get him on the telephone immediately."

Stauffenberg was well known at the Wolfschanze. When the commandant was not found, Captain of the Guards von Moellendorf gave the sergeant permission to let the count pass. They were out! Haeftenger mashed the gas pedal to the floor. With Hitler dead negotiations for an armistice to this terrible war could begin.

Chapter Sixty

The SS detachment guarding the Wolfschanze sprang to seconds after the explosion rent the air. Feldwebel Werner Voelker was the first to dart into the briefing room building. The inside was a shambles of split wood and shattered glass. By all appearances, no one could have survived this blast uninjured. He darted into the map room, his eyes watering and burning with pain. There, lying in a pile of furniture were the map room occupants. Some lay still, others were writhing in pain. One man was on his hands and knees.

Sgt. Voelker sprang to the man on his knees—it was the Führer! He held out his hand, but the pain in eyes become. intense. They watered so furiously he could hardly see. He rubbed them viciously, then blinked away the tears and grabbed the Führer's arm. The Führer looked at him dumbfounded, still in a total state of shock. Voelker pulled him to his feet. Then his desperately watering eyes glazed over and he could see nothing.

He pulled the Führer in the direction of where the exit should be. He could still make out the faint light of the entrance. Next he realized the Führer was guiding him. Fresh air hit his lungs; he had not realized how fiercely his lungs were burning. People were running around shouting. "The Führer is alive. Hardly injured at all. God is certainly watching over him." One voice said. "My god, his eyes look at his eyes." Voelker heard another man next to him mutter to some one else: "Will you look at the Führer's eyes—like two clots of phlegm."

In the tumult Voelker felt the Führer's arm being removed from his own. "Voelker, you're a hero," a voice he did recognize, blurted out. "You've saved the Führer's life!" someone shouted at him.

"Wunderbar," Voelker coughed. "But my eyes are killing me. I can't see a thing."

Chapter Sixty-One

Ballard sat by the window of his apartment in Weissensee overlooking the small pond across the street. The pond was a part of the small park that also contained the "Gymnasium" a public school of grades 5 through 13.

There was little traffic on his little street-the Woelkpromenade. Every twenty minutes an autobus, would pass by the connecting street down the road.

Occasionally a truck might drive by toward the nearby cemetery, or—very rarely—a taxi. Ballard hardly noticed the Mercedes driving along slowly until it stopped in front of his apartment. Some big shot no doubt, stopping off to visit his mistress.

The driver of the car jumped out and ran to the rear curbside door. A big shot all right, Ballard mused. Only people paid out of personal purses jumped to with such alacrity.

An SS corporal, he noticed. No wonder. And Totenkopf at that. Ballard awoke from his reverie in a flash. It must be Frau Freund-Pergolesi, being dropped off at his flat. Good God, where was she to sleep? Ballard had been feeling so sorry for himself, he had done nothing useful since his meeting with Hitler. Except to get himself fitted with a pair of reading glasses.

Wearily he turned from the window and made his way down the stairs. Just as the front bell rang, he opened the massive oak door. Standing there was an officious SS officer with clip board. The old woman, head bowed, stood meekly behind him, followed by the corporal.

"We seek one Herr Robert Ballard," the officer said in clear, perfectly-accented high-German. He and his spit-and-polish was straight from central casting.

"Then you've found him," Ballard said morosely. "Where do I sign?"

"This woman has a residence permit for only thirty days," the officer continued. "Here is her exit visa, made out in the name of Frau Ballard, and her Standesampt permission to marry, a waiver of the race laws and Marriage Banns, and a protection notice of the Geheimpolizei, also good for thirty days. After that, if this woman is found in Germany, she will be immediate1y arrested and resettled. Permanently. Sign here please."

Ballard signed in stupor. Marry the mother. Right. What had they not screwed up, these clowns?

"Heil Hitler!" the officer saluted him. Reflexively, Ballard returned the salute. He turned to face Frau Anna Freund. The officer stepped around the sunken woman and quick-marched to his car—a smirk of pride on his face that, in spite of the quality of the audience, he had been able to carry out his, duty to the letter.

The stooped woman who raised her head to look up at him was not Anna Freund, it was Sabina.

She looked up at Ballard with the wide eyes of a dog that had been beaten regularly, and yet still, inexplicably, returned to its master. Ballard felt his legs grow weak.

"Sabina!" he gasped. "My God, my darling Sabina. I was expecting your mother. I was told you had been shot." He grabbed her shoulders to make sure it was really her. He fell onto his knees on the brick front porch, and clutched her waist, pressing his head into her belly to keep the earth from spinning around him.

"Sabina, my darling. I love you. I love you. I've been a terrible, unforgivable asshole, I know. Please, I beg your forgiveness." Tears flooded his eyes, and he held on to the woman's waist with a frightening grasp. She felt so frail. When she remained silently immobile, he looked up at her face, unable to see anything through the flood of tears. He released his grip. What right had he to hold this woman? If she deigned to speak with him at all, it would be a privilege for him to listen.

"Robert," a voice said. "You don't seem yourself."

"I am not myself, Sabina, darling. I am a different man altogether. I swear it. I beg you to forgive me for realizing—much too late, criminally too late—that I love you, and that I've treated you abominably."

"Robert," she said weakly. "Are you sure you're alright?"

Ballard supported the arm of the wan Sabina up the stairs and into his apartment. She had circles under her eyes and she walked, it seemed to him, with a slight hesitation, as if she was suffering from sore muscles. She had to stop at the landing to catch her breath. A thousand confused thoughts boiled in his mind—thoughts about what he should say, how he should apologize about his treatment of her, to commiserate about the death of her mother, whether she would marry him, where they should go.

"Have you eaten Sabina? Are you hungry?"

"If I could have some soup, Robert" she said without looking at him. "And then some sleep. I'm absolutely exhausted."

He quickly heated up some canned chicken soup. When he returned to the living room. Sabina lay in an armchair, fast asleep. He lifted her up. She seemed even lighter than before—and carried her to the bed. He lay her down and took off her shoes. They were terribly cheap, he noticed, without a label, a travesty of the stylish shoes Sabina usually wore. He realized with a slight shock that they were probably made by the inmates of Ravensbruck.

He loosened the collar button of her blouse and, still fully clothed, spread the cover over her. It was 4 p.m. He kissed her gently. Perhaps she would nap a few hours and then they could talk. They really needed to talk.

Without knowing why, Ballard found himself embroiled in cleaning his apartment. He began by rolling up the living room rug and washing the floor—something he couldn't recall every having done in his life. He looked in on Sabina, asleep in the same position he had left her. He washed every window, inside and out. "Mathematical genius for hire; does windows" he thought to himself with bitter irony. He took his Swedish Electrolux vacuum cleaner and vacuumed the rug from east to west and then again from north to south. It was 6:30. He looked in on Sabina who had shifted her position to sleeping on her right

301

side—the side she slept on next to him. He cleared his throat, but got no response, so he started cleaning his kitchen.

It was after eleven before Ballard finished in the kitchen. He had cleared out all his cabinets and scrubbed them thoroughly. In the back of the overhead cabinets, he discovered ancient dried herbs, pencils, matches, candle stubs, paper clips, rotted rubber bands, a small kitchen knife, pen quills, the entire detritus missed in twenty years of superficial cleaning. He returned all the dishes, pushed back the oven which he had cleaned behind, inside and out.

He washed up and entered the bedroom. Sabina was on her right side and purring. He sat down on top of the bed and put his hand on her. No, he could not bring himself to touch her yet. He was not worthy.

Ballard went to the closet and pulled out a blanket. He lay down on the living room couch and was asleep in an instant.

The next morning Ballard awoke with start at 6 a.m. He tried to maintain a drowsy state, hoping to stretch-out the time before he got up to a decent hour, but it was no use. Sabina was back, sleeping in the next room! They were to get married, had to get married by the Führer's order! He brightened at the thought.

Ballard knocked gently on the bedroom door. Hearing no answer, he peered inside. Sabina was lying on her back, the covers twirled around her, still fast asleep. Ballard rolled her over to unfurl the covers she had wrapped herself up in, and recovered her smoothly. He kissed her gently. She smelled of stale cooking fat.

He made himself a hasty breakfast of sausage and yesterday's rolls, and then started on the bathroom. He used steel wool and soap powder and scrubbed down—God, he never realized how filthy it was—every square inch of the enormous bath tub. He was cleaning the outside of the toilet bowl when he heard a nose. It was Sabina, standing in the door way in a full-length cotton night shirt.

"May I use the bathroom, Robert?" she asked softly.

"Of course, yes. I just cleaned the tub." Ballard said proudly. "Are you hungry? I can go to the market and get breakfast."

"I'm simply starving" she said. Tenuously she stepped forward and touched his arm. He saw her eyes fill with tears. He seized her in his arms and hugged her gently, afraid if he clutched her too tightly, something might break.

"Oh, Robert," she said. He felt her body convulsing with sobs.

Shaken and unable to say anything, Ballard excused himself to run to the market. As he stepped outside, he noticed a man sitting on the park bench throw his newspaper into the wire trash bin and saunter casually away.

To give Sabina plenty of time to bathe and get dressed, Ballard walked, rather than drove to the food black market at the back of the Reichleben & Sons Hardware Store. Frau Reichleben cast a harried, appreciative glance at one of her most regular customers.

Back in the kitchen he fried up a half-dozen "mirror" eggs—eggs sunny-side up. They had been bartered for thirty American cigarettes. He discovered that he too was ravenous. He threw in the wonderful German bacon—so pure that it could be eaten raw with no fear of trichinosis. He heated their plates and four large 'Knüppeln' rolls in the newly-cleaned oven.

"Sabina, darling," he called as he set on the dining room table a meal that, despite of the easing of rationing, the average German family had not eaten in years.

She appeared now wearing her bathrobe. Her eyes grew large at the repast spread out in front of her. But she fingered the front of his shirt shyly.

"Robert, I've been a terrible, stupid fool, and I wish to apologize . . ."

"You apologize to me?" Ballard exclaimed. "Sabina, darling. You certainly have nothing to apologize to me about. I'm the complete idiot who . . ."

"No, Robert," she said firmly. "If I hadn't been so paranoid, and so false to you and my faith, if I had trusted you, which I didn't, then maybe none of this would have happened."

"Sabina, my darling. Let's set our priorities. First of all, there's a delicious breakfast growing cold in front of our very eyes; and second, you want to talk about what religion our children are going to be raised. Now I ask you, which is more important?"

"Why, Robert," she said, her black eyes lighting up, for the first time. "Of course the children are more important. But if you mean which is more urgent . . ." Sabina quickly sat down and began dishing herself the eggs.

After they had eaten, Sabina forced Robert to sit down—she immediately noticed the fresh-scrubbed living room—and listen to her `apology.'

"Robert, I am a Jew. From the moment that awful Hitler came to power, being a Jew in Germany became more and more difficult. Month after month, year after year, I saw the property of my Jewish friends confiscated, their shops forced to close, them fired from work. In the last few years they have simply disappeared.

"My father, a Lutheran, died a few months after he retired as a professor at the Humbold University. I was twenty-one at the time. His name was Stellmann, and not Jewish, which protected us for a while. But Goebbels got more and more crazy, and soon Mama and I were to get our identity papers stamped with a 'J.' In desperation I married a casual university acquaintance, Signor Pergolesi, the Italian diplomat. It was a simple seduction on my part and he was a kind, ineffectual man. But his citizenship was not ineffectual.

"Through his position, Mama and I both were able to become Italian citizens. But, of course, you never lose your German citizenship. Perhaps foolishly, but like so many of us, we chose not to believe all the clues of the ultimate aim of the Nazis until it was too late to get out.

"We are all Germans, after all, we told ourselves. As ruthless as they are, the Nazis took great pains to hide the real horror as much as possible. And of course you couldn't read a word about what they were doing. While my husband was alive, we were protected and it was easy to shut our eyes. As soon as he died, the protection began to waver and, name and citizenship change or not, we were once again nothing more than German Jews.

"You know the bureaucracy in Germany grinds slowly but exceedingly fine. It was only a matter of time before our name-change would be unraveled and they came after us. I was desperate once again. I thought by marrying a well-placed officer in one of the security services I might achieve some safety."

"Stumpfnagel," Ballard interjected. "Then I came along. Another foreign safety net."

"Yes, Robert. I tried to use you, too," Sabina said somberly.

"But because of their great interest in you, I was immediately noticed by the Gestapo. So, instead of being protected by you, I was discovered."

"They're still interested. When I went to the market, I noticed that we're being watched."

"F-Faulheim will never let us go, Robert, no matter what the Führer has allowed us to do. That monster will find a loophole or arrange an accident. He put me up in that apartment in hopes of getting information on you—but he wouldn't say what he was looking for. And I went along with it. When I didn't get anything, wouldn't pry, he . . . he raped me." She lowered her head and shook with sudden sobs.

Ballard's face hardened and he reached. out to hold her.

"No, Robert," Sabina said firmly, pushing him off and wiping her eyes. "Let me finish. Just as I found out that even you couldn't help us, I also realized I had fallen in love with you anyway. That's why I cried so. But instead of opening up, I became even more desperate than ever to prevent you from finding out about my, my . . ."

"About your being Jewish." Ballard said.

"Yes," Sabina said quietly. "I was certain that once you found out, you would never see me again—or that you couldn't see me again. Abwehr security would somehow interfere. It was a terrible mistake. By deceiving you I thought to save my life, but I lost my soul in the process. You can't deceive those you love. I moved back in with Mama. Then that Gestapo thug took Mama away."

"So once again he had you over a barrel," Robert said.

"Yes. That horrible man had me go up to visit Mama. He had put her up at a small inn, and the SS Captain who met me at the station gave us both a tour of the work camp nearby. Robert, you wouldn't believe the appalling . . ."

305

"I know all about it Sabina," Ballard said with downcast eyes. "You mean you didn't travel to Ravensbruck with your dance instructor?"

"Roland Uhl? No, he brought me to the train station. On orders, he said. SS Hauptsturmfuhrer Hartnack picked me up. They know everything about everyone, and use it whenever it suits them.

"The captain made our situation quite clear. Either we find out where you were getting your intelligence information from, or first Mama, and then I would become permanent guests of the camp."

"So you had to chose between me or your mother," Ballard said.

"And this was just at the time you began behaving so . . . oddly towards me, Robert. I realized then that my hope of seducing you into marrying me and getting my mother and me out of Germany was a barbarous deception and would never work."

"So why not play along?" Ballard asked.

"You forget, your confession at Scharfenberg would have made marrying you—who was to become a German—just another blocked alley. So I realized I must stop the deceit. When I did, it cleared my mind and I noticed for the first time that I, too, had fallen in love . . ."

"But not enough to tell me the problem . . ."

"Robert, I was so confused. And so ashamed of keeping our situation from you. Of not trusting you. It was so faithlessly selfish. So . . . dishonest."

Ballard looked into Sabina's eyes. She returned his gaze wide-eyed and open. He saw none of the veil of feline craftiness. It had been replaced by enormous vulnerability, and still-fresh scar tissue.

"Maybe there was not yet anything to trust, my darling," Ballard said. "For the longest time I was just interested in you for . . ."

"For the sex," she said flatly.

"Yes. Then I fell in love, too. Very much against my will. Only I was too stupid to realize it until after getting back from the Oak Ridge mission."

"I remember when you fell in love. On Scharfenberg," she smiled briefly, awkwardly. It still didn't come easy to her. "When you began to tell me that very strange story about your father discovering your mother. I still don't understand where that happened. I pushed you away because I realized that even if I did ensnare you, all I would have

306

had to do was remain quiet a little longer and then say 'yes'—as a German you wouldn't be able to protect us at all. I would have married for convenience once again, and been right back where I started: helpless. Thinking that over made me realize how plans laid in deceit always betray the cleverest of designs. It was the memory of your genuine tenderness toward your mother that made me realize that only trust works—no matter what the apparent disadvantages . . ."

"Oh, Sabina," Ballard interrupted. "The story about my mother is nothing compared to what I'm going to tell you now!"

Chapter Sixty-Two

Hitler's marriage to Fräulein Eva Braun was heralded on the front page of every newspaper in Germany, of course. But it was done with odd restraint. A gala wedding had been out of the question, the editors intoned, as the announcement would have attracted Allied bombers literally by the hundreds, and the potential for suicide squads was also high. Yet even the newspapers could not conceal that the wedding ceremony had been a rather ad hoc affair.

The rumor mills buzzed at how Eva Braun finally managed to make an honest man of him. The Berliner joke mill—the sharpest in the land—opined that Adolf Hitler, whose girth had started to draw invidious comparisons to that of Göring, had so often promised Fräulein Braun that he would not eat any more of the delicious Viennese pastries to which he was addicted, that when she caught him at it once again, she had put more than her foot down. Further promises were unavailing, and, she had declared with typical feminine logic, that if he did not marry her at once, even she would no longer have him, given his recent weight problem.

She told him, so the rumor mongers insisted, that he was making a joke of the master race: "Tall like Goebbels, slender like Göring, and blond like Hitler," she said the joke went. "Well," Eva Braun was rumored to have shouted at the Führer, "At the rate you're gaining weight, they won't need Göring to poke fun at any more! Unless, of course," she is said to have purred, "you have someone sensible around you who will see to it that you pay more attention to your diet."

It was the most banal of middle-class arguments that trapped Hitler. What could any honorable man do, he is said to have asked his closest friends rhetorically. But if Hitler believed that marrying the jail

308

keeper was going to mean she would no longer guard the key, well, a lot of people felt this was just another of the Führer's grand strategies that, like most of the others, had not been thought out past the next step but one.

Some wags managed to insinuate that Eva Braun was tired of being left home for the ceremonial dinners and the concerts that the Führer attended more and more often. All those movie stars she saw fluttering around her man. That would stop, too. Or at least she would be there to maintain decorum.

And now that the war was going so well, appearances at social functions were becoming more common. There was no longer the embarrassing matter of how to refer to the presence of Fräulein Braun. Nor was she content to remain in the Berchtesgaden retreat in South Germany.

Although it was never written about, the sources closest to the Reich's Chancellery claim it was a darker event that caused the sudden change of Hitler's heart. These pundits claimed that Eva had called the Führer in the middle of the night to threaten suicide again. Only this time she wouldn't miss! And, indeed, it was probably her first threat of suicide that convinced Hitler to permit her to move into a private apartment at the Reich's Chancellery. Hitler surely remembered his first true love's successful suicide—that of Geli Raubal—some say in jealousy over Hitler's new acquaintance at the time, of Eva Braun.

Whatever was the cause of Hitler permitting her to make an apartment in the Reich Chancellery, once ensconced, no one dared refer to Eva as Hitler's 'consort.' A 'friend' left far too much to the imagination. 'Acquaintance' was too distant to be acceptable to her. And 'fiancée,' which was the closest description, was not yet a fact.

Thus, commentators wrote archly, the leader of the greatest military power on the planet had succumbed to the oldest of strategies in the oldest of battles—the "war" between the sexes. It was not so much a battle lost, the boldest were to say, as one in which the stronger party surrendered willingly to the weaker. This was a propaganda theme cleverly scripted by Goebbels himself, and it quickly made up for the years of the official invisibility of their illicit relationship. The emphasis on the domesticating sanctity of matrimony appealed strongly to

Hitler, who picked up on the theme quickly, and expanded it in many kitch-laden homilies.

"Yes, I was first captivated and now finally captured," Hitler joked frequently to any gathering of the faithful, with Frau Hitler now finally able to stand at his side for official photographs.

Unbeknownst to most, there were some embarrassing details that needed to be papered over for the wedding. German racial laws were quite strict. Had Herr Hitler obtained a certificate of racial purity, the minister officiating the hasty wedding had asked, red-faced with embarrassment. He was only a bureaucrat doing his duty. Hitler, who to this point had a dreamy appearance, became suddenly angry. His response was that his background was public knowledge and well-known to the high-level witnesses—Joseph Goebbels, Martin Bormann, and Arthur Axmann, head of the Hitler Youth. This question of provenance evoked anew memories of Hitler's magical one-day transformation into German citizenship from his native Austrian.

Fräulein Braun wore a gown of mauve silk taffeta. White was never worn at civil weddings. Hitler muttered the answers to his vows in a barely audible mumble. Eva Braun was cheery and spoke clearly. The ceremony took only twenty-five minutes. Afterwards, word of it was passed out to the rest of the Chancellery staff. Soon singing took place, dancing in the halls, and the forbidden smoking of cigarettes. To the faithful, it almost unbelievable—as if Jesus Christ had taken Mary as his bride—but certainly a cause for great rejoicing. Hitler joined in the merrymaking, leaving the celebration from time to time to get updated dispatches. The war, though going well, was far from over.

Chapter Sixty-Three

In spite of their freshly minted exit visas, the problem of Faulheim did not go away. Then Stumpfnagel had the brilliant idea of forging duplicates of Ballard and Sabina's exit permission and applying for train reservations from Hannover and Berlin at the same time. Faulheim would instantly learn of the Berlin travel arrangements and make his plans to intercept the couple accordingly. Then, Ballard would slip back to Hannover the day before his Berlin exit visa date, and proceed to Switzerland from there. It would be months before the simultaneous submission would be discovered. The Munich and Swiss boarder crossing check points would simply get duplicate visa confirmations for the couple, coming from different location a day apart, and recognize them simply as common, official last-minute alterations, either date being valid but not, of course, both. If Faulheim sent anyone to stage a pickup, using the Berlin dates, he would be a day late. Even Canaris had smiled at that one.

Ballard pulled away from the stoplight, shifted into second gear and turned to Sabina, sitting beside him. "Just like old times, isn't it darling, having lunch at the Neva Grill."

"Oh, it's so exciting to be doing this again, Robert. Do you think the waiter will remember us?"

"How can he forget," Ballard smirked. "It's not every guest who brings her own dessert."

"Whatever do you mean, darling?" Sabina asked. Then her face turned bright red. "You don't mean he saw . . . what we were doing . . . ?"

"No question in my mind," Ballard smiled.

"But darling, then we can't . . ." The car lurched forward with a mighty jolt.

"What the hell? That idiot behind us—he ran into us. Jesus Christ, he's going to hit us again." Ballard mashed the gas pedal. Another jolt, this one less forceful as Ballard had almost matched the lunatic's speed.

He spun the steering wheel and slid around the corner into a side street. The car behind them slammed on the brakes, bumped up onto the sidewalk and turned back into the road, intent on ramming them again. Ballard felt an enormous welling up of fury at Faulheim. The bastard was hoping to stage a car accident. The closer his and Sabina's exit visa approached its expiration date, the more brazen Faulheim was getting in his dirty tricks. As if he was worried that the couple would simply disappear on the final day. Ballard's anger turned to vindictive hatred at the thought that his wife was also a target of Faulheim's vengeance. Ballard saw immediately that the driver was not practiced at high speed maneuvering. He slowed down.

"Robert, why are you stopping?" Sabina was white-faced with terror.

"I'm not stopping," he answered curtly. In moments the other car began gaining on them. Only then did Ballard pick up his speed, but the other car was closing the gap. Sabina glanced at the speedometer—one hundred km/hr through the crowded suburbs of Berlin. By now the other car was only ten meters behind them and closing fast. At the last instant Ballard spun the steering wheel sharply to the left. A split second after the car began to swerve, he jerked hard on the emergency brake. The rear wheels locked and lost traction instantly, whipping the car around in a perfect half-circle. They came to an abrupt stop pointing back the way they had just come. The mysterious pursuer roared past them, brakes squealing. Ballard put his car in gear and sped off. He glanced in the rear-view mirror. The other car skidded sideways into the curb. Both wheels hit and the car rolled over on its side. A man jumped out the top door and rushed around to push the vehicle back on its wheels. Ballard made a skidding turn into the next street. He found a short driveway and pulled into it.

"Get out, quickly," he said, and guided Sabina around to the driver's side of the car. She crouched down behind it while he, standing outside, rummaged in the glove compartment. He pulled out a flashlight and jammed it between the transmission hump to hold down the gas pedal. With the gearshift in neutral, the motor roared unfettered.

Screeching tires alerted them to the arrival of their pursuers, racing around the corner.

"Step back," Ballard ordered, as he leaned into the cabin of the car. He waited a moment, coolly estimating the closing distance. With a forceful jerk he threw the gearshift lever into reverse. The transmission uttered a terrible clunk and bolted the car backwards into the street, directly into the path of the speeding pursuers.

Ballard and Sabina saw the looks of terror of the two men as they crashed squarely into Ballard's Opel. With a rending shriek of tearing metal, the two cars become one and skidded to a halt.

Ballard ran up to their pursuers. Blood flowed freely from the nostril of the driver slumped over the wheel. His passenger had slipped into a heap in his foot space, and was vaguely moving his arms.

Ballard's face was set in a grim mask of determination. The time for fair play was long over. Faulheim had long ago crossed the line. He pulled out his Swiss Army knife. Selecting the awl, he stepped to the rear of the car and, reaching underneath, punched upward with his tool. A trickle of gasoline dribbled out. On the dashboard of the car lay the smoldering cigarette thrown out of the passenger's mouth. Ballard plucked it up and flipped it under the car. In an instant waves of invisible heat surrounded the vehicle.

Spectators began to run hesitantly toward the burning car. Ballard pretended to shield his face. "Watch out," he cried. "It's about to blow up." The men pulled back. The Allied bombings were dangerous enough. No one wanted to die because of someone else's car accident.

Reaching through the open window, Ballard pushed the door handle down to the "locked" position while pretending to be struggling to open it. He gave the appearance of trying to pull the victim through the window. The man opened his eyes and gazed at Ballard uncomprehendingly. Ballard felt the man's strength returning.

He gave him a short, sharp jab to the temple, knocking him sideways and unconscious.

A searing wave of heat billowed forth. Now the fire was getting hot. He ran around to the other side. That door was crushed shut. He placed one foot on the frame and heaved at it, deliberately but ineffectually, giving the appearance of a desperate struggle. A whooshing roar of yellow flames signaled the ignition of the engine oil. Ballard stumbled backwards, tripped and scrabbled to safety. In seconds the entire car was consumed in flames. A blazing hand calmly reached out the open window, then stopped moving.

A police officer pulled Ballard to his feet. "Are you all right? God in heaven, man, that was unbelievably brave of you to try and rescue those two unfortunates. That's a Gestapo vehicle, you know. You'll certainly get a medal for this."

The crowd cheered as Ballard made his way over to Sabina. He hung his head as if exhausted, and stumbled slightly.

"I'll be all right," he said, waving wanly to the witnesses. Yet he realized that killing these two assassins would not stop Faulheim. He would have to move against the man himself.

Chapter Sixty-Four

"Herr Ballard," Lieutenant Stumpfnagel said. "Permit me to introduce to you Feldwebel Matthias Hetzenauer, the leading sniper in all of Germany. He has just over three hundred certified hits to his credit."

Ballard shook the ruddy young sergeant's out stretched hand. The handshake was firm, but not excessively so. It seemed more controlled than spontaneous. The pleasant smile, too, was a practiced one, hiding the face of a loner. The self-contained man, totally self sufficient, needing little in the way of companionship.

"So pleased to meet you Herr Feldwebel," Ballard said. "In addition to being Germany's leading sniper, I understand you are also an accomplished gunsmith."

"Ja," the sergeant answered. "It helps to get a good score if you have a good gun."

"What model sniper rifle do you use?"

"Most of us use the K98k made by Mauser and others," the young man replied. Ballard bade him sit down. The young man declined a beer. "Some use the G43, but once anyone shoots the K98, no one ever goes back to the G43."

"And a telescopic sight . . . ?"

"Oh, there are many—Kahles, Ajack, Dialytan. I think most use the Voigtlander in four or six power."

"And what kind of accuracy can you get at, say, six hundred meters?"

"The better shots could hit a man in the chest four times out of five, I think."

"What if you were required to hit a soccer ball at that range?" Ballard asked.

"Na ja, you mean a man's head. That would take probably three shots to hit. But most targets don't wait around after the first shot."

"So you couldn't guarantee to hit a man's head at six hundred meters with a single shot?"

"No. We could hit it at four hundred meters."

"What if I wanted to be able to hit a man's head at six-hundred meters? What would it take?"

"Maybe it could be done with a very finely-tuned model."

"Tuned?"

"Ja. We check all the dimensions to make sure they are not just within specifications, plus or minus some allowable tolerance, but hair-perfectly so. This means building up some parts, removing a little metal on others. 'Stoning,' we call it, followed by lapping, perhaps just like a jeweler."

"And the barrel?"

"The lands and grooves must be sharp. We check to make sure it's straight. If not we bend it."

"Bend it?"

"With a special machine. But, ja, we just pull on it until it's straight."

"Anything else?"

"It would be very important for such a rifle to have the barrel completely relieved from the stock, so it is nowhere touching the stock. It must be completely free to vibrate. And, of course, you would need to shoot special, precision-manufactured ammunition. Something you loaded yourself."

"Herr Feldwebel, I have a proposition for you. How would you like to manufacture such a weapon for the Abwehr. In exchange for a two-week leave of absence. And, say five hundred Reichsmarks spending money? I would need it in five days."

"Oha, wunderbar. Jawohl, I'd love that."

"But the finished rifles will have to hit a fifteen centimeter target at six hundred meters four shots out of five."

"I'll shoot them myself, Herr Ballard."

"Oh, one more thing," Ballard added. "Suppressers."

"Well, for the K98 we have been using a Soviet design, the same as they use on their Mosin-Nagant rifle. But it's not perfect; you can't get rid of the supersonic crack with high-powered ammunition. Still, they work pretty good. You still hear the shot, but it's much harder to tell where it's coming from."

Chapter Sixty-Five

They drive to Hannover was made in near silence. Sabina lay against his arm for much of the four-hour trip.

"Robert, won't it be difficult to get an apartment on such short notice?"

"I have had an apartment there for almost four years-since 1941," Ballard answered. "It's where I've been keeping my time machine."

Sabina gave him an odd look. "It's so hard to comprehend your really being from the future," she said.

"You still don't believe it yet, do you my love?" he asked. He was not bitter.

"It's not that I don't want to believe it, Robert. But the more incredible something is, the more you have to see it for yourself."

"Well, see it you will. Just don't fiddle with it," Ballard joked. "You don't know when you might end up." They both chuckled at his lousy joke.

Ballard showed Sabina the time machine sitting in the empty dining room. It made no sense to her, looking like just so much apparatus. Later he introduced her to the local tradesmen at, the market, and to his black market contacts—the young girl at the shoemaker's store for milk, cream and eggs, and the old man at the spirits store for meat and fish without ration cards.

Sabina and Robert also got married in Hannover, the waiting period of the Marriage Banns being waived as was commonly done with soldiers on short leaves, and the special SS permit alleviating—although not without raised eyebrows—the racial discrepancy. Sabina had bought herself a ring even before Ballard realized one would be needed.

Ballard and Stumpfnagel had agreed that as long as Ballard was seen regularly in Berlin, Faulheim would assume that Sabina was simply being kept hidden nearby, and he would never expect they would leave for Switzerland from any place but Berlin.

Ballard and Sabina kissed good-bye outside the apartment. They had not yet made love since Sabina's return from Ravensbruck. Ballard was content to let the wound of their separation heal at its normal pace. On the lonely drive back to Berlin, he found himself singing the Star Spangled Banner.

Ballard had to shout into the telephone receiver to be heard. Then, suddenly, he could hear perfectly. Sabina had called him each day from their apartment in Hannover via the Abwehr in Berlin, which telephone lines could not be tapped. He was not in the office, so the Abwehr operator patched the call through to his apartment in Weisensee. The Gestapo might intercept the call to Ballard, but could only trace it back to Abwehr Headquarters. Sabina continued talking, unaware of the poor reception.

".. . come out here by train tomorrow night? It should clean up by then. I have a little surprise for you."

"I'm sorry darling, I didn't hear the first part of what you just said."

"It's very cloudy right now, and we'll probably have a terrible downpour any second," she repeated. "Oh, look, the sun just came out. My goodness it's astonishingly bright. I've never seen . . ." The telephone went dead. Ballard's mind blanked out. It refused to compute. Color drained from his face. It's not possible, he thought. Then he yelled it out. "It's not possible!" He looked outside. A faint glow seemed to illuminate the dark heavens to the west, as if the distant city had turned on all its lights to ward off the continuing gloom of war.

Ballard's hands were shaking. He tried to dial Stumpfnagel, but could not make his fingers behave. Finally he achieved the task. Inge answered pleasantly.

"Inge, get me Stumpfnagel immediately, wherever he is," he cried into the telephone. "I don't care. Yes, put me in to Canaris. This is extremely urgent. Yes, I'll wait."

Ballard paced back and forth in extreme agitation, each walk being halted by the length of the telephone cord. Finally Stumpfnagel answered.

"Stumpf, give me Canaris, immediately. I think Hannover has just been hit with an atomic bomb."

A few moments later he heard the admiral clear his throat: "Canaris here. What's going on Herr Ballard?" There was a sense of courtesy strained in his voice.

"Herr Admiral, I was just talking to Sabina, my fiancée in Hannover. She described a bright light in the sky which she thought was the sun coming out. Then she remarked it was much brighter than the sun. Then the telephone went dead. I think Hannover has been nuked."

"'Nuked?' How is that possible? Herr Ballard, what makes you think that the sun coming out is . . . hold on a moment, I'm getting a Priority-One call on my special telephone." There was a long pause. "Ballard. You were right, Hannover has been hit with a massive air strike of unknown origin. No aircraft were reported. You're sure the attack was nuclear? What do we do?"

Ballard felt his stomach begin to retch with fear. He straggled to control himself. "Evacuate everyone immediately from the city in an upwind direction. Everyone who is still alive must get away from the fallout. You know fallout—its the debris the bomb made radioactive that will settle out of the sky over the next few hours and days. No heroics. You won't save anyone by having healthy people remain behind to look out for the sick ones. You'll just end up with more sick and dying. Those who can't be moved, God rest them. Quickly put them in basements, or sealed rooms. They'll need food and water for two weeks. It won't be easy."

Ballard felt his knees starting to give out on him. His stomach was a torment of twisting pain. He flopped to the floor and threw up. "Shit. Excuse me, Herr Admiral," he said, wiping his mouth. "I just got sick. Burns. You'll need as much medication to treat burns—terrible burns, broken bones. And diarrhea. Aspirin. I ..I can't think of anything else right now, Herr Admiral. I think I'm going to faint."

Canaris turned abruptly to Stumpfnagel. "Ballard just passed out from fright. He says we have a national emergency on our hands. Have the radio room contact the Americans to find out their intentions. Good God, this could mean the end of the war, with Germany losing again."

"But Herr Admiral," Stumpfnagel objected. "How could the, Americans have recovered so quickly from the destruction of Oak Ridge and Hanniford?"

Canaris looked up sharply, his face rigid in thought. "Is it possible they had more than the two bomb plants?"

"Ballard would certainly have known," Stumpfnagel answered, sitting down. Then he looked up. "Whoever's responsible will be making demands." They both left the office and climbed the stairs to the top floor. Inside, the room was abuzz with activity. Radio clerks were transcribing messages in shorthand. The few wire recorders were hooked up and running.

"Major Hartkopf," Canaris shouted out. "Was ist Los?"

"Oh, Herr Admiral, the news is terrible," the radio officer said. His face was white. "We're getting the news on most Allied channels. Winston Churchill claims to have dropped a so-called 'atomic bomb' on Hannover. They are demanding an immediate cease-fire, and a staged withdrawal of German troops back to the prewar borders. If this is not visibly begun in forty-eight hours, they plan to bomb another city."

"Does the Führer know?" Canaris asked.

"He must know, Herr Admiral. The Chancellery also monitors most foreign transmitters."

"But he won't know the extent of the damage one of these bombs can cause," Canaris said. "Nor the after-effects. Only Ballard knows, and Bormann would never let the Führer get his answers from a foreigner, especially this one."

Canaris thought for a moment. "I'll call the Chancellery myself and request an audience. He must see me, or we'll just see another German city wiped out."

Canaris lifted the telephone and asked to be put through to the Führer. He got through to his all-powerful secretary, Martin Bormann.

"Herr Bormann, you are aware that the raid on Hannover was caused by a single uranium bomb which probably destroyed most of the city, and that the British threaten to drop another unless we begin an immediate halt to Operation Sea Lion?" Canaris paused to listen to Bormann's reply.

"What do you mean it's not determined who dropped it? What difference does that make? Does the Führer know what has happened, and that the cause is an atomic bomb?"

Canaris put the phone down momentarily, a stunned look on his face. He put the instrument back to his mouth.

"Are you insane, Herr Bormann? An entire German city up in smoke from a single bomb—maybe 50,000 to 100,000 casualties—and you don't think you should wake up the Führer and tell him until its proven who did it? When the second bomb drops on Nuremberg, what are you going to tell him then? That you wanted to make absolutely certain this wasn't just a little British joke?"

There was a longer pause this tune. Stumpfnagel could just make out the sound of a wheedling voice, but he could not hear the words.

"I have no idea which city is going to be next on the list, Bormann. That was just an example. Are you people living in another world? There's a war on, and we've just been dealt a crippling blow. You want to ignore what this means to the conduct of the war and instead examine the situation reports for political acceptability? Goddammit, Bormann, you can't be telling me you won't wake the Führer at the cost of 50,000 German lives. Who's side are you on for God's sake? I don't care if he is in bed with Frau Hitler, I demand you put me through to him immediately. Yes, entirely on my own responsibility."

Canaris stood there with a look on his face that Stumpfnagel had never seen before. He looked like he was going to cry. He caught Stumpfnagel's curious look.

"Do you realize what this means, Herr Leutnant?" the admiral asked. "Once again the German army is not defeated on the battlefield, but stabbed in the back. Just like, the First War." Canaris choked. "The people won't stand for it again."

An "atomic" bomb! Good Lord. Canaris looked at the silent telephone with disgust. Bormann was stalling. He slammed the received down. The two men took the lift back to the top floor and the radio room. They wanted to get as much detail about the bombing of Hannover as possible. They had to figure out the German response. Hitler would demand an intelligence appraisal.

Chapter Sixty-Six

Ballard slowly recovered his senses, lying draped against the window radiator. His jaw ached from where he had fallen onto it. One part of his mind swirled with confusion and hurt. His stomach was a knot of pain. Sabina in an atomic attack in Hannover. Could she have survived?, Another part of his mind became hard and calculating. It was the combatant part of him, disciplined to shut out fear and analyze what to do next.

Hannover. Sabina was in Hannover. If she was still alive, he, more than anyone, would know what to do. He must go there to rescue her.

He staggered out of his apartment to his new Opel. The street seemed perfectly normal. Down the cross street he saw the Nr 71 streetcar pull away from its stop. In the opposite direction a military convoy of trucks heading out to resupply troops in the East. A knot of women carrying their net sacks were arguing about where they could buy meat. The war was over and no one knew it.

Ballard drove to the corner Apothecary to stock up on first-aid supplies. The owner looked askance at the quantity and type of medical supplies the tall foreigner was hurriedly buying. He was on the brink of asking whether this was for precautionary measures, or perhaps the tall customer whom he occasionally saw, knew some thing more ominous. Foreigners always seemed to be better informed than the German public. This customer was an odd one, always asking about unusual formulations, or pharmaceuticals never heard of. How many times had he at tempted to make up some unheard of concoctions. But the harried expression on Ballard's face held the pharmacist back. Ballard paid and bolted out the door.

Hannover lies 285 km due west of Berlin—the same distance as Hamburg lies to the northwest. Ballard pushed the Opel unmercifully, driving at 140-150 km/hr—as fast as the car would go on a level stretch. On moderate hills its speed would drop to 110 km/hr, with Ballard mashing the gas pedal to the floorboard. He cursed the great German Autobahn; it was nothing more than what a state highway would be in the 1990's in the United States. The Meritt Parkway came to mind. Narrow, and of poured concrete, its only advantage was it was reasonably straight and had no speed limit. A lot of good no speed limit was to him; scores of times he came up behind other traffic at high speed, only to have to slam on the brakes because a slow truck was passing one slower yet. Once he could not stop in time, skidding into the rear of tractor trailer and bouncing the front of the Opel off the truck's rear tires. The driver, an Army private jumped out in fright, and then shook his fist at Ballard as he accelerated away.

The sky in the west was heavy and dark, as if a terrible storm was brewing. Ballard knew it was a huge cloud of hot debris, swirling up in the grip of hot air being sucked into the upper atmosphere to be irradiated with radioactivity. As the cloud cooled, the dirt and stones and bits of matter would settle out, transformed from fertile earth to a killing precipitation from Hell.

Ballard looked at the trees racing by. They were being whipped in great gusts. He could not tell from them which way the wind was blowing, whether there was a general direction in which the fallout would be carried. Ballard rolled up his windows. His mind was racing too. What was he going to do? Was the time machine intact? It had only enough charge for a single trip back to 1990. Once back, it would take a year to construct another lithium-niobate singularity lens. Longer, as he would need three full charges; one for him to come back to 1945, and two more to bring Sabina and him forward to 1990. But, with their visas expiring, if he didn't get Sabina out of Germany in the next few days, she would be as good as dead.

There was another alternative: he could go to the future, build some more lenses, and then return before the nuclear explosion. But as the thought surfaced, so did its antithesis. The Sabina he picked up then would not be exactly the same Sabina he was racing to save now.

325

In a flash he realized how it worked. Time ran in parallel tracks all right, but these tracks were only parallel, not the same history repeated and rerun differently. Different time tracks were not exact duplicates. Everything would be slightly different. He would be leaving this Sabina behind once again. Returning to the new Sabina would not save this one who he would be abandoning. He realized finally that time travel is the ultimate illusion. No amount of fourth-dimension travel can change reality. Time travel could only create an endless successions of new realities. Like a series of different movie versions of the same story. He could not abandon this Sabina and pretend the one he returned to rescue would be the same one. Not and live with himself. Betrayal, he realized, is the greatest sin. And he did not want a slightly different women to be his wife.

He gnashed his teeth at his lack of options. He, with the greatest power of the universe at his command, and still he was helpless—as helpless, he realized suddenly—as every man is who gets his power from objects rather than from the human spirit. Cars, money, futuristic gadgets, nothing counts, he realized, except how I behave toward the one who loves me.

Ballard recognized his exit intersection coming up. He slowed down. A traffic policeman was waving him down. He rolled down his window and came to a stop.

"You can't go any farther," the policeman shouted. He did not recognize the official "V" license plate of Ballard's car. He was an old man, sixty at least. His face was ravaged with hopelessness. This was his second World War. "There's been a colossal air attack. Worse than Hamburg. The entire city is in flames. People are desperate to get out. They'll kill you and steal your car."

"I'm with the Abwehr. Step aside and thanks for the warning." Ballard flashed his number shield and drove on. He reached under his seat and pulled out a Parabellum P-08 pistol—the German Luger so beloved by Hollywood for its timelessly svelte cures. It had been essentially replaced by the Walther 9mm P-38 which was cheaper to make, and more reliable under field conditions. But Lugers were still manufactured for those who could afford them. He pulled back the two knurled toggles of the bolt. The cartridges stacked in the magazine slid up in a tight column, with the top one protruding above the restraining lip of the clip. He released the toggles and the triple-hinged breech block snapped forward, stripping the top cartridge out of the magazine and into the breech. Ballard clicked the safety lever off and lay the pistol on the seat next to him.

As he turned off the Autobahn exit ramp, Ballard save the first signs of the disaster. Ragged lines of civilians hobbling along the road with all the possessions they could carry. Some had large bundles on their backs. Other used baby carriages, wheelbarrows, bicycles, anything that rolled. Most were too dispirited to even look up at his passing.

Two youths carrying bundles brightened as they spotted Ballard's car. They dropped their loads and leaped onto the hood, banging their fists against the roof.

"Stop instantly," they screamed. Ballard sped up, whipping the steering wheel back and forth sharply. One of the men, laying on the roof and holding on to a windshield wiper, slithered off, still clutching the wiper in his hand. He rolled on the street, covering his head with his arms. Ballard slammed on the brakes. The other man, clinging to the hood fell off forward, raking his belly on the hood ornament. Ballard, his face a tight mask of anger, accelerated and brutally ran over the attacker.

Approaching his apartment on the Hubertstrasse, Ballard kept his speed high as he rounded the curve, only slowing as he approached the apartment entrance. A soldier sitting in a sullen group at the side of the street stood up and broke out in fast run toward the car as he saw Ballard screech to a halt. In his hand he waved an axe.

Opening the car door and standing up behind it, Ballard stared impassively at the soldier who was closing in rapidly. At twenty meters separation, Ballard stepped out from behind the door and wordlessly raised his Luger. Shocked to see a civilian with a firearm, the man took a desperate leap, raising his axe overhead with both hands, a bloodthirsty scream issuing from his lips.

Ballard fired two quick shots. The pistol barked twice, kicked back twice and spit out two spent cartridges. The man's body shuddered at the impact of the bullets thumping into his chest, and crashed against

327

the Opel, his axe clanging off the roof. He bounced backwards and fell to the curb. Ballard stepped out from behind the door and, before the stunned soldier could rise, shot him in the forehead. He pitched over backwards, his legs kicking spastically. Down the street, watching the scene, a few of the man's companions stood up, uncertain of what to do.

"Why not stay where you are?" Ballard screamed out. The men sat down. Ballard raced up the stairs to his secret apartment. He fumbled with the key, his hands shaking so hard he was unable to stick it into the lock. He jiggled it desperately torn between jamming it in, and frightened that he might break it off. Why wasn't his body working right?

He took two deep breaths, and slid the key into the lock. He burst through the door. The living room was littered with broken glass. Sabina had left a note:

Dearest,

Feel a little sick after the terrible air raid. Look at the mess!! Went to pharmacy for some Togal. Back to clean up by 13 hours.

S

It was already 1500 hrs—3 p.m. She was two hours overdue.

"Christ, the pharmacy . . ." Ballard realized it was a half-mile toward the city center.

He dashed down to the Opel and drove off. The men on the corner were just climbing into a wagon they had relieved a farmer of. The farmer lay writhing in the road, bleeding from his mouth. Ballard did not slow down.

As Ballard drove toward the center of the city, he was surprised to see that the roads were still free of heavy debris. Leaves and small tree branches lay everywhere, but he could drive over or around most of them. A few had to be moved. There was glass everywhere, but it lay in flat shards. Even many telephone lines were still up.. He judged himself to be about two kilometers from the center of the city. Perhaps the epicenter of the explosion was farther west.

A thin line of people was trudging in the opposite direction, but not nearly as many as he expected. Twice he saw the glint of opportunity light up in a man's eyes. Each time he raised the Luger in his hand and saw the hope extinguish.

The pharmacy lay ahead. A small mob of people were milling around it. He drove on, looking for a garage into which to hide the Opel. A man was sweeping glass away from the front of his store: Ballard screeched to a halt.

"You, open that garage door," Ballard demanded, the Luger pointing at the old man. He dropped his broom and his arms extended out from the waist, making a sign of helplessness while shaking his head. Ballard fired a shot over his head. The man scurried to the garage, pulled out a huge set of keys and struggled to raise the overhead sliding door. Ballard parked the car and approached the old man.

"I won't be long. If there's anything wrong with the car when I get back, or if you think you can siphon off a few liters of gasoline, you won't live long enough to have made it worthwhile. Understand?"

The man gave a sickly smile and nodded his head.

Most of the people besieging the pharmacy were women, desperate to buy medicaments for their children. Ballard shoved his way through the crowd, shouting out, "Make way. Abwehr, official business."

"Official business, of course," a surly women shouted back, unfazed by the drawn pistol. "Why not wait in line like the rest of us, mein Herr?"

"You call this mob scene a line?" Ballard quipped grimly. "where's your Germanic sense of discipline?"

"A foreigner, no less," another women rejoined, catching his slight accent. "High and mighty."

Ballard could not help but smile at the cheek of these women.

"Look, he chuckles," a third women piped in. "Obviously not a German official," another piped in. Reluctantly, the women broke ranks to let the American through.

Inside the pharmacy was as crowded as a train station during rush hour. The female owner of the shop was on a ladder pulling down the remaining supplies from the upper shelves. There, at the cash register, parceling them out, was Sabina.

"I'm sorry, only one package of bandages per customers. No, I don't care how much you're willing to pay. Next, please." She looked up at Ballard with placid eyes. Suddenly they sparked with recognition. "Robert," she cried out. "Thank God you're here. I'm exhausted."

"We've got to get out of here, Sabina," Ballard said in low tones. "Hannover is going to get radioactively 'hot' in the next few hours."

She nodded in agreement. "Frau Heinkel, how much more is there?"

"Only this top shelf," the older women shouted back.

Ballard raised his pistol in the air. "Ladies, your attention please." The hubbub died down instantly. "There are only just enough bandages left for all of you in here. We are going to give them to you for nothing, but outside, in the front of the store."

The mob turned and bolted through the door.

"Give them away, mein Herr?" the older women asked pointedly.

"Look, Madam, you've got two hundred marks worth of goods left. If you were to run out with a store full of desperate people, they'd take the place apart to make sure you're telling the truth. This way they're leaving the store quietly and you can lock up. Cheap at the price,"

Ballard reached up to take the remaining armful of bandages. Pushing at the remaining stragglers, he followed them outside.

"OK, here's all we have," he said, and threw the armful into the air. With shrieks, the mob clawed at the packages. Ballard stepped back into the store and bolted the door. Inside, the older women glanced at him appreciatively. She turned to Sabina.

"Is that your man?" she asked as if Ballard wasn't there.

"Jawohl," Sabina said and rushed to collapse in his arms. Ballard hefted her up. She felt so wane. Ballard looked at the older women with alarm.

"She's exhausted from helping me for several hours," the women said. "And becoming doesn't help her either."

'Becoming'? Ballard thought, looking for a place to set Sabina down. He had no idea what else that meant in German. "Becoming" what?

"Which is why she came here to get her Togal," the women continued. "After that the mob scene outside and all over town, she became afraid to take the streetcar back to your apartment alone."

She walked over to the window shutters and began to crank them down. There was a knock at the door—three raps followed by two and then one.

"That's Alphonse, the housekeeper," she said and let him in, It was the man Ballard had threatened to let him park his car. The man he had shot at. They looked at each other in confusion.

Ballard made up his mind. He had his woman. He needed to get out of here as quickly as possible. His own medical supplies were back with the time machine. He would pick them up and get back to Berlin.

"I'll take my car now," he said.

Sabina fell into an immediate deep sleep in the back seat of the Opel. Ballard pulled up to his apartment building entrance. The dead axe-wielder still lay on his back in the gutter in a pool of blood. Ballard stepped around him and opened the rear car door and lifted Sabina into his arms. He saw how angrily pink one side of here face had become. It would peel, but the skin was not broken; it was still only a first degree burn.

With the woman in his arms, he struggled to stand up, stumbling on the curb. Turning clumsily, he bumped into someone.

"Excuse me," he said automatically. He looked over his shoulder and almost dropped Sabina.

"General von Hoescht, what are you doing here?" Ballard was shocked again to notice that von Hoescht was pointing a pistol at his middle.

Von Hoescht stumbled backwards to prevent Ballard from getting too close to him. Awkwardly and slowly. Something was wrong with him, too.

"Get inside," von Hoescht rasped, motioning with his pistol. He staggered in after them.

Ballard had to lay Sabina on the hallway floor to get out his apartment key. He propped her up and unlocked the door. Von Hoescht remained a few steps down, eyeing the American balefully. As Ballard entered, dragging Sabina behind him, the general bolted up the remaining stairs. He staggered into the living room just as Ballard lay

Sabina on the couch. The window glass had been blown out and the room was littered with glass shards.

"Stop!" von Hoescht screamed. "What are you doing?"

"I'm putting a bowl next to her head. She may get sick and vomit when she wakes up."

"Vomit?" von Hoescht asked. "What kind of sickness is that? What's going on, Amerikaner?" He leaned heavily against the door, his eyes fluttering with fatigue.

"You're sick, too, aren't you Herr General?" Ballard asked.

The general turned his head. His belly heaving twice. Finally he could restrain himself no longer. He dove toward the bowl set out for Sabina and ejected a stream of vomit at it. His gun hand never wavered in Ballard's direction.

Von Hoescht wiped his mouth with his sleeve. "Where's your device?" he asked. His eyes were steady now, They bored into Ballard.

"Device?" Ballard asked.

Von Hoescht slapped Sabina in the face with his Walther, opening a cut under her eye. She moaned. "Don't toy with me Amerikaner. Your time traveling machine."

"Oh, that," Ballard said. He stopped and thought for a moment. "Of course. It's this way."

Ballard led the way into the dinning room. There sitting in the center of the otherwise empty room sat Ballard's machine. Von Hoescht's pallid eyes rose momentarily in awe. It was equipment the likes of which he had never seen before. An upright stainless steel cylinder large enough for a person to sit in with a belt-like seam around the middle set on a metal platform. It had a curved window on each side. Arising from the platform was a control stand with instruments and a flat display screen. At the far side of the cylinder was a box the size of a car battery.

"This . . . is really all there is to it?" he asked. "You came from the future with this?"

"You've already figured that out, it seems, Herr General. How did you manage to find us?"

Von Hoescht spun on his heel. He fired a shot between Ballard's legs. "I'll ask the questions here. The next shot will put an end to your very prolific manhood, if Faulheim's pictures are any guide." Then he smirked and relented. "When your Jewish whore was returned to you, you lost all sense of discipline. Knowing listening devices were in your apartment, you nevertheless told her about this secret apartment." His face was illuminated by a sneer of utter disgust at Ballard's obvious weakness.

Ballard froze in place. "What do you want? There's only enough charge left for a single fifty-year trip."

"Fifty years?" von Hoescht asked. "I want to go just thirty-one years."

"To . . . 1976?" Ballard asked. Sabina began to moan. She was moving on the couch, trying to sit up. Ballard started toward her.

"Stop where your are, Herr Ballard," von Hoescht barked. He pointed his pistol at Ballard's groin.

Ballard turned to face the general. "Look, you Goddamned Aryan asshole, if you shoot me you're not going anywhere except to a hospital—if you're lucky. You want to time travel to 1976? Be my guest. There's not enough energy in the machine to take Sabina with me back to 1990, and I'm not going back without her, so we're staying here. She is sick and I'm going to her side. You decide what you want to do." He turned his back on the general slumped against the machine and walked over to Sabina.

Sabina was struggling to sit up. She recognized Ballard and lifted her arms to him. "Oh Robert, she sobbed. What happened? What's wrong with me?"

He embraced her gently and then backed off to look at her. Ballard made some calculations.

"Sabina, when the bomb went off, where were you?"

"Why . . . I was blinded, momentarily. I was talking to you on the telephone, standing over there by the window. I staggered back. I must have tripped on the rug. The next thing I knew, I was lying on the floor. What happened?"

"Hannover was hit by an atomic bomb. Your face got burned by the intense light from the explosion on the left side."

"I know. It . . . it feels very tender," she said, placing her hands delicately on her cheek.

333

Ballard got up and walked over to the window. He looked outside. "How high in the sky was the light you saw, darling?"

"Now that you mention it, that was odd, Robert. I thought it was the sun coming out. Even though it was about one o'clock, the light was lower, like it is at five p.m. Does that mean anything?"

"So you fell down and lay where—about here?" He stood two meters from the window.

"Yes. You can see on the floor, there, where there's the least amount of glass. It showered on top of me!"

"What difference does it make where she lay, Ballard?" It was Von Hoescht, standing in the bedroom doorway, holding his pistol weakly in his hand.

Sabina sat up, shocked at the realization they were not alone. She stared at Ballard with questioning eyes.

Ballard shrugged. "We're his guests for the moment. He wants to use the machine." Sabina lowered her eyes. Ballard continued. "The initial danger from an atomic blast is from the flash of light. Light that is so intense it burns anything it its way. Your sunburn is from the light flash, in which case all you've got is an unpleasant sunburn . . ."

"Or what else?" von Hoescht asked.

"Gamma rays are also emitted a few seconds later," Ballard admitted. "Roentgen-type rays, that, ah, can do more permanent damage."

"The woman looks worse off than me," von Hoescht said belligerently.

"But once she fell down, she was shielded from the subsequent irradiation by the brick walls of this building," Ballard said. "Where were you when the bomb went off?"

"Near the city center. But I was completely inside a concrete building. In the basement, in fact. As you can see, my skin has not undergone any color change."

Ballard stared at the general. "So you were lucky. When do you want to go?" Sabina saw by his look that Ballard was lying.

"When? Right now," he answered irritably.

"No, I mean do you really want to go to 1976?"

"Of course not, you idiot. I want to go backwards, to 1914."

"1914 . . . ? Ach so. The beginning of the First War." Ballard's eyebrows raised. He almost smiled. Of course. This was von Hoescht's great passion—to prevent the diplomatic betrayal of Germany in the First World War. He was just as crazy as himself. As he had been, Ballard corrected himself.

"Let's go. What's involved?"

"You can't take anything with you. Clothed or not, you'll end up stark naked. But any clothes you wear will be burned off during the transition."

Von Hoescht's eyes dropped. Nakedness was disgusting, but he was willing to do anything for the sake of the Fatherland. He swallowed hard. "Los," he motioned with his pistol.

With von Hoescht watching carefully behind him, Ballard set the controls so the date August 5, 1914 was prominently visible on the liquid crystal display. Von Hoescht reached over to run his finger tips over the smooth plastic surface of the flat LCD display. Ballard helped von Hoescht into the cylindrical time capsule. "Take as much off as you feel comfortable with, Herr, General. It will make the transition, which is uncomfortable, easier."

Von Hoescht looked Ballard in the eye. He judged that he was telling the truth. Standing in the open cylinder, he striped down to his shorts. He did not give up the pistol. "Start the machine," he ordered. Ballard pressed the start button. "We've got three minutes to get you sealed up. Be sure the pistol is not touching you," Ballard said, setting the top half of the cylinder down on the apparatus, enclosing the General. He slid it shut with a quarter-turn. Von Hoescht kept his pistol pointed at Ballard as he moved about.

A humming noise filled the air. Ballard stepped back into the doorway. "Sabina, come and watch." They looked at the German general sweating inside the capsule. His skin began to take on a pale color. The pistol lay at his side,

"Robert, I think I can see through him," Sabina said in wonder. In the next moment, the capsule appeared empty. The humming stopped.

"That's it," Ballard said. He unscrewed the top of the capsule and retrieved von Hoescht's pistol. His crumpled undershorts lay in a sweaty pile.

"Is he . . . did you really send him back to 1914?" Sabina asked.

Ballard checked the instrument panel. The remaining power level was forty-four per cent. Nineteen ninety was lost to him forever. "Yes," Ballard said slowly. "And as long as this building was here then, he'll be fine. Otherwise he's going to have a three-story fall to the ground."

"Robert, I told you I have a surprise for you. I'm not sure this is the right time to tell you . . ."

Ballard looked up with a harried expression. "Sabina, I'm sorry to interrupt you. If you're feeling all right, we should leave the city immediately. With the center of Hannover destroyed, no one will be leaving by train from here for quite a while. And I want you to see a doctor. We'll go back to Berlin and either leave from there, or figure out what we can do." His expression darkened.

"What is it darling," Sabina asked.

"The British said they would drop another bomb if the Germans don't begin an immediate pullback to its prewar borders. I'm not so sure Hitler will come to his senses in time. The question is, where will the next bomb be dropped?"

"You think it might be Berlin?"

"That would certainly get the Führer's attention," Ballard replied, slowly. "Sabina, There's something wrong about this atomic bomb attack. I noticed it when I drove in toward the city center to pick you up. I think

I should just drive around briefly to check the extent of the damage. Lord knows, I'll be getting enough questions about it from Canaris."

"Do you want me to come?"

"No, darling. You'll be much safer here. Take the general's pistol. Do you know how to use it?" Sabina nodded.

"Don't let anyone in. If anyone except me tries to open the door, shoot through the door to discourage, him."

Ballard went out to the car. A small group of men had been approaching it, but the body of the axe-wielder still lying nearby caused them to keep their distance.

"Anyone entering the building will be shot by the general," Ballard said curtly. "If you don't belong here, get out." The men turned away sullenly.

Ballard drove off, hoping to survey the center of the bomb blast by circling around it on secondary roads. The streets were filled with debris. Tree limbs lay scattered about, glass was everywhere, thousands of articles lay strewn about, pots and pans, shoes, wash that had been hung out to dry, newspapers, soccer balls, china, even pieces of furniture blown out of verandas. The masonry houses and buildings themselves seemed essentially intact, although often the wooden window frames facing the explosion were still smoldering. As he got closer to the center, he began to see the first evidence of heavier damage.

Wooden buildings—there were not many in Germany—such as unattached garages, garden sheds and kiosks had been pushed over or split open.

On his left, Ballard saw the first sign of significant structural damage. Concrete building with roofs partially caved in; masonry buildings with the roofs blown off and no windows intact but all the walls still standing.

He drove over a slight rise in the road. Before him, lay a scene of intense destruction. He stopped the car at this vantage point. Spreading out below was a scene from Dante's inferno. All masonry buildings were gutted, many still burning. Yet their walls were standing. The few wooden buildings—garden shacks and garages mostly—were completely flattened, lying as splinters on the ground. Everything had been scorched. Cars, trolleys trucks and buses lay turned on their sides. Even objects that did not appear mechanically damaged were black with fire damage. At this close range the thermal radiation of the bomb had reached out with deadly effect.

He saw some corpses lying on the ground. Each was bright red or black, many with skin shredded off as if they had been caught in some huge flaying machine. A few had sections of normal color where

337

the actinic light of the blast had been blocked. A shadow of life to anyone completely shielded from the light. A useless patches of health to those caught in the brilliant rays of the exploding bomb.

Ballard felt an enormous welling up of guilt arise, a feeling as if his mind was about to emotionally throw up. All his efforts—developing the theory of time travel, building a time machine, coming back and personally trying to alter the course of this catastrophic war—all to stop atomic bombs from being used. He was such a genius, and he had failed completely.

A few civilians were puttering aimlessly about, walking through the rubble of their property. Many seemed in a state of shock. A few Red Cross ambulances picked among the streets, searching for important party members and military personnel. His thoughts dwelt on his mother being plucked up out of the ruins of Hiroshima. It was for her sake that he had started this quest. He had failed her. He thought of Sabina, and how he failed her, too. No, a voice in his mind stated sharply. He had almost failed Sabina. He was making good. The affront was to think a mere mortal could alter the powerful current of history by time travel trickery, instead of like Hitler—by force of enormous will. Time travel was a fake, his whole life in Germany was a fraud—giving an enormous illusion of power, he realized—but accomplishing nothing except giving him a momentary big thrill. He'd be better off taking drugs. At least the after effects would not be so deadly.

But not Sabina, Ballard realized. She is not a fake; she is real, and she is true. She alone was his salvation from his own cosmic stupidity. He, the Faustian genius saved by love. God, it was so trite, but, he hoped, still possible.

His eyes tearing with shame, Ballard noticed that buildings at the far side of the slight valley he was looking at seemed to have escaped the fiercest damage. He estimated the distance across the slight valley at something over a kilometer.

He slowed down, edging the car carefully around the wreckage of vehicles that had been stoved into trees and buildings. He saw very few people wandering around. He swung right, and then right again. His next two turns were completely blocked by wreckage, and he had to back out. But within an hour he was able to make a complete circle. A square kilometer of maximum damage, and no total obliteration. Even at what he reckoned to be the center of the blast, the walls of concrete buildings remained standing. Even some trees, though shorn of their limbs, remained upright. Ballard was troubled; something didn't make sense. He stepped on the gas to return to his apartment.

It struck him that except for this small valley, the damage was not nearly the same as the vast desolation over tens of kilometers square that had visited Hiroshima. Outside the circular epicenter of the Hannover blast, tree branches were down everywhere. Power lines were down and the streets were littered with broken glass. A few smaller buildings had their roofs caved in. There were many small fires smoldering, but no inferno. Something didn't make sense.

Back at the apartment he tried to telephone Canaris but the line was still dead.

On the drive toward Berlin, Sabina fell in and out of sleep—or was it unconsciousness due to radiation sickness? He left the Autobahn at Magdeburg to fill up with gas. The military depot was just off the town square. Here everything here seemed normal. He spotted the post office across the square and walked over. Inside he asked the operator to connect him to the Abwehr. He got put through to Canaris immediately.

"Herr Admiral, the damage in Hannover is extensive—much too much for a single conventional bomb, but I am baffled by the lack of damage compared to the Japanese atomic explosion."

"What are you saying, Herr Ballard?"

"Von Hoescht found me at my apartment. He was obviously suffering from radiation sickness, but he was only a half-kilometer from ground zero."

"And he wasn't injured?"

"Not externally. He was in a basement shielded from the flash of the explosion that burned Sabina's face. But I suspect he got a good dose of gamma rays. They easily pass through twenty centimeters of concrete at such close range. He looked weak, and he kept scratching himself—a sign of acute radiation sickness. Yet the fact, that he could walk out so close to ground zero is almost unbelievable."

339

"Where is the general now?"

"In 1914, if everything went all right."

"1914? You sent him..?"

"At gun point, Herr Admiral. He wants to change the course of the First War."

"Ha! You mean he wants to be the Robert Ballard of the First World War," Canaris said coldly. "But if he fucks up things the way you have, maybe we would all be better off if everyone had just stayed home."

"Herr Admiral, surely you don't think I am to blame for this . . . this tragedy?" Ballard said, flushing with shame.

"Who else was to blame? Before this, we were winning the war."

"This is exactly what I've worked so hard—WE'VE worked so hard— to prevent."

"And you've botched it good, Herr Ballard, haven't you? Maybe with all your 1990 science you can only rearrange the furniture of history, but not really change it."

Ballard squeezed his eyes shut to follow that idea through to its logical conclusion. Yes, it was possible that the flow of time is too powerful to do anything else but to divert it in the mildest ripple. But it could not be stopped or diverted too far. Not by the mere trickery of tine travel.

"I hope to God that isn't true, Herr Admiral. But the British had practically no A-bomb effort. Like Germany, they couldn't afford it. And there's something odd about Hannover. That's why I'm calling. There just wasn't enough damage."

"Meaning?"

"There was clearly radioactivity. I think . . . I think the British bomb might have been a near-dud."

"A dud?"

"A bomb that just barely got to criticality. An atomic bomb uses conventional explosives to get the atoms to avalanche into fission. I wonder if the Brits only got a mud slide."

"We'll soon find out," Canaris said sourly. "The Führer doesn't believe them or you. He's moving Operation Sea Lion up to take place next week."

"The invasion of Britain?" Ballard said. "But surely he doesn't want to give the Brits the German invasion force as a target?"

"The Führer is taking that chance. He figures if this was the best they could do, they've shot their bolt. By the time they get another uranium bomb ready, we'll have overrun their factory. Where is their factory, by the way?"

"I have no idea. They didn't have a production facility the last time around. Cavendish Laboratories in Cambridge. Birmingham and Glasgow Universities were the sites of a lot of university work. The project goes under the code name of 'Directorate of Tube Alloys.' Imperial Chemical Industries was the major company involved. But if they've dropped one bomb, they're likely to have another. The Americans had four, one test bomb, two for Japan and a spare. It's crazy to take that risk with the German people."

"Crazy?" Canaris shouted. "Of course it's crazy! War is crazy, and this war is the ultimate craziness. But what choice does Hitler have? If he quits now he'll lose by humiliating surrender. The German High Command won't permit that again. If he carries on and has guessed wrong, at least he'll lose on the battlefield. And the Brits might be bluffing, in which case Hitler will be a braver god than ever. He's got no choice but to blunder on."

"Christ . . . this is just what I tried to stop, this senseless . . . nuclear devastation . . ." Canaris heard Ballard choke back a sob.

"How does it feel to be just like us, Herr Ballard?" Canaris said somberly. "To whom the future is nothing but a featureless blur?"

Ballard waited for the post office operator to render his bill. If the British are bluffing, he had to admit to himself, Hitler is making the right move. When threatened with annihilation, attack. Although brilliant scientists, the British never were that good at solid engineering. like the Germans or the Americans. They just might have slapped together a theoretically fissionable contraption that half fell apart on the descent. Or maybe it exploded too high in the atmosphere. Or—and this was the most likely explanation—they just hadn't produced enough plutonium.

In that case, the next bomb might not have enough either. They expected a big, convincing blast, but it hadn't come off. Now their second bomb was much less of a threat. Hitler is tactically right about launching Sea Lion. Ballard shook his head. It still didn't make complete sense. The British claimed they would follow-up within forty-eight hours—so short a period as to make dropping the second bomb nearly inevitable. How can the British expect the huge German military apparatus to completely change course in such a short time period?

How could the British tell it had changed? It almost seems as if the British wanted an excuse to drop a second bomb regardless. A secret "revenge" weapon that puts the V-1 bombings to shame. And pays the Germans back.

Where would the second target be? Berlin? In that case he should remain here with Sabina. But Ballard doubted it. Even the Americans didn't A-bomb Tokyo. As the center of the country's administration, the capital city would be needed to bring the country back from the stone age into which it would be bombed. And with Berlin evaporated, who would be left to surrender? The Wehrmacht and other services would splinter into scores of holdouts fighting from desperate redoubts. The war could drag on for years.

Magdeburg itself would make an ideal second target. A giant, nuclear footstep in the direction of Berlin. Ballard shuddered at the idea. He trotted back to the car and sped toward the Autobahn.

Sabina had awakened. She sat up and folded her arm into his. "Robert," she said softly. "What is to become of us?"

Chapter Sixty-Seven

"There's nothing anyone can do for your wife with this condition, Herr Ballard," Doctor Albrecht von Hohenratt said. "We have so little knowledge of the effects of ionizing radiation on the human body. Only with Professor Doktor and Frau Roentgen from all their x-ray experiments. Very ugly. But they received many doses over many years. Some very strong, especially around the hands and face. From what you say, your wife has had a single, weak, half-body exposure. Above the waist, fortunately. She'll be fatigued for a week or two. She should rest as much as possible and avoid any source of infection and she'll be fine. The child should be fine as well."

"The child?" Ballard asked uncomprehendingly.

"Ja. She's becoming. About three months along, she thinks. It doesn't show at all."

"So that's what it is," Ballard said with a tone of mild shock. "'Becoming' means 'pregnant.' I'm going to be a father."

"Ho-ho," the doctor laughed. "Yes, Herr Ballard, the Abwehr said you were an American. 'Pregnant' is for animals. Humans 'become.'"

Ballard waited for Sabina to get dressed and escorted her out of the clinic. He congratulated her on her 'becoming,' hardly able to keep his hands off her, kissing and petting her on the way out.

"Robert, this is not America," she said, slapping his hand from her breast. "And besides, you know what the doctor said: 'Lots of rest.'"

Ballard's lower lip curled out like an adolescent caught with his hand in the cookie jar. "Well, maybe just once," Sabina relented. "If you promise to be gentle." They both left the clinic beaming.

Ballard and Sabina returned to their apartment and embraced. Sabina pushed him away and after pulling the blinds, began to undress.

343

Ballard nearly strangled himself in his haste to get out of his clothes. The lay naked, side-by-side in bed, holding each other. He stroked her hair and her back while she lay comfortably in his arms. He was acutely aware of his intense desire, but he closed his eyes and lay still. He felt the liquid pressure of her breasts hot against his belly. After nearly an hour of wordless cuddling, Sabina rolled him on his back. Carefully she fit the tip of his rigid erection into the opening of her sex. With her weight on her knees, and straddling him, she slowly wriggled her hips in gentle rocking motions, not easing herself down, but just letting him nuzzle her entryway.

Ballard lay still in an ecstasy of pleasure. Watching her move her body around on top of him in the half light, her head down, her face covered with her unbound hair, her lush breasts wobbling in front of him as she delicately fitted him inside of her, the sight and sensations of all this together caused him suddenly to ejaculate.

"Ohhh, darling, so soon?" she purred. He felt the beginning of detumescence set in. Sabina sensed it too. "No, no, my darling. You've brought me this far. You're not going to get out of your husbandly duty that easily."

She kneeled next to him and let him watch her stroke him in long, slow pulls, using both hands as if she was milking a particularly large cow's udder. The sight, of her blatant ministrations sent a shudder through his body. In a few minutes they both felt a stiffening of resolve.

"That's a nice boy," Sabina said, straddling him once again. This time she removed her hand after fitting him in, and let him slip inside her full length. "Hmmmmm," they murmured in unison.

Sabina began a slow wiggling on top of her husband, rocking her hips this way and that, twisting her self backwards and forwards, but never up and down. Ballard lay his hands on her hips, urging her to raise and lower herself on him, but she continued only to squirm around. Suddenly, as if an internal switch had exceeded a pressure threshold, she moved her feet forward, pinning his shoulders down and began to lift herself up and lower herself down. With the change in position, he felt himself enter her even deeper.

Ballard lay back, fascinated. This was their first love-making since being reunited. He had been worried that Sabina had been so badly treated that sex might no longer interest her, but he felt sure if he did not push himself on her, she would slowly recover her sensuous nature. Now she was thrusting, herself on him with an ardor that was thrilling beyond belief.

Sabina began humping him in earnest. She grabbed his hands and pulled them against her breasts, urging him to stroke them and pinch her nipples, now grown stiff and erect. Her head was thrown back and she was bouncing up and down on him, pounding and rubbing her flesh against his with animal savagery. A low growl began to emanated from her throat, changing to an ululating chant of orgasmic overload.

For long seconds her groin seized his member in a furious grip. Then she collapsed on his chest, crooning and blubbering, stroking his chest with her breasts, her loins still quivering spasmodically. Ballard felt himself ejaculating spastically—a little late and almost incidentally. Sabina felt it too, and sat up once more to thrust her hips from side-to-side, as if sucking his life juices fully into her womb. He felt her quivering in post coital spasms.

Sabina slowed her rotational motion and lay still on top of him. She pulled the sheet over them, and nipped at his chest with her teeth. She reached between her legs and coddled his balls in her hand, preventing his rapidly diminishing member from slipping out just yet. In a few moments she was fast asleep.

Ballard gently slide out from under his wife. They were both wet with perspiration. He looked down at her in amazement. Covering her with sheet and blanket, he kissed her and went to take a shower.

345

Chapter Sixty-Eight

"Some good luck at last, darling," Ballard said, hanging up the telephone. "We have an appointment to get our travel papers signed off and stamped at the Foreign Ministry Travel Office tomorrow at 3 p.m."

"Thank God. We really are running out of time," Sabina replied from the kitchen. "But do we both have to go? Usually married couples can just send a single partner."

"Darling, you know very well that with Faulheim watching us like a hawk, they're going to handle this one by the book."

The next day the two drove to the Foreign Ministry. A crowd of civilians were milling about in a state of excitement. A policeman was urging people to move on. Ballard pulled over to the curb.

"What's the problem, Officer?" he asked.

"Can't you read the sign? The Foreign Travel Office has been closed until next week," he replied with a harried glance.

"Next week?" Ballard said. "But our visas will expire by then."

"So get them renewed by the person who issued them," the officer said.

"That was Adolf Hitler," Ballard replied in a daze. "He's rather hard to get to see."

The policeman gave Ballard's off-color joke a disquieting grimace and turned away from the car. Ballard pulled away from the curb. He drove slowly, uncertain what to do next.

"Darling, look, it's that awful man," Sabina cried out. She pointed to a tall, lanky figure slowly crossing the street fifty meters in front of them.

"Faulheim!" Ballard barked.

As if he could hear them, Faulheim stopped in the middle of the street, ostentatiously checked his wristwatch, shook it with a worried expression, pressed it to his ear, and then continued to amble across the street as if traffic were of little concern to him.

"The bastard knows we're watching him," Ballard said with disgust. "He can hardly keep from smiling."

"He is smiling," Sabina growled. "Can't you just run him over, Robert?" Her face was tight with anger. "I'm serious."

"Of course! That's it. That's exactly what he's hoping for," Ballard answered. "He had the office closed just on our account. For God's sake, this whole thing is a set-up. Look at the goons on both sides of the street, pretending to be part of the crowd. He wants us to try to run him down. They're waiting to spear us like fish in a barrel if we get within twenty meters of him."

Ballard pulled over and waited for Faulheim to set foot firmly on the sidewalk before continuing on at a crawl.

"What do we do now? We've only, got seven more days," Sabina asked.

"I've got to think on it, darling. But not to worry. I'll come up with something." But Sabina did not relax her face.

"Sabina," Robert said over supper that evening. He had prepared the standard German evening meal—sausage, potatoes and sauerkraut. He had even learned to like sauerkraut by rinsing out the vinegar and adding cloves. They split a beer.

"I have an idea."

Sabina looked at her husband with amusement. "But darling," she quipped. "We just did it a few hours ago. Aren't you satisfied? I mean for today . . ."

"Not that, you licentious women," Ballard replied, He stopped talking and got up around the table to kiss his wife on the neck. It was true—he could not get enough of her. "This is about getting out of here to Switzerland. We've only got three days left on our visas. We can't spend the days lying in bed, no matter how pleasant that might be."

Sabina looked at him inquisitively.

"Come with me to the office tomorrow," Ballard said, waving his arm around. "The enemy is listening."

"Robert, you must be completely mad. This is the craziest idea you've ever had. You expect me to go with you to meet Hitler's wife so you can ask her whether we can travel with her and her disgusting fiend of a husband on their private train down to Berchtesgarten? Have you gone out of your mind? It was that criminal whose henchmen who caused the death of my mother . . ."

"Sabina, darling. She is not a criminal. She is a nice, pleasant girl. She fell in love with the wrong guy. Just like you," he jested. "And, besides, Stumpfy and I can't think of any other way to get down to the boarder. The SS controls all long distance travel; the Abwehr can't help us. And if we get on a train out of Berlin by ourselves, you-know-who will be waiting for us."

Sabina's face fell and her eyes clouded. "That monster would wreck our train to get us back into his clutches," she muttered. She looked up at her husband. She still did not feel quite herself and it was difficult to tell if the queasiness she felt each morning was the remains of her atomic bomb exposure or the fault of "junior," as Robert called the baby. She didn't know what to do either. Except trust her husband.

"All right dear. I'll play along."

Chapter Sixty-Nine

Stumpfnagel grabbed Ballard's arm from behind. "Herr Ballard, come back in. The admiral is waving to us."

Ballard turned around and re-entered Canaris' office and sat in his stuffed leather chair. The two dachshunds ran up to him demanding to be scratched. The admiral was standing erect, listening intently on his "special" telephone. His face looked bleak. Slowly his arm pivoted downward, the telephone handset falling back into its cradle.

"The second uranium bomb," he muttered. "It was dropped on the Nordhausen rocket works . . ."

"The huge underground factory?" Ballard asked.

"Jawohl," the admiral muttered, sitting down slowly, bending awkwardly at the waist like an old man. "Initial estimates are that over 15,000 skilled workers have been killed or horribly wounded. Our entire V-1 and V-lb production destroyed. Most of the Messerschmidt jet fighter production . . ."

"But most of those workers are foreign slaves," Ballard interjected.

"Not so much any more," Canaris said gravely. "The production had become so specialized we had to use German workers and scientists, especially for the highly-skilled metal working of the jet engines. We built the factories to survive any direct bombing hit the allies could throw at us."

"Good God," Stumpfnagel interjected. "That means as soon as the Allies shoot down our present fleet of Me-262s and V-lbs, they'll be able to rule the skies again. German troops will once again be pinned down."

"It means the war will finally be over," Canaris said bleakly. His eyes filling with tears. "That is if those monsters in the Reich's Chancellery can gather together twenty grams of brain matter amongst themselves. I'm not so sure that they can."

Chapter Seventy

Bormann was on his feet, pacing in small circles in front of Hitler. "I tell you, the man must be taken out of the succession list, mein Fuhrer. It is bad enough that he is a total morphine addict and can vacillate from dopey to a raging maniac in a matter of minutes. But this business with Count Bernadot why it's nothing more than a poorly disguised surrender negotiation."

"And not proven," Hitler muttered without meeting Bormann's gaze. Göring was his longest, most trust-worthy comrade. Yes he had quirks—who hadn't in this business. But such a mind. There was no one, not even Speer, with a quicker mind than Göring. The man knew everything and forgot nothing. He possessed the ruthlessness required to get a job done. And his bravery was also beyond question.

Bormann would not be deterred. "The Fat One is not only your immediate successor, which adds great credence to his treasonous behavior—people may think he is your secret emissary—but he is also still head of the Luftwaffe and the Reich Defense Council, President of Prussia, Reich Minister, Reich's Marshall, and who knows what else. I'll tell you one thing, mein Führer, if he survives the war, he'll be a millionaire from what he's put away. Yet you, you who created the entire Third Reich, you who have given everything of yourself, you have taken nothing!"

"That's absolutely true," Hitler growled. It was recurring sore spot with him. He had no money. Yes, he could get anything he wanted—although his wants were always quite modest. Yet if he were to step down from his office he would be reduced to receiving a meager pension, and own nothing: no vast hunting estates in Prussia, no factories producing concrete, construction materials, mattresses, furs. No, Bormann, was right about that part of it. Göring was the businessman among them, that's for sure. And what had he done to earn his fabulous wealth?

"He's outside now waiting to see you with some new cockamamie scheme for saving the Reich at the same time it enriches his pocket, you can be sure," Bormann continued, recognizing that he had roused Hitler's ire at Göring. "Why not tell him to finance it himself—he should have been made to pay for all those jet fighter planes he got you to build."

Hitler shifted his weight on the couch. The report on Göring's suspicious connections to the Swedish businessman Birger Dahlerus had come from Himmler himself. It was not likely to be completely wrong, although lord knows how these guys went after each other like little kids constantly tattling on one another.

"Well show him in," Hitler agreed. "I'll see him, alone."

"Jawohl, mein Führer," Bormann said dubiously. He knew, what a fast talker The Fat One was, and, the hold he still had on Hitler.

Bormann left Hitler's study. Without looking at him, he motioned to Göring to enter.

"Mein Führer," Göring blurted out ebulliently, charging up to him and shaking hands roughly. He was dressed in his white presentation uniform—the golden pheasant version with the ceremonial dagger dangling at his side. "It is a miracle from heaven that you escaped that cowardly attack at the Wolfschanze."

Hitler nodded noncommittally.

"Your escape was more than providential. Did you know that you were the only person who survived who was not permanently blinded?"

"Is that so?" Hitler asked. Now that was interesting. "What about that private—Voelker? He was just in and out."

"Also legally blind, mein Führer," Göring effused. "He can see light and dark, so there may be some future improvement. But right now he's on full pension and uses a white cane to walk down the streets."

Göring swiveled his massive bulk down and perched the edge of a stuffed chair facing Hitler's couch, coiled like a tiger ready to spring forward—a position from which to regale Hitler with another great new idea. He was sweating slightly even though the room was quite cool.

"Look at this photograph of you two coming out of the briefing room," Göring said, pulling an envelope out of his briefcase. He showed the photograph to Hitler. Hitler held, it at arms length. Göring was momentarily puzzled. Where was the phenomenal improvement in eyesight he had heard about? Or had there been some damaged after all?

The photo showed a hatless Hitler, his hair disheveled, clutching at the arm of Private Voelker. Hitler gasped at what he saw. His eyes were two featureless disks, as if his pupils had been erased. He looked like a vampire.

"Gott im Himmel," Hitler said. "I don't want that picture getting out."

"No of course not, mein Führer," Göring lied effortlessly. "The negatives are already burned and this is the only copy." He folded it and ripped it, folded it and ripped it again.

"Mein Führer, I have just been to the rocket research facility in Peenemünde . . ."

"How much is whatever you're trying to sell me going to cost, Herr Reichsmarshall?" Hitler asked testily. He could tell the Fat One was excited beyond normal. Opiates. That obese fool had the nerve to prop up his courage with drugs before coming to see him. It was outrageous.

"Cost, mein Führer?" Göring said, astonished at the cold reception. "This is a chance to bomb America from German soil. That Ballard stunt took over thirty days and kept six U-boats out of commission. They could have been sinking Allied ships. Now we have the chance to do the same damage—as much damage as we want—in Thirty minutes. How can we talk about cost?"

"Because it takes money to run the war, Herr Reichsmarshall, as you always seem to forget. And you've always got a disproportionate share of that money—for the air war over Britain—which you lost; for your jet fighter fleet, which is still letting the bombers through, and for your personal use, if appearances are to be believed."

353

"Personal use?" Göring said in disbelief. "Ach, ja. I should have known. That coarse dwarf has been stabbing me in the back again. He has made quite a career of it, No one he doesn't like is safe, which means almost everyone who has any field experience beyond being a flak private like himself. Of course! He's still burning because I failed to invite him to a hunting weekend. As if he would fit in with the officer corps types that I did invite. Junkers all of them. You know that the last time he rode a horse he fell off and broke his collar bone?"

"It's quite an estate, 'Karinhall,' one hears tell," Hitler added. "Thousands of acres . . ."

"Acres of overgrown forest, mein Führer. Much of which was already in the family. A perfect nature preserve for future generations of German children to see stags, wild boar, geese, ducks, rabbits, wolves in their natural habitats." Göring was gesticulating wildly to emphasize the size of the stag's antlers—"instead of in the zoo when that terrain gets carved up for workers' settlements." Göring wiped his mouth with his sleeve. He was drooling slightly, so agitated was his response.

"He's told you about his own so-called farm, hasn't he? 'Agricultural Estate North,' he calls it, in Mecklenburg. Ten Thousand hectares in his own name. 'To guarantee the Führer's food supply.' Hah! Enough land to supply food for the entire Luftwaffe. He'll be sitting pretty after the war. But I didn't want to dwell on Bormann's many perfidious shortcomings, mein Führer. Rather I want to tell you about a new development, a development that will let us strike those damnable cowardly Americans on their own soil from here in the German Reich!"

"So what are you talking about, Hermann," Hitler asked irritably. Göring was in a state. There is nothing so annoying to be on the brunt of a person's attention when. he is intoxicated and you are not.

"I'm talking about the A-9, a three-stage rocket that will reach New York. We could finally give the Amis a taste of their own medicine"

"What? And frighten them out of the war, Herr Reichsmarshall? How would dropping bombs on New York help its win the war? It would merely infuriate the American people—perhaps enough to turn their fury from the Japanese to us," Hitler said, deliberately baiting his old comrade. "And now this British monster bomb on Hannover. Where were your Messerschmidts then?"

"For God's sake, mein Führer," Göring said, switching from a bellicose bluster to a bathetic blubber. "You have to see the survivors of the Hannover attack. Some of them look like roast pigs that have been taken off the spit. They wander around like zombies. You must show yourself to the people, mein Führer: Let them know that we still have a chance of winning the war . . ."

"A chance at winning the war?" Hitler blurted out. "A chance, only? What kind of defeatist talk is that? Next you'll want to send signals to the Swedes for talks about a negotiated surrender! If your defense of the Reich hadn't been so porous, that so-called atomic attack on Hannover would have been prevented. That was in broad daylight, I remind you. Where were your expensive jets then?"

Hitler wore a hooded expression that Göring had never seen before. Göring felt his heart beating in his chest with frightening arrhythmic pulses. Was he going to faint, right here in front of the Führer? Hitler snapped put of his momentary lull.

"I'm not so sure you are any longer capable of defending the Reich itself against Allied bombers today to be bothering yourself with quixotic schemes to bomb the USA tomorrow. What does Speer think of your idea? And that Ballard person?"

"Ach, those two," Göring sighed. "Ballard thinks the entire V-2 program is a waste of time, but what does that oddball traitor know about German strategic interests? And besides, as an American, have you ever noticed in him any expression of hatred toward the Americans? It's very strange why he wants to help Germany so much—and to what extent. And Speer, the devil take him, he'll do whatever you think best and thank you very much. He says we could skip building the V-2 and go right to the A-9 'intercontinental' rocket. Intercontinental, mein Führer. The A-9 is just two smaller rockets sitting on top of the V-2. In concept at least. Naturally the bottom stage is by necessity quite a bit bigger. I have a fantastic film showing it."

"So Speer is against it, too," Hitler volunteered. "That leaves you and those moonstruck propeller-heads on the Baltic as the only ones who are pushing this project—General Dornberger and his crew. And that charmer, von Braun. Ever since Professor Doktor Lusser developed the V-1 and its fantastic seeing-eye guidance system, the rocket-scientists

355

at Peenemunde have been desperate for a way to come up with a project to top that. Not to help the war effort, mind you, but to justify their existence. Delivering a ton of explosives four hundred kilometers away at Fifty-seven hundred kilometers an hour instead of only at seven hundred kilometers an hour is hardly an advantage at fifty times the cost!"

Göring knew Hitler well enough to realize the Führer had something else on his mind. He was working himself up to broaching the subject. It might take a rage to get it out. God, this could go on for hours. Göring had a group of pilots to decorate. They should be back in the air shooting down bombers, not hanging around waiting for the Führer to come to the point.

"I want to see better results against the Allied bombers," Hitler blurted out. "I gave you General Galland and his pick of the pilots with their new jets. That was not cheap to put together, that jet fighter, and it was the American who urged me to do it. At least they've reduced the bombings somewhat. But the reports show only a half-dozen or so bombers a day are being shot down. What happened to the twenty-five and thirty a day we used to shoot down?"

"Mein Führer, surely you are aware that the Me-262s are working fabulously! They're sitting around just waiting for engagements. The Allies are afraid to show their heads."

"So the reports of the bombing of Darmstadt yesterday and Frankfurt the day before were just hoaxes?" Hitler said.

"No, they were hit, but at night," Göring said. "Eisenhower has called off daylight bombing." With this turn of the discussion, Göring knew any further talk on the A-9 was doomed. The program itself was probably doomed. And all because of that God-accursed American. Von Braun would be furious.

"The jet fighter is not ready for night operations, but we're working on it," Göring said defensively. The truth was pilots skilled enough to fly at night were the real problem. There just weren't enough of them. And it was just not possible to send inexperienced pilots up in the hottest fighter in the world at night. Half of them couldn't find the runway after an engagement, even if their didn't shoot each other down or crash into each other.

"So instead of solving the problem of how to keep the Allies from bombing Berlin, you're working on how we can spend a fortune now in order to maybe be able to drop a few kilos of bombs on New York in two of three years. You know, old friend, Bormann may be right. I don't know if I can trust your judgment anymore."

"Bormann right? About me? Can't trust my judgment?" Göring said, the look of incredulity slowly replaced by one of fear. God, if he could only pop a morphine tablet into his mouth. They were in his breast, pocket, just inches from his mouth. But he knew Hitler strongly disapproved of this little indulgence, and he was watching him, like a hawk. "That odious creature hasn't earned the right to cast any judgment about me. Where was he when you and I were being shot at on the streets of Munich? Where was he during the Great War while you and I were on the front lines, risking our lives and earning our Iron Crosses? The only medal that creature ever got was his Blutorden-and even that was done retroactively just like his backdated party membership. Number 555! How he hoodwinked you to permit that, mein Führer, I'll never know, but every one of us who fought with his bare hands in the streets resent it when that little orangutan sports one of our most honored decoration . . ."

"I'll thank you not to libel the Deputy Secretary, Herr Reichsmarshall," Hitler said, his voice rising. "He may not be a war hero, but he is a tireless worker who helps me at every turn. He solves my problems instead of enlarging them, as your crazy new rocket bomb to America scheme proposes, and your inadequate defense of the Fatherland—no matter how much money I shower on you."

"A tireless worker, yes, mein Führer," Göring replied, his own voice rising. "But just who he is working for—you, or himself—is another question . . ."

"Stop blaspheming the Deputy . . ."

"Blaspheme that little toad," Göring shot back. He broke out into a profuse cold sweat. He was trembling and hardly knew what he was saying. "Nothing I can do will be blasphemy enough for that little coward. You know he's doing everything in his power to take over your position when . . ."

357

Hitler's eyes sparkled as if ignited from within. "When what?" he snorted. "When who attempts what? Is that what's on your mind . . . ?"

"Mein Führer, of course I have no intention of taking over—unless you are completely incapacitated. As written in the codicil of June 29, 1941 . . ."

"Taking over? You can sit here and tell me to my face you intend to take over?" Hitler sprang to his feet. "This display of brazen arrogance is outright treachery, Herman. You would have failed completely to protect us from Allied bombers: Only the American's suggestions pulled your coals out the fire on that one with his push for the Messerschmidt jet fighter. And having failed to protect the Fatherland, you have the nerve to come in her with another crackpot scheme to spend millions of Reichsmarks to drop a few kilos of bombs on New York city in 1948. Then, in the same breath you tell me you're going to take over as soon as I'm 'incapacitated.'"

Hitler was shaking all over. "You know, Herman, I have been extremely patient with you, in spite of your vile habits and the advice of many other generals. But I can tell you one thing: you are not going to take over for me now, in the future or ever. I'm changing my will at this instant. I'm writing you out of the will, out of the succession. I'll, put Doenitz in your place. He knows about loyalty and keeping his nose to the grindstone. Doenitz doesn't come in here whining about how little support he gets, or how much money he needs for uranium-powered U-boats for the year 1950! And as far as your leadership of the Luftwaffe . . ."

"'Out of the line of succession?'" Göring couldn't believe his ears. That was impossible. He had worked so hard, put in so many years, accepted countless humiliations without complaint.

"Mein Führer, you can't do that. Please reconsider what you're saying . . ."

"And now you have the gall to tell me what I can do," Hitler raged. "Oh, such perfidious treason. And from you of all people. You, my old friend, telling me to my face that you're going to take over."

Hitler moved toward the door. "I'm getting a stenographer this instant. I want you to sit here and witness me cutting you out . . ."

Göring sprang to his feet. "Mein Führer, please don't be so hasty. Consider what you are doing . . ." He clutched at Hitler's arm to hold him back. Hitler sprang aside, shocked at being seized. Göring reached down and unsheathed his ceremonial dagger. "I swore an oath and dedicated my life to you on this dagger, mein Führer," Göring bellowed. "Don't take that away from me."

His face was red with hysterical tension, his eyes bugged with fear. He was waving the dagger aimlessly.

"You dare threaten me like that, you disgusting drug-sopping Schweinehund." Hitler screamed. "Bormann is right—you don't know what you're doing anymore. You'll be lucky if I don't have you shot for this affront." Hitler pulled his arm, trying to break Göring 's frantic grip.

"Nein, mein Führer," Göring shouted. "I can't let you do that." He drew his arm back and spun the Fuhrer around to face him. For a split second the two faced each other like boxers squaring off for a fight. With powerful upward stroke Göring plunged his golden dagger straight into Hitler's solar plexus, lifting his victim off the floor. A horrible groan escaped from Hitler's lips.

"Hermann," Hitler gasped, grimacing at the incredible pain. "You betray me . . . thus?" His mouth continued to move, but no sound came out. He fell on his knees, clutching feebly at the ivory handle sticking out of his body, driven in up to the golden hilt, but to weak to pull it out. There was no blood. Then he fell forward, catching himself by his hands. His face was purple and horribly twisted. He huffed and gulped in small gasps, even breathing was intensifying the acute agony.

Hitler fell on his side, moaning loudly and thrashing around on the floor. Göring 's face had gone pale with the enormity of what he had just done. What had come over him? His mind had completely blanked out. Taken out of the succession? That was what did it. After all he had done for the Führer—no one had suffered more humiliation and returned a more loyal service, time and time again. All to maintain the right of succession. Now Hitler was going to strike him off the list! All because of the constant whispering of that poisonous toad.

Göring kneeled down and put a meaty hand on his old comrade's quivering shoulder. He knocked the Fuhrer's trembling hands aside and jerked the dagger out. A spurt of blood squirted onto the oriental carpet. Göring got down on his knees and rolled Hitler on to his back. He stabbed him again, in the same vulnerable spot just below the sternum, this time angling the blade upward, searching for the heart. But the blade refused to find the vital organ. Impaled by the dagger, speechless in the most terrible agony, Hitler began to writhe and squirm on the rug, trying to free himself from the Fat One's iron grip. Göring held onto the dagger, searching upward with the blade.

"Help!" Hitler shouted weakly. His diaphragm was severed so he could not expel enough air to shout loudly.

"Shhhh. Don't cry out, mein Führer," Göring crooned. Göring pulled the writhing Hitler to an upright sitting position and brought the knife to his throat. It all made sense now. This was his destiny, to rule Germany and rule it correctly; to remove all the doubt and equivocation that had plagued the Fuhrer's office ever since that swine Bormann and his counterfeit medal had got control over him.

"I do this for the good of the Reich," Göring said animatedly. "Heil Hitler." In a single maniacal stroke Göring pulled the knife blade across Hitler's throat. Released from Göring 's bearhug, Hitler lunged forward, butting Göring 's hand—the knife only severed his esophagus. Blood gushing from his throat, Hitler pitched forward, gasping air out though his gaping wound—air no longer able to reach his vocal cords which made a sloshing sound as blood clogged the slippery wind pipe sticking out of his neck.

Göring rushed to the study door. He came to a complete stop and then opened it and looked out. "Orderly," he called out calmly. The young man leaped to. Entering the study his eyes refused to believe what he saw—the Führer crawling on the carpet like a broken dog.

Göring slammed the door shut. "Gott im Himmel," the aid muttered, stupefied. His face contorted to a mask of fear.

"Du Schweinehund," Göring screamed. "You killed the Führer!" He grabbed the young man and spun him around, holding him from behind. In one violent stroke he slit his throat with his ceremonial dagger. This time his stroke was strong and sure. The man raised his hands to his neck to staunch the pulsing squirts of blood. He struggled to free himself, but Göring held him with fanatic strength. Suddenly the young man wilted.

Göring released him and let him slump to the floor, stumbling to get up, incomprehension written on his face. He stared at Göring until terminal shock set in. His, face turned white, his eyes glazed over and he slumped to the ground.

His eyes twitching nervously, Göring gazed at his handiwork. What was he doing? Good God—but this was no time to be fainthearted. At last he could take a morphine tablet from his breast pocket; no better make it two. What a sense of relief just the knowledge that he had taken them provided a comfort.

Göring scooped up some blood and slathered it on the front of his white uniform. Quickly, he frisked the young orderly and found his service pocket knife. He unfolded the three-inch blade with a worried look. Hardly long enough to do the job. He threw the open knife next to Hitler's body.

"HELP, FOR GOD'S SAKE HELP!" Göring bellowed at the top of his lungs. He lifted the orderly up by his armpits and dragged him to the door, opening it by pushing the handle down with his elbow. Awkwardly, he inserted his toe in the crack of the door and flung it open.

"HELP! FUHRER ATTACK, HELP IMMEDIATELY."

Göring heard a responsive rush of activity and immediately drew back into the study, falling down on his back, drawing the dead orderly on top of him. As two SS officers burst into the room he flipped the orderly's body one way and then the other as if engaged in a furious struggle. The orderly was plucked up and a pistol thrust into his dead face. Göring stared at another pistol.

"Gott sei Dank, you got here," Göring blubbered, pushing the pistol aside. "See to the Führer immediately. This maniac attacked him right in front of my eyes."

One of the two officers was already at the Führer's side. The three of them saw Hitler's eyes bugging, trying to look at Göring standing half behind the officer. Hitler's arm moved as if to point.

"He's trying to say something to me," Göring blurted out, pushing the attending officer away. "Let me get next to him!"

The SS officer moved aside. Göring dropped to his knees. He put his ear next to Hitler's mouth. He heard a frothing gurgle. Suddenly his ear was seized and bitten with an unholy pressure. Göring winced, but managed to contain himself.

"Jawohl, mein Führer," he said somberly, the pain of his ear being gnashed by Hitler's teeth bringing him to tears. "Oh God," Göring cried in agony. "Of course I'll do everything in my power to carry out your will. I swear it in your name."

"Herr Reichsmarshall," one of the officers said "Please let me get to the Führer. He must have immediate medical assistance."

Göring could not move. His ear was still tightly clamped in Hitler's mouth.

"Be still," he hissed. "The Führer is still talking to me." Abruptly Hitler's mouth fell open, releasing his painful hold.

"That's it, I'm afraid," Göring said with a somber face. It was all he could do not to take his mangled ear in his hand. "The Führer has breathed his last." He turned to the two officers. One dropped to his knees next to the Führer.

"Halt," Göring Bellowed. "He is finished." Uncertain of what to do, the man backed off. "By right of the Codicil of 1941, and the terms of Hitler's last will and testament, I, Hermann Göring, now assume the position of Reich's Führer and Commander in Chief of the German Reich, and all the armed services. Gentlemen, you are released from your personal oath to Adolf Hitler. You will swear an oath to me, right now. Begin." He pointed to the first officer who was holding Hitler's head in his hands. "Let go of him. I am in command now."

The head dropped to the floor. The men sprang to attention and in unison began to tone: "I swear by God this holy oath, that I will render to Adolf—Herman Göring, leader of the German nation and people, Supreme Commander of the Armed Forces, unconditional obedience, and I am ready as a brave soldier to risk my life at any time for this oath."

Chapter Seventy-One

Eva Braun held Ballard back for a moment as he and Sabina entered her apartment in the Reich's Chancellery.

"She doesn't know anything, does she?" Eva whispered reproachfully.

"No, of course not," Ballard assured her. Sabina turned to face Eva Braun and be introduced.

"Frau Hitler," Ballard said. "Permit me to present to you my wife, Sabina Pergo . . . Sabina Ballard. Sabina, please meet Frau Eva Hitler."

They shook hands all around, the two women eyeing each other in a series of rapid calculations that instantly divined the other's class, trustworthiness and emotional makeup.

"Since both you ladies are now honestly married, I though it might be nice to meet," Ballard said cheerily. "We are trying to arranged transportation out of Germany."

Eva ushered them into the drawing room. Sabina noted that although Bauhaus design was forbidden as Jewish art, Eva had decorated the room as modern as current prejudices would allow. The wood of the furniture was honey-blond. She had laid an oriental rug on the floor. Only the stark photograph of a brooding Fuhrer marred the light, airy decor.

"It's so nice to meet you, having seen pictures of you in the newspapers so often," Sabina said earnestly.

Ballard noticed the background wrinkles of the strain of the internment had not yet disappeared from Sabina's features. Would they ever?

"I understand you're also a fan of the movies. Did you catch Willy Birgel in 'The Traitor'?"

"Did I catch him?" Eva replied. "It's one of my favorite films. I have a copy here in the library. And doesn't he look like Clark Gable?"

"Yes, he is very handsome," Sabina said, warming up. "And if the leading lady what's her name, Lida something, hadn't made such a fool of herself, it could have been his best film."

"Yes, Lida Baarova, the Czech," Eva answered. "A terrible lens hog. But at the time she was Goebbels' girlfriend, you know. So the producer couldn't do a thing to keep her from trampling away with every scene, or try to." Eva guided Sabina over to one side of the couch and sat herself at the other end. Their knees almost touched. "But you know I really like Willy Fritsch better. Did you see him in 'Women Are The Better Diplomats'?"

"Oh, he was wonderful, as usual. But I didn't like it that much," Sabina said. "Maria Rokk acted the way a man might think a women would act. I don't think Josef von Baky is a dramatic director. He should stick to his Münchausen stories."

Eva sat back in pleasant surprise. "Why Frau Ballard, that's a perfect description. I never cared too much for that film either, and I could never put my finger on why. Would you care for a glass of wine?"

"Oh. Some tea would be nice," Sabina replied.

"Yes, tea would be perfect," Eva said to the white jacketed attendant who had appeared. "And you, Herr Ballard?"

Ballard turned from the bookshelf where he was studying the titles. They were all cinema books—Hollywood, Leni Riefenstahl, "Gone With The Wind," the Ufa studios in Munich. "I'd love a glass of wine, if that's all right," He answered. "White and dry."

"Whatever the Herr desires," the waiter murmured and disappeared as silently as he had come.

"Well, Herr Ballard," Eva said with mock severity. "You mentioned transportation. Have you come here to ask me to get you another six U-boats?" A telephone rang in the background. "That effort caused a bit more excitement than I'm used to."

"No, Frau Hitler," Ballard laughed. "This is purely a personal transportation problem. Sabina and I are on our way to Switzerland . . ."

The attendant rushed up to Eva with the telephone. His face was white. Eva looked at him in shock. She had never been interrupted like this before. She put the instrument to her head. "Eva Hitler here . . ."

There was a moment's pause. Ballard could hear an excited voice on the other end. Eva gave a loud shriek of pain. The telephone dropped from her fingers and she fell back on the couch, wailing in horrible screams.

Ballard rushed to her side. "Frau Hitler, Eva, what's wrong?"

"The Führer has . . . been killed. Just now. Göring is sending SS troops—to arrest me."

"Damned shit," Ballard said, his face tightened into a mask of concentration. "He's worried that your marriage might cloud his succession. We've got to get you out of here. Buy some time. Eva," he said, shaking her to get her attention. "We must escape. Is there another way out of here?"

"The emergency exit . . . a tunnel, to the Ministry of Propaganda across the street," she moaned. "In the bedroom." Ballard ran to the entrance door of Eva's apartment and locked it. He sprang back to Eva, pulling her to her feet. "Show me," he barked. "And come on. We've got to move fast." He saw Sabina grab her pocketbook and Eva's.

Supported by Ballard, Eva stumbled toward the bedroom. She pointed to an armoire. Ballard handed her off to Sabina, who was just barely able to keep the heavier women on her feet. Ballard pulled the side of the armoire away from the wall. It slid easily. There, set in the wall was an oval-shaped steel door, just like on a navy ship, complete with two lever locks. He flipped them both up and pushed the door open. It creaked, but swung easily. They heard a banging on the front door and violent shouts.

"Quickly, get in," Ballard whispered. He grabbed the semiconscious Eva from Sabina and carried her through the door, then propped her against the dank tunnel wall, using Sabina to keep her from falling down. As Ballard returned to the room, he heard the sound of the front door splintering. Ballard pulled the side of the Armoire up against the wall. At that instant he heard a loud voice in the bedroom: "No one in here." He hesitated, then slowly eased shut the steel door. It creaked, but he heard no acknowledgment from the other side. Quietly, he put

365

Eva's arm around his shoulder and began to move down the dark tunnel, with Sabina leading the way.

They had been walking a considerable distance, a hundred yards at least, Ballard estimated, and Eva Hitler was weighing him down. Every fifty feet or so dim yellow emergency lamp burned to show the way, but in-between lamps it was pitch dark. He felt as if he had passed dozens of them. They must have already passed completely under the Wilhelmstrasse.

Eva began to come around. "My God, Herr Ballard," she said, removing her hand from his shoulder and standing on her own feet. "This is crazy. That I, the wife of the Führer, should be running like a rat for its life. I feel like a character out of Les Miserable."

Sabina handed Eva her pocketbook. Eva nodded her thanks. Ballard estimated they had walked at least two hundred yards by now. Where did this tunnel end? He motioned for them to continue.

"Göring had something to do with it, you can bet," Ballard and said. "He was scheduled to decorate some pilots with Hitler to be standing by. Something must have, happened."

Sabina uttered a grunt. She had bumped into an other steel blast door. Ballard pushed the door open very gently. It was well-oiled and swung open silently. They heard two men arguing. Ballard recognized one voice—Albert Speer.

"I'm telling you, that is nowhere in the construction contract. Show me where it says . . . what?" Ballard heard a scuffle as someone else had entered the underground room. "The Führer—murdered?"

Ballard swung the door open. There facing them, a look of shock on their faces by what they had just heard, were Albert Speer and Martin Bormann.

"Ballard," Bormann shouted out, startled by his unorthodox appearance. "You had something to do with this." He reached for his side arm and drew it out, a look of tremendous exultation growing on his pudgy face. He had caught that American pain in the ass and the likely murderer of the Führer. With a smirk of glee, he tightened his finger on the trigger. Kill the bastard now and he would fix the board of inquiry's result later. Just then Eva Hitler stepped into the room.

"Frau Hitler," Bormann said amazed once more. His trigger finger relaxed slightly. "Is he . . . is the American kidnapping you?"

"No," she replied. "He helped me to escape. It's your friend who's after me—me the Führer's wife."

"But who would be after you?" Bormann asked, his bureaucratic brain struggling unsuccessfully to keep up with one shocking event after another. "What 'friend?'" It was too much.

"It's your bosom buddy Göring," Ballard interjected. "He's trying to take over the government. And he knows that Eva Hitler is the one person who can stop him from assuming the title of Reich's Führer."

"But the will?" Bormann said uneasily.

"The will, the will," Ballard mocked. "Are you going to let an old scrap of paper overrule the current realities? Frau Hitler is the heir apparent. She's a Hitler now. The real thing, not an old foolscap. She's going to need your help to rule the German Reich. But she won't be able to let you take control of anything if Göring catches her and kills her, too."

"Göring killed the Führer?" Speer asked.

"I don't know for certain," Ballard replied, "But he was with him."

Bormann lowered his pistol, his face taut with concentration. He knew one thing—his ancient adversary, Göring, was not going to usurp the Führership. Ballard was an acute embarrassment, but that minor score could wait.

"That drug-addict Schweinehund is no more fit to rule the German people than any other insane asylum inmate," Bormann said. "He spent a lot of time in a mental institution, did you know that?" he asked Ballard solicitously, holstering his pistol. "Now, what should we do?"

"We need a car," Ballard said. "To escape to Bavaria. Eva has many friends there. Then we can get in contact with you. Begin an underground movement to depose the Fat One. The 'Bormann Brotherhood' we'll call it. When we gather our forces, we'll strike like lightning and without mercy."

"Ja, perfect," Bormann said, his chest swelling at the thought. It was his favorite phrase. "Follow me." He glanced up at Ballard gratefully for having come up with a plan. "You can use my car."

Bormann's own car might also become the target of an hysterical Göring, ready to lash out at anyone who might oppose his rule. But driving it the half-kilometer to the safety of Abwehr Headquarters was a chance the three of them had to take. To throw off any subsequent inquires, Ballard dropped the women off at the Abwehr and then parked the car on the Prince Albrechtstrasse, right outside the Gestapo Headquarters. Let Himmler convince Göring that Eva Hitler was not being protected by the Gestapo.

Chapter Seventy-Two

As they entered the Abwehr, the sergeant receptionist told Ballard that Lieutenant Stumpfnagel was in the command post. Ballard rushed the ladies into the elevator and into the map-covered room. As they entered, Stumpfnagel was on the telephone, his face stricken.

"An assassination attempt has been made against the Führer," Stumpfnagel said. "Stabbed by an aid, according to Göring." He spotted Eva. "God in heaven, Frau Hitler!"

"Herr Leutnant Stumpfnagel, meet Frau Hitler," Ballard said rapidly. "Stumpf, you better seal up the building. No telling what the crazies of the Gestapo might try to do in the confusion. And if Hitler is dead, it's anyone's guess who will try to seize power."

"Seize power?" Stumpfnagel said. "There are laws of succession . . ."

"Which don't mean a thing. The fat one has already tried to arrest Frau Hitler: We just escaped out of the Reich's Chancellery in time. This is the opportunity of a lifetime for Göring and his private armies," Ballard said grimly.

"You mean . . . the SS?" Stumpfnagel asked uncertainly.

"Do I ever. Especially as their blood oath to the Führer has now expired. And Bormann is not going to be sitting around on his fat ass for long, either. We have to get out of Berlin as quickly as possible. Göring can't let Frau Hitler escape It is the only thing that could cloud his succession."

Something he saw outside the window caught Ballard's eye. "Herr Leutnant, you take Frau Hitler to Admiral Canaris. Figure out an escape plan. I'll catch up with you in a moment." Ballard pushed Inge, Eva

369

and the lieutenant cut the door. He held Sabina back. "Wait here a moment," he said tersely.

Ballard pulled the K-98 Karabiner rifle out of the closet. It had been fitted with a six-power DDX telescopic sight and at the end of the barrel was a long fat tube with Russian markings. He pulled up a chair next to the open window and propped his elbows on the sill. "Quickly, Sabina. Use those binoculars on the cabinet." She hefted the large Navy-issue optic and peered through them. "Do you see that group, of men filing out of the back door of the last large office building six hundred meters from here?"

She could not figure out what had got into her man. "Just a moment," Sabina said, focusing and scanning the buildings. "Yes, I see them."

Ballard lifted the Mauser rifle and aimed carefully. "Now tell me when your friend shows up."

"My friend?" Sabina said, lowering the binoculars to give Ballard an odd look.

"Watch the men!" Ballard shouted. "We will never get this chance again."

Sabina scanned the group. Most were milling about for a few moments, enjoying the fresh air. A few lit up cigarettes.

"There's General Stanezwitz . . . and—oh God, the monster— F-Faulheim standing in the doorway."

"I have him," Ballard said quietly, peering intently though the telescopic sight. "He's yelling at the men. Probably telling them about the attack on the Führer. Watch him closely now . . ." Ballard took a half-breath and held it.

A loud "chuff" noise shoved Ballard's shoulder backward roughly. A full second later Faulheim—his mouth open, shouting urgently to the assembly—fell over forward, his legs knocked out from under him by rude explosion below his waist. He sat up bewildered, a red stain spreading from the shredded trousers of his crotch.

"You didn't kill him, Robert," Sabina said reproachfully.

"He didn't kill you dearest," Robert replied grimly. "Come-on. Let's go. It won't take that animal long to figure out what happened."

Sabina held him back for a moment, as bewilderment slowly metamorphosed into comprehension. A dawning smile transforming the tenseness in which it had been gripped since their reunion. "But he'll have a long time to think about it, won't he, Robert dear," Sabina said, a gleeful grin now forming on her face. It was just beginning to sink in what her husband had done. She felt inexplicably giddy. It was the first time since her return from Ravensbruck that Ballard had seen her really smile.

Chapter Seventy-Three

While Eva Braun set at the sink having her hair dyed brown, Ballard instructed Lieutenant Stumpfnagel to drive toward the Avis highway leaving the city, to see whether any roadblocks had been put up. Stumpfnagel returned in half an hour.

"The entire city's been more or less sealed off by the Leibstandart Adolf Hitler SS Division. I had no trouble getting through, but they're stopping absolutely everyone. And they wouldn't show me their list."

"You asked to see it?" Ballard said, incredulous.

"Sure. It's normal for the security forces to cooperate on such roundups," Stumpfnagel said. "But they wouldn't give me the dirt under their fingernails on this one,"

Ballard sat down and thought. "What about the trains—the S-Bahn and the U-Bahn?" Ballard asked, referring to the Stadtbahn, the city train system, and the newer underground.

"That's a good question, Stumpfnagel said. "Usually they would be covered, too. But they can't do everything at once. With the caliber of people they're looking for, they'd be covering the roads and the airports first. Then the express trains, and finally the locals."

"They're going to come snooping here pretty soon," Ballard and said. "Especially Faulheim's boys. We can't count on the Abwehr to shield us much longer. The three of us have to get out of Berlin before the net is cast too tightly. Can you spare us four or five men, armed, but dressed as civilians, as an escort?"

"Sure, if you think it would help," Stumpfnagel replied. "But you're taking a chance . . ."

"Being alive is taking a chance, Herr Leutnant," Ballard declared. "But I think I've got a plan . . ."

Ballard felt like a circus performer. His hair was dyed a distinguished gray, and his false mustache was black. He stooped over with a cane, escorting the now dark-haired Eva Hitler, her features made up to add twenty years to her age. Sabina, their "daughter," had blond hair.

They drove to Pankow, a section of Berlin due north of the Abwehr and entered the S-Bahn at the a local station. Four Abwehr agents in civilian clothes entered different cars and casually made their way to the vicinity of Ballard and the two women. Ballard noticed a Gestapo checkpoint being hastily set up for the express trains going north, but local trains were still unwatched. Forty minutes later, at the last station but one, the three got out with their guards following at a distance.

Ballard looked around. There, parked on the street below, was Stumpfnagel. He saw them—and waved.

"They've set up an automobile checkpoint at Tegel next to the airport which is also covered," Stumpfnagel said. "That's where I was stopped. But your plan seems to be working. Leaving Berlin for Munich by going north on the local train was a clever idea. I'll bet you wouldn't have got through if you had made a run for it by going directly south. Herr Major Hilflich says they've got the southern exits closed up as tight as a drum."

Ballard said nothing. He took the car keys from Stumpfnagel and gave him a serious handshake. "You take the train home with your men. We'll call you when we arrive. But I think this is the last time we'll ever see each other. And give my regards to Inge Schmidt."

Stumpfnagel stiffened. "Oh, Ja, Donnerwetter, I hadn't thought of that. Well good luck, Herr Ballard. And to you, too Gnädige Frau Hitler and Frau Ballard."

Stumpfnagel saluted and turned to leave. But he could not tear himself away from watching Ballard depart. So much had gone on. The man from the future, the man who would save Germany and the world from atomic war. Like Hitler, he was a genius who had failed. Instead of bringing about its salvation, Germany was once again going down in flaming ruins. Was Ballard a mirror image of Hitler? Hitler, who was brilliant and could be (so he was told) a likable guy. Was Ballard just as mad? Here he was, on the run with Adolf Hitler's wife and his own wife, a Jewess plucked out of a concentration camp. Good Lord could there be a more unlikely scene? Would his children ever believe it?

Ballard put the car into gear and drove away sharply. He struck north, following the route toward Orangienburg. After fifteen minutes, Eva turned to him.

"Aren't you going to turn around toward Munich, Herr Ballard?"

"I'm not taking you to Munich, Gnädige Frau. That's the first place Göring will search for you. He's probably already got the entire area alerted to be on the lookout for you and us."

"But I have friends there," she protested. "And Herr Bormann will . . ."

"Göring hates Bormann, so he's as good as finished. And your friends are no match against the Gestapo or the SS. Göring controls both."

Eva thought about his answers. They made sense. "So where are you taking me?" she asked finally.

"To Friedenthal just up ahead. To the 502nd Commando school. You'll be in good hands there, I can assure you."

"The 502nd Commando school. I've never heard of it. Who is in charge?"

"You've never heard of it because it was authorized by your husband without any written orders. And he put in charge of it the one man you can count on to see you safely through the end of the war, dear lady—SS Standartenfuhrer Otto Skorzeny."

"Skorzeny!" both women said simultaneously, in awed tones. But Eva Hitler's reply included a half-hidden smile.

Chapter Seventy-Four

MAY 1, 1945

The afternoon had shifted to twilight by the time Ballard finished his story of the death of Hitler, Göring 's attempt to arrest Eva Hitler and her "presumed escape to the south," and the eighteen-hour flight of himself and Sabina past Hamburg here to Flensburg, the northernmost city of Schleswig-Holstein on the Jutland peninsula shared with Denmark. Wolfgang Luth looked at Ballard with a cynical smile.

"My, my, how the mighty have fallen."

Ballard snorted. "Well, if you mean Hitler probably killed by Göring, Frau Hitler on the run, Bormann's fate undetermined, but he's undoubtedly on the lam, and me a complete failure in stopping the use of the atom bomb—then you're right, we've all come down a bit."

Luth continued to observe them with his superior gaze.

"And you want me to take one of our precious remaining U-boats out to drop the two of you off the coast of England? Can you give me one good reason why I should do that? Especially when Admiral Doenitz is hinting that if Göring does take command, the Navy may not follow his orders."

"Doenitz said that?" Ballard asked, amazed. "He was always the good soldier."

"That's why he said it," Luth continued.

"Herr Fragattenkaptain," Ballard said, with a sudden seriousness in his voice. "The war will be over as soon as Germany's current stock of jet fighters are destroyed. That will take a month or two. If you take us out of Germany, I will tell you your destiny and what you must do to stay alive."

Luth smiled condescendingly. "And you know my destiny?"

"I know that next week on May 13, at 0300 in the morning, you will be challenged by a young, inexperienced sentry and will inexplicably not respond with the password. Perhaps you will be deeply preoccupied with other things. Perhaps you won't hear him in the storm. The terrified sentry, under your written orders to shoot at the first failure to respond with the password, will challenge you two more times and then—still unable to make you out clearly—will shoot you dead with a single shot."

Luth's face turned to stone. Everyone knew the war would be over soon. The country was in chaos, with disbanded troops on the prowl for food. All sorts of terrible crimes were being committed daily. Luth had indeed just changed the sentries' standing orders to exactly that, to shoot after a single missed challenge. How could the American possibly know about that? The orders were issued but had not yet been distributed.

Ballard saw Luth's face assume the same cold, assessing stare that he had seen on General Guderian. Years of combat had taught him to recognize that when logic and instinct clashed, the experienced soldier must count on instinct. Thousands of routine life-or-death situations had inculcated a sense of decision making in these commanders that bordered, as far as Ballard could tell, on the supernatural. Luth had long ago realized he would never understand Ballard, but he had learned to trust the man's judgment. Logic said to turn him in. His instinct caused him to pause.

Luth tuned to Sabina. His features changed from those of exhaustion and deadly cynicism to one of an almost ethereal smile.

"My dear Frau Ballard," Luth said. "What do you think of all this scurrying about?"

Sabina smiled back at the famous U-boat commander with a warmth that lit up the chilly office. Then her smile modulated to one of serious purpose. "Herr Frigattankapitan, two weeks ago I was released from the Ravensbruck KZ camp due to the efforts of my husband." 'Mein Mann,' Sabina said—'Mann' being the German word for both 'man' and 'husband.' Hearing himself referred to as a husband still struck Ballard as odd.

"We have been under continuous Gestapo surveillance since, or on the run from them. Oskar Faulheim of the Gestapo will not rest until he captures us. But I simply thank God for every day that we have with each other."

Luth looked away, unwilling to show the moistening of his eyes. Just like Ilse, my wife, he thought. True-blue to the end. And this one Jewish to boot! The amazing American, who could have had anyone from a thousand safe German women, had gambled everything to pull this one out of the devil's cauldron. From her courage and beauty, he could see why. The fact that the Gestapo was after them was just a confirmation of his worthiness.

Luth sat back and took in the couple before him. Good men stick together come hell, deep water or politics. And women, far better then men, knew who the good ones were. They had the ability to spot in a flash the ones worth saving. He saw in that moment that just as he was blessed with a loyal wife, so too was this crazy American. If the American is good enough for this tough beauty, who was he to gainsay her. And besides, he had made the Oak Ridge operation possible—and he had put his money where his mouth was; he had gone along on a dangerous mission. And the operation had been a triumph.

In spite of Luth's suspicions about the American, he had shown cool courage. And he had given up unasked his priceless store of penicillin that had certainly saved Lieutenant Richter's life. What to do? Luth's instinct won out.

"All right," Luth said wearily. "We'll leave tonight on the outgoing tide at 2200 hours. The U-309, on Wharf Number 4."

Ballard stood at the bottom of the ladder as Sabina was helped down the hatch from above by a crewman.

"Oh, Robert. It smells, so." She wrinkled her nose.

"Maybe we could wait on shore for them to deliver a new, unused one," Ballard suggested, his eyes rolling backwards. Women!

Sabina spotted the look. "It's just that I've seen so many newsreels about the famous U-boats, I feel I really know what they're like. Not like this."

"Just like little girls and horses," Ballard exclaimed.

"What?" Sabina said.

"You know, dearest," Ballard said. "Young girls always go through a stage where they fall in love with the horses they see in the movies. Then they smell them at the stable—and in most cases it's all over. They turn to boys who smell much nicer."

"Oh Robert, you're quite crazy, did you know that?" She said. Captain Luth appeared from below.

"I'm glad the words came from your lips, madam," he said with mock severity. "Otherwise I would be more hesitant in agreeing."

Why Herr Fragattankapitaen, your are most perspicacious."

Would Madam care to explain the meaning of that word?" the captain asked, good-naturedly.

It means you're right, Herr Kaleunt," Ballard broke in. "But only because you accidentally happen to hold the same opinion as that firmly held by the entire female race—that all males are uniformly crazy."

"Oh, it's a matter of race, now, is it? I thought the race master died underground."

"You didn't know what killed Hitler?" Ballard asked astonished.

Luth looked at the American perplexed. Had he finally gone completely batty? He shook his head.

"It was the shock of learning of the indisputable scientific discovery that it is not Aryans but women who are the master race," Ballard said straight-faced.

Luth and Sabina snorted with laughter. Batty for certain, Luth thought.

"Herr Kaleunt," the bosun's mate shouted down the hatch. "A Gestapo agent asks to see you."

Luth looked up sharply at Ballard and Sabina. "You weren't joking about Faulheim, were you?" he asked with a worried look. Ballard dropped his eyes.

Luth put on his white Commander's cap and climbed up the ladder, emerging on the submarine conning tower.

"Yeah, what do you want?" he said to the leather-jacketed man standing on the wharf beside a super-charged touring Mercedes.

"Good evening, Herr Fragattankapitan," the man said smoothly. "We are here to pick up an escaped criminal, Herr Robert Ballard, and his half-breed wife."

"Really," Luth answered. "So why have you come here?"

"We were led to believe that the two are on board your U-boat. We don't want any difficulties. We just want those two troublemakers."

"On what authority do you seek them?" Luth asked nonchalantly.

"Why, by the authority of the Führer . . ." the agent said reflexively.

"Oh. So the Führer now speaks to the Gestapo from the grave?"

"Well, no. I mean the new Führer, Hermann Göring." The Gestapo agent was uncomfortable. He was not used to having his authority challenged so cavalierly. And he was clearly still uncomfortable with assigning the word "Führer" to a man who but recently, had been the butt of many coarse jokes.

Luth called Ballard and Sabina up onto the tower. He handed them each one of the five huge binoculars used by spotters. "Do you recognize who is sitting in the back seat?" he asked.

"It's Osakar F-Faulheim," Sabina answered, her face flushed with anger. "He violated me. In his office." Luth's eyebrows raised a millimeter.

"Are you armed?" Luth shouted out to the agent.

"Why, yes," he answered. "Of course. I'm on duty."

Luth stuck his head down the hatch and called for a crew to man the deck canon. The men popped put of the forward hatch and quickly loaded the 8.8 cm antiship canon.

"Herr Fragattenkapitan," the Gestapo agent cried, alarm in his voice. "What are you doing?"

"Well, I'm armed, too," Luth answered. "Put your weapon on the dock and tell the pervert in the automobile to get out. I want to see him eyeball to eyeball."

"Herr Kaleunt, it's just a severely war-wounded veteran . . ."

"Gun crew, fire one round at the boot," Luth shouted out.

"No wait," the agent screamed. It was too late. An 8.8 cm anti-ship round blasted out of the canon. Instantly it struck the Mercedes in the center of its rear tire, blowing the back of the vehicle into the air by kinetic energy alone. The target was too close for the shell to arm itself. The car fell back to the wharf with a harsh jounce.

The Gestapo agent drew his pistol and ran behind the smoldering Mercedes. He began firing at the gun crew. Suddenly a wave of heat exploded around the crippled Mercedes. He staggered back but then fought his way to the rear door. He pulled its occupant out by the collar and dragged him away from the burning car. It was Faulheim, wearing what looked like a large baby's diaper. Seconds later the car exploded, knocking both men into the oil-soaked water.

"Herr Kaleunt, you can't do this," the Gestapo agent cried out from the black, frigid water. "A helpless war-wounded is drowning. He is too weak to swim."

"Do tell," Luth answered, and then shouted down the hatch. "Make way, three knots forward." The diesel engines of the Type VII U-boat burst forth into song. Giving over the harbor navigation to his first mate, Luth slid down the ladder to the control room. He turned to Ballard and Sabina. "I've had business with that Gestapo Schweinehund Faulheim before," Luth said matter-of-factly. "Gave my wife Ilse a hard time when we were to get married. Didn't like the odor of her grandfather. Doenitz had to set him straight, but I've held a grudge against him ever since."

Sabina put her hand on the captain's shoulder, and kissed him on the cheek. She returned to Ballard and took his arm in hers, smiling like the cat that had just lapped a dish of cream.

Chapter Seventy-Five

The main hatch swung open noiselessly and a puff of fresh, salty air flooded the inside of the U-boat conning tower.

"Quickly, men," Captain Luth whispered to the crew dragging an inflatable boat up through the small hatch. Ballard fastened the May West around Sabina's middle, swinging one loop between her trousered legs.

"Robert!" she said in an annoyed tone, trying to push him away. What was he up to now?

Luth looked over, saw the nonstandard fastening and grunted his assent. After Ballard was finished, he grabbed Sabina's life jacket and tugged it back and forth and up and down to assure himself it was snugly fastened.

"Between the legs is smart," he said to Ballard, making sure Sabina. heard him. "Too many men have slipped out of the vests . . ."

"Herr Kaleunt," a voice whispered from the hatch. "The inflatable boat is ready."

Ballard directed Sabina up the ladder, following closely behind her. Once outside, he was surprised to find the water level only a foot below the conning tower deck. The U-boat was just barely sticking its nose out of the sea. Ballard looked at the coastline a half-mile away. He could just barely distinguish the dark streak of land from the blue-black sky.

"It's been an exciting adventure knowing you, Herr Ballard," Luth said rapidly. "I hope things turn out for you and Madam. Good-bye." He saluted briefly and disappeared beneath deck. Two crew men with worried faces held the rubber dingy up against the periscope.

"Please hurry," the one man said. Ballard stepped in first, his foot sinking precariously on the slippery rubber floor. He turned, ready to receive Sabina as she was handed to him. Ballard saw that both crew "men" were seventeen year-olds.

"Good trip," the older one said and threw the rope to Ballard. In an instant they were separated from the U-boat, which sped silently away. The wake bobbled the boat, threatening to topple it.

"Oh," Sabina gasped, falling to the soaking floor. "Why did they pull away so fast?" She sat upright, wet from the waist up.

"We were always moving. They just let go of us. A submarine can't maintain its height in the water unless its moving," Ballard said. He was placing the wooden oars into their locks. He pulled on the oars and spun the clingy around, his back to the dark shore. "They are desperately afraid of being seen by radio beams that can see metal objects." Ballard watched the tower slip under water. For a moment the periscope made a white flag-like marker on the surface of the water. Then it too disappeared in the enveloping blackness.

After numerous attempts to synchronize the rowing of both oars, Ballard finally got into the rhythm of it. After a few minutes, he felt his shoulder muscles start to loosen up. The exercise felt good.

They heard a roar in the distance. Ballard stopped rowing and looked around, listening.

"Is that an airplane?" he asked.

"No," Sabina replied. "It sounds like the surf."

Robert continued to pull on his oars. Soon, in response to the waves rushing into shore and receding, the clingy began to heave upward and plunge down. Ballard felt his old nemesis arise like the stench from a bog.

"Arrgh, I'm getting sick," he groaned.

"Sick?" Sabina, asked. "Robert, we're finally escaping from that maniac Adolf Hitler and his Gestapo henchman, we're both in one piece and newly weds, and you can think about being sea-sick?"

"Sabina, darling. I didn't think about it," Ballard said angrily. "I'm getting sick and trying not to think about it."

"Oh Robert," Sabina said with a chuckle. "You're just worried about what's going to happen to us. Sea sickness is all . . ."

"Don't you dare say it, my darling," Ballard growled.

"Say it?" Sabina asked. She had never experienced him being so unaccountably angry. "Say what?"

"Say that it's all psychological," Robert said, his voice grown weak.

"But I'm sure that's the case, darling—oh no." Sabina moved quickly aside as Ballard lunged for the side of the dingy.

"Du Schweinehund," Sabina cried out angrily, wiping his bilious chyme from her knee. "Oh, you're disgusting." She pummeled him on the back with her tiny fists. "You did that on purpose."

Ballard hung over the side weakly. It was the only time in his life he had ever been able to smile after throwing up.

Chapter Seventy-Six

It was five o'clock in the morning by the time Sabina and Ballard managed to hike into a small village. They had no idea where they were. Captain Luth had refused to tell them where he was dropping them off, "So as to protect the U-boat for as long as possible in case of English torture," he had said jovially.

In the chilly predawn they searched around for a police station. Ballard had given Sabina his jacket to keep her soaked body as warm as possible and now he found himself shivering as well.

Ballard stopped and banged on the front door of the lion's Head pub. After a few seconds, he banged again. A wooden window creaked open above them.

"What's the racket govn'r," a voice called out.

"We're German spies and we want to give ourselves up," Ballard answered.

"Oh, right then," the voice said and the window slammed shut. They heard nothing more.

"Do you think h-h-he doesn't b-b-believe us, darling?" Sabina asked after a minute of waiting. Both of them were shaking with cold.

Ballard began to get angry. He looked around for something to throw. He tripped on a cobble stone and pulled it up, but it was too heavy. He shuffled his feet along the side of the building. His foot struck something; a heavy stick, probably one that had been fetched many times. He cocked his arm and hurled it at the window. It splintered the glass with a satisfying crash. The face popped back out.

"Eh. Why don't you go home nice an peaceful before I call the police?"

"Becauz vee vant you to call ze poliz. Vee're not kiddink," Ballard said sternly.

"Oh," The voice said, mollified. "Why didn't ye say so."

"Und open upp to let us in. Vee're freezink to des."

"Keep your shirt on Jerry," the voice said. "I'm down in a flash."

Police Constable Hubert Pembroke was not nearly as put out by having to arrest German spies only to find out they were merely DP civilians, as Gregory R. Mullins was in demanding that someone should pay for his broken window.

"Now look `ere, Mullins," the constable finally said, "Ooh these people are is up to Scotland Yard to determine. But yer window can wait until daylight, can't it?"

"Well, I don' know," Mullins said defensively, realizing he was being shown the door and would have precious little gossip to reveal at his pub.

"So why not just be gettin' along and I'll be by to discuss the damages," the constable continued. "Now be off wit ya'."

The constable handed Sabina a large mug of tea. "More's on the make," he said amicably. "Now that Mullins' is gone: Let's go over it one more time."

Ballard nodded. "I'm an American who has been living in Berlin—trapped by the war, really. I married this lady a few days ago, who is German and we got smuggled out by submarine and dropped just off shore. You can find our rubber dingy an hour or so down the road when it gets light. We're not spies, we're refugees."

"Not a lot of refugees get escorted by a submarine," the constable said, scribbling notes as Ballard spoke.

"I know," Ballard said. "We've had a . . . a varied existence. I'll be glad to tell Scotland Yard the whole story . . ."

"Well, ye'll get yer chance at that," the constable said, flipping his pad shut. "I'll call them and report. In the meanwhile, you're welcome to sleep in the cell—or take a room at the inn down the road."

"You'd let us leave here to stay at an inn?" Ballard asked.

"Only if yer promise not to escape."

"Oh, of course," Ballard said. They were truly in England. And the Kaleunt had warned about torture.

Ballard woke suddenly to the sound of shooting. He leaped out of bed and ran to the window. He could hardly believe his eyes: a group of British soldiers had surrounded four Americans in a jeep. The Americans had their hands in the air!

"MR. BALLARD!" a loud British voice shouted. Ballard struggled with the window and pushed it open. He stuck his head out hesitantly.

A beefy sergeant looked up from his gun pointed at the Americans. "You Ballard?"

"Yes . . ." Ballard answered.

"Well get your arss down here before the Americans reinforcements arrive. We don't have much time."

"Time? Time for what?"

"Your fellow Americans are after your arss, pal, unless we stop them. Now get moving."

"What about my wife?" Ballard asked.

"Your wife?" There was nothing in his orders about a women. "Bring her," the sergeant barked.

Chapter Seventy-Seven

Robert Ballard stood behind Sabina as she curtsied and shook the hand of the Prime Minister of England, Winston Churchill Ballard shook his hand and reflexively knicked his forehead. He caught the sparkling eyes of the rotund PM eyeing him with frank curiosity. The eyes darted about with acute intelligence. Behind the appraisal Ballard detected. a twinkle of joy. During the introductions, Ballard noticed the subdued, superior smiles of the small coterie of high-ranking British officers. At least he believed they were high-ranking. Ballard had never been able to figure out the British method of signifying rank. But they all sauntered about with the same awkward carriage that passed as high-class reticence. He heard a lot of low-voiced "Oh, may I . . . ," "Here please let me . . ." and "Oh, not at all . . ."

There was a very feminine air of cut and parry. It made him realize in an instant one sharp cultural difference between the German and the British High Command. Polite and snide. The Germans were just civil and blunt.

"Mr. Ballard. You are undoubtedly wondering why you've been invited here," Churchill said in a dry, laconic voice.

Ballard shook his head rapidly. "Yes, Mr. Prime Minister. I would dearly like to know. According to your very competent men, a few hours ago the Americans were going to fly me back to the United States to stand trial for high treason. Your man assured me I would face the firing squad."

"And well you would have," Churchill replied. "The American government is very angry at you for destroying their atomic bomb plants in Tennessee and Oregon. You put them completely out of the business of making atomic bombs. It will be years before they repair the damage."

"Which I admit I set out to do. The atom bomb is a horrible weapon. It must never be . . ."

"Now, now, Mr. Ballard, you've been through a lot, we know how you feel, but surely your realize with all the scientific effort going on, somebody had to make one." The Prime Minister stood up from his chair. Everyone else in the room did so immediately. "Come," he said, amicably. "Let's move into the study where we can speak a little more privately." He looked up at the assembled group of generals and admirals. "Gentlemen, I'd like to have a few words with Mr. Ballard. General Mountbatten, would you escort Mrs. Ballard? We will join you for dinner in thirty minutes."

The door to the study closed. Ballard nearly grinned at the grand coziness of it. An academic's dream. His dream. Books from floor to twelve-foot-high ceiling, full length French windows with white drapes showing behind the blackout curtain, now drawn aside to let in the evening light, Two sofas facing each other in front of a fireplace. What a place. Just like he wanted to have. Maybe now he could.

"Mr. Ballard," Winston Churchill said with great enthusiasm, taking the American's arm and guiding him to the sofa. "The British Government cannot adequately express its thanks to you for what you did."

"Which was what?" Ballard asked, still puzzled.

"Well first it was the information about the German heavy-water plants in Vemork, wasn't it?" the PM asked. "Thanks to that little note—and by the way, I can tell you receiving that letter did raise some eyebrows—we were able to completely gut the German nuclear bomb program. In a sense, Mr. Ballard," Churchill said after lighting a huge cigar, "You can be said to have prevented the Germans from A-bombing Great Britain."

Blue smoke billowed from the Prime Minister's mouth in successive puffs. "Her Majesty's government is grateful."

Ballard looked at the Prime Minister. So that's what they think. Good lord, he had better keep his mouth shut about the actual progress the Germans had made with their uranium burner project. Heisenberg had so skillfully kept it a research project, it had no chance of attaining practicability. At least not in the next ten years.

"And by crippling the American effort you forced the Americans to transfer most of their technology to build-up the nascent British effort. With enormous help from the Americans, and very painful expenditures of our own, we succeeded in manufacturing four atomic bombs. Now that the war is practically over, or will be as soon as, we drop the last bomb, the Americans won't be able to rebuild their Tennessee plant in time to complete a single bomb. The place is a radioactive glut.

"During peace time, the urgency to rebuild the plant will evaporate. And the money, thus leaving Great Britain with the only operational atomic bomb manufacturing capability, for, say, the next ten years at least." Churchill said. "And the only ones with operational experience in using them. You can't imagine how that has improved our relations with the colonies. The first reversal of fortunes with that rebellious breed since it all started back in the '70's."

"You mean 1770's?"

"Quite," Churchill replied expansively. "A most satisfying reversal of fortunes."

He puffed deeply on his smoldering cigar. "The Americans are acutely jealous, of course. And they are begging us for a few atomic bombs to use on Japan. They'll pay dearly for them, of course; probably in exchange for our entire lend-lease debt! But the reversals of how they are treating us has undergone a most profound change for the better. No longer is the British Empire their poor doddering parent ready for the nursing home."

"But I can't go home again," Ballard said, realizing how parochial his complain sounded.

"Quite right," Churchill said. "You would be arrested instantly and most certainly executed. However, Her Majesty's government is extending to you the full force and protection of British statehood, Mr. Ballard, for you and your wife. The papers will be completed by week's-end."

"I'm honored, Mr. Prime Minister," Ballard croaked. "Thank God." At last they would be safe. And together.

"Oh no, Mr. Ballard," the Prime Minister said reprovingly. "It is we who will be doing the honoring. Her Majesty intends to knight you shortly after your citizenship papers are completed. Knighthood is only possible for a British subject."

"Ooh," Ballard said with a pained expression. "Mr. Prince Minister, there's something I have to tell you, a very unpleasant fact to save us both a lot of embarrassment."

Churchill took the cigar out of his mouth in surprise. "Frankness? In time of war? Now that is a surprise. Yes, do go on . . ."

Ballard stood up and paced nervously. "Do you, ah, remember Bletchley Park?"

"Bletchley . . . that awful German sabotage led by that Frankenstein Skorzeny?" Churchill blubbered. "Over six hundred of our finest mathematicians horribly burned to death. Our entire code-breaking effort halted in its tracks. You don't mean to tell me . . . ?"

"Yes, I'm afraid so. I planned that operation too," Ballard said.

"But why, man?" Churchill asked plaintively.

"The Allies were crushing the Germans too rapidly," Ballard said, the story rushing out frantically, his face red with shame. "I had to buy time so the Germans could perfect the V-1. And construction of the Oak Ridge refinery had to be far enough along so that bombing it would do irrevocable damage. If Bletchley had been allowed to decode everything the Germans transmitted, the German war would have been nearly over before the equipment I needed to destroy Oak Ridge would be ready.

"Nor would Oak Ridge have been far enough along to worth destroying. I have not been for or against the Allies or the Axis, Mr. Prime Minister. I am against any use of atomic bombs!"

Churchill fell back into his sofa, chomping furiously on his stogy. "Good God, Mr. Ballard, you are really serious." He puffed sharply on his cigar. There was a long pause. "This puts the whole affair in an entirely different light." He puffed rapidly again, but the disgusting black object had gone out. He took a sterling silver Ronson lighter and re-lit it, blowing huge clouds of smoke into the room.

"This begins to make more sense now, too," he muttered, his brow deeply furrowed in thought. "You were always were too good to

390

be true. We're dropping the third one, you know. Tomorrow morning. On their Operation Sea Lion."

Ballard gasped. He realized he could marshal no military argument against it. The genie was out of the bottle. Without using the A-bomb, the war would continue indefinitely. Göring would just begin to consolidate his power, and grow to enjoy it even more than his drugs. Absolute power is the absolute high. Another A-bomb would bring the war to a quick halt but at what terrible human cost? Once again the full extent of the failure of his mission sank in.

"The Hannover bomb was, not very powerful. What happened?"

"You know that?" Churchill barked. "How could you know that?"

"I was there right after it went off."

"I'm told that a huge area was demolished," Churchill said, sitting up and swiveling in Ballard's direction. He peered sharply at Ballard. A most unusual person he sensed. Unnaturally so.

"I'd say a square kilometer was demolished. That would mean the bomb only had a yield of, say, a couple of kilotons. I'm sure you were hoping for ten or twenty."

Once again Churchill stared at the American. "You know, our embassy people in Washington haven't been able to find out who the devil you really are. We don't think the Americans know either. And not for want of trying . . ." He flicked his head as if bothered by a fly.

"They used enough uranium in the first bomb estimated to get a yield of twenty kilotons. We believe we got five. We doubled the uranium and think we got twenty at Nordhausen, but that was a surface burst and the damage was difficult to assess. The crater was quite small. Tomorrow's bomb will be greater still. We're combining the amount from the two remaining bombs into one. But it will be an air burst. With the troops masses at the Pas de Calais, we could kill a half-million German soldiers. It will break the back of the German fighting forces."

Ballard paled at the realization of his failure. "Ten thousand were killed instantly at Nordhausen," he volunteered. "The rest either severely wounded by the hurricane of the blast, or heavily irradiated by the radioactive soil. People and machinery were blown out of the hundreds of tunnels into the countryside like grapeshot, Some for over

391

a mile in the air. How did you ever find me to rescue me?" he asked, anxious to change the subject. "And the Americans?"

"Oh, that. You can thank your Gestapo friend Faulheim for that," Churchill replied absently. "He sent a signal in the clear to all German forces to prevent the escape of one Robert T. Ballard for the assassination of Adolf Hitler. He just happened to mentioned you as the head of the Oak Ridge raid, too. Nice touch."

"But why would he do that? The Germans think I'm a hero for that action."

"Oh, it wasn't the Germans he wanted to tell. It was the Americans."

"The Americans . . ." Ballard repeated. "Of course. That's why when they learned we had landed they were in such a hurry to capture us. How did they learn?"

"My friend," Churchill said gravely, "although I don't know, if I can call you a friend anymore. Not with Bletchly Park on your tally sheet. When we heard from Faulheim's broadcast who it was that was coming, the entire Royal military establishment in southwest England was alerted. Of course, the Americans were too. And they were as frantic to capture you as we were to celebrate you. If you had fallen into their hands, you would be hung for treason. They are already demanding your extradition.

"The man whose window you broke couldn't wait to tell all who would listen about the German spies he had turned over to the constable. He runs a pub and an American officer happened to stop in the morning after his stint at all-night guard duty. He realized right away who you were, so he telephoned his commanding officer—they're encamped a few miles down the road. Our boys first got the report from Scotland Yard. They had a bit farther to travel; they both arrived at the same time. Caused more than a bit of a stink, our boys holding the Americans at gun-point."

Churchill's face had fallen into a deep scowl, his mind roiling with thought. "Now we can't have any celebration—not with the murder of six hundred British souls on your conscience." Churchill eyed him bitterly. He had still to figure out what to do with the American.

"Get me another cognac out of the cabinet, would you please?" The British leader chewed on his smoldering cigar. "Your admission of guilt, however honest—and I commend you for your honesty—introduces a factor into the equation which brings her Majesty's government to a point of great vexation." Churchill looked into Ballard's eyes. "Your entire . . . almost supernatural adventure sorely tries the soul."

He averted his gaze and shook his head vigorously. "Any decoration is now out of the question. But citizenship, yes. Otherwise the Americans will kill you; and we owe you much, regardless of how it was accomplished."

Churchill looked up at Ballard with rheumy eyes. "Well, Mr. Ballard," Churchill said gruffly, "There's quite a lot about this war that neither you or I will ever understand. But this much is clear: you can't remain in Britain because of your involvement at Bletchley—that will come out sooner or later, of that you may be certain—and you can't remain an American citizen because the Americans will hunt you down."

Churchill moved his portly frame from side to side as if he was sitting on something uncomfortable. He took a quick final sip from his cognac. "So here, then, is what Her Majesty's government is prepared to do . . ."

Chapter Seventy-Eight

The agent took the boarding passes from the couple as they reached the top of the gangplank and handed them off to the chief steward. "Mr. and Mrs. Jones, welcome on board. Mr. Royce will show you to your cabin."

The two followed the steward, the tall man rather reluctantly, the short women with a light step. They were shown to their cabin on the top deck with four large portholes. There was a sitting room, a large closet and a separate bedroom with two beds. There was even a separate powder room. The women beamed at the accommodations. She checked the closet: all their luggage had been delivered beforehand: their entire new wardrobe hung carefully arranged in the large closet. She pulled out an evening dress and twirled around, holding it in front of her. He lay down on one of the beds and tried to take a nap, but he was continually pestered by her chattering, as she felt compelled to show him every dress in the wardrobe.

Half an hour later they heard the deep blasts of the steamship horn signaling the departure. They left their cabin and walked to the railing. A Royal Navy petty officer was standing near the gangplank. "Mr. Hubert," they called out. He looked up and saw them waving to him. With a relieved expression, he waved back. The moorings were cast off and the boat slowly pushed away from the dock. His job done, Petty Officer Hubert turned and walked away.

"Oh, Robert," the woman beamed. "Just think of it—a whole new life. No more Faulheim—see, I can say his name. No more Hitler or that Eva Braun women who you so fancied . . ."

"But Sabina . . ."

394

"Don't play innocent with me, you impossible lecher. One look at that tramp's face when she saw you was enough for me." She turned to look him full in the face. She gave him a passionate kiss. Other passengers looked at the odd couple askance.

"Aaargh," her companion pushed her away. "Sabina, please don't squeeze me like that. The boat is rocking and you're knocking me back and forth."

"Rocking?" Don't be silly dear. The water is as calm as a mirror and we haven't even left the harbor. Oh, you know, you don't look so good. But honestly, you can't be feeling badly already, Robert, we've hardly moved a hundred feet. Come on, let's dress," she said gaily. "We've been invited to sit at the captain's table for dinner."

"How can you even think of food?" he asked querulously.

"You can't be serious," she replied. "We haven't eaten since breakfast. It's nearly seven p.m. and besides, I'm eating for two."

"How long is this trip going to take?" he asked morosely.

"Three weeks," she said primly. "A wonderful honeymoon. Now let's go back to the cabin, dearest. I know, just what will fix you up."

Ballard's eyes lit up momentarily.

"No, not that, silly. At least not before dinner. It's a new pill the Americans have invented—Dramamine. It's said to work miracles against your silly seasickness."

"I've used it for years, my darling," he protested. "And instead of being sick and alert, I'm sick and stupid. Take your pick."

"Hmmmm," she said, her brow wrinkled in heavy thought. "That would be a difficult choice."

He swatted her on the rump, but she did not scamper away. "Well maybe we don't have to be in quite such a rush for dinner," she said dreamily, facing him and fingering the lapels of his jacket. She looked at him and then shyly averted her gaze.

His eyes flared with pleasure. His nausea suddenly vanished. Hells bells, he thought. Maybe this seasickness business is all psychological.

NNN (The end.)

395

Afterword

I tried to make this story as accurate as I could regarding the major historical characters, historical events and the details of everyday life. But this simile could only be maintained for so long. Nor could I include everything, or even such very important aspects of daily life as the furious pace of Allied bombing as early as 1941, or the ravenous sweeps of Jews and other social undesirables into the concentration camps. To have given those two aspects their proper weight would have resulted in better history but a different story.

In Ballard's War, the first major departure from history occurs after Hess's flight and before Stalingrad. Von Stauffenberg's brave attempt to assassinate Hitler occurred in July 1944, not near the end of the war as I detail it, and, of course, the addition of mustard gas was Ballard's idea.

It was instructive to learn what technology did and did not exist in Germany in 1940-1945. Berlin had excellent direct-dial telephones. Television transmission had been demonstrated during the 1936 Olympics, although no one owned any televisions sets. The ball-point pen had been invented but not yet brought to production. When it came out in America after the war, it sold at a great premium as a technical marvel, and smeared terribly.

Aerodynamic streamlining occurred during the war as ever greater speed was sought from aircraft, although American automobiles obtained their swoopy looks long before; a styling statement, or of necessity? The ubiquitous German Type-VII U-boat was festooned with railings, deck guns, conning tower, ack-ack guns. It was really only a boat that could submerge, and so could manage only four knots under water—a deadly deficiency. A serious effort to streamline resulted in the

396

modernistic Type-XXI U-boat and the few that were made could cruise under water at seventeen knots. Like the revolutionary Me-2621 jet fighter, the Type-XXI was nearly invincible. Had either been introduced two years earlier it is likely Britain would have fallen, denying it to the Allies as a staging point for an attack on German's Western Front.

But, had the Germans fared better in prosecuting the war, the pressure to come up with these radically improved weapons would have lessened. In Germany's case, desperate necessity, even blind hope in the face of hopelessness (along with engineering genius), was certainly the mother of invention.

Is there any way the Germans could have won the Second World War? The answer lies in the numbers. Even had Hitler done everything right, that is, listened completely to Ballard, in the final analysis Germany did not have the industrial might to compete with the United States. If Hitler had destroyed Oak Ridge (and got the Japanese to destroy the Haniford nuclear plant in Washington State), and switched to a secure code—both big "ifs," the war might have lasted an extra two years. By then German war production would have been exhausted just as the US manufacturing would have reached its peak. One Me-262 might take on two or three Mustangs but it could not take on six, or ten. And, with Russia conquered, a stalemate might have been negotiated.

With the development of the atomic bomb, however, all of Germany's high-tech gadgets could not have saved it. And, of course, Germany was nowhere in sight of developing its own nuclear bomb. Even if Ballard had given them the plans, the small, war-exhausted country could not have afforded the immense effort.

With a half-century of hindsight, the only wonder was that the end took as long as it did. When Germany was defeated, it fell apart like the fabled one-horse shay—everything wore out at once, and the country collapsed into a heap of rubble without an ounce of reserves.

German Glossary

The initial word in quotes following the German word is the literal translation. The words in parenthesis are the phonetic pronunciation. Then follows the meaning.

Abwehr. "Dis-arm." (UP-Vair) The German Counter Intelligence Service, equivalent to our Secret Service. It was a Navy operation, run by Admiral Canaris who was implicated in the 1944 von Stauffenberg assassination attempt of Hitler. Canaris was executed in the last days of the war.

Donnerwetter. "Thunderweather" (DUN-air-vetter), a mild expletive like `darn it.'

Engländer. "English person" (ENG-lender). Since this is a masculine form, it means an Englishman. All German nouns possess gender—either masculine—Der Engländer-the Englishman), feminine—Die Engländerin, the English woman) or neuter—(Das England—England). All German nouns are always capitalized (unlike English where only proper nouns—peoples' names, etc., are capitalized). However, adjectives are never capitalized, so one can he "a German boy or a Jewish woman," and that is written: "Ein deutscher Junge, oder eine jüdische Frau." To make it even less accessible, German adjectives must also reflect the correct gender and inflectional case (objective, subjective, accusative, and nominative) of sentence construction.

Frau. "Woman" and "Mrs." (Frow) A woman is only called Frau after she marries, which means an eighty-five year old women could still be addressed as Fräulein Jones (Miss Jones). However, if a woman's marital status is not known, she is referred to as Frau after about the age of thirty-five, similar to the way English speaking people refer to a woman as "Miss" or "Ma'am." The diminutive is "Fräulein," (Froy-line), girl or Miss, the umlaut changing the sound of Frau, and—lein being a catch-all suffix that minifies the noun, just like chen (as in Mädchen "MAID-schen") or the south German suffix "-li" diminish the noun. Mädchen means "little maid," or girl.

Führer. "Leader," "Guide" (FOOR-rare). The umlauted ü is hard for English speakers to pronounce. The sound lies exactly between "ee" and "oo." The word comes from führen to lead. In German, the context indicates when it was applied to any leader, or to Adolf Hitler. Mein Führer (mine FOOR-rare) means "My Leader" and is how Hitler was always addressed.

Gestapo. Acronym for GEheime STAts POlizei, "Ges-STAPO" Secret State Police, the most powerful (and most feared) of the many German enforcement agencies. Heinrich Mueller, an ex-policeman, was its head. The Gestapo was closely aligned with the SS and had as a major part of their charter the rooting out of Jews, as well as all social undesirables and their deportation to concentration camps.

Gnädige Frau. "gentlewoman" (GNAY-dig-a-frow). A polite way of an underling addressing a lady of higher station. Often pleasant flattery.

Herr. "Mr.", "Lord" (Hair).

Herr Leutnant. "Mr. Lieutenant" (Hair LOYT nant). You can only say in German "Lieutenant Jones," without the Herr if you are being rude, because "lieutenant" is just a rank. Adding Herr makes the reference to a person who is a lieutenant. Although some SS units later thought it more soldierly to drop the Herr suffix.

Himmel Herr Gott noch mal. "Heaven Lord God once more," a common curse. Germans can string a lot of expletives along for very long, often highly creative curses.

Hochactungsvoll. "High attentiveness" (HOCH achtungs fohl, both ch's being soft. A standard sign-off like "sincerely yours."

Ja. "Yes" (Yah)

Jawohl. "Yes-good" (yah-VOLE. A stronger or more respectful yes, similar to "yes sir," or "Very good, sir."

Kneipe. (Ka-NIPE-eh), a noun meaning a seedy bar or dive. The verb kneipen means to go bar-hopping.

Leutnant. "Lieutenant" (LOYT-nahnt)

Liebchen. "Loved one" "Dearest" "Sweetheart." (LEEB-chen)

Luftwaffe. "Air weapon" (LUFT-vaff-eh) The German air force.

Nein. "No" (nine)

Nicht Wahr? "Not true?" (nicht Vahr?-soft "ch") Very common catch-all phrase meaning "Isn't that so?" "Ain't it," "Don't you think", etc.

SS. Abbreviation of Schutzstaffel-"Guard Staff." The SS was an army-like organization that was highly ideologized and completely separate from the normal military, and commanded by Heinrich Himmler. Extensively equipped, trained and brain-washed, SS members earned the reputation of undertaking any task, no matter how difficult or horrid. The Totenkopf SS (Deathshead SS) ran the concentrations camps. Although it is not popular to say so, the training, discipline and fanaticism of the Waffen SS—the armed SS earned them the reputation of being the most effective infantry force fielded in WW-II.

Umlaut. "Change sound" (UM-lout) The two little dots placed only over the vowels "a", "o" or "u" which change the sound from "ah", "oh" and "oo" to "aaah", "er" (without the r-sound) 'and "eu"—the halfway between "ee" and "yew" sound. A way of slightly changing the pronunciation and, therefore, the meaning of a word. An alternate way of inserting the umlauted sound is to add an "e" after the vowel. Mädchen can also be written Maedchen. An umlaut is sometimes put over one vowel of two to indicate each is pronounced distinctly.

Voelkische Beobachter. "Peoples' Observer" (FELL kish-eh be-OH-bachter). The official Nazi Party newspaper.

Was ist los? "What is going?" (Vas ist LOHSS?). Another catch-all phrase expressing any variation of "What's up?" or "What's going on?" etc.

Wehrmacht. "Armed Power." (VARE-macht) The German army.

Zeitung. "Time-ness" (TZEI-tung) ['Tzei' rhymes with 'high] Newspaper.

Zu Befehl. "To order." (TSOO be-FAIL). A standard answer to a superior acknowledging compliance, e.g., "as you order, sir."

All Letters are pronounced in a German word, no matter how awkward and always in the same way. Pflanze,(plant) is spoken p-ff-LAHN-zeh. Schnorchel," (snorkel) is said SH-NORCH-hel (soft "ch".

The letter combination ei is always pronounced "aye" as in Einstein (not Eensteen), and ie is always pronounced "ee" as in Knie "Keh-NEE," or "knee."

The German letter "z" is always pronounced as "tz." Mozart is pronounced MO-tzart.

"W" is always pronounced as the English "v." Wasser (water) is said "Vass-air."

The German "v" is pronounced as "f." Vater, meaning Father, is spoken "FAHT-tair"

The letter combination of "sch" is common. "Sh" without the c does not exist. The English word "school" is a carry-over from the German Schule-"SHOO-leh."

The letter "e" at the end of a word is always pronounced. Porsche is pronounced POR-Sheh. ee is pronounce to rhyme with "hay") as is Kaffee "KAH-fay (coffee) or Tee "Tey" (tea).

There are no German words (as opposed to imports) that begin with the letter "C."

About The Author

Born in Berlin in 1940, Tom Holzel escaped out of the Russian Zone at war's end with his mother and brother, and emigrated to the U.S. He has returned often and developed a fascination with the last days of the war, as well as with the disappearance of Mallory & Irvine on Mt. Everest in 1924. The latter saga resulted in the book he co-authored: *The Mystery of Mallory & Irvine*. In 1986 he mounted an expedition to Mt. Everest to search for the cameras of Mallory and Irvine. He lives in Boston with Dianne, his wife of 43 years.

Made in the USA
Lexington, KY
29 January 2012